EPIDEMIC OF CHOICE
A DEA STORY
(a novel)
By
DON NELSON

Epidemic of Choice – A DEA Story, is a novel based upon actual events which occurred during the course of official government investigations. The names and descriptions of the individuals mentioned in this novel are not factual. Any resemblance between the identified characters of the story and people in real life is coincidental and wholly unintended.

ACKNOWLEDGEMENTS

My eternal gratitude goes out to my wonderful wife, who scrutinized each page as I wrote. Her assistance and keen eyes were invaluable to me as I put thoughts to print.

I also am forever in debt to several other family members, who made unique (and clever) contributions to my writing.

Finally, I want to extend my heartfelt thanks to Paul Alme, aka Whitey, originally from Moorhead, Minnesota, who gave me direction in a life which later became filled with amazing experiences.

Thank you Whitey. Rest in peace, my friend.

PROLOGUE

FACT: The decades of the '70's and 80's marked the beginning of an era of grave challenges presented to the drug law enforcement community, both in the United States, and throughout the world. Post Viet Nam gave smugglers and traffickers new opportunities at gaining unheard of profits from their illegal ventures. Heroin began pouring into the United States from the Far East at historic levels. Cocaine and marijuana provided enormous riches to organized crime in South America, as those drugs began saturating the social strata of this country. Money flowed, and the drug addict population increased exponentially.

The escalating profits enabled newly established drug cartels to expand their horizons in South America as they gained in power and resources. In the '80's, South America became increasingly involved in the production of heroin, much of which came into the United States via the same trafficking routes as had been established by the cocaine smugglers.

FACT: During the '70's, a strange phenomenon began in the outskirts of Kindred, North Dakota. Farmers and other citizens reported sightings during the night time hours of what appeared to be people carrying lit torches in strange processions, moving about the farmlands. This was later referred to as "the Kindred lights." The authorities responded with aggressive investigation.

NOT QUITE FACTUAL: In the early 1980's, veteran DEA Special Agent Jake Shaunessey was transferred from the DEA office in San Diego to Minneapolis, where he was asked to provide insight and expertise to a number of relatively new and inexperienced agents.

THE REST OF THE STORY: FACT, FICTION, OR SOMEWHERE IN BETWEEN?

You be the judge.

CHAPTER 1

Minneapolis, Minnesota

The DEA agents wasted no time. Travis swung the twelve pound sledge hammer, shattering much of the front door to the house. He side-stepped, moving out of the other agents' path, dropped the sledge hammer and drew his Sig-Sauer 9mm. Jake and Kiel sped into the house. Moments later a grim reality stopped them in their tracks. The narcs had been primed for most anything. Or so they thought.

"Blood!" Jake's voice echoed throughout the walls in the room. "It's all over the place." He and Kiel slowly approached the hallway. The scene told them they were too late. They had already lost this one. Blood spackled the hallway floor, its trail leading into both of the bedrooms. Bloody palm and finger prints streaked down the white painted walls. The agents entered the first bedroom. Void of people, but blood pervaded the room. They approached the second. More of the same.

"Jake, down here!" Lisa's voice rang out from the basement.

Jake and Kiel followed the voice and the blood trail to the kitchen, down the stairwell to the basement. The ghastly scene awaiting them would have shocked even the most hardened narcotics agents.

A fluent stream of obscenities burst from Jake's mouth as he holstered his pistol.

On the floor the headless torso of a man, its clothes soaked in blood from gunshot wounds, lay in a crimson puddle. Perched on a table, its head stared down at the body. Tied to a chair, a woman faced the gruesome corpse. A bullet hole perforated her forehead. Her skull and brains splattered the floor.

The agents gazed, wide eyed at the lifeless carnage.

"My guess is they made her watch while they lopped off his head. Then they shot her," Jake said.

"What's this about, Jake?" Lisa asked.

Jake's entire frame bristled. His nostrils flared, and his veins swelled. He fought to retain his composure. "Heroin. The woman lived here. My snitch told me if we caught her dirty she'd talk. I had a lot of questions for her."

Lisa's eyebrows arched. Curiosity drew creases on her forehead. "Such as?

"Like, 'who the hell is this guy they call "Frenchy"? Where does he live?' She knew him. Knew him well."

Lisa nodded. "Who's the snitch?"

Jake made a head gesture towards the body on the floor. "He was."

Lisa pursed her lips. "Oooh. And somebody didn't want your questions answered."

Jake grimaced. "Yeah. It looks like Frenchy's people got here first."

CHAPTER 2

Rural Kindred, North Dakota

The terrified young girl looked up through the chain link grids at her only source of light. The single light bulb, dangling from an aging ceiling beam, hovered over the middle of the dim room. At one end of the room a large steel door opened to stairs leading up to the barn. Across the room a second door mirrored the first. The dank cellar, with its dirt floor, cinder block walls and musty ceiling, held a repulsive odor. The stench betrayed the overwhelming presence of vomit, human waste, and death.

Beneath the light bulb two cages, each the size of the interior of a Volkswagen, took up half the room. A heavy chain and padlock secured the door of her cage, ensuring Andrea would be going nowhere. A bucket and a plastic water jug sat next to her, and a steel collar had been securely fastened around her neck. Two chains led from the collar to a metal stake imbedded deep in the dirt. A young cow's severed head lay nearby, with a length of hide forming a brown cape. Slits cut in each side of the cape would soon accommodate the girl's dirty arms.

Before her abduction, the teenager's face had been fresh and bright, her hair shiny, and her jeans and sweatshirt clean. Posters, now being taped to store windows and fastened to lamp posts throughout the Minneapolis metro area, displayed Andrea's easy going smile. One that hinted of a pleasant, yet vulnerable, personality.

These desirable attributes had since been stolen; the captivating smile replaced by stressed, red eyes drenched in fear, the hair stringy, the innocent face dirty. Tears marked trails down pale cheeks, while her soiled clothes reeked of urine. The once beautiful high school cheerleader now more closely portrayed the image of a street urchin.

Cowering in her cage, her head now buried between her knees, Andrea heard a key rattling. Petrified, the fifteen year old gathered enough courage to look towards the sound. It took all the energy she could summon. Sitting on a cold steel floor for the past two days had drained her strength and spirit, leaving her shivering as she wondered how she could have allowed those animals in Big Al's clan to abduct her as she left the shopping mall.

When Big Al entered the room she trembled violently. Her pleading expression begged for mercy, while revealing her sense of horror, loneliness and desperation. The large man looked at her menacingly, soaking in the messages she conveyed. He liked what he saw. The young prisoner quickly looked away, realizing she had no hope.

One Month Later

On the map, Kindred is a tiny dot. Located twenty miles southwest of Fargo, North Dakota, the farming community boasts a population of barely over five hundred. On the east edge of town sat a small Mom and Pop motel. Its proprietors constantly struggled to make ends meet, but they remained there because they liked the quiet, easy going life North Dakota offered. Along Kindred's short main street the town offered a gas station, a farm implement dealership, two bars, a small grocery store and a few shops. For anything else, you went to Fargo.

Manfred Alfonse Culpepper made his home on a spread a few miles west of Kindred. Well educated, he felt equally comfortable in the presence of both intellectuals and thugs. People in either category found him intimidating in size and persona. Beneath his dark thinning hair, wide face, and square jaw, a set of broad shoulders and massive arms gave notice he should never be taken lightly. Those features, combined with a heavy dose of cunning woven into his DNA, gave him an uncanny ability to manipulate and control. His followers called him Big Al, partly because of his physical size, but also because they believed his qualities mirrored those of the late notorious Chicago gangster. He liked the nickname.

His prison record, a haunting problem, caused him much consternation. Big Al knew if his name ever popped up during a routine inquiry by the law, red flags would wave, raising it a few notches above routine. To solve the dilemma he devised elaborate steps to become invisible. He now believed his organization and security precautions were vastly superior to those of his cohorts, Frenchy and Black Jack Mike.

Perched on a comfortable chair in his office, Big Al propped his feet on his desk. Earlier that day, just before sunset, his large bay window boasted a relaxing, panoramic view of a peaceful meadow loaded with wild flowers and prairie grass. It extended all the way to the tree line bordering the Sheyenne River, which flowed along the south edge of the farm. The thick growth of trees displayed buds, soon to be replaced by leaves. The meadow comprised a small part of a productive farm Al purchased three years earlier. After he took over, the farming stopped.

But the full moons didn't.

It had been cloudy and overcast for most of the day. The morning began with a gentle rain. Al liked the spring rain. It washed off the winter's dirt, making everything cleaner and brighter. He also liked the full moon, which would show itself that evening.

Big Al considered the full moon a fascinating ally and a powerful tool. The night of the full moon provided him a grand opportunity to renew his power and authority over his clan, ensuring their loyalty and obedience. Its compelling influence on people, an accepted scientific fact, remained a mystery. Scientists didn't understand it and neither did he. But he took advantage of it. A bright and shiny full moon, along with the power of suggestion and hallucinogenic drugs, gave him access to psychological keys. Knowing how to manipulate these keys enabled him to draw upon the strongest of human emotions.

His farm, his clan, and the full moon, important elements in a deadly and highly rewarding scheme, combined to bring him wealth beyond his wildest dreams. But he wasn't satisfied. Big Al was driven to watch the stacks of drug money pile up in his vault.

Tanya, his most trusted of the clan members, was tough as tempered nails on the outside, but ultimately proved very susceptible to Al's manipulation. She had been a challenge, but in time he accomplished complete dominance over her. His control over the other clan members had come easily.

Grabbing his phone Big Al dialed Tanya's pager, punching a code instructing her to come to his office. Minutes later she knocked on his door.

"Come in." His deep voice echoed.

Tanya stepped into the office and closed the door. A tall, slender individual, she liked the Gothic look. It broadcast her mentality. She wore her jet black hair in a short punk style, and her deep purple eye shadow and black lipstick completed her message. Her face was pale, but her eyes keenly focused. She carried a black, hooded robe.

"Is it time, Daddy?" she asked.

"Yes,Tiggy. It's time to punish your young mother. Is her hood prepared?"

"Her hood is ready."

Al stepped to the refrigerator and grabbed two zip lock baggies. One contained psilocybin mushrooms, the other jumbo sized joints of high potency sinsemilla marijuana. A twisted, sadistic smile formed on his lips. One hell of a dangerous combination, he thought as he walked back to his desk. He handed Tanya twelve marble sized mushrooms, one for each of the clan except her. She didn't need anything extra.

Then Al opened up the second baggie, withdrew thirteen thick joints and examined each as he placed them on his desk top. Their pungent aroma wafted up to his nostrils. The best marijuana he could find, it held a bright green color and represented many years of scientific cross-breeding and tender loving care by the Mary Jane experts. Al didn't hesitate to pay two thousand dollars an ounce for the supergrass. For him, this stuff was worth much more than its weight in gold. He nodded to Tanya.

Grinning, she snatched up the doobies. She liked to toke on a joint once in a while.

"Begin the ceremony. I'll be there at midnight," he said solemnly.

Minneapolis, Minnesota

A devout thirty-two year old Baptist, Ken Washington dedicated his life first to his family, and next to his career. A detail oriented individual, he felt quite comfortable being the sole black DEA agent in the Minneapolis office. But several weeks after a second black agent, a rookie straight out of the DEA academy, came to Minneapolis, a cloud of uncertainty began to complicate Ken's life. Robert Little, the new kid on the block, became his partner. Ken considered it important that any partner of his, especially another black agent, would fulfill Ken's lofty notions of what makes a Special Agent with the DEA.

"Okay, I'll do it," Ken told his supervisor when given the directive. "But I'll need the latitude to teach the kid in my own way, and that'll be piece by piece. He probably won't like me too much at first."

"Ken, you do what you gotta do," Harold replied. "But you were a rookie once too. I want you to remember that when you put him through the paces."

One major element of the job, dealing with informants, always presented a challenge. A month after Robert's arrival in the mini-apple, Ken made arrangements for a second meeting with one of his CIs, Baby Duke, who had promised him information about Black Jack Mike's heroin operation. Ken believed continued exposure to Baby Duke would make a good addition to Robert's short list of experiences as a Special Agent. But fate had other plans for Ken. His wife and pre-school age daughter were stricken with a harsh stomach virus. Their condition demanded his presence at home.

Looking at his wife's distressed, gaunt face, Ken grimaced as he called Jake Shaunessey to explain the situation. His friend wasn't gonna like what he had to say.

"I know your attitude about Baby Duke," Ken said, cutting Jake off before the man could swear, "but Robert can't do it alone."

He could almost see Jake's frown through the phone. Jake had controlled Baby Duke as a confidential informant, or 'CI' as they were called, several years earlier, and Ken knew no love was lost between those two.

"Hey, I'll cover for you," Jake groaned. "But man, you're gonna owe me."

"Yeah, I know," Ken lamented. "Nobody said this job was easy, right? I'm tellin' ya, I'd rather be hittin' the streets than staying home. I've spent half the day cleaning up puke, and the other half trying to hold down my own lunch. Look, I'll call Robert and tell him. He'll be waiting for you in the morning."

"Okay," Jake said half-heartedly.

Ken knew Jake was probably trying to figure out which was worse: Baby Duke, or a toilet full of vomit. "Appreciate it, Jake," he said.

"You'd better."

The next morning started like any other. Jake didn't suspect it would be a morning to haunt him like a Charles Dickens' ghost. Melissa stood at the front door, waiting to say good-bye. He had to bend over to kiss her. A petite woman with short dark hair and a small up-turned nose, her head reached mid-way up his chest.

"Don't forget, next week is Melanie's birthday," she said. "Hard to believe she'll be fourteen."

"Fourteen? I thought she was just turning ten!"

Melissa thumped his chest. "Fourteen, goofball! And you know what she wants? A horse! I said, 'Where would the horse sleep? The boys have the basement, and even though I can't imagine a horse making a bigger mess than those two, there just isn't room down there. There's nowhere to keep one. The bathrooms are too small.' I don't think she appreciated my humor," she finished, grinning.

Jake chuckled, trying to picture a horse living in their bathroom, eating hay out of the sink. "I think she'll have to wait until she can pay the boarding fees. Until then, she can ride a horse from the stables."

"Yeah, she'll have to be content with a stuffed horse on this birthday." She kissed him. "Love you. Take care of yourself."

They were words from the bottom of her heart, words she never took lightly. Melissa knew all about the risks and responsibilities conjoined with Jake's position as a DEA agent. After sixteen years, she couldn't even begin to count the number of nights he hadn't come home until the wee hours because "the street" demanded his presence. And she recalled too many times when he hadn't come home at all for two or three days running. The reality that came with the territory in his chosen field required he had to work when the bad guys worked. Drug dealers sure as hell didn't work long hours, but they often worked *strange* hours. A common goal of narcotics agents was to catch the dopers dirty, which meant to catch them doing their thing. Melissa knew her husband was damn good at achieving that goal. Upstairs in their bedroom, safely tucked away in a corner of their closet, sat a large box stuffed with citations, awards, and official looking certificates commending Jake for his accomplishments as an agent over the years.

But those awards didn't come cheap. Signs of wear and tear had surfaced on Jake's face and six foot plus frame. The signs derived from stress that accompanies continuously dealing with slimeballs, long work hours, being subjected to life-threatening situations, and a habit of irregular meals. Melissa believed the crow's feet planted near his eyes, and the creases on his brow were chiseled too deeply for a thirty-seven year old face. And she wasn't wild about his wiry mustache either. It made him look even older. But she did like his broad shoulders and his thick chest. And she loved cuddling next to him in bed, tucking her head into one of his muscular arms on those nights when he did come home before "Oh dark-thirty," as he would say. He made her feel safe and secure; and all the other things a wife hoped for, or expected from her mate.

When he worked the long hours to which she had become accustomed, she missed those things. And when he came home fairly early on a Friday evening and told her he would probably be home the entire weekend, she cherished the moment. They didn't come very often. As she watched him drive off to work that morning, she wondered what the day would bring.

Sitting in his office chair, Robert, a recent college grad, exhibited an athletic build but a small, boyish looking face. Raised in Atlanta, he considered making the adjustment to this foreign climate about as difficult as jumping off a warm, sunny dock into a glacial lake. For the past month it had been cold, cold, and more cold. Damn! he thought, every time he watched the news. Does this state know the meaning of Spring? He liked his weather hot and sunny. The hotter the better. He sometimes wondered how the hell he'd ended up in one of the coldest states he could name. Maybe Alaska could have been worse. Maybe.

But a rookie out of the DEA academy didn't have much say about where he went. The school was tough. A genuine, bonafide, made in the USA just to fuckin' piss you off tough. He was damn happy to graduate and tell his grandmother he made it. And finally, another area of his life promised some relief. It began with the weather forecast: lots of sun and warming temps. While fifty degrees was a far cry from warm, he rejoiced over what that attractive meteorologist with long blonde hair and a big set of lungs said on the tube the previous evening. Then came the phone call from Ken, and he realized he might finally see some action.

Sitting at his desk, waiting for Jake to pop through the office door, Robert wrestled with the relationship he had with his assigned partner. Working with Ken was like breaking in a stiff pair of new shoes. Even though the size was right, the fit sure wasn't, and it seemed like a fifty-fifty shot blisters were in the making. Ken always seemed, what was it, up-tight? Aloof? Not exactly condescending, but always leaning towards wary. Robert didn't understand Ken's attitude, and he brought it up with his Grandma during one of their regular phone calls.

"Sounds like a perfectionist, that's all," she told him. "Just make sure you do what he wants, and you'll survive. Nothing lasts forever. Soon as he sees what you're made of, he'll come around."

Of course, she was right. Grandma was always right. Maybe he just over-reacted. Hell, who wouldn't? All he had seen so far was cold weather and horse-shit, menial assignments. Plus a whole lot of Ken's nit-picking. But Robert now saw a bright spot. During their phone conversation, Ken told Robert to tag along with Jake the next day. Ken would be busy doing something else. What that was, the man hadn't bothered to say. Although irritated at being left in the dark, Robert couldn't help but feel a sense of relief knowing he would be with Jake for a day.

His muscles tingled as he sat at his desk. If things worked out he'd hit the street with the other guys and finally watch them do their thing. Impatient to make his mark, Robert eagerly anticipated the first case in which he would be actively involved. "About damn time!" he thought out loud. For the third time he checked his watch. Ten o'clock. Jake should arrive shortly.

Robert knew Jake's seniority and experience in the office made him big dog among the street agents. Everybody spoke highly of him. It seemed Jake could hone in on a pusher like a compass could find north. Robert looked forward to working with him as they dealt with Baby Duke.

Only two agents in the office were senior to Jake: Harold Sampress, Jake's supervisor; and Alan Ravich, the head of the office. Robert heard a few mutterings in the office about the two bosses, but didn't yet have a handle on that. It seemed all the agents liked Harold. They considered him a good guy as well as a top shelf supervisor, one who did what he could to help and tried to stay out of the way when his presence would hinder.

In the academy, Robert heard whisperings that the DEA was similar to every other law enforcement agency in one respect: It had its share of tyrants. Robert suspected Alan Ravich to be one. He knew the man didn't command respect. While Ravich had only been in town for six months, it was obvious the only person in the office who liked the man was Scott. And nobody in the office cared for that guy either. Robert didn't have a handle on that situation, but knew he would over time.

And he had been told something else. The two bosses seldom went out on the street, only when it was something major. Major big, or major bad, Ken said. Robert had the strong impression their thing was administrative schmoozing and PR work. They could have it.

Jake finally came through the door, and Robert threw him a quick greeting. "Mornin' Jake."

"Morning," Jake mumbled.

Robert's natural smile strained. Jake seemed a bit grouchy.

The fading smile caused Jake to realize he had sent negative signals, and he immediately switched frequencies. "How's it going, Robert?"

Back on track, Robert said, "Going good. Can we talk when you get settled?"

Nodding, Jake strolled to the coffee bar. Retrieving his cup from a collection of mugs, Jake filled it and walked slowly back to his desk. The rookie was waiting.

"So what's up with the meet. Where's it at?" Jake asked.

"Eleven-thirty at Wirth Park."

"Wirth Park?"

Jake's expression turned serious, and Robert struggled to figure it out. "Yeah, that's where Ken set it up."

Jake shifted his thoughts to a major hurdle, something he would have to cover with the rookie. *Might as well do it now.* "Robert, do you know this CI?"

"Baby Duke? Yeah, Ken and I met with him a couple weeks ago at the park. He spoke about some new shit coming into town. Said he'd stay on top of it. Ken gave him some bread. Had the feeling he'd be after more."

Jake thought about it. Yeah, for sure. Cash was that snitch's MO. Jake didn't know how much Ken gave the mope, but would've bet most anything the DEA didn't get its money's worth. Baby Duke had never been productive as an informant, and his file had been passed around like a bad penny.

He took a quick mental inventory of what he could remember about Baby Duke. The man lived on the near North Side, the roughest section of Minneapolis. An ageless-looking guy, he could have been thirty or fifty. Jake recalled the grisly tracks scarring both of his arms, and the gold earring that always decorated his left ear. One daunting thought: after several years of snitching for the DEA, Baby Duke had probably picked up enough savvy about probable cause and search warrant affidavits to make him dangerous.

Jake downed a slug of coffee as he considered the scheduled meet. "I'll help out any way I can, but I've got to give you a heads up on Baby Duke. I used to control him, but when Ken arrived here I turned the snitch over to him. I figured the guy would be more effective if a black agent controlled him. Sometimes that works."

Robert listened closely. "That's what Ken told me. So what do you think? Does the guy have anything going, or is it all bullshit?"

"That's always a fair question when you're dealing with a mercenary snitch like Baby Duke. Is it jive or is it for real? Usually, if a CI is working off a beef I like him better. Those are the ones that have a lot to gain. Or lose. Baby's a hard guy to figure. His sole motivation is money, and that's how he weighs his risks. He's a junkie, so he's got to be dealing behind our back. Any dope dealer will make more on that end than he would through us. When I handled him I thought he had potential, but he really never did shit. The mope is probably into some heavyweights, but he's never turned us onto them. The last time I worked with him I got tired of his crap and threatened to cut him off. That's when Ken took over."

Robert frowned. "What's Ken's done with him?"

"Nothing news worthy. Basically a lot of small timers. But it's his call. If he wants to give Baby Duke another go, we'll move on it."

He quietly watched Robert and hoped their talk hadn't been too discouraging. What the hell. Rookies had to start somewhere. If this whole thing went nowhere, at least the guy might learn something. He smiled. "Go get some money. We'll meet him and see what he's got. We've got an hour, so I'm going to try and find the top of my desk."

CHAPTER 3

Tanya left the house to do Big Al's bidding. She quickly joined the other clan members milling outside around the two double-wide trailers that served as their living quarters. They wore black hooded robes similar to hers. Motioning them to follow, she led them over to the large, red dairy barn a good yelling distance from Al's house. There, she put on her robe, raising the hood over her head. The others raised their hoods, and the ceremony began.

"Light the torches," Tanya commanded.

Each member held a wooden baseball bat, its fat end covered with a thick wrapping soaked with kerosene. One of the clan, Frankie, went from torch to torch, lighting each with his cigarette lighter. The group formed a circle and Tanya gave each clan member a magic mushroom. Within minutes of eating their mushrooms, a charged, mystical ambiance developed, quickly dominating the spirit of the group.

Tanya handed out the joints, and everybody toked for ten minutes. Then, holding the torches high, they formed a procession behind Tanya.

Their torches created crooked shadows on the ground, pulsating, bobbing and weaving, like tall, black flames licking out of a huge bonfire. The moon, the darkness, the ghoulish shadows, and the hallucinogenic effects of the drugs all combined, giving the clan members the feeling they had entered another dimension. Their vulnerability, Big Al's key, hit its peak.

Tanya led them, single file, around the barn, then the trailers and the house. Next she followed the tree line and marched across the meadow to the wooded area bordering the river. They ambled amongst the trees and bushes, careful not to disturb the slightly elevated mounds of earth dotting a large area within the woods.

As they walked, their chant pierced the cool night air. A loud, chilling, monotone chant, they loudly recited the words during every ceremony.

"Lucifer. Satan. Beelzebub. We've sharpened the knife. It's in your honor we'll snuff out a life.

"Lucifer. Satan. El Diablo. We ain't gonna fail. Come pay us a visit. There'll be blood in your pail."

Following Tanya's lead, the group repeated the verse over and over in unison. On they trooped, while the drugs percolated in their veins and their psyches moved into synch. Finally they staggered back to the barn. Tanya looked them over. Yeah . . . they were ready. She led them in. The tromping noise of their stumbling feet echoed throughout the tall, cavernous barn. They placed their torches into holders mounted along the walls, then shuffled into a half-circle formation where they resumed their chant, now almost deafening within the confines of the barn.

Shifting his attention away from Robert, Jake sat down, turning his chair towards his desk where a stack of papers awaited him. Looking above the clutter, he saw Lisa Sanchez at her desk, chomping on some miniature carrots she had in a plastic baggie and dictating a report between swallows.

A strikingly pretty Hispanic mid-way through her twenties, Lisa's short, dark hair complemented her alert brown eyes and spunky attitude. When she first reported in at the office, Jake heard comments from some of the other agents about her hour glass figure. He didn't like hearing that talk because he didn't know how it would set when it got back to her. And it would. As it turned out, his concerns were for nothing. She could handle herself quite well in the office, thank you, and she sure as hell wasn't inhibited. In any event, the comments ended as the agents got to know her and saw what the woman could do on the street.

It didn't take her long to be accepted as part of the family, important in a setting where survival meant watching out for each other. A few weeks after her transfer to Minneapolis, Jake and Lisa had a heart to heart and she told him about her experiences in Florida. He hoped they would help her grow, not be a millstone around her neck. After a few deals, Jake knew the woman had what it takes.

"Hey Lisa, Que Pasa?"

She turned off the recorder. "Morning Jake. Same old shit."

Chuckling at her approach to the new day, he pulled his chair in close and looked at the overflowing pile of memos and bulletins in his inbox. A number of agencies throughout the Midwest regularly submitted bulletins regarding new developments. Much of it didn't directly concern narcotics enforcement. Indirectly however, anything of interest to one law enforcement agency could potentially concern the others. Good to see them cooperating on some things, at least.

Jake plucked a memo from the top of the heap: a list of statistics regarding hospital ER admissions for heroin overdoses and deaths throughout Minnesota. He found the figures, highlighted by Harold Sampress, shocking. Looking up at Lisa he said, "Have you seen this memo?"

"Not yet. Something earth shaking?"

"Pretty close."

Lisa scooted her chair across the floor, coming to a stop close to Jake.

"Take a look at these numbers. They divide Minnesota in half, north and south, comparing heroin stats for the past three years. The north has seen an increase in heroin overdoses by 450 percent. Staggering!"

"Hmm."

"And check out the southern half," Jake continued, pointing to the next set of figures. "A 200 percent jump. This is serious stuff, Lisa. It looks like a major organization has snuck up on us."

Leaning back in her chair, Lisa had a puzzled look on her face. "Yeah, I think we just been ambushed." Furrows creasing her forehead, she studied the statistics.

Jake pushed his chair back. "You know that snitch I lost a while back?"

Lisa grimaced. "How could I forget?"

"That had the makings of a big heroin case. Frenchy is big time. If we could just get a handle on him. What a difference a few hours can make." Jake shook his head in disgust. "What about that heroin operation you've been working. Anything from your CI about all the junk flooding the state?"

She shook her head slightly. "Everybody knows there's heroin out there. Never seems to be a shortage of the shit. But none of my intelligence pointed at a problem this big. These figures jump out and bite you on the ass."

"Yeah they do. This keeps up, the crime problem in Minnesota is going to turn the entire state into a war zone. Looks like we've got an epidemic brewing."

Lisa thought about it. "I guess heroin is the latest drug of choice."

"I'd say it's the epidemic of choice."

Lisa returned to her desk. Jake scratched his initials onto the memo, tossed it into his outbox and snatched the next one, a statistics tally on the rising crime rate. No surprise there. He initialed the memo and grabbed another. This one held more gut wrenching information. An alarming increase in missing person reports had been submitted during the past year involving teenage girls. He knew many runaway girls from Minnesota gravitated to New York City, where they hooked up with ever-ready pimps. The media referred to it as "The Minnesota Pipeline." As a narc, he generally didn't investigate missing person reports. But what the hell was going on? Were they all runaways, or was it something else? If so, what? Sex-slave ring? Serial killer? His thoughts automatically shifted to his teenage daughter. Jake shivered, then pushed it out of his mind.

Looking at the next item, a bulletin submitted jointly by sheriffs of several counties in eastern North Dakota, Jake's face formed a puzzled expression. Cattle rustling? What the hell? Rustling and livestock mutilation were on the rise, and the sheriffs requested all the agencies to be alert for any information that might help their detectives. The bulletin seemed way out of place in a DEA office. It undoubtedly posed a serious problem for some, but it wasn't his bag.

Putting the bulletin down, Jake shifted his attention back to his priority: Heroin. How in the hell did Minnesota's junkie population in the northern half of the state grow by a whopping 450 percent? He had never seen such a pronounced increase. His stomach growled in protest, but he wasn't sure if it was against the news or the coffee. Maybe both. Or maybe it was the thought of working Baby Duke again.

He pushed the box away like a plate full of moldy food, and focused on Baby. Supposedly the guy would provide them with new information about a big-time heroin dealer. *Frenchy?* he wondered. *Nah. He'd be talking about a dealer in the hood.* Jake motioned for Robert to get ready. Time to get it on.

Jake looped his cuffs under his belt and grabbed an extra magazine for his nine-millimeter. Robert did the same. Baby Duke was a CI, but as far as Jake was concerned the guy was a devious dirtbag without loyalties.

Seeing Robert's pistol, Jake said, "Beretta, huh? They issue them at the academy now?"

"Yeah. They're big on Berettas."

"Beretta's a great piece, but I like my Sig Sauer better." Jake patted his shoulder holster. "This pistol just don't jam. I've put over twenty thousand rounds through it and never a mis-fire."

Robert nodded. The semi-automatic pistol was the only way to go; an obvious fact they drove home at the DEA academy. If you didn't carry one, you were probably out gunned. But those pistols have a lot of moving parts. As one of the instructors said, "There are two kinds of semi-automatics. The ones that have jammed, and the ones that are going to jam." That guy was a wheel gun man, but he knew he was a dying breed. Yet for a street agent, having your piece mis-fire at a critical moment was a nightmare scenario. Something they all talked about. Gun fights were more common place with narcotics agents than in other areas of law enforcement, and an agent often found himself one-on-one at close distance with the bad guy. If the pistols came out and yours didn't work, well . . .

All the agents in the office went regularly to the firing range to hone their marksmanship skills. They were excellent shots, and Ken told him Jake consistently scored the highest in their combat shooting drills. Robert wanted to see him in action.

Walking out of the building, Jake said, "You drive. Give you a chance to learn the streets."

"Sure enough. My car's over there." Robert pointed to the far end of the parking lot.

They pulled onto Olson Memorial Highway, which took them west toward Theodore Wirth Park, one of the many parks built around the lakes of the metro area. The light traffic made the drive go quick and easy. A half mile into the heavily wooded park they spotted Baby Duke, crouched low in his car.

Robert said softly, "Same old jalopy, sitting in the same old place."

They went by without slowing down and crept another two hundred yards to a secluded area. The plan called for Baby Duke to walk to their car and hop into the back seat. If someone else came too close, they'd move.

Baby Duke had been watching the narrow paved road carefully, and within minutes the agents saw him slowly sauntering towards them. He slid into the back seat, giving Jake and Robert a wide toothy smile, and shook their hands.

"My man," he said to Jake. "How you doin?"

Jake noticed a wary smile on the informant's face. "Just fine, Baby. I think you know Robert."

"Oh yeah, we're tight." The CI shook Robert's hand, then said, "Say, what happened to Ken? Wasn't he supposed to be here too?"

Jake nodded. "Yeah, but something came up and he couldn't make it. Guess it's just like old times, Baby. Play it straight and you got no problems."

"I hear that."

Robert readied his notepad, and Jake got down to business. "So what's happening, Baby?"

"Well it's like this. You know a dude called Black Jack Mike?"

Jake knew a lot about him. He had always figured that heroin peddler to be way out of Baby Duke's league. "What about him?"

"Black Jack Mike has a crib on Newton with his old lady, Maureen. He's one bad dude. Does ounces of junk. Sells right out of his pad. Makes deliveries too, just like the pizza man. Has a regular door to door service. People call him and order up. He brings the dope out to 'em. This dude is making big time bread. You gotta see the inside of his place. Everything's expensive. First class. It's a fucking palace, see what I'm saying? He's got guns around the house, and a dude named Jeremy shadows him for extra security on his deliveries. That guy's a mean little weasel. Carries a MAC-10 and another pistol."

Baby Duke took a deep breath. "BJ's got a bedroom way in the back. Does his business there. Jeremy hangs around the family room. Watches over anybody who's waiting while Black Jack's handling the product."

The CI paused again, and Jake looked into his glassy eyes. He didn't like what he saw, but couldn't get a good read on the guy. The informant was talking about a real heavy weight. That had to cause the little snake some bonafide anxiety. But was something else squirming around inside this mope's brain? "What's he charge for a quarter, Baby, and how's he sell 'em?"

"It's like this. He gets fourteen hundred for the quarters. Got it packaged in balloons, quarter and half ounce. Pretty good shit. You can cut it in two easy."

"Okay. What's Maureen's action?" Jake asked. He noticed Maureen's name brought an immediate but brief reaction to the CI's face. Jake's mind did a double click on her name. *How does Maureen fit into this puzzle?*

"Maureen. Shit. She shoulda been called 'Marine.' Fuckin' drill sergeant. Takes care of business for Black Jack when he's gone, but only for special people."

Baby Duke settled back in his seat, trying to relax. Jake sensed increased anxiety in the CI's body language.

"She likes me. We go way back. Yesterday I heard BJ was sitting on a few ounces, so I stopped by to see what I could learn. Her old man was gone, but Mo and I had a long talk. She'll tell me what's going on, see what I'm saying? So she takes me to the back bedroom and shows me half an Oh Zee from his bag. I wasn't really in the market for a half, but I did get a dime's worth for you."

The CI retrieved a small paper packet from his pocket and handed it to Jake. It was folded, refolded, and tucked into itself, forming a lock. On the street, people called it a bindle. Jake opened it. It contained a small quantity of beige powder, just enough to cover a person's thumb nail. Looked like heroin, and probably was. Jake would field test it in the office.

"You got this from her?"

"Yeah."

Jake intently studied the man. The sample spoke loudly, something he couldn't ignore. Although uneasy about it, he decided he had to pursue this. After quizzing Baby Duke a little longer about Black Jack Mike's operation, he gave the informant some money. With the meeting over, the CI moseyed back to his car and drove out of the park.

Some of Baby's information looked good. The fact the CI turned over some dope, along with a story to back it up, was something a narc could, and usually should, take action on. Jake considered the heroin sample. Black Jack Mike sold quarters and halves in balloons, but Baby had only given Jake a hit, contained in a bindle. Jake tossed it around in his mind, comparing what Baby said with what probably really went down. Most likely Baby had scored some, probably a quarter but maybe a half, from Black Jack Mike, cut it, sold a chunk and shot up the rest, except for the sample he set aside for the DEA with his eyes on a reward if Black Jack Mike went down. Jake didn't like it, but informants often did things that way. On the other hand, his office had a thick file on Black Jack Mike. The sample might be just what they needed to get a warrant and hit the guy's door. It could be a good case if they caught him dirty. Jake wished it were someone other than Baby Duke giving him this dope, but he'd make do.

He looked over at Robert. "Let's take a spin past Black Jack Mike's crib. See if there's anything we can add to this."

Robert pulled out of the park, and five minutes later they drove past the house. At the end of the block Robert turned onto another street, then glanced at Jake with a "what next?" look.

Jake grinned. "You know the way back to the office from here?"

Robert nodded.

"For now we've done everything we can. Call Ken and bring him up to speed. If he can come in, he can take over. If not, I'll handle it with your help. Black Jack Mike is a major heroin figure. Make a case on him and we've earned our pay. The guy is a prime suspect in several unsolved murders in the city. A lot of guys in law enforcement would love to see him go down."

Making another right turn, Robert headed back to the office.

As they approached the city's business section, Jake asked, "Seen much of the downtown area yet?"

"No, I haven't," Robert replied.

Jake nodded. "Okay, Hennepin Avenue is next. Turn right and I'll show you something."

Hennepin Avenue, a well traveled street noted for its nightspots, theaters and restaurants, stood out from the rest of downtown. Robert made the turn and drove past a nightclub with a large neon sign over its entrance blinking, "Saddle Club."

Motioning towards the club, Jake asked, "Ever hear of this place?"

"Nope."

"It's a notorious strip joint. Real popular with big time dopers in this city. On any given day you'd see major players inside. But you'd be wise to stay out of there. Go inside and someone recognizes you as a narc, the word spreads fast and you'll be burned. Could be bad news if you came across one of them when you're working undercover."

CHAPTER 4

At ten-thirty AM, six DEA agents gathered in the war room to prepare for the raid. The room, separate from their common office space, looked unkempt, with no windows, smoke stained ceiling tiles, and drab, gray walls plastered with street maps. A long table at one end of the room held a collection of gum wrappers, ash trays, and several used Styrofoam coffee cups. An assortment of mangled paper clips littered the aging tiled floor.

Waiting for Jake to begin his briefing, Kiel McIntyre munched on a jumbo size Hershey bar while describing the antics of an idiot driver he encountered on his way to the office.

Travis Shepherd, alone in his personal space, leaned back on a rickety old office chair that squeaked in protest to his every move. Finding a comfortable position, he began twiddling with a deformed paper clip which he intended to toss onto the pile on the floor. He had a distant look: the mess he had been making on the floor shadowed what he had done with his life.

Noticing Travis, Lisa Sanchez couldn't resist. With a mischievous grin on her face, she plopped down on a chair and slid next to him. Pressing her nose close to his shoulder, she took an exaggerated sniff. "Hey, Homeless, you take a shower this morning?"

Travis braced himself, wondering which shoe she would drop next.

"Yeah," he said cautiously.

"So, you installed a shower in the back of your van, huh?"

"Actually, I went to the 'Y,' but I got a deal for you."

"And, what's that?"

"You let me use your shower, I'll let you scrub my backside. Might be the closest you've come to having sex for a long time."

Lisa shook her head in feigned disgust. "You too. How long's it been since your last flame kicked you out?"

The jab knocked Travis out of his state of semi-contentment. Irritated, he struck back. "Lisa, is this a proposition? If it is, I can understand you're probably tired of rejection, but I'm still in mourning over my last break-up. The most I'd be willing to give you is a one-night stand, and you'd have to throw in a dinner."

"You wish." Lisa's eyes narrowed as she groped for another avenue of attack. This one had crashed and burned.

Jake finished at the photocopier and joined the group just in time to rescue the two from each other. "Okay, stop your dueling before you two forget who the enemy is. Here, take a run sheet. This is the bad guy." A mug shot of Black Jack Mike took up half the first page.

Jake handed Travis and Lisa copies of the raid plan, then went on down the line until everyone had one.

"I just got a search warrant signed for Black Jack Mike's pad. If any of you didn't know, his real name is Michael Roosevelt. This doper is 'Mister Big' on the north side, and it looks like we can catch him dirty. When it's over, if all goes well, we'll make every effort to flip him. His cooperation is really important. The heroin problem we've got is way out of hand. We're playing catch-up and this might be our jump start. We've got to do this right. I want to lean on him heavy, and then watch the scumbag squirm for a deal."

He paused, giving the agents a chance to look over the run sheet which held crucial information on their target, along with a sketch of his house. Jake was about to resume when Ken Washington entered the room.

A large man, he wore blue jeans, a purple jersey that said 'Vikings,' and a Twins baseball cap. The crimson tinted whites of his eyes, and his drawn face were a quick giveaway he probably hadn't slept in days. Everybody could tell he felt surly by the way he walked into the room.

Jake sent him a friendly greeting. "Hey, you made it. Good. We can use your help. Wife and daughter doing better?"

Ken sat down. The chair groaned under his weight. "Yeah, they're back with the living. What an ordeal. Did I miss much?"

"Just starting."

Jake handed Ken a run sheet, then faced the group. "The informant on this deal is Baby Duke."

The agents were all familiar with him and his dealings, and just mentioning his name re-opened some old sores.

Sal frowned. "Baby Duke? That worthless piece of crap hasn't come up with anything hot in his life, except for the TV set in that shit hole where he lives."

Lisa chimed in. "Jake, something's wrong with this picture. Baby Duke's about as useless as a car without wheels. All he's ever done are nickel-dimers. No way could he set up Black Jack Mike. Roosevelt is a major player."

Taking offense, Ken couldn't hide his aggravation. "Okay, okay you guys. Baby Duke is for real. I've been saying that for a long time. When this raid's over, you'll be eating those words like fat folks at a food fest. And don't be coming to me for any Tums."

Jake tried to stifle a laugh, at the same time irritated at the direction the briefing had taken. Ironically, he felt the same as the others about Baby Duke. But he had committed himself to this effort.

"Enough already!" Jake's voice rose above the chatter. "Correct me if I'm wrong, but I believe everybody in this room is a narc. So what the hell is the issue? It isn't whether you like Baby Duke. Our concern is Black Jack Mike, and like it or not, Baby Duke has given us what we need. Are we all in sync here?"

Everyone nodded.

Satisfied, Jake resumed. "Okay. Yesterday the informant went to Black Jack Mike's house and scored some junk from Maureen, Mike's wife. Baby says Mike is dealing large quantities of junk out of a back bedroom. Timing is everything. We've got to secure the heroin before Mike's toilet eats it. He's got a guy for security named Jeremy. A real bad ass. If he could, he'd hold us up while Mike ran to the bathroom. We're not going to let him. I've come up with a ruse to get Jeremy out of the house. Two uniforms from Minneapolis are going to handle it."

Jake explained the plan, spent ten minutes covering the raid, and summed up with individual assignments. After fielding questions, he said, "Okay, grab your gear. Our rendezvous is the parking lot of the North Side precinct station."

Ken, Robert, and Travis drove to the site in a van. The others were in cars.

Driving to the meet spot, Ken used the time to give his partner a few last minute instructions. "You'll be the last one through the door. Remember to keep your pistol pointed down at the floor, not at my back. Stay behind us. Travis and I will secure the rooms along the hallway, and you cover us. Don't let anybody run out of the house."

It was more than Robert could handle. He moaned to himself, shut his eyelids and rolled his eyes. *Keep my pistol pointed downward, not at his back. I can't believe this. If Grandma were to see me now. A few weeks ago I was telling her how much I learned in the Academy, and now this guy is acting like I'm a complete idiot.*

He looked straight at his partner. "Hey, Bro, I know it's tough for you to put your confidence in a guy fresh out of school, but believe me, the Academy taught us a lot. I sure as hell know better than to point my nine millimeter at your back."

Two days without sleep left Ken irritable and he had little patience. His eyes narrowed. "It's like this, Rookie. You don't know if you can handle it, 'cause you've never been there. After I've seen your work I'll decide how much I should trust you. Until then I don't take nothing for granted. Do as you're told. Stay low key. Watch us do the job."

Robert realized he had to prove himself, just like when he first arrived at the Academy. Must be my baby face, he thought. Nodding his head, he looked out the window, frowning as he watched the traffic.

At the precinct station, they were greeted by two uniforms leaning against their squad car. One, Juan Rodriguez, was a diminutive Hispanic with a pock-marked face and a pencil mustache. He was working on a final drag off his Marlboro. His partner Wayne Brady, a black cop who looked like a body builder, chomped intensely on a wad of gum. Jake knew Rodriguez, who at one time had been with the PD narco unit.

When Jake decided on the ruse, he called Rodriguez, who in turn recommended Brady's help because Brady had dealt with Jeremy in the past. Brady was as large as Ken.

Seeing Brady and Rodriguez stand next to one-another reminded Jake of David and Goliath. He quickly made the introductions, everybody checked their weapons, and they were on their way.

Jake drove, with Kiel riding shotgun. They had been paired up for four years, since Kiel reported to Minneapolis fresh out of the DEA Academy. They clicked as partners and the boss kept them together. Jake considered Kiel a stand up guy, the kind of agent you could trust to back you up and watch your back. Kiel held the honor of being the shortest agent in the office, with Lisa beating him out by an inch. His blond hair, cut short like many athletes prefer, made him look even shorter. His size never held him back.

Jake parked his car around the corner and a few blocks down from Black Jack Mike's house. They couldn't see the house, and would rely on the van to be their eyes and ears. The area was quiet.

"Looks good so far," Jake commented as he studied the street.

They parked directly in front of an old two-story house with a large screened-in porch. Kiel glanced up at the house and saw someone peer out the window, then quickly disappear behind closed curtains. "Hope that doesn't mean trouble. People in the house are checking us out. Might be putting the word out in the neighborhood. This thing better go fast or we may be burned."

Before Jake could respond the screen door opened, and a girl, probably in her late teen's, came out of the house, walking towards them on the walk way. She was attractive, and as she approached the side walk she gave them a cheerful smile and then a thumbs up signal before turning down the walk and heading down the block. Her bottom showed a slightly exaggerated wiggle, which the two narcs figured was for their benefit.

Kiel smiled. "She had to know we're cops, and it sure as hell doesn't bother her we're here," he said, closely following her strut.

Jake nodded. "I don't get the feeling she's going to sound the alarm. Maybe her dad's a cop."

"Yeah, maybe. Or maybe she's just on our side for whatever. Look at that tail move. What a tease. Reminds me of my wife a few years ago . . . before we were married."

"Lucie was a tease?"

"Nah. But she sure knew how to walk. Maybe she still does, and I just don't notice it any more, I don't know. Things haven't been the same for a couple years. Can't figure out if it's me or her or what the hell. I get the feeling she just doesn't give a shit anymore."

"You've been working a lot of long hours, Kiel. Why don't you give it a break? All those surveillances you've been doing on your own time? You don't need to do that stuff. Go home early once in a while. Get re-acquainted. It works for me."

"You and Melissa ever have problems?"

"Yeah, sure, just like everybody else. But nothing we couldn't get through. You gotta make an effort. Nothing's easy."

Kiel nodded. "Ain't that the truth."

Jake looked down the sidewalk where the girl was walking. Now a block away, she stood at the corner. Jake remembered there was a bus stop there and surmised the girl was on her way to work, or maybe school. He looked back at Kiel. "Say, how old's your daughter?"

Kiel brightened up. "Lucinda just turned four. Man, is she a cutie. She'll be starting kindergarten soon. Hard to believe, you know. She really gets excited when she sees me in the mornings." He paused for a minute, as though considering what he had just said. "I suppose you're right. I think I'm . . .

Ken's voice came across the radio, and Kiel stopped mid-sentence. He and Jake went on high alert.

Sitting at the desk in his darkened office, Big Al looked out the window and eyed the torches which signaled the progress of the ceremony. Time to join in.

He opened a drawer, pulled out a nine millimeter Beretta and tucked it under his belt near the small of his back. A little insurance policy to guard against a bad trip.

Next came the hooded robe. Unlike the black robes worn by the clan, his was crimson, its hood tight against his head. He looked into a mirror and liked what he saw.

Around his waist, he wore a wide leather belt with a sheath. Al opened another drawer and took out a twelve inch blade knife, sporting a thick, polished, white bone handle. He carefully moved his thumb along the blade's cutting edge. Satisfied with the razor sharp feel, he slipped it into the sheath. Everything was set. Moving quickly, he went down into the basement and entered his secret room, closing a hidden door behind him. Unlocking two dead bolts in a solid steel door, Al followed a tunnel to the cellar, located underneath the barn, where he had to open a similar door. He paused before entering the cellar. The stale, rank air got his attention. Making an effort to ignore the pungent odor, he walked over to one of the cages. Quickly disconnecting the chains from a thick stake imbedded in the earth floor, he unlocked the cage door.

Roxanne, a sixteen year old runaway whose face and raggedy blonde hair were evidence of her three days captivity in the dirty cellar, looked up at him in sheer terror. She began screaming, "Please, oh, no!"

"Shut up," he yelled, giving her a vicious look. Big Al hated it when they howled, and most of them did. But all their screaming hadn't changed anything. It only deepened his resolve.

Pulling her out of the cage, he removed the steel collar from her neck. She continued to shriek, and Al put a strip of duct tape over her mouth. Roxanne's screams converted to muffled, yet loud, rebellious moans. Big Al pinched her nose shut. She surrendered and he allowed her to breathe. He found the sudden silence gratifying. Next, he placed the remnants of the cow's head over hers, with the cape extending down her waist. Then he fastened steel bracelets with heavy, five foot chains onto her wrists. Finally, he swooped her up, cradling her in both arms. With the dangling chains rattling loudly against the steps, he carried her up into the interior of the large barn.

The clan listened, mesmerized as the sounds of clattering chains progressed up the stairs. Watching the trap door slowly rise, they resumed their chant, now louder in anticipation of the climax. El Diablo finally appeared through the trap door with their lamb in his arms. Unable to contain their eagerness, the furor of their chant increased, its hollow echo resounding throughout the barn.

"El Diablo, El Diablo! Bring on the knife. This is your night. Come take a life."

Al walked over to a heavy wooden table, dark with stains. On the floor next to this altar sat a metal pail, partially filled with cow's blood. The bushy end of the cow's severed tail, about twelve inches long, lay next to the bucket. Al laid Roxanne face up on the altar. The heavy chains clanged onto the floor, and the chanting peaked. He turned to face the group. The chanting ceased.

"Satan is with us," he thundered. "I am Satan's servant. I have served him well and he speaks through me. You will not doubt me. You will obey. Satan has selected this lamb as a symbol. You will share in the lamb's blood. Defy me and the blood will seal your fate."

Grabbing the cow's tail, he dipped its bushy end into the blood and painted Roxanne's arms.

The effects of the hallucinogens on the clan were compelling. The group repeated the chant, which now had a noticeable slur as the words spilled from their drooling mouths.

"El Diablo, El Diablo! Bring on the knife. This is your night. Come take a life."

All but Tanya entered into a state of drug induced delirium, which brought powerful, ghoulish visions. Phantoms embraced the physical features of Al. Some saw horns on Al's head. Some envisioned him with a long tail. Frankie visualized Al's body with a diabolical likening of a goat's head, complete with horns, cloven hooves, and a wicked face. In each case, the loathsome spirit called up the darkest fears from the forgotten depths of their psyches, while at the same time their deepest lusting.

Al pulled out his knife, and with two quick strokes slashed Roxanne's wrists. Blood poured onto the floor. He moved the pail to catch some of the blood stream. Roxanne struggled slightly, but the weight of the heavy chains plus the valium in her system impeded her efforts. Al and the group watched as the blood flow finally slowed to a trickle. Her body quivered, then stopped.

She was gone.

Big Al studied the members of his clan. Their eyes were wide, their faces frozen in awestruck adulation. His feelings of omnipotence were never so great as during moments like this. He thrived on those feelings, lived for them, and wished life could always be this way. Time to capture the moment and ensure his control.

The group removed their hoods and stood in a row, shoulder to shoulder, facing their leader. Al picked up the pail with the blood, along with the cow's tail, and walked to the end of the line. Stopping in front of each person, he dipped the tail into the blood and slopped globs of the red liquid onto the person's face. They moaned and bellowed as they smeared the blood over their faces, noses and hands, like crimson colored sunscreen, then licked the slippery liquid off their fingers. Their lips and mouths, dripping in deep red blood, resembled the mouths of carnivores fresh off a kill.

This was their toast to El Diablo.

CHAPTER 5

Ken Washington watched the street intently as the action started to unfold. He keyed the mike which he held out of sight on his lap. "Heads up! I've got the squad car driving down the street. They've pulled up to the house. Both uniforms are out of the car . . . walking up to the house . . . knocking on the front door. Waiting. Now one of them is talking to someone. The uniform is holding up a clipboard. The door is still closed. I can't see who he's talking to."

The sprawling one story house, built in a "L" shape, had a new brick facade front. Inside the front door was a large dining room, then a huge sunken family room with a bedroom behind it. To the left of the dining room loomed a long hallway. As the squad car approached, Black Jack Mike, Jeremy, and Maureen were relaxed in the family room.

Black Jack Mike felt comfortable having Jeremy at his side for security. The two had hooked up several years earlier. He knew the skinny man with long legs and a short torso sometimes tended to be a little crazy, but he never doubted Jeremy's loyalty. Some time ago, after Jeremy shot and killed two people in a drug deal gone sour, Mike knew if he ever came into a threatening predicament, Jeremy would be at his side with his finger on the trigger of one of his guns. Obviously the man wouldn't hesitate to shoot. In the beginning of their partnership, Mike had occasionally wondered if Jeremy's trigger finger would be reliable if the threatening situation was brought on by the cops. He had since cast aside any doubts. Mike also concluded that if Jeremy had to drop the hammer on a cop or two, it would be very wise for Mike to get the hell out of the country.

No way would Mike ever go peacefully to the joint. Not with the options he strongly believed were available. His man had super heavyweight connections in South America. Mike had never met them, but he had certainly done them okay. On more than a few occasions, when fits of paranoia began to thump on his brain, he always found solace in the belief the people down south would surely open their doors to him if he came knocking. Wasn't it reasonable to expect assistance if he was in a bind? Wouldn't they show him some gratitude for helping them get rich? Bet your ass! Black Jack Mike's contingency plan, should he ever start feeling the heat bearing down on him, called for a quick rendezvous with Eddie, his ticket south.

Jeremy, a hyper guy whose life had always been right on the edge, had a natural tenor voice which raised an octave when he became angry or agitated. Flipping through the pages of a skin book, he alerted to the sound of slamming car doors. He jumped to his feet, scrambled to the front door and stood on his tiptoes, peering out one of the small windows.

"Hey Mike, check this out, man. Two cops coming up to the house. Don't look like they're in a hurry. Hey, one of em's Brady. Now what the fuck is he about? Don't know the other guy. Carrying a clipboard or some fucking thing."

Mike and Maureen sprang off the couch. She bolted to the back room. He joined Jeremy and stared out the window. They weren't narcs. It didn't *look* like a raid.

Damn strange. "What the hell. What the fuck do they want?" Mike muttered.

The drug dealer had to make a decision. How much time did he have? Maybe just a minute or so. Or maybe there wasn't anything going on. Maybe . . . maybe what? Flush it or stash it. Which? A struggle swamped his brain, as greed and paranoia neurons fought a high stakes duel. A clipboard must mean it's some kind of routine bullshit. He was probably okay. But still, cops at the door *might* mean a raid. Then there would be hell to pay.

Greed won. Gotta hide the dope. He grabbed Jeremy's shoulder. "Look, you handle 'em, got it? Don't let 'em into the house. I'll go move things around, just in case." Turning around, he yelled, "Hey Maureen, hide your shit." If Jeremy did his job, the cops wouldn't see him or the old lady.

He raced down the hallway to his office. Entering the room, Mike looked towards his desk. Bags of heroin, a pistol, a shoe box filled with money, a drug scale; it all sat out in the open and he stood vulnerable. Sweat began sliding down his forehead, clouding his eyes, dripping off his chin. He wiped his eyes with his sleeve. *Fucking cops!* Moving quickly, he scooped up the heroin and the box and scrambled to the closet with its false wall on the opposite side of the room.

Jeremy stared out the porthole while Officer Rodriguez, with Brady next to him, knocked loudly on the front door. Reluctantly, Jeremy opened the heavy inside door, leaving the outside storm door, with its thin glass window, locked.

Seeing Jeremy, Rodriguez said, "We need to talk to Jeremy Anderson."

"You know I'm Jeremy. What's this about? What you want?"

"Jeremy, I've got a summons from Hennepin County. You missed your last two child support payments. The judge wants to know why."

Jeremy's first impulse was of relief. Not a raid, just some kind of bullshit court thing. Then he was irritated. "Child support payments! What the hell you mean child support payments?" His anger increased, his eyes flashed and the tone of his voice went up a few notches. "What the fuck is this shit? I ain't got no fucking kids. Hey Brady, this is bullshit."

Brady's stone face mirrored that of Rodriguez. He was familiar with this character's short fuse. "Hey Jeremy, settle down. If you got no kids, it's just a mistake and you won't have to pay a dime. But you gotta tell the court."

"What the fuck, man! I'm busy! I ain't got time to fuck around going to court to talk to some judge about a bunch of fucking bullshit!" Sneering at Rodriguez, Jeremy snarled, "You said it was a summons?"

Rodriguez stayed cool. "That's right, it's just a summons."

"Let me see that fucking thing," Jeremy ordered.

Rodriguez said deliberately, "Hey Pal, we came here to give you this summons, not show it to you. You gotta sign a receipt for it."

Sensing things were about to get out of hand, Jeremy decided to cooperate. "Fucking bullshit crap." He cautiously stepped onto the porch.

Rodriguez showed lightning quick reflexes. He grabbed Jeremy's left arm and flung him onto the lawn. Air exploded from Jeremy's lungs as he landed squarely on his chest. His chromed nine millimeter fell out of his belt and slid across the grass. The small cop leapt off the porch, and his knees were digging into Jeremy's back before the gasp had ended. Following Rodriguez, Brady jammed his hand onto the back of Jeremy's head, smashing his face deep into the grass, while Rodriguez slapped on the cuffs. A quick pat down revealed a MAC-10 machine pistol still in its sling under his arm.

Ken and Robert had black ski masks, designed to protect their identities. As soon as the door opened they pulled the masks down over their heads, and Ken gunned it towards the house.

"It's going down," Ken reported. "We're on our way."

Within moments he could see the other cars squeal to a stop in front of the house, with agents jumping out even before their cars stopped.

Jake and Kiel were in the lead car. They arrived just as the two officers pounced on Jeremy. Jake bolted out the door, pistol ready, and sprinted to the house with Kiel right behind him. They bounded up the steps to the porch, followed by Lisa and Sal. Slamming his shoulder into the door and shoving it wide open, Jake yelled, "Police!" then rushed inside, followed by Kiel, Lisa and Sal. They raced towards the rear of the house.

Ken, Travis and Robert were next. They were to secure the rooms along the hallway to the left. Stopping at the first door, Ken glanced at Robert and said tersely, "Cover us." He then moved quickly into the first room on their left, while Travis took the first door on the right.

Moments later Ken announced, "This room's clear," and stepped back into the hallway. Methodically, he and Travis went through the doors along the hallway as they searched for people and weapons.

Robert soon found himself alone at the end of the hallway, staring at a halfway open, large oak plank door. Fuming how Ken treated him, he felt insulted at his given assignment in this raid. He could hear the others yelling from the far side of the house. It seemed that's where the action was. That's where the dope was.

That's where he wanted to be.

"Fuck this and fuck Ken," he muttered, deciding to secure this last room himself and then hustle to the other end of the house where he could be part of the action. Walking slowly through the doorway, Robert followed classic combat protocol: his arms straight out, pointed slightly downwards, his Beretta locked firmly in his hands, ready to fire.

The bat slammed down like a wrecking ball against a brick wall. A shrill yelp burst through Robert's lips as a shard of bone tore his skin, leaving his arm dangling like a Basset Hound's ear.

A curious thought flashed through Robert's brain before the pain registered: *A damned baseball bat?*

Black Jack Mike, pumped with adrenaline, whipped the bat around again, this time striking the rookie's shin bone. Robert moaned, seeing stars as he crumbled to the floor. His body quivered, fighting to absorb the pain. Then, brutally yanked off the floor, his feet hung a couple inches above the carpet. He tried to scream. Only a half-hearted gurgle escaped. The drug dealer's thick forearm pressed tightly against his larynx. Struggling to breathe, he knew he was being used as a shield. Robert fought for air. Then he realized his problems had only just begun as he felt the cold steel of a gun barrel shoved into his ear.

The agent focused on remaining conscious. Every move by Black Jack Mike tightened the stranglehold. Robert's vision blurred. His glassy eyes felt like they were ready to explode. He began drifting off. Vaguely, he heard shouts between his partner and Black Jack Mike. His eyes closed but he forced them open. What he saw wasn't good. Ten feet away, his partner's pistol pointed directly at his forehead. *This is it. I'm going to die. I love you, Grandma.*

A large, beefy man, Black Jack Mike had a bowling ball head and a bushy, fu-man-chu mustache. On his knees, he had just replaced the false wall when the screaming agents burst through the door. *A fucking raid! Damn it! Should've flushed the shit.*

Angry at his bad decision, he was ready for a fight. He sprang to his feet and looked across the room at his gun on the desk. Just a few feet away, but might as well be a mile. If he crossed the room to get the pistol, he'd be in view of the hallway. The cops would see him for sure, and they'd be on him like black on coal. No way would he reach the gun. His mind reeled. Fuck! Why didn't he jam the pistol under his belt before he grabbed all that shit.

He spotted a baseball bat propped in a corner. Remembered taking the bat from Maureen weeks earlier. Then it had been *her* weapon. Not a gun, but what the hell. It would do. Picking up the bat, he held it high and hid behind the door.

The bat did its damage. He dropped the bat and reached down, his thick fingers surprisingly nimble as they snatched up Robert's pistol. Cocking the pistol, the drug dealer shoved the muzzle into Robert's right ear.

Hearing the noise, Ken rushed to the doorway of the room he just secured. He saw the predicament and his adrenaline surged. Disaster in the making. Not even thinking, Ken simply reacted to his training. Tearing off his ski mask, he used the doorway as cover, cocked his pistol and trained its sights a few notches above Robert's head at Black Jack Mike's shiny, sweat soaked face.

Roosevelt saw Ken's head and pistol edged around the corner of the doorway. "Fucking drop it, Motha fucka! Drop the fuckin' piece! I'll do him! I'll fuckin' do him!" Roosevelt yelled, jerking on Robert's neck with each word.

Ken growled back. "Roosevelt, you want to come out of this alive you better be real fucking careful. *You* drop the fucking piece. Let him go and you'll be okay. If you don't, we'll be carrying you out of here in a body bag."

"Shut the fuck up, Fed! I'm calling the shots now." Mike's face flashed hostility. His yellow stained teeth bared ugly like the fangs of a cornered wolf.

Ken kept his finger snug against the trigger. "The only shot you're calling is whether you live or get riddled with lead. I'm telling you, let it go. We're sure as hell not letting you walk away."

"Hey, Motha fucka, it's your choice. You want this guy's brains splattered all over this fucking room or you gonna do what I say?"

Everything Ken saw and heard churned in surreal, slow motion, while his mind raced. Robert's life was doing a delicate tap-dance on a tombstone. A pool of blood collected at the rookie's feet while the kid moaned, obviously seriously injured. A twitch of Roosevelt's trigger finger and the rookie's brains would be blood pudding. How much stress had wormed its way into that finger?

Jake had been adamant about bringing Roosevelt in, getting him to cooperate. It was a big priority. The investigation was real important given the heroin explosion in this state, and this would be an ideal starting point. But even more importantly, Ken had to try and save his partner's life. He was positive Roosevelt wouldn't surrender, and with Robert's blood pooling on the floor there wasn't much time. The standoff must end quickly.

The agent focused on the drug dealer. His big head provided the best target. In this case, his mouth would be the bull's eye. The bullet would shatter the back of Roosevelt's head, instantly halting any signals to his gun hand. But the pistol screwed into Robert's ear was cocked, and the odds of it firing were high. At the academy the instructors discussed similar scenarios. It was fifty-fifty. That meant a one-in-two chance Robert's brain would catch a slug. Not good, especially from Robert's point of view.

Something had to be done about that weapon.

Ken said a quick, silent prayer. "Okay Mike. We'll do things your way, but one step at a time. I have to know Robert's alive and breathing. Take off his ski mask."

Roosevelt, desperately grasping for a thread of hope, eagerly felt a tinge of relief sail through his body. His mind raced. Yeah, he had played it right. He had a heavy bargaining chip with this knuckle head that walked straight into his arms. With one narc locked in his grip, the others had no choice but to accept his demands. If they didn't, they'd be scooping up this guy's brains and they knew it. Now if he could only trade this narc for some assurance the law would back away for a few hours. He had to meet with Eddie.

Black Jack Mike's left arm was busy holding Robert up off the floor. His right hand held the pistol to his prisoner's ear. Frantically, he yanked the ski mask off Robert's head, and for a brief second the gun pointed towards the ceiling.

POW! A nine millimeter hollow point bullet screamed through the drug dealer's mouth and out the back of his head. Blood, bone, and brains spewed onto the wall and the carpet, and Black Jack Mike fell, slamming to the floor with a loud *WHUMPFF,* the impact shaking every wall, rattling every window in the house. He didn't know he was dead.

Robert also fell, landing on top of Black Jack Mike's body. Using his good arm and leg, he wriggled off Roosevelt's quivering corpse, trying to get away from the grisly remainder of the drug pusher's head. The pain made him want to scream but he fought it off. *Yeah, my arm and leg are broken, but I can handle this, damn it.*

Ken and Travis were instantly at his side. Ken rolled up his raid jacket and placed it under Robert's head. "Hang on, Kid. We'll have an ambulance here soon. You'll be okay."

He then looked the other way. *What a mess.*

Seconds after hearing the gunshot, Jake and Kiel charged to the front of the house to see what the hell was happening. Seeing Jake hustling down the hallway, Ken yelled, "Black Jack Mike is dead. Robert needs an ambulance."

In the back bedroom, Lisa and Sal kept a tight lid on one very distraught Maureen. Her chubby wrists sported handcuffs. She looked down at the floor and moaned in self-pity as she eyed the evidence the agents found in the room. Several balloons of heroin lay on a dresser, next to a scale. Two guns, a pistol and a sawed-off shotgun, were on the floor, safely out of her reach.

Outside, Jeremy sat in the back seat of the police car, while Brady leaned against the car door and watched the house and wondered what the hell. Hearing the gunshot, Rodriguez had scrambled into the house and followed Jake and Kiel down the hallway. Using his portable radio, Rodriguez requested an ambulance, backup units, and a homicide team.

"An ambulance is on the way," he told the agents in the bedroom.

Kneeling next to Robert, Travis pulled a knife out of its sheaf to cut Robert's pants leg and expose the wound. As Ken watched, he told the others what happened.

Jake took over. "Don't touch anything. Homicide will have to look at everything before we start our search." He left the room and went to the back of the house to talk to Maureen.

In her late thirties, Maureen carried some extra pounds. Her tight blue jeans looked obscene over her huge buns, and her blouse was taxed to its limits. Long gold earrings dangled from her ears. A blue scarf, knotted in the front, covered much of her hair. Staring at Jake, she looked like a deer caught in the headlights.

"Maureen, your husband's dead. We had to shoot him," Jake said, trying to sound sympathetic, but actually pissed off and frustrated.

"Serves him right. He got me into this pickle. This is all his dope," Maureen stated with a smile.

Her reaction surprised him. "So, I take it you didn't much like him."

"Well, it's not like that's a big secret. Yeah, we're married, or were, but it was all about money. Mike was a real jackass, but he knew how to make bread." Her eyes lit up as an idea struck her. "Say, being as he's dead and all this dope is his, does that mean you can let me go. I won't be selling no more dope for him, I promise you that."

"Nope. That's not how the system works. Sell dope, you gotta face the music."

"Well, how about taking off these bracelets? Where the hell could I go? I mean, you got me surrounded." Maureen frowned.

"Not a chance. Lisa and Sal will keep you company until we leave. The cuffs will come off when you get downtown."

"Uh, okay."

The ambulance arrived and the paramedics placed Robert on a gurney and took him to the hospital. Ken and Travis followed. Minutes after they left, the homicide detectives arrived. Clearly upset Ken and Travis had left, the detectives completed their investigation of the scene, had the coroner remove the corpse, and then headed to the hospital to get statements from the only eye-witnesses.

With the detectives gone, Jake and Kiel stood back and surveyed the room where Roosevelt made his last stand. The room was sparsely furnished, with only a desk, two office chairs, and a closet filled with clothes.

Jake walked over to the desk and picked up Black Jack Mike's .357 magnum revolver. The homicide detectives had unloaded it and left it there for the narcs. "This could've done us some damage."

Kiel nodded. "If he wanted to do something with the dope, why was he here and not in back with Maureen, or in the john putting the toilet to work?"

Jake looked at the other side of the room. "Yeah. And if he was squaring off for a fight, why did he leave his gun on the desk and attack us with a damn baseball bat? You don't bring a baseball bat to a gun fight."

Eyeing the closet, Jake crossed the room. He swung open the two over-sized closet doors and looked inside. Black Jack Mike had been a clothes hound. Jake looked thoughtfully at the array of expensive suits, shirts and ties, all hanging from rods or lying in a closet organizer. Several dozen pairs of high dollar shoes were neatly arranged on shelves stacked from floor to ceiling, taking up nearly half the closet's twelve foot length. Apparently the room had been a bedroom, but Mike converted it into an office. Possibly he kept all these clothes in the closet because their bedroom lacked space. Then again, maybe he wanted to conceal something. Jake snatched an arm full of suits and sport coats and carelessly tossed them onto the floor, unconcerned when some landed on the globs of blood and grisly residue. Next went the shirts, then the ties.

He got down on his knees and closely examined the closet.

Nothing.

He stood up and examined the shelves holding Roosevelt's collection of shoes. The organizer was made of narrow, white steel rods and heavy gauge wire. He looked at the carpet where the posts met the floor and noticed an outline, barely discernible, where one of the posts appeared to have rubbed against the carpet, leaving a ghost of a trail. His heart started pounding. He was on to something.

Scrutinizing the organizer he noticed a board, several inches long, butted up against the inside corner of the closet. The whole affair was a professional piece of work. But the board, slightly canted, was trying to give up its secret. Gripping the board with his hand, he gave it a tug and heard the unmistakable sound of Velcro. So, that was it! He pulled it off the wall and grabbed the organizer. It pivoted out of the closet like a door on hinges. Behind it, a paneled wall. Jake noticed tiny nicks along a seam. He took out his knife and jammed it into the seam, coaxing a piece of paneling away from the wall. His work exposed a compartment, about four feet long, three feet high, and a foot deep. It concealed the evidence that would've put Black Jack Mike away.

"Well, how about that," Jake said smugly.

Looking into the space, Kiel flashed a grin. "Black Jack Mike's career was at a dead end, and he knew it"

"Yeah, the only question was where he'd be doing his time? In the joint or the grave yard? Help me move this stuff to the desk where we can check it out. Roosevelt wasn't big on talking to us, but we can learn something here."

The agents shuttled Roosevelt's stash over to the desk. Kiel placed the zip lock baggies filled with powder onto the scale one at a time, while Jake tallied the weights and added the numbers. Then he nodded approvingly. "One and a half kilos of junk the street's not gonna see. Some people around here will feel that."

Next they started on the money, counting the hundreds first, then the fifties and on down the line. It totaled $82,000.

"Not bad for a day's work," Kiel said, grinning. "How about that ledger? That might tell us a lot."

Jake glanced through the pages. "Sometimes we get lucky. We wouldn't want Black Jack Mike to have died for no reason." Then he spotted four safe deposit box keys lying in the shoe box, and put down the ledger. "It's a safe bet a chunk of his profits went into these safe deposit boxes. The eighty-two grand is just a start."

Lisa walked into the room. "We finished searching the rest of the house. Did okay in the back bedroom, but nothing like we expected. A couple ounces of junk, $9,000 cash, a safe deposit box key and a couple guns. How'd you guys do?"

Before they could answer, she approached the desk. "Hey, the mother lode. Congrats, guys. That's the biggest junk seizure I've seen since I came to this icebox."

Jake wasn't that impressed. "It's a good seizure, but it can't stop here. If we can't take this to the next level, we're nowhere. Wish I could've talked to that asshole."

Lisa looked at the slurry on the floor and the wall that a few hours earlier had been Roosevelt's brains. The scene evoked some grisly memories, and a shiver ran through her shoulders and down her spine. Sensing Jake and Kiel noticed her reaction, she willed it to stop, adopting a macho posture. Turning her back on the mess she said, "Fuckin' idiot. Any fool knows you don't take a federal agent hostage at gun point and live. This almost looks like a suicide by cop."

Kiel studied her closely, then lightened up. "Yeah. Inconsiderate bastard. Only thinking about himself. If he wanted to die, he could've had the decency to talk to us first. What did he have to gain by taking what he knows to the grave?"

Jake decided he'd had enough. "Let's get this stuff loaded into the van and get the hell outta here."

Lisa and Sal took Maureen, and Jake and Kiel took the van.

Heading downtown, Kiel became concerned. "I wonder how Ken's going to deal with this. Killing someone's damn tough to live with. He's gonna need some time to regroup."

"I know. He did it right, did what he had to do. But he's going to pay a price. Might have a few nightmares."

Kiel nodded. "So, what's with Lisa? I was surprised by her reaction. She always comes off hard, but the mess in that room sure grabbed her crotch. You think it had to do with what happened in Florida?"

Jake knew. But if she wanted the entire office to know, it'd be up to her to tell them. He gazed out the window. "I guess you'll have to ask her."

Kiel juggled those words for a few seconds. Yeah, something was going on. Something about Lisa made him feel uneasy. Something he hadn't noticed before. But then this was their first shooting since Lisa arrived in Minneapolis. "Huh. Maybe I will." He let it pass, returning to the image of Robert, lying helpless on the floor, his arm and leg bloody and mangled. "Hope they can patch up Robert. Those were some ugly wounds."

"Yes they were." Jake's voice was matter of fact. "The poor guy just got here, raring to go, and now he'll be hung up at home. What a career starter."

"Yeah," Kiel murmured quietly. As they reached Olson Memorial Highway, Kiel turned onto the street, smoothly merging in with the flow of traffic. He switched lanes and passed a truck.

Jake's mind moved back to the raid and Baby Duke's information. The commotion back in that house brought on a sensory overload. Now, riding shotgun in the van, he finally had time to think. An alarming thought nudged his brain. Something didn't fit.

"You know, going through Black Jack Mike's records I saw a number of entries to *Duke*. It seems *Duke* regularly bought half ounces. I'm thinking *Duke* has got to be our one and only Baby Duke. Baby told us he got his shit out of the back bedroom. But it appears Black Jack Mike dealt out of that room in the front."

Kiel thought about that. "I hope Robert didn't get busted up because that snitch scammed us. When we hit the house, the back bedroom was our first priority. If you're right, and if Baby had told us that, we would've done it differently. Maybe nobody would've gotten hurt."

"Yeah. As it turned out, Roosevelt had too much time and he used it to make one hell of a desperate decision. Must have been damn scared of going to the joint. That's the kind of person that flips. With all the stuff we found, we had him cold. We really could've laid on the pressure. My gut tells me he would've talked, told us all about his connection. Could've been a whole different world. When I get Baby Duke back in the office we're going to put him through the grinder. He's holding something back. Maybe he knows something that could help us move this thing along. I want to know what's going on."

Over the years, Jake had controlled many informants. They ran the gamut as far as color, shape, and personality. But typically they had their own agendas, and lying was part of their game. Jake always watched for it, but this time, as suspicious as he was, he had missed something. That cost them. One agent hurt, another would be hurting, and someone dead. All on Jake's deal. He gnashed his teeth, upset he might have dropped the ball.

As soon as they arrived at the office, Jake, Kiel, and Lisa secured the evidence and then focused on talking to the two prisoners who were locked up in separate detention cells. The interview room was down the hall. Its contents were simple: A gray, steel table with two long steel bench seats, all bolted down.

They first brought Jeremy to the room. Without expression, he looked at the three agents on the other side of the table as Jake read him his rights. "I'll do my talking to my lawyer. Leave me alone."

The man was hard core, and Jake wasn't surprised by his attitude.

Next came Maureen. Lisa showed her through the door and she sat down on the bench seat, waiting for Jake to start rolling the ball.

He looked into her eyes, sizing her up. He'd done this a thousand times, was familiar with the range of attitudes and looks dealers tossed his way, and within a few seconds could see where her mind was. She was thinking about her two options: Fight it or cooperate. But Maureen knew damn well fighting it would lead down a dead end street. She got caught sitting on a couple ounces of H, along with a basket of evidence that proved she'd been dealing. Her body language told Jake she'd bust her ass to get the hell out of this jam. Before he even started talking the game, he knew how it would play out. First off, the woman would tell him what she knew so she could get back onto the street. Then, to make sure she stayed there, Maureen would hire an attorney; one who could help her grease the skids to freedom with a shit load of cooperation, while making sure the feds held up their end of any agreement.

Maureen's voice carried a husky sing-song tone, and Jake could see she wanted to quickly put her vocal cords to work. Without prompting she repeated, no, she didn't like her late husband. Yeah, it was a business partnership, not a *real* marriage, and even the business end was getting rocky.

"So tell us about it," Jake said curiously.

She got straight to the point. "Okay, you know I was a heroin dealer, but I was a honest heroin dealer. Not a crook like Mike. Of course, he always wanted to be called 'Black Jack Mike,' like he was something special. Huh! Black Jack Mike. Once in a while I'd call him 'Nigger Mike,' just 'cause I liked riding his ass. Other people couldn't do that, but he was afraid of me. I'd call him whatever I want. He was just a crooked nigger, trying to cheat everybody.

"I'd buy his heroin an ounce at a time, you see. Sometimes I'd pay him right up front, sometimes I'd pay him later. A couple months ago I got an ounce from him and paid him up front. I made good notes of that particular transaction, you understand? My records was always good and accurate. His records weren't shit. So a week or two later he tries to cheat me; tells me I still owed him for that ounce. I tell him I already paid him. So he doesn't believe me and starts going through my personals looking for money. That got me mad. I kept a baseball bat in my bedroom, just in case, you understand? So I grabbed the bat. I was going to start thumping on his head, but he ran out of the house with Jeremy behind him."

"The baseball bat from hell," Lisa said, grimacing.

"So, what you're saying is there were two separate drug businesses operating in the house?" Jake asked.

"Yeah, you got that right."

"And you had your business going in the back bedroom?"

"That's right. He slept in the back, but he never did any dealing there. That's where I did my business, and he knew that. And I never went into his office except once when I caught that fucking Baby Duke trying to steal some of Mike's stash. I went in there that one time and chased his black ass out of the house. I used the same baseball bat. It sure got his attention."

Kiel raised his eyebrows. "So you're saying Baby Duke wasn't one of your regular customers?"

"Hell no, child. I wouldn't ever want to do no dealing with that snake."

Jake dug a little deeper. "So, Baby Duke always bought his heroin from Mike?"

"Child, isn't that exactly what I've been telling you the last ten minutes?"

"Yeah, but we have to make sure we got it right."

"We've got Mike's drug records," Lisa said. There's a number of entries that say a person named 'Duke' was buying halves. Would that be Baby Duke, or was there another Duke?"

"Well, that would be Baby Duke, buying half ounces. There weren't no other Duke dealing with Mike."

"Okay. All this junk Mike was getting. Where did he get it from?" Jake turned the page on his notepad.

"You mean *who* did he get it from?" Maureen's face showed more than a trace of apprehension. Maybe even fear. She didn't want to get into it, but knew there was no choice if she was going to get some relief out of these narcs.

"Yeah."

"Well uh, a few months ago he told me they had a different connection, and the new stuff came from South America. Colombia, South America. Same place where all the cocaine comes from. The heroin came from one of them CARtels. You want somebody that's big? Those people are big. Mike didn't have enough sense to make simple change, but he had a dynamite connection. One of the people you'll be looking for is a guy named Eddie. I think he heads up the smuggling end of their operation. There's two others that I heard Mike talk about. A dude named Frenchy something or other. He's the main supplier of the white folk around the cities, an' he's supposed to be one vicious mother. The other one they call Big Al. I got the impression that guy is even badder than Frenchy. I know Mike was afraid of him. He supplies the northern half of the state and I think North Dakota too. Mike said Big Al's got some weird looking white bitch doing a lot of his dirty work."

Jake kept a poker face. *Eddie! Frenchy! Big Al!* Maybe he was making some progress here. "You know her name?"

"No, I don't. But I remember Mike telling me the organization stretches all the way from South America to

the top of Minnesota. Said they have a new jet plane. So
new it still smells fresh, just like a new car. You know how
a new car smells before folks start smoking inside it? He
said that's what the plane smells like. At least that's what
Eddie told him. I don't know what they do with it. Maybe
that's something you ought to look into. Maybe they use it
to smuggle their dope. They bring in coke too, but Mike
never dealt snow. Strictly a junk man. That's where the
demand is, and the way they talked, the demand is getting
bigger and bigger. Mike bragged that he did his share to set
that up. Yeah, those people are big all right.

"Say, I'm giving you guys some good information
here. I should never have to go to no jail now."

CHAPTER 6

Jake's boss considered the Black Jack Mike shooting an opportunity to advance his personal agenda. Sitting at his desk, he pondered over his next step. Alan H. Ravich had his name embossed in gold on a heavy sterling name plate occupying a prominent place on the desk. The name plate looked rich, a hint he must be quite an important person. Beneath the name, in slightly smaller letters, were the words 'Resident Agent in Charge.' The position was called 'RAC' for short. Sitting behind the desk, filling his high-backed leather chair, Alan's appearance was highlighted by a head of reddish-blond hair and a well manicured, rusty colored goatee. Early in his career he was thin, but now he resembled a wooden barrel with arms. Divorced and never re-married, (rumors had surfaced he was a wife beater) he spent much of his off-duty time occupying a booth in one of his favorite watering holes. His disposition was generally as sour as his drinks.

As RAC of a small DEA office, Ravich hadn't yet made it to the senior management level, and a few of the senior bosses weren't happy he made it this far. He didn't care what they thought. He got to this desk thanks to some shrewd and well timed ass-kissing. In spite of all the ballyhoo, the DEA's good-ol'-boy system was alive and well. Alan had spent the last ten years assigned to DEA Headquarters where he played the game. He preferred office work to getting his hands dirty, and the tower always had a variety of positions for agents who didn't want to work the street. But finally he came to grips with the reality that without supervisory experience in the field he wouldn't go any higher. He decided he needed a good drinking buddy who had influence with the heavy weights. His plan worked, and within a couple years he got his promotion and reassignment.

Minneapolis was a step in the right direction, but he was going to be out of there as soon as he could swing it. At fifty years old, he was seven years away from mandatory retirement, and if he continued to play it right he might get a shot at the big leagues. Alan dreamed of landing a real cush job; being top dog, or at least second in command, of a major office like Chicago or Los Angeles. Those jobs paid damn good and led to a fat pension, a whole lot better than this desk offered.

In the meantime, he would look after one of his special interests. Ravich was elated he could swing Scott Hookman's transfer from the Big Apple to Minneapolis. Yeah, Scott's short assignment to New York hadn't turned out, but things would change now that Scott had a Rabbi of his own. As head of the office, it would be easy for him to steer a career case to Scott's desk. Harold would be a good mentor for advice and direction to make the case successful. One good case, a few well-placed words, and the kid's fledgling career would sky rocket. Too bad Scott hadn't been in a position to take the lead on this heroin case. Simply a matter of timing. Alan must've been looking the wrong way when that lead came in, or it never would've gone to Jake.

Alan didn't like Jake. The man was a leader, no doubt, but there was friction between them. Jake kept his distance from both Alan's office and his favorite watering holes. It concerned Alan that Jake's attitude might bleed onto the other agents. They all liked Jake except Scott, who marched to Alan's drum. If Jake would get with Alan's program, the others might follow. If not, then he was a threat. After six months as RAC, Ravich had decided Jake wasn't going to play the game. Alan felt as head of the office he certainly deserved an occasional smooch planted firmly on his ass. If that wasn't to be, then Jake might get something shoved up his.

Ravich couldn't simply yank the heroin case away from Jake and assign it to Scott. That could adversely affect Jake's career, so Alan would need some justification. But he would scrutinize Jake's work with twenty-twenty eyes, and if at any time it didn't measure up, well then, maybe . . .

Having decided on the course of action that best fit his short term plans, he called Jake into his office.

As Jake approached the man's desk, he could sense where this meeting was headed. Alan's bloodshot eyes and crimson nose were beacons of animosity. What followed wasn't exactly warm and fuzzy.

Alan looked at Jake closely, taking his time before speaking. "So, how is it that you allowed a rookie agent to get hammered by a fucking baseball bat, lose his weapon, and then seriously jeopardize the entire raid team. What makes it even worse, you should be talking to Black Jack Mike, not burying him."

Ravich noticed Jake's eyes narrow. Yeah, some hostility there. The time was right to impress on this guy, lest he ever forget, who called the shots and who did the grunt work.

Jake tried to explain the problems encountered in the raid. "Well, boss . . ."

"I'm doing the talking now. This was your raid, wasn't it?"

"Yes, it was. I . . ."

"Don't interrupt me. You met with the informant, you made the assignments . . .

Returning to his desk, Jake fumed over his private meeting with the boss. Ravich hadn't worked the street for so long he had no clue. The man's assessment of the raid was way off. Yeah, an agent was hurt. And okay, killing Black Jack Mike certainly didn't help the cause. But what choice did Ken have? They *had* seized a hell of a lot of money from the house and those safe deposit boxes. And what about the dope they found? One helluva good seizure. Now there was one less heavy weight prowling the streets of north Minneapolis. Anyone with experience in knocking down a door knew executing a raid was one of the most dangerous elements of this job. Intelligence helped, but what hid behind that door was always a big question mark. DEA agents were the best trained narcs in the world, but damn it sometimes shit happened. Sometimes you took a hit.

The meeting added insult to injury, and Alan had made a point to mention the lengthy, negative newspaper article. Jake knew the north side was in an uproar over the shooting, but wondered where the press got all their information. If that shooting wasn't justified, what shooting was? After reading the article, Jake had the impression its author must have been one of Black Jack Mike's customers. He sure had a burr up his ass. Whatever, the boss really took it personally.

He stared at his watch. Yeah, it was time to get Baby Duke into the office. Set his ass down on the hot seat and watch the little parasite wriggle. It wasn't a case of shit flowing downhill, but, well, okay, maybe it was. What the hell. That's part of life. Jake had to accept responsibility for the raid because it was his deal. But Baby Duke was a major contributor to the problems.

Jake planned his strategy. When he got Baby on the phone, he'd talk vaguely about the CI's reward. That would get the scumbag downtown. Jake believed there were two ways to control informants: Carrots and sticks. Depending on the informant, cash might work as a carrot. But the stick was generally more effective. Nothing like the threat of prison to keep someone motivated. Baby Duke didn't have prison to worry about, at least not now. Maybe that was part of the problem. But he wouldn't get any cash either. Jake wasn't interested in working the informant again, and he intended to substitute a lot of heavy talk for the carrot. Baby Duke lied and for that he would pay. Jake wanted to know the truth, and he knew to get the facts he would have to make the little maggot squirm.

Ken wasn't available to join Jake in the confrontation. He was on administrative leave following the shooting, and hadn't yet been cleared to return to duty. Kiel eagerly volunteered to fill in, saying if Jake wanted to chomp on Baby's miserable, drug-dealing ass, he wanted a chunk too. When it came to ass-chewings, there was always room for another shark.

The informant arrived and they plunked him down in the interview room. Jake's eyes, narrow and needle sharp, made it obvious handing out rewards didn't occupy a spot high on the drug agent's list. Baby felt the heat as soon as his butt touched the cold steel bench.

"Black Jack Mike is dead. Jeremy and Maureen are in jail," Jake said resolutely. "We seized a lot of heroin and cash."

Baby Duke shifted in his seat. "So I heard. You guys cleaned up. I guess we make a good team, huh."

"We need to clear up some details," Jake continued brusquely, ignoring the CI's lame attempt to fade the heat. "You told us Black Jack Mike did all his dealing in the back bedroom."

"Well, yeah, I had that impression. Say, when do I get paid?"

"But you got that sample from Maureen, isn't that right?"

The informant squirmed some more. He hadn't figured on this. "Well uh, yeah, that's the way it was," he muttered nervously. "She gives me a little of her product when I stop by, you know."

"Did you ever do any dope deals with Black Jack Mike in his office at the front of the house?" Jake's voice was confrontational, his face stern.

Baby Duke took it all in. He knew where this was going, and frantically searched for a way to get these wolves off his back. He wanted to take his paltry reward and make for the door. The money was a whole lot better on the other side of the fence. Why screw around over here? Fuck Black Jack Mike and his bitch of a wife. Fuck Jake. And fuck being an informant. "Well, I went to their crib a lot over the past year. I don't remember. Maybe we did and it just slipped my mind. That's a long time to be remembering things, you see what I'm saying?"

The trap was set. Time to pull the trigger. "Well, looking back over the past few months, do you remember ever being in that office at the front of the house?"

"Well, I might have. Can't remember right now."

Stepping over the bench seat and picking up a covered object, Jake raised the baseball bat from hell high over his head and slammed it down heavily on the thick steel table. The loud crash reverberated in the small room, and nearly jolted Baby Duke off the seat. He grabbed the edge of the table.

"So when was the last time you saw this fucking bat?" Jake yelled.

Baby's eyes, a world away from calm, expanded to half dollar dimensions and stared at the bat, and then Jake. He took a few seconds to regroup and catch his breath. "Hey man, let's don't get violent, okay? Be cool. I'll tell you about it.

Jake sat down to let Baby Duke talk, but kept the bat on the table for incentive.

"I been scoring dope from Black Jack Mike's crib for a couple years. His stuff has always been good, but man, six months ago it exploded. His connection changed. I'd go there every week or so to score a quarter or a half. Always got it from him. Look, his old lady is a real barracuda. We hate each other.

"So a couple months ago I'm sitting in the dining room waiting for BJ. He's in his office, getting my bag ready. Then he heads past me towards the back. I know Maureen was there and I hear them arguing. Suddenly BJ comes running past to the front door. Jeremy jumps up and takes off trailing him. Then Maureen storms out of the back, holding this big fucking baseball bat over her shoulder. She really can't run very fast, so she throws the bat at them just as they're opening the door."

Jake and Kiel exchanged glances, both frowning, but let Baby continue without interruption.

"That bitch has one hell of a temper. She walks past me, picks up the baseball bat, swearing and muttering, and waddles back to the bedroom. Doesn't even see me. So now BJ is out the door, forgot all about me, and I need to hit some shit real bad. See what I'm saying? Maureen is out of sight, and she sure as fuck wouldn't give me anything. I decide to go into BJ's room and see if he's got my bag ready. I wasn't going to steal anything you know. I wouldn't do that."

The atmosphere thickened as the tension between the CI and the agents seemed to draw the walls in even closer. Baby Duke's eyes darted nervously between Jake, Kiel and the table in a futile effort to find a safe haven.

"So I'm in his room and I see he's got a scale on the desk next to a bag fulla junk and a box stuffed with money. I don't know how much junk. Looked like over a half pound. I figured I'd just take a quarter ounce or so and pay him later, you know, like the next time I saw him. I don't see any balloons on the desk, so I scrounge through the shoe box. Like maybe there's some balloons under the money or something, you know. Anyways, I'm looking and I hear this noise behind me. I turn around and it's the fucking bitch, about to crack my head open with this motherfucking bat. So I start talking to her, trying to settle her down. She calms down and we make a deal. See what I'm saying?"

Jake glared into his eyes. "You were dealing behind our fucking backs, weren't you?"

"Yeah, I was dealing. I'll be straight with you guys. That's how I paid for my shit. But now Maureen's telling me every time I score from Black Jack Mike, I've got to give her a full fucking third of what I got. And if I don't, she'll tip him that I was going to rip him. He finds out and he's going to pound me into a bloody stump, probably kill my ass. So I got no choice. I gotta pay the bitch. But now, with this whore holding me up, I'm hardly able to get through the week. What the fuck could I do about it? Then I think, what the hell, I got you guys. You're always hungry. Give you guys a case, I can make a little bread and move on to a different connect. But I can't blow my cover. No fucking way.

"So I know how you write those affidavies. I tell you I got the shit direct from BJ and that goes down on your affidavie, then sure as hell they'll know it was me turned on 'em. But hey, Maureen's dealing heavy too. Got her own customers. She's just as dirty as BJ. Why not set 'em both up? Just tell you I got it from her in the back bedroom. She'll think the informant was one of her people and nobody'll even be looking my way. And I know you guys won't miss BJ's stash, 'cause you'll tear the house up once you're inside. Then I'd have my reward, you'd have your case, and they'd be in the joint. Could've worked perfect."

Feeling the blood throbbing in his head, Jake wanted to reach over the table and grab the man's throat. The raid had been plagued by problems. Baby Duke couldn't be blamed one hundred percent. But if they hadn't been misled, the agents would've focused on BJ's office. They would have been ready for anything, and Black Jack Mike's nose would've been putting a dent in one of the walls. But as it turned out, Robert went to the hospital and Ken would have to come to grips with a killing.

Jake's eyes met Baby Duke's watery pupils. "Listen you fucking toad. One of our guys is busted up and somebody is dead because you decided to play fucking games. I want you gone. If I see you again, I won't need any excuse to toss you into the slam right alongside Jeremy."

Somehow, the CI managed a defiant expression. "Okay, I hear you. But I risked my ass to give you guys some information. You got a mess of dope out of it and you owe me some green."

Kiel was more than ready to kick the guy's butt. He reached over and grabbed Baby Duke by the front of his shirt, pulling him nearly across the table. "Hey, you little sack of shit. You're not getting a fucking dime. What you are getting is the fuck out of town. If you're still around tomorrow, I'm putting the word out you were the Black Jack Mike snitch. Everyone in the fucking Hood will know it. You hang around, we'll be finding your ass lying in an alley."

"All right, hear me out." Baby Duke's voice quivered. "One of your guys got hurt. That's not how I thought things would go down, but the damage is done. You see what I'm saying? If you guys'll stay off my ass, I got something for you. It's big. Bigger than BJ, for sure."

Jake and Kiel glanced at each other sardonically, both rolling their eyes.

"Let's hear it," Jake said skeptically.

"The guy you wanna look at is a white dude named Eddie. He was BJ's main man. BJ let that slip a couple months ago. Said Eddie had a solid connect in Colombia. The dude's bringing huge amounts of junk into Minnesota. Once he gets the dope here, he's got three people doing the distributing. Now, I guess with BJ gone, Eddie's only got two. I heard BJ say the name 'Frenchy' once. He might be one of 'em, but I'm just guessing. I'm thinking it won't take long for Eddie to find a replacement for BJ. That's all I know about him, but that's some heavy shit. You find Eddie, you're on the right track."

They escorted Baby Duke to the back door and he headed for his car. Watching the CI's jalopy disappear down the street, Kiel turned to Jake. "What do you think of this South American heroin thing?"

Jake shrugged. "Baby Duke's not the most reliable guy ever walked through that door, but Maureen told us the same thing. The Colombian drug cartels have poured enough coke into this state to fill half our lakes. Why not heroin? They've already got the machinery in place. For sure we're dealing with an epidemic."

"You got that. We've got to find out more about Eddie."

Jake nodded. "Yeah. And Frenchy and Big Al, if we can believe what we're hearing. At least we got some names."

Jake's thoughts shifted in a different direction. "Went to see Ken last night. Wanted to see how he's holding up. Told me he's been having nightmares. Said the whole scene keeps churning through his mind. He didn't join the DEA to be an executioner, but that's how he feels. The man is eaten up by guilt and anger. He's not dealing with this very well."

Kiel shook his head, not liking what he heard. "I've read studies that say over half the people in law enforcement who kill in the line of duty turn in their badge within five years. It can scramble a person's career and life."

"Yeah," Jake said, concerned. "When I worked in San Diego we had two shootings in one year, just a couple months apart. The first agent really changed . . . got depressed, never got over it. He quit, went off the deep end, started hitting the bottle. The second agent went back on duty. Didn't seem to faze him. I guess fifty-fifty is pretty close. I don't like where that puts Ken. I saw the look in his eyes. There was more there than just lack of sleep."

Jake found Ken's road map eyes to be especially disturbing. They revealed much about Ken's struggle; guilt, anger, depression. Bad things. Ugly things. Things that could reduce Ken to a hollow shell. Or worse. Jake recognized the signs. Agent burn out wasn't uncommon, and it happened for a variety of reasons. Too much undercover work, long hours without positive results, and inept supervision were just a few of the culprits. Killing somebody ranked pretty high. A cop never knew how he'd handle that until it happened. Ken had no choice in shooting Black Jack Mike. He did his job and the results were ugly. And then, like Jake, he got his ass reamed by Ravich. A double whammy. Little wonder Ken wasn't himself after the Black Jack Mike raid. Jake wondered in which direction Ken would ultimately go.

CHAPTER 7

A week before the next full moon, Tanya, Frankie and Charlie scouted the Minneapolis metro in search of their next lamb. Their searches weren't especially organized. They simply drove around shopping malls, movie theaters, parks, or wherever and looked for girls or young women who were alone and vulnerable. Once in a while they got lucky. Other times it would take a few days hard work before they had their prize. Mindful that Big Al wouldn't tolerate failure, they always allowed themselves extra time.

Early one evening the trio watched the sunset approach as they entered the parking lot of a mall in Edina. Tanya drove the van, with Frankie in the passenger seat. As they drove past a row of cars, Frankie spotted a target. A teenage girl who had just gotten out of her car walked towards the mall.

"Check it out," he said as Tanya drove past the girl. "She's by herself."

Tanya grinned as her adrenaline rose. This marked day one of the hunt. She loved it when luck smiled on them.

"She got out of that beetle at the end of the row, didn't she?" Tanya asked.

Frankie nodded. "Yeah."

"Okay. She comes back, we'll snatch her when she gets to her car." Tanya looked back at Charlie. "I'll park so her door is right next to you. Be ready. I'll tell you when. If you gotta punch her, don't kill her." She turned to Frankie. "Keep your eyes peeled. Tell me if there's anybody who can see what's going on."

Frankie and Charlie both nodded. They knew the drill.

The three sat in the van, anxiously waiting for their victim to return. The sun edged deep into the horizon and the parking lot lights came on. The clan members welcomed the sunset. During these operations, darkness worked in their favor.

Mary Dee had dimples, freckles, and wavy brown hair. The sixteen year old had just acquired her drivers' license, and relished her first taste of independence. She coaxed a set of keys out of her parents and drove to the mall.

With summer around the corner, Mary Dee purchased a bikini swim suit, sandals and sun screen. Elated at the day's purchases, she happily strolled out of the mall and hoofed it to her car. A security car stopped at the cross walk to let her pass, and she smiled at the guard. He smiled back and continued on his way, turning into a parking lot serving an adjacent section of the mall.

Tanya and Frankie both spotted Mary Dee as she walked towards them.

Tanya's crisp voice blurted, "She's coming down the aisle, Charlie. Be ready."

"I'm ready."

"How's it look to you, Frankie?"

"Don't see nobody around."

Finding it difficult to contain her excitement, Tanya said, "She's about twenty feet away. Remember, don't kill her."

Charlie nodded. "Don't worry. El Diablo will be pleased."

Busy searching through her purse for her keys, Mary Dee looked up when a car full of high school boys turned down the aisle and stopped.

Two of the boys stuck their heads out. "Hey Mary Dee," the driver said. "You got your own wheels now?"

The girl's eager smile betrayed her answer. "Hey, Smitty. Hi guys. Yeah, got my license yesterday, and now I'm good to go."

The boys looked at each other, all grinning.

"Want to join us for a burger?" Smitty asked.

"Love to."

"Great. Get in your bug and follow us."

Mary Dee followed the boys out of the parking lot.

The deflated clan members all cursed angrily as they left the mall to continue their search.

Meanwhile in the Southwest, Jose Garcia de Lopez, driving a semi loaded with leather jackets and boots manufactured in sweatshops in Mexico, knew all about the six kilos of pure heroin concealed underneath the bed of his truck.

He cleared Customs at the US port of entry without a hitch, and proceeded to the first Chula Vista exit off Interstate 5. Parking his rig near an outside pay phone, he punched in a pager number and sent the message "12121." His next stop came a short time later in the Chula

Vista industrial area, where he entered a large parking lot near an import warehouse. Parking his rig between two trailers, he jumped down and waited.

Sandra Walton arrived within minutes and slipped her car in behind Jose's rig. Her driver's license said she was twenty-four years old and from San Bernardino. She had a plain face and board straight, light brown hair. As an added touch Sandra wore glasses with thick, ugly frames, a bulky, oversized sweatshirt, and baggy levis. Above her right eyebrow, a small birth mark resembling a miniature Mickey Mouse wasn't particularly appealing. She wasn't a knockout, but when dressed up she wasn't the same homely woman who had just parked behind Jose's truck. Except for the birthmark her coarse appearance was deliberate; a makeover she worked on in preparation for each trip. She had it down to a fine art. Shortly, she would board a Greyhound destined for Minneapolis. Sandra considered it imperative to be an unnoticed ghost for the next couple days, as inconspicuous as the drab, worn fabric covering the seats on the bus.

In drug smugglers' lexicon, Sandra was a mule. As a courier for large quantities of dope, she cherished anonymity as much as a snowman needs snow. The risks were high, but the rewards good. Sandra's fee brought her a thousand dollars a kilo, plus expenses. Each trip took five days; two and a half uncomfortable days on the bus, thirty-six hours in a Bloomington hotel room, and the relaxing plane ride home. She made the trip once a month. It was better money than stripping.

Sandra got out of her car and with a brisk, business-like air, approached the smuggler. Her schedule set, she didn't consider Jose worth a lot of friendly chatter.

"Hello, Jose. Everything okay?"

"No problems." His thick, heavy Latino accent made speaking English difficult for him, and he kept it short and simple. He felt uncomfortable in her presence.

Sandra nodded, indicating, "show me."

Almost home free, Jose wasted no time scampering under the truck. He unfastened the cover to the hidden compartment and tossed a compact leather tote bag to Sandra, now on her knees watching.

Sandra anxiously unzipped the bag holding six rectangular shaped packages, each inside a zip lock bag and strapped in white paper tape. "PRODUCTO DE COLOMBIA" had been stamped in black ink in several places on each package. Nodding her approval she said, "Okay, looks good. See you in a few weeks."

As she started towards her car, Jose walked jauntily into the warehouse and handed his brown manifest for the legal cargo to the manager.

Leaving Jose, Sandra drove directly to a dumpster a quarter mile away. She retrieved a medium sized suitcase from her trunk, promptly transferred the heroin into the suitcase, and tossed the tote bag into the trash.

The suitcase matched a second bag. Both displayed tags identifying the owner as Barbara Sheffield. The address and telephone number on the tags were bogus, although she didn't really believe anyone with the bus line would give them a second glance. In her mind, traveling via bus provided an extra layer of security for her activities. A pain maybe, but so far everything had gone like clockwork. And okay, her boss demanded sex every time she came to Minneapolis. But what the hell? The money fit her needs, and so did a good screw every month. Especially with him. He did things for her that nobody had ever done.

Recently their relationship had become an obsession with her. Did she love him? She didn't know. Never having loved a man, she had no experience in that arena. But the monthly meetings with him sure as hell lit some fires in her belly. What was it? The risks of her occupation? Her boss's good looks and physical endowments? Maybe the great sex they always enjoyed.

(She considered him a genuine stud. Cool, sophisticated, and totally different from her loser friends in California.) Whatever, she always looked forward to checking into the hotel, and wished this arrangement would go on forever.

Sandra headed toward the freeway and the bus depot. Arriving at the terminal, she parked the rental car in the adjacent garage and carried her suitcases into the building. The television screen indicated her departure was on schedule. She nodded her approval. Purchasing a one way ticket to Minneapolis, she wanted to be the last to board.

The bus route twisted through Las Vegas and Salt Lake City, making numerous stops as they headed eastbound on Interstate 80 to Des Moines. From Des Moines, a direct shot north took the bus to Minneapolis. By the time Sandra arrived she was tired, smelly, and felt fur on her teeth.

Walking out of the terminal, she saw refreshing bright rays of May sunshine peeking around tall buildings. The fresh air felt pleasant, but not enough to make her change her opinion of Minnesota. Looking around, she hailed a Yellow cab.

Seeing her, the cabby jumped out. "Need a cab?"

"Yeah," she said, and handed him the suitcases.

He slipped her luggage into the trunk and opened a rear door. "Where to?"

"The Medallion Suites Hotel in Bloomington."

"You got it."

Beaumont Lenihan, a minor cog in the heroin organization, came on duty at the Medallion Suites at 4:30 PM. An assistant manager at the front desk, he sported a mysteriously smug face. He had occupied that position for years, with assurances from management of upward mobility, future career potential, and on and on. But none of this happened. He stagnated, while many people hired after him were receiving promotions and transfers to larger hotels.

Three years ago he had made plans for a career change when a girlfriend helped him with a life altering introduction. She put him together with a man who had serious money. The man was tall and trim, with an olive colored complexion and coal black hair. He presented Beaumont with a most interesting proposition.

"All you have to do is watch for the police. I'm talking plain clothes types. It'll be for four days every month. Your contact will stay in touch and she'll let you know when it's over. Tell her if you notice anything suspicious. Each day you're on guard I'll pay you two hundred and fifty dollars."

Beaumont liked what he heard. An extra thousand a month. Talk about easy money. How could he turn this down? He now lived on an easier street, the money was always there, and never a problem.

He knew it involved drugs. But so what? In his opinion, his minimal role presented minimal risks. After all, a guy couldn't get into trouble just for being observant. His hotel job, keeping his eyes and ears open and making sure the guests' needs were met, made his other job quite simple. Beaumont made it a game identifying his other boss's "mystery guest." There had been three so far. Lately, his eyes had settled on Barbara Sheffield.

Sandra's cab dropped her off, and she carried her suitcases into the hotel's cavernous lobby. No bellhops here, one of the things she liked about this place.

"I'm Barbara Sheffield," Sandra said as she brushed up against the front desk. "My husband has a room here, but I don't know the room number."

With an ambiguous smile, Beaumont said, "You've got room 304, Mrs. Sheffield. You know how to get there, don't you?"

"Yeah," she replied as the clerk handed her a pass card.

Sandra headed directly down the hall to a bank of pay phones, where she methodically dialed a number and punched '30303.' Then straight to her room. The hotel room was the standard run of the mill: two beds with the usual lamp table in between, a dresser beneath a large mirror, and thick draperies concealing a picture window overlooking the parking lot. On one side a door led to the neighboring room. Sandra always tested that door immediately upon entering her room. That done, she could breathe just a bit easier. While she didn't like it, the door had never caused her problems. Every room in the hotel had a connecting room. Kind of a poor man's suite, she supposed.

She checked her watch. Five-thirty. Sometimes he didn't show up until late the next day, but she never knew for sure when to expect him. Anxious to take a shower, she stripped down and scurried into the bathroom, taking the heroin with her. After a long and relaxing shower, she felt clean but not refreshed. Too tired to eat, she crawled into bed. When she woke up she'd clean her contact lenses and do some magic with her hair.

At seven-thirty the next evening the man entered the hotel. His contact had spoken with Beaumont. Everything looked cool. Time to go to work. Outside of Sandra's room, he noticed a room service tray on the floor with dirty dishes and food scraps. Good! He liked that she followed his explicit instructions. He knocked lightly on her door.

After a quick peek through the peephole she let him in, smiling seductively. "Hey Stallion," she said cheerily.

She wore a delicate, sheer gown. Her face wasn't something to win pageants, but her body would've been a worthy competitor.

Looking at her, his eyes couldn't decide where to focus. They finally gravitated towards her breasts. "Hi. Everything okay?"

"Yeah."

"Good. Come on, let's play," he said with a grin, gesturing towards the bed.

Sandra squealed with delight, slipped off the gown and jumped into bed.

Within seconds he was naked against her. Slowly he savored her clean, lightly scented body, as he explored it with his hands, his lips and his tongue. She began to sigh and moan almost simultaneously, as she eagerly surrendered herself. They made love enthusiastically, each holding nothing back, and when finished both were satisfied it was everything they wanted.

They lay on their backs, catching their breath and enjoying the moment. Finally, he forced an impassive expression and said, "That wasn't bad."

She playfully punched his wash board stomach. "Huh. Wasn't bad? I'd say we had it timed perfect. But you know my timing could have been better last night. I was dragging ass when I got in. First I took a well-deserved shower. Then I intended to take a short nap but I totally zonked out. When I woke up at nine-thirty room service was shut down, and was I hungry."

"So, where did you eat?" he asked cautiously.

"Didn't. Stayed in my room. Hope you appreciate how I follow your rules."

Sensing martyrdom, he reached over and began stroking her flat tummy.

"Maybe these long road trips are good for you. Keep you from getting fat."

She pretended to ignore his hand. "You know, maybe I should charge you for the great action I give you."

He took his hand away. "Yeah? With the good screwing you always get, maybe I should pay you less."

Sandra became serious. "Okay, time out. Look, these bus rides seem to get longer every trip. Is there any other action besides the cross country tours?"

"Don't tell me you're overworked."

"Those damn bus rides sure get old."

"Okay," he agreed. "So you're underpaid. Look, I know reliable people are hard to find. We've had people who tried to cheat us. We got rid of them, and I'm glad you're aboard. Just don't cross us."

"Eddie, you know I'd never do that. Don't say that to me after we made love."

"Yeah, I suppose that was insensitive, but right now we're talking business, not pleasure. When you combine the two, you assume the risks. I like you Sandra. I'll talk to my people about kicking in another two-fifty a key. Sound okay?"

Her heart did a giant flip-flop. Eddie never went overboard with affection, but at least he appreciated her. And the extra money would be a good salve for his occasional aloofness. "Sounds good for now."

"Great. Let's see the packages."

They dressed and Sandra pulled out the suitcase. He examined the packages thoroughly, especially interested to see if the words stamped on the tape, across the seams, were intact.

"Everything looks fine." he said.

"Yeah. I checked it all out just like you told me. Jose seemed okay, too." She always mentioned Jose. If she forgot, Eddie would ask. He was the kind of person who always kept his fingers on the pulse.

"Okay. See you next time around."

"Bye, Eddie."

Eddie handed Sandra an envelope and left the room carrying a suitcase.

CHAPTER 8

In another part of the metro, Sudden Sam O'Grady, the middle aged owner of the Saddle Club, was hard at work. The club was his life. He spared no expense making the Saddle Club the best strip joint in the city. Sam brought in Las Vegas and New York talent, who alternated on the dance floor with the homelier local strippers. The locals doubled as barmaids when not on the stage tantalizing customers.

His patrons found lots to like in his club. It featured a top notch sound system, its softly padded Italian leather chairs were comfortable, and the drinks generous. A well-stocked mahogany bar dominated one end of the club, the stage the other. The club's cover charge, highest in the Twin Cities, never discouraged a packed crowd from gathering. Blue and white collars gleefully mingled to the catchy sounds of the music and the rhythmic grinding of the stacked beauties on stage.

Sudden Sam held two beliefs close to his heart. The first: Drugs are bad. The second: Prostitution is good. Outspoken in his opinions, he never missed a chance to expound his views on both issues.

Sam saw drugs as the scourge of the world. His establishment witnessed frequent visits by state legislators, local judges, a prosecutor, defense attorneys, cops and at least one federal agent. All of them were clients who eagerly met with him in the privacy of his office as he conducted his other business, 'Sudden Sam's Sex Services,' as they liked to refer to it. While taking their money,he always seized the opportunity to tell them how he felt about the drug problem.

"Drugs kill people. Thousands and thousands of people die every year from drugs. And some people are trying to legalize dope. I say no fucking way."

His opinion on prostitution received equal attention, and even though his clients already shared his viewpoint, he couldn't help but lobby them. "I'm providing the good citizens of this community a needed service. What I can't figure out is why it's illegal. It's not illegal in the state of Nevada. Why should it be illegal here? It's the oldest profession, and it's not going away. We should make the most of it. After all, morality can't be legislated."

His captive audience had heard this monologue more than once. While in their private conversations the legislators always sympathized with his cause, they nevertheless made no effort to change the laws.

Sam embraced their money, but hated their hypocrisy. Yet his definition of hypocrisy seemed to have its limits. Drug dealers were welcomed to his club along with everyone else, as long as they didn't deal on his turf. As he said when the subject arose, "I'm not a cop."

Frenchy Deveroux, like many others, frequently came to the club to experience the best of both of its worlds. The night Frenchy died, Sam sat in his posh private office talking to Karen, his newest employee. She had been stripping for a month when, like most of the girls, she decided to supplement her income.

"So, you made the big decision did you?" Sam asked.

Karen looked across the desk at the big Irishman and flashed him a warm smile. She found the man fascinating. His congenial smile made her comfortable. His large head, topped with short, curly brown hair, reminded her of her father. And his barrel-sized chest and pro-wrestler's shoulders gave her a sense of security while on the dance floor. Karen reported to work that day wearing a floral, silk mini-skirt, and made no effort to conceal her crotch from Sam's view.

"Yeah," she answered, lightly massaging one of her thighs. "I can see some of the other girls are doing really well. I'd like in."

All business, Sam's mind never succumbed to distraction. "Okay. This is how I operate. Prostitution in my club is real discreet. I handle it solely by referrals, and all business is arranged in advance. The payments are made directly to me. I pay you, and I keep half."

Explaining his rules, Sam cautioned any violation would send her out the door. His first rule: No hooking on the side. And then he talked about his pet prohibition. "Another iron clad rule is no drugs in the club, and I watch real close."

She nodded in agreement and smiled brightly at her meal ticket. "The girls talk about you all the time, Sam. You have my word, I'll definitely play by your rules."

"That's the only way it can be, Karen. It's my show. I'll be straight with you as long as you're straight with me. Welcome aboard."

"Thank you, Sam. You know, everyone says you're a solid guy. But could you tell me something? How does your reputation tie in to your nickname?"

Sam chuckled. "Sudden Sam?"

"Yeah."

"I don't know that the two are related, but it's like this. When I was younger, I was a champion golden gloves boxer. Most of my matches ended fairly quick."

Business was brisk as Frenchy Deveroux entered the club in his typical showboat style. He saw Sam at the end of the bar and bellowed out a greeting. Sam nodded and walked back to his office. Deveroux followed.

Frenchy took a seat opposite Sam and cut to the chase. "Sweet Candy on tonight?" His eyes betrayed his exuberance for the evening.

Sam found the man's eagerness amusing. "She'll be here in an hour."

"Any chance she can get off around eleven?"

"If the money's right." Sam's pearly teeth gleamed through a friendly smile.

Frenchy reached into a pocket and withdrew a wad of hundreds. He counted ten, folded them in half and gave them to Sam. "Here's a thousand. Me an Nikki need her for the night."

"I'll let her know."

Frenchy left the office and found a seat close to the stage. In his mid-forties, the man had thinning hair, fat cheeks, and a sizable paunch. Although obviously in poor shape, he dressed rich. Thick strands of gold hung around his pudgy neck and dangled off his right wrist. Flashing a gaudy diamond ring along with a Rolex watch, he displayed an air of self-confidence associated with wealth.

A saucy looking blonde waitress came and took his order. She returned shortly with a tall drink. Giving her a wide smile, he sat back eager to relish all the flesh soon to parade across the stage. Candy's image stirred his imagination, and his groin tingled in anticipation of what the night would bring.

A few minutes later three men entered the rapidly filling club. They paid their cover charge and managed to find an empty spot a few tables from Deveroux. In his early thirties, Curt Haug, the leader, was a tall, skinny man with stringy, dirty looking hair held captive by a red headband. The long, tapered bridge of his hook nose contributed a hatchet-like bearing to his narrow face. His weasel eyes, which even in the dark liked to hide behind tight slits, were those of a practiced predator. Curt had done time.

The other two, Eric and Desmond, also on the thin side, were five years younger. Like Curt, they were junkies.

Sam quietly noted their arrival. A successful club operator remembered faces, and he always tuned in to the arrivals and departures of his patrons. He had seen Curt and Desmond a number of times, but didn't know their names or background.

Looking toward the stage, the three took care not to attract Frenchy's attention, speaking quietly and stopping their conversation when the music quit.

Curt glanced over at Desmond. "Tell Eric what you learned," he directed.

Leaning towards Eric, Desmond filled him in. "The guy has a huge place out in the country by Elk River. He comes here a couple times a month and takes one of the strippers home. Got a nymph named Nikki living with him and they're big into threesomes. Nikki likes to talk, and she's got a relationship with a chick I know. That's where I get the skinny. The two get it on once in a while when Frenchy's out of town."

Grinning at Curt and Eric, Desmond continued. "Fatso has big bucks. Deals in heavy quantities of junk, and he's always holding. He's also got coke in his place for the skirts, but nothing big. This looks as good as it gets. Checked out his place yesterday. It's perfect. Has a few acres surrounded by trees. You can barely see the house from the road, and it's out of sight from the neighbors."

Putting his elbows on the table, Curt leaned forward and took over. "Desmond's chick said Frenchy would be coming here tonight. Looks like her information is solid. We'll watch him and get a feel for when they're about to leave, then we take off." He lowered his voice, almost to a whisper. "There's dope, money, and a pile of gold coins in his place. This could be the fucking mother lode."

A tall, shapely twenty-one year old blonde, Candy liked to strut her stuff, and knew how to put her curves into motion on the dance floor. As a part-time hooker, full-time stripper and barmaid, she made serious money. Recently, however, much of it went towards a habit.

Candy reported to work conservatively dressed in a white blouse and dark pants, looking more like a bookkeeper than a stripper. Seeing her arrive, Sam beckoned the stripper to his office. Until a month ago, Sam could set his watch by her arrival. But now she was about as predictable as next year's weather. Sam didn't like fog in his club's forecast.

"You're late again. That's twice in the past week. You never used to come in late. Ever. Is everything okay?"

"Yeah, everything's fine. I guess I just lost track of time or something. I'll try harder. Sorry."

"Good, we need you around here. You're one of the best," he said enthusiastically.

"Thank you, Sam. Is that why you called me in here?"

"Just part of it. Frenchy is here. I told him you'd be available at eleven o'clock. I'll pay you tomorrow, like always."

"Okay. I'll take good care of him," she said agreeably.

"Great. Now give us a good show. They're hanging from the rafters out there."

"You got it."

Candy went into the dressing room and prepared for the evening. Ten minutes later, approaching the stage, she caught Deveroux's attention. He looked at her with an eager smile, which Candy returned.

CHAPTER 9

About ten to eleven a waitress, showing off ample cleavage, checked on Frenchy, asking, "You ready for another?"

Staring, he said, "Nah, I'm leaving. But this is for you, Sweets." He laid a C-note on the table and watched her wide blue eyes light up.

At the same time, Candy walked to the dressing room behind the bar.

Curt watched. "Heads up. They're ready to split. Let's go."

As if on cue, they got up and walked out. Sam mentally noted three paying customers leaving.

The trio headed to Curt's van in the parking lot, where they noticed Frenchy's car, a red BMW.

"That's his Beamer," Desmond said, entering the van.

After paying the attendant, Curt drove west on I-94. Taking the Elk River exit, he turned onto a dark county road, drove a couple miles west, then north.

"It's coming up soon," Desmond cautioned.Moments later they were in front of Frenchy's place. Curt stopped. "Big house, three car garage," he commented. "I'll pull over to the left side of the house, out of sight from the driveway."

Turning off the headlights, he studied the house. Bright yard lights illuminated the drive. "Frenchy will drive into one of the garage stalls. We'll just walk in behind 'em."

The stillness of the country night was complete. The darkness behind the shadows of the large, two story structure was total. Curt stuck his head out the window and listened for any activity. Nothing. They were cool.

He turned and whispered, "Quiet as a whore in church. Get ready. Remember, keep your masks on and no shooting. If they don't get hurt, the cops will never know about this."

Following Curt's lead, Desmond and Eric put on their ski masks and crawled quietly out of the van. Peeking around the corner, Curt had a bird's eye view of the illuminated driveway.

Fifteen minutes later the Beamer pulled into the garage. The trio crept towards the open door. Frenchy was partially out of the car when Curt jammed his nine millimeter into the side of Frenchy's head.

"Okay Fats, you do exactly as I say and maybe you and the whore will be alive to talk about it," Curt said brutally.

Knowing this meant big trouble, Candy remained frozen in her seat. Eric, pumped and impatient, wasn't as polite as his leader. Tucking his pistol under his belt, he opened the door and yanked her out by the hair. She attempted a scream, but he slammed his fist into her mouth, knocking out several teeth and welcoming her into the world of the junkie. Then he cocked his pistol, pointing it at her head.

"Listen you fucking cunt," he snarled. "No noise. Just do as we say."

Candy's mind and body enveloped in terror. Her muscles quivered violently while globs of blood poured out of her battered mouth, spraying her skimpy outfit and the floor.

Frenchy knew what they wanted. His mind raced, searching for a way out.

Desmond didn't like what he saw and punched Frenchy hard in the stomach. Cushioned by layers of fat, the punch had minimal effect. He round housed Frenchy's gut three more times and got the man's attention. Frenchy doubled over, his lungs desperate for air. Desmond bent down and looked into the man's bulging eyes. "Pay attention, Asshole. Try anything and it'll be the last thing you do."

Satisfied things were under control, Curt said, "Inside." He activated the garage door and led them into the house.

Inside, Desmond said, "I'll find the other bitch." He bolted upstairs.

Nikki, a living Playboy image, sat on the king size bed in the master suite and casually applied a sparkling crimson polish to her toe nails, awaiting the pleasures of the evening. Her long, glistening dark brown hair complemented her high cheek bones, large, soft brown eyes, thin nose, and brilliant white teeth. A sheer Barbie Doll teddie stopped just above her navel, covering her smooth shoulders, and barely concealing her picture-perfect breasts. Seeing Desmond enter the room with a gun, her shriek pierced the air as she pulled the sheet up to her neck.

Desmond raced to the bed, pulled the sheet off and gruffly yelled, "Shut your mouth, bitch. We're not here for you. Do what we say, and you'll be okay."

Walking into the house, Frenchy had caught his breath. But his brain continued to struggle for a way to turn the table. He noted their ski masks. A solid sign these assholes had no intention to kill him or the girls. They simply wanted his dope and money. He didn't keep a fortune in the house, but neither was it small change. Add that to the value of the junk and coke, it would take months to recover the loss. No way would he turn it over to these fucking rip-offs without a fight. Did Nikki know where the safe was? Maybe. She was home alone much of the time. But he had never shown it to her. Frenchy gambled only he knew about the safe. The guy jamming the pistol into his back had to be the leader. Any way to take him out? Yeah. It'd be damn risky, but if he failed they wouldn't kill him. Beat the hell out of him, sure. Shoot him and they had nothing.

A stairwell close to the kitchen led to the second floor. Resting on a pedestal at the base of the stairway, a two foot pewter statue of a nude woman pointed one of its arms up the stairs. *Probably my best chance.* When he reached the stairway he grabbed the statue, hoping to spin around and use it to knock the gun from Curt's hand. He didn't come close. Pulling back sharply, Curt over-reacted and shot Frenchy. The bullet caught the man square in the side of his head, going straight through and narrowly missing Eric and Candy. Frenchy's head exploded, plastering Eric's back with blood, brains and skull bone fragments. Eric flinched, accidentally squeezing the trigger of his nine millimeter, and sent a bullet into Candy's shapely torso. Her mouth opened wide, but like a mime, there was no scream. She crumpled unceremoniously to the floor.

The two gunmen stared at each other. "Aw fuck," Eric moaned. "Now what the hell we going to do?"

Curt was stunned. They were just getting off the ground, and it seemed his plan had already crashed. He had to get things back under control. "Shut the fuck up. Let me think."

Desmond had just shoved Nikki out of the bedroom when he heard the shots. Fuck! A shoot out! He grabbed Nikki by the shoulder, spun her around and punched her hard, breaking her thin nose. Bleeding and moaning, she fell to the floor.

"Stay where you are, Bitch," Desmond quietly hissed, pointing his gun at her head. He cautiously approached the top of the stairwell. Peering down he saw the two bodies, lying in pools of blood, with Curt and Eric standing over them.

"Son of a bitch," Desmond cried. "I thought you said no shooting."

Curt and Eric both looked up, and Curt said quickly, "Bring the bitch down here. We gotta make this fast."

Desmond picked her up and shoved her down the stairs.

Seeing the two bodies, Nikki totally freaked. "Oh no! Oh my God! Oh no!" Bleeding profusely over her partially nude body, she stared numbly at the body of her dead sugar daddy.

"This way, Bitch. Hurry up," Curt yelled. He pushed her towards the kitchen where she sat on a chair, with a wide, blank look, staring at the floor. Curt dropped down to one knee and looked into her face. "Frenchy's dead 'cause he wouldn't talk," he lied. "The girl was an accident. There's a big stash of dope in this place and lots of money. We want it."

"Oh! Oh!" Nikki sobbed hysterically.

He slapped her face, trying to get her attention. "Listen bitch, just show us where it is and you won't get hurt. You don't even know who we are. We'll leave you alone if you promise not to call the police until morning. We just want to get out of here."

Nikki blubbered and wailed incoherently, totally incapable of speech. But she understood what had been said and cooperation seemed her only ticket. Why not? It wasn't her stuff. Nodding, she pointed down at the floor.

"Good girl. Are you saying it's in the basement? Show us," he said, pulling her onto her feet.

Walking unsteadily to the stairs, she led them down to a large unfinished basement. On one side stood some wooden storage cabinets, the furnace and a water heater. Against the opposite wall, a washer and dryer. She led them to the dryer. Curt looked at the appliances. They looked like they had never been used.

Nikki finally regained her composure enough to talk. "Underneath the dryer is a floor safe."

Eric and Desmond moved the dryer and saw their prize. The expensive looking safe had a stainless steel door with a spin dial lock.

"Do you know the combination?" Curt asked. His harsh, crisp voice echoed throughout the cinder block interior.

Nikki nodded, then meekly walked to one of the storage cabinets on the other side of the room. With shaking hands, she opened up a door and pointed to one of the sides. "That's the combination," she said, sniffling. "I guess Frenchy must've wrote it there in case he forgot it."

Looking inside, Curt saw the combination written in very small print. "Yeah, this is it. Real good," he said with a grin.

He returned to the safe, knelt down, and opened it on his first attempt. "All right," he said with satisfaction. "Let's see what we got."

Reaching in, he pulled out a large paper sack, then another. Opening the first, they all looked inside. "This one's full of cash. Looks like all hundreds. We'll count it later." Curt set the sack aside and opened the second. He pulled out a gallon size zip lock. "I'd say a couple pounds of smack," he said, examining the beige powder. "What else we got?" He retrieved a second baggie. "Coke."

Desmond nodded and said, "Let's get the fuck out of here."

"Right. Just one more thing," Curt said. He stood up and took his pistol from his belt, then looked at Nikki. "I lied," he said, and fired three times.

They pulled off their ski masks, and Eric stared in disbelief at the bloody young woman. This was the first time he had ever done anything with these two. "Motherfuck! None of this was supposed to happen," he muttered. He walked to a corner of the basement and puked.

Curt didn't like the idea of killing anyone. Murder meant life in the joint, and he sure as hell wasn't going back there. But it was done, and nothing would change it. "Knock it off. I knew we'd have to kill her when I saw her on the stairs. We didn't have no choice, you guys know that."

Walking over to Eric, he grabbed his shoulder. "Come on. You can be the first to try some of the junk."

Eric retched again. Finally finished, he nodded.

Looking at him, Curt sneered. "Let's go!"

He grabbed the paper sacks, and they ran up the stairs and out of the house.

Driving towards the Cities, Desmond sat in the passenger seat, next to Curt.

Eric, sitting on the bench seat in the back, dug through a satchel for his works, hoping to shoot up right away. Looking for his syringe and cooking spoon, his muscles quivered and his hands shook. "Look, I'm a fucking mess," he said, clearly upset. "I got blood and brains all over me. The shit's even in my hair. I got to get back to my place to clean up before we split this stuff. How about handing me that bag of smack. I'm going to do some now."

Desmond crawled to the back with the bag. "Here. Don't take it all." Then he returned to the passenger seat, opened the sack of money and stared at it contentedly.

Safely on the freeway, Curt asked, "Hey Eric, whereabouts you live?"

"Just off Lake Calhoun Park." Eric was cooking some junk with a lighter.

"Okay. That's our first stop," Curt replied. Looking back he saw Eric ready to shoot up.

It was total silence in the van as Curt motored to the Lake Calhoun area in south Minneapolis. Turning onto the Parkway, he looked around again.

"Hey Eric, which way now?"

No response.

"Eric, pay attention. We're at Lake Calhoun. Where's your place?"

Nothing.

Curt looked over at Desmond. "Go see what the fuck!"

Desmond again crawled to the back of the van, pulled out a penlight and shined it on Eric's face. Eric lay on the bench seat, his head and shoulders slumped against the side of the van, his eyes blank and a slight smile on his face.

"Motherfuck," Desmond said loudly. "Hey Curt, Eric's dead!"

Curt grinned. "Hey, that must be some pretty good shit. Well, that means you and me get a bigger cut. Where you want to dump him?"

Desmond thought about it. "He wanted to go home. I guess this is as good a spot as any."

Driving past a stretch of sandy beach, Curt said, "Here's Lake Calhoun. There's a concession stand next to that entrance. How about dumping him behind it?"

"Yeah, whatever."

Curt pulled in and they looked around. Thirty feet away were clusters of shrubs and trees.

"This'll do," Curt said. He drove up next to the concession stand, turning off the headlights. "Nobody'll see him at least 'til morning."

Neither of them noticed the teenage couple making out behind the shrubs. With the bright moon overhead and the city's lights as a backstop, the kids could clearly see everything.

CHAPTER 10

Big Al beamed as he looked into the briefcase stuffed with bundles of currency. Two of his clan had just returned from a road trip, and gave him the cash as their evidence of a successful week. Closing the briefcase, Big Al brought it to his basement. Spacious and partially finished, its walls were paneled with rich, wooden mosaic squares. Its ceiling had white elongated tiles. Its concrete floor, hidden beneath colorful and intricately designed oriental rugs, was the only unfinished part of the large room. In one section of the basement a physical conditioning center with two weight benches, a punching bag hanging from the ceiling, and a treadmill awaited Big Al's pleasure. A billiards table occupied another section. A long, comfortable looking leather couch sat next to a long wall.

He shoved the couch away from the wall. Stepping up onto the couch, he moved a ceiling panel revealing a toggle switch. Flipping the switch, an electric motor started humming softly as a portion of the paneled wall behind the couch moved slowly inward, exposing a three by three foot opening. Getting down on his hands and knees, he pushed the briefcase into the opening and crawled through. Inside, he stood up and surveyed a concealed room.

Two walls in the room had heavy steel doors leading to tunnels. The room compared in size with that of a two car garage. A walk-in vault, featuring a standard combination dial, occupied much of the space. A gun cabinet loaded with an arsenal of weapons and ammunition stood guard next to the vault.

A quick glance reassured him everything was in order, and he opened the vault door. The vault, constructed with steel-reinforced concrete, had eight foot high walls, and was as big as a full-size van. Currency had been stacked in rows from floor to ceiling along the length of one wall. On the floor, nearly four hundred thousand dollars contained in a tote bag waited to be counted. Looking at the money, he felt relieved he had the money counter. Even so, counting all the cash he had just taken in would be time consuming.

Recently, Al had been strongly considering moving his money to another location. A place the Feds could never find. The vault was well hidden and secure, but ultimately this money was his life.

The mountain of money, however, didn't come without its share of serious baggage. His vigilance had paid off, but at the same time it deprived him of his mobility. Relocating the cash occupied the top rung on his wish list, because his home held him hostage. With so much at stake, his fingers had to remain on the pulse and he could never be away from the farm for longer than a day. The clan members, with the exception of Tanya, lacked the sophistication needed to deal with problems as they arose.

But where could he move the money? He really doubted his clans' ability to move large amounts of money across borders. They were very good at selling dope, but smurfing? Probably not. Money leaving the country in amounts exceeding ten thousand dollars had to be registered with Customs. Failure to do so constituted a felony, and the Feds were alert to this requirement. In any event, he had not taken any steps to deal with money in another country. He didn't have any trusted foreign contacts.

Banks? No way. Enormous deposits like he would have to make would attract big time attention. Safe deposit boxes were also out. It would have taken more safe deposit boxes to accommodate all his cash than existed in the local banks.

Still, Al knew at some point he would have to move the money. And when that time came, he would need help from someone he could trust explicitly. Could Tanya be that person? Maybe. Everything she did exuded her loyalty. The fact she loved him cemented the relationship. Yeah, if he knew one person who would unfailingly do his bidding, it was her.

After considerable thought, Al had decided to do nothing until the time came to shut down his operation and move on to fresh pastures. Closing shop meant dealing with the witnesses, and that would take some planning. He figured one more year. Until then, he would stay close to the farm. It wasn't a bad place to roost.

Scott Hookman's career with the DEA began three years earlier in New York. After he and another agent argued over a woman, a feud developed including vandalism, harassing phone calls and anonymous threats. While proof had eluded them, most of the agents placed Scott at the top of their suspect list. The Special Agent in Charge of the New York office totally agreed.

Somehow, Scott managed a transfer to Minneapolis, but his transition didn't go smoothly. It wasn't long before the Minnesota agents were clued into his lack of motivation. They also noted his condescending attitude, something the agents assumed related with his disquieting friendship with the boss. It all added up to an icicle office relationship.

Several days after the Elk River murders, Cindy, an office secretary, developed her own opinion of the agent.

With fiery eyes, she stormed out of the unisex restroom muttering, "I should have known."

Scott was the last to have used the john. Sitting at his desk he found himself confronted by the highly irate woman. Glaring at his slicked back red hair, then his evasive blue eyes, she unloaded on him.

"So, Scott, just how old are you anyways?"

"Twenty-six," he answered, puzzled.

"You've been pissing for twenty six years and still haven't figured out how to aim that damn thing? Worse yet, you apparently don't know how a toilet seat works. Tell me, how would you like to go in there and sit your bare ass down on somebody's urine? Didn't your daddy teach you nothing?"

Just then the phone rang. Scott reached for it thankfully.

The voice on the phone sounded somewhat stressed. "Scott, this is Sudden Sam O'Grady. I feel uncomfortable calling you at your office, but I may have some important information for you."

"Yeah, Sam. What can I do for you." Truthfully, he hoped this would come to nothing. A client of Sudden Sam's other business, Scott didn't want his job to muddle his social life.

"It's about Candy. You remember her don't you? Of course you do. She disappeared, and after reading today's paper I think I might know what happened, but I don't want to go directly to the police. I got my business to protect, and thought you would be the best place to begin."

"So, does this involve drugs?" Scott hadn't read the paper.

"Yeah, heroin. Lots of it. And missing people too."

Scott's mind quickly shifted into overdrive, looking for an angle to avoid work. Just then Jake came through the door, solving Scott's problem. "Sam, I have to refer this to our heroin expert," he bullshitted. "I'm going to put Jake Shaunessey on the line."

Sam was a little put back. Strange, his friend passing the buck this way. Scott always talked a good game. Well, what the hell. Who knew how the DEA did things? "Uh, okay. Thanks Scott. We'll be talking."

Scott turned to Jake. "I've got a call that involves what you're working on."

Picking up the phone, Jake introduced himself.

"Jake, Sudden Sam O'Grady. You may have heard of me. I own the Saddle Club. I've got some information you might find real interesting. It's about a pound of heroin, some cocaine, and one of my employees who's missing. Can we meet?"

"Sure," Jake said. "Where are you?"

"At the club. It's not open yet, so nobody's here and now would be good."

"I can be there inside of twenty minutes."

"I'll be waiting," Sam replied.

Ending the conversation, Jake turned to Kiel. "Hey Bud, can you join me in a meet?"

"Sure thing. What's up?"

"Just talked with Sudden Sam O'Grady."

"The Saddle Club? What's he want?"

"Says he's got information on a pound of junk and a missing employee."

Locking his desk, Kiel said, "Let's go."

Jake grabbed his battered briefcase and within minutes they were on their way.

Getting into Jake's car, Kiel appeared amused. "You know, I think we've rubbed off on Cindy. She's become a pretty fair investigator."

"Yeah, how's that?"

"She collared the toilet seat ghost. Just as you were coming in, she was reaming Scott's ass."

"So, Scott's the one?" Jake chuckled.

"Cindy seemed pretty positive. And now I've got a good idea why they transferred him out of the Big Apple."

"And what's that?"

"He's not a straight shooter."

Jake laughed, then changed the subject. Scott wasn't at the top of his list. "How's the heroin investigation going?"

Following the shooting, Alan Ravich decided to shake things up. His plan included reassigning Kiel, who became Lisa's partner. Kiel's immediate responsibility involved helping her with an undercover heroin operation that seemed to have targets located all over the Metro area. Kiel wasn't happy with the new assignment. He would miss working closely with Jake. But he figured working with Lisa would probably be okay once he got to know her.

Kiel thought about Jake's question for a moment. "I'd have to say it's moving, but at a snail's pace. Our informant knows lots of people and the list of defendants is growing with Lisa's UC buys. So far it's just a bunch of small-timers, but I try to be optimistic. It's kinda like playing the slots at Vegas. You never know what's gonna happen with the next pull of the handle. There's always a jackpot out there somewhere. We might get lucky."

"I guess luck has its place in this job. Personally, I think good agents make their own luck. You going undercover with her?"

Kiel shrugged. "If we can work it. Right now the dealers don't want to meet anyone new. I'm just playing second fiddle, doing surveillances, helping where I can. Hey, speaking of help, I've got a deal tomorrow. Controlled delivery. Could use some help if you're available. Most of the guys are tied up in court."

"Count me in."

Jake turned onto Hennepin Avenue and they could see the Saddle Club's blinking neon sign. Spotting a lot across the street, Jake parked and they made their way to the club. Jake tried the entrance door. Locked. Not surprised, he banged on the door.

Sam opened it within seconds. "Come on in. Thanks for coming." He pointed to the back of the club. "This way, please."

As promised the club was empty, and lit just enough so they could find their way through the maze of tables and chairs. He led them to his office.

"Sam, I'm Jake Shaunessey and this is Kiel McIntyre."

They flashed their credentials but Sam barely gave them a glance. Who else would they be?

O'Grady produced a warm, sincere smile. Expecting the owner of a strip joint and call girl operation to be hard-nosed, the man's style surprised Jake. Before talking, Sam retrieved a newspaper from the far corner of his desk. He opened it to page three and laid it on the desk, then paused as if searching for the right words. Obviously, something of importance concerned him.

"Look, this is delicate for me. I'm sure you're aware I got a number of call girls working out of this place. We all know it's not legal, but up to now the cops have been closing their eyes. Maybe 'cause I do business with a few of 'em. Now I'm afraid there might've been some murders. If I'm right, they're connected to my business. Indirectly that is. That means the police will probably be taking a close look at my club. I'm hoping if I get any heat you might put in a good word."

Jake answered. "Let's see what you got. It might be possible."

"I guess that's the most I can expect," Sam said. "It's about these two guys arrested in Hudson, Wisconsin." He slid the newspaper towards them.

The agents immediately recognized the headline.

"Yeah, I've been following this," Jake said. "It's about a dead guy found on the beach at Lake Calhoun. You seen this, Kiel?"

"I read it this morning. His name was Eric Butterfield. Lived just a couple blocks away from the beach. Strange deal. He was splattered with blood, but a heroin overdose is what killed him. Figure that. Witnesses saw two guys dump his body on the beach, copped the tag on their van and called the police. They arrested Curt Haug and Desmond Reinhart in Hudson. This is them." Kiel pointed to two mug shots displayed at the top of the article. "Cops caught 'em dirty. One and a half pounds of heroin, half pound of coke, and a hundred thousand cash. Good seizure."

"Yeah," Sam interjected. "The police think some other people were killed because the blood on Butterfield's body wasn't his. They're asking the public to come forward. I may know whose blood was on his body."

Jake looked across the desk intently. "Tell us about it."

"Last week Frenchy Deveroux, one of my regulars, came in. He paid for a night with one of the girls, Candy

Almond." Noticing their expressions, Sam added, "Yeah, that's her real name. I arranged for her to leave at eleven with him. I noticed three guys came in at the same time as Frenchy. Then, as he and Candy got ready to leave, they just up and left. That's them in the photograph. I gotta bet the third guy is the body on the beach."

Jake and Kiel exchanged glances. "You said 'Frenchy Deveroux?' Jake asked.

"Yeah. You heard of him?"

Jake shook his head. "Not exactly."

"Hmmm. That surprises me. Anyways, I haven't seen Candy since they left. She didn't report to work Saturday and didn't call. I phoned her place several times. No answer. So now I read about these two pieces of slime and how the police think maybe there's other people dead. Look, Frenchy's a big tipper. He's got bucks. I've heard bits and pieces that he's a big time heroin dealer. Got a place near Elk River. You oughta check it out. If everything's okay, please don't mention my name."

Jake and Kiel looked at each other, nodding their heads in acknowledgement that Sudden Sam's information might be pretty damn significant.

"Okay. You think Frenchy took Candy to his place?"

"Always does. Has a girlfriend lives with him. They like threesomes."

"How do you spell his name?" Jake asked, pen in hand.

"That's Deveroux." Sam spelled it.

"You ever see these guys before the other night?" Jake studied the two photographs.

Sam nodded. "Yeah. A few times. Always

came in together. Didn't cause any problems. Never saw the third guy before though. Don't know anything about him. But if I saw a picture of the dead guy, I could tell you if it's the same person."

Jake and Kiel stayed for a while, getting as much info as they could, then left.

"What do you think," Kiel asked as they walked across the street.

"I try to be optimistic. My money says this guy is the Frenchy we've been looking for. Let's check it out. I'll call the Sheriff in Sherburne County and get a couple of his guys to go to Deveroux's house with us. If it's bad in there, we'll talk with Minneapolis and Hudson."

The Sheriff assigned four deputies to help, two uniforms and two plain clothes. Two hours later Jake and Kiel, accompanied by the four deputies, drove to Deveroux's house. Jake and Kiel pulled up the long driveway, followed by the deputies. It looked bad from the start.

"Check out the garage," Kiel said, concerned. "Door's up, and we've got a Beamer inside with its doors wide open."

"Yeah, something's wrong here," Jake answered.

With guns drawn, everybody got out of their cars. One of the detectives approached the uniforms. "You guys do a walk around and then watch the perimeter. We're going in."

Jake, Kiel and the two detectives entered the garage.

"Look at this." Jake pointed to the floor. "Blood." It felt like déjà vu.

The others nodded, grim faced.

Jake approached the garage entrance to the house and knocked loudly on the door. No answer. He tried the doorknob. It opened.

An overpowering, rotting stench gagged them.

"Whew, this is bad," Kiel exclaimed. "Sam was right."

They all grimaced as they tried to deal with the powerful odor. They slowly followed Jake into the house. Within a few seconds Jake saw the bodies of Candy Almond and Frenchy Deveroux lying on the floor.

Jake felt a strong urge to retch, gulped, then looked back at the others. "Blonde. Fits Sam's description."

Kiel placed his hand over his nose and mouth. The stench was horrible, but the sight of the two bloated corpses bothered him more.

Sidestepping the bodies, they moved on.

Entering the kitchen, Jake pointed to a chair and the splotches below it. "Somebody was bleeding heavily. Look at the blood trails."

Their eyes followed the trails, first the one leading upstairs, then the other leading to the basement. He turned to one of the detectives. "We'll check out the basement. You got the upstairs."

Halfway down the stairs Jake recognized the smell. The pungent odor in the confined area was even more intense. Nearing the bottom, he knew why.

The Sheriff's office began its homicide investigation.

Jake and Kiel assisted in the search of the house, beginning in Frenchy's office.

Kiel opened a desk drawer and pulled out a ledger. He turned randomly to a page, gave it a cursory look, and caught Jake's attention. "Hey, check this out."

Jake moved over to the desk. "Hmm. Kilos, pounds, dollar amounts, dates. Any names?"

Kiel turned the pages. "Guess not, but plenty of initials. There's another ledger in there. Let's take a look." He pulled it out and opened it. "Same stuff. Frenchy was doing pretty good."

They remained in the house late into the evening, then accompanied the detectives to the Sheriff's office where they reviewed their evidence. Jake and Kiel were particularly interested in the ledgers.

"We can't let you have 'em. Got to keep the evidence intact. But you can have copies," one of the detectives said.

While Jake and Kiel made photocopies, the detective called the homicide bureau in Hudson and asked them about the two dirt bags they had in their jail. Hanging up the phone, he joined the agents at the copier. "Haug and Reinhart both got attorneys and aren't talking. No big surprise. I'd bet my wife's bingo money that DNA testing will match the stiffs at Deveroux's place with the blood they found on the guy at Lake Calhoun. I think our killers are sitting in the slammer in Wisconsin."

A couple hours later, Jake and Kiel headed back to their office, both deep in thought. Approaching the freeway, Jake said, "There's some big quantities entered in those ledgers. Lots of money. Sound familiar?"

Kiel nodded slowly. "Frenchy's records read a lot like Black Jack Mike's. We found three million in Mike's safe deposit boxes. Maybe Frenchy was sitting on something like that."

"Yeah, I hear ya. When we get back let's compare 'em."

It was eleven-thirty by the time they got to their desks. The office was dark and Jake flipped on the lights. "Nobody home. How often does that happen?"

It surprised Kiel too. "It's late, but usually someone's here, catching up on paper work, finishing a deal or something. Come to think of it, that's usually me," he said with a tired look. He could feel the strain that accompanies long hours.

Kiel wasn't alone. The day's activities had Jake's nerves as taut as a guitar string, and he didn't like the feeling. He reminded himself it wasn't that the murders needed solving. In all likelihood that had been done. (Jake personally believed Frenchy deserved exactly what he got, and he sure as hell wasn't going to mourn the doper's demise.)

Corralling his thoughts, he tried to separate the fog from the smog and regain his perspective. The death scene, while gut wrenching, comprised only a small part of a big picture. His major concern dealt with the epidemic tearing at the state's bowels, and the gruesome realization that unless he succeeded in this investigation, bodies would keep stacking up.

Jake went to his filing cabinet and pulled out Black Jack Mike's ledgers. With Kiel peering over his shoulder, he turned the pages and compared them with the photocopied records from the Deveroux house.

The records brought a smile to Jake's face. He looked over at Kiel, seeing the same expression. "How about that. Looks like Maureen told us the truth. They had the same source. When a shipment arrived, they were both ready and waiting. Identical payments on the same dates, month after month. I'd say he brought in money on the same scale as Black Jack Mike."

Kiel nodded. "Frenchy's floor safe couldn't hold that kind of cash. The money the cops took from the two screws in Hudson was just a small part of it."

Jake thought about it. "I'm thinking there are some safe deposit box keys hidden in that house, and we missed 'em."

"I'm thinking you're right."

"I'll call the Sheriff's office. Let's go back."

Jake didn't relish going back into the house. With the odor of death still strong in his nostrils, pores, and clothes, he felt a strong urge to go home, pour a tall glass of bourbon and, what? Maybe gargle with it? (Something he had never done, but what the hell, anything to purge that stench from his sinuses). But now wasn't the time to go home and confer with Jack Daniels.

They headed back to Elk River, arriving at one thirty, and met for a second time with the two detectives. Inside the house, the smell of death welcomed them back. They did their best to ignore it. Kiel began his search in the office, and Jake took the basement. About an hour later Jake heard Kiel yelling, "Bingo." Jake went to the office to join him.

"Found these taped to the bottom of a file cabinet," Kiel said, displaying six deposit box keys. "They're at four different banks."

They rejoined the deputies and showed them the keys. "We'll check these out as soon as we can," Jake told them. "I think I know what we're going to find. It's been one hell of a day, Gentlemen."

The deputies agreed.

Jake and Kiel got home around five in the morning.

CHAPTER 11

Back in their office by nine, the two agents displayed expressions that could only mean they wished they were someplace else, preferably in a reclining position.

"I feel like I'm hung over," Jake groaned. "Kept dreaming about corpses. Probably got an hour's worth of sleep. And that stench! Can't get rid of it." His glassy eyes looked raw and swollen, and two days worth of stubble sprouted from his face. He went to the coffee bar and poured his first cup of the day.

Kiel looked just as bad. "I hear ya. I wanted to sleep in, but the postal inspector arrives in a half hour. We made arrangements to do that deal. Couldn't beg off."

Jake spread the morning paper across his desk, turning to the Metro section. "It's in today's paper."

Kiel walked stiffly over to Jake's desk and read the heavy sub-titles. "Triple slaying in quiet Elk River. Police investigation points to drugs."

He and Jake, each with a grim look, began quietly reading the article. It focused on a press release given by the Sherburne County Sheriff.

"We're in the news again," Kiel said. "That's twice in two weeks, all of it pertaining to killings. Nice of the Sheriff to give us full credit. The reporters would be doing acrobatics if they knew it was all related."

"You got that right." Jake yawned and looked at his watch. "You said the postal guy is coming at nine thirty?"

"Yeah," Kiel answered. "He's bringing the package with him. It's a mail parcel, originated in Bogota. Somebody concealed a pound of coke inside the covers of a large book and mailed it to Angela Lurtz in Brooklyn Center."

"We know her?"

"Nope. Ran her through our computer. Everything's negative. Driver's license records show she's twenty-six years old. No criminal record."

"How'd we get onto this?"

"A sniffer dog alerted to the package in Miami. The Customs people checked it out and found the coke. Turned it over to the postal people. The inspector brought the package to me last Friday. I field tested the coke. Looks like good stuff. We removed all but a couple grams and substituted lactose. We've got a search warrant affidavit almost completed. All we got to do is deliver the package. If someone at the house accepts it we'll finish the search warrant, get it signed, and hit the place." Kiel took a couple chugs of coffee, set the mug down on Jake's desk and stretched.

Controlled deliveries often involved drugs intercepted by a government agency, generally Customs or the Postal Service. The strategy was to put the drugs back into the hands of the ones who were expecting them. The trick? Do it in a way that produced evidence the recipient knew he possessed dope, and intended to sell it.

Jake rubbed his red eyes. "Which inspector we got on this?"

"Mattson."

Jake nodded. Mattson was an okay guy as far as postal inspectors went. And Kiel knew his stuff. But after the Black Jack Mike raid Jake had to be sure of the arrangements, so he went a little further. "Okay. How'd you set it up?"

"Mattson will be riding with Sal. They'll meet with the regular mail carrier down the street from Lurtz' house and give him the package. The carrier will knock on Lurtz' door, and if she answers he'll tell her there's postage due. If nobody answers, we'll try again later."

"Who else is going?"

Kiel looked around the room at the desks. "Lisa, and Travis. I'll be with the prosecutor, getting the warrant signed. Soon as it's signed I'll let you know and then meet up with you."

Jake would be in the van with Travis, keeping a close eye. That meant only three vehicles, enough if everything went according to plan. But if the package moved, three cars would be on the light side. Jake wanted to do better. "How about Ken?" Jake nodded towards Ken, now back on duty and sitting glumly at his desk.

"I'll ask him. See if he feels like going out."

Mattson arrived promptly at nine thirty, and Kiel gathered the agents for his briefing. Ken joined them.

"You all know Inspector Mattson."

Mattson scanned the group of agents and nodded.

"Here's your run sheets," Kiel continued, handing a sheet to each of the agents.

He paused, giving them time to read, then continued the briefing. "Jake and Travis, you'll be riding together in a van. You've got the eye. Sal, let us know when the carrier's got the parcel. Ken and Lisa are solo. Lisa, you carry the shotgun."

The agents all nodded.

Briefly, Kiel went over the raid plan as outlined on the run sheet. Pretty basic stuff; they'd done it many times. Then they hit the street.

Jake drove while Travis manned the radio. With a year and a half behind him as a DEA agent, Travis had made great headway in proving himself and was well liked. In his late twenties and slightly shorter than Jake, Travis had close cropped hair, like Kiel's except dark. His narrow face and deep set blue eyes gave him an appearance women always looked at twice, but he could no longer afford to act on the opportunities that frequently came his way.

Travis' personal life looked like an obstacle course, littered with pissed off women groping for his already thin wallet. With two ex-wives and a young daughter, he had to shell out a huge portion of his paycheck for alimony and child support, with very little left over. Unable to even pay rent, his van had become his home. While his plight was amusing to everyone in the office, they also felt sympathetic.

"How you getting along in your new home?" Jake tried to stifle a smile.

Travis took Jake's poorly concealed grin in good humor. He knew it was a joke around the office and could appreciate that, even if it wasn't funny to him. "You know Jake, I'm hurting. I spend my nights in parking lots, usually a truck stop or a convenience store. In the morning I stop off at the 'Y' for a shower before going to the office. It's a bitch right now. I don't know what I'm going to do next winter. Sure as hell can't spend a Minnesota winter living in a van. I've either got to get promoted or transfer to the deep south."

Jake thought for a moment. "Why don't you move in with someone. Share expenses. That would work."

"The only other agents living alone are Scott and Lisa. Scott's afflicted with a serious case of RDD."

A question mark took over Jake's face. "RDD?"

"Yeah. Realization Deficit Disorder. He just doesn't fucking realize that if he wants to get along around here, he's gonna have to roll up his sleeves and do some actual work, not just buy the boss drinks in the evening."

Jake shook his head, smiling. "RDD. Huh."

Travis continued. "Now Lisa, yeah, I'd go for that. But she's been real cool towards me. I think she's wary 'cause of my history."

Jake didn't have a suitable answer, and just nodded in agreement.

Arriving at the target street in Brooklyn Center, the two agents studied the street numbers, looking for the right house. That stretch of Earl Brown Drive featured older, two story homes. They found the house, noted the address, and continued down the street to the end of the block. Jake circled around and set up a block down on the opposite side of the street, where they had a good look at the house.

Travis keyed his mike. "We're set up with a good eye. We're the only vehicle on the street. Hope that doesn't spook anybody."

Sal and Mattson parked around the corner on a side street, where they waited for the mail carrier to arrive. Lisa found a spot a couple blocks away and slumped down in her seat trying to look invisible. Ken sat three blocks north, well out of view.

Fifteen minutes later the mail carrier parked behind Sal and Mattson. Sal got on the radio. "The carrier's here. He took the package and he's moving."

As the carrier walked up to the target house, Travis called it. "Mail carrier is at the house, knocking on the door. Waiting. Someone opened the door and they're talking. The door closed, but the carrier's still standing there with the package."

A minute later. "The door's open again. He gave them the package. He's walking away. The package is in the house."

Looking at Mattson with satisfaction, Sal said, "Let's rendezvous with the carrier. See what he's got to say."

After talking with the carrier, Sal and Mattson met with Jake and Travis. Then Jake called Kiel. "The mail carrier said a woman, mid-twenties, came to the door, paid the postage and took the package."

"Okay," Kiel replied. "I'll get the warrant. Let me know if anything changes."

Jake and Travis sat directly behind a dark curtain, watching the house. "Now comes the wait," Jake said. "I remember a couple years ago working one of these when we saw the guy come out of his house and throw the wrapper into the trash. We hit the house and caught him weighing the dope. Too bad it doesn't always go that way, catch 'em doing something that'll convince the jury. If it's not clean and simple, the attorneys have a way of hiding the evidence behind a mountain of chaff."

Travis agreed. "It's nice when there's a trip wire, something clicks and tells us 'okay, hit it.'"

"Yeah. Timing is huge. It's pretty damn frustrating when we hit a door and find the package sitting untouched. We search the place, don't find anything else, and then we got zip. You know what? I hate these damn controlled deliveries."

"Huh. Some of the guys like 'em. I guess they have the impression they're actually in control of something."

Travis stretched out his legs and yawned. It was one of those hand over your mouth, wide gaping yawns that demand all your attention. Sleeping in a van meant long, uncomfortable nights, and he presently spent a big chunk of his time in one. He now hated vans, which made this surveillance a bigger pain in the ass for him than for Jake. "I wonder what Angela Lurtz is doing now. Is she going to make it easy for us, or are we going to be pissed off?"

Jake gave him a sideways glance. "Don't get me started. I've seen too many of these turn sour."

At that moment, Lurtz was on the phone with David O'Neal. "It's here," she said nervously. "Make it quick."

Several minutes later, peering out of the rear window through a slit in a second black curtain, Travis reported, "A car's coming down the street. Going real slow." The new activity gave Travis a much needed shot of adrenaline.

Jake watched O'Neal's car through the dark side windows. O'Neal drove even slower as he passed the van. "It's a male driving. Gave us a double take. This guy might be involved."

Travis scooted up front to get a better view as the car passed the van. They watched O'Neal continue for a block, then do a U-turn in the middle of the street.

"Huh. He's coming back. This is interesting," Jake said in a low voice.

"He's parking in front of Lurtz' house," Travis said.

Travis got on the radio and updated the others. "He just went inside. Somebody met him at the door. The guy is a white male, probably in his early twenties. He's got long blond hair in a pony-tail, wearing a ragged looking T-shirt and blue jeans. He's about six feet, one eighty. Looks in good shape."

Lisa came on the radio. "Yeah, he drove past me just as I was getting ready to move. I don't know if he noticed me. I'm in a different spot now."

Travis called Kiel and had him run the car's plate. It was registered to David O'Neal, who lived less than a mile away. Giving Travis the info, Kiel added, "I did a records check. He's never been busted, but his name's cropped up several times. We've got intelligence on him. He's definitely dirty."

Five minutes later O'Neal walked out of the house. Travis called it. "He's out and walking to his car. He's got the package under his arm. You guys take the eye when I call him away. We can't leave 'til he's out of sight."

As O'Neal pulled away, he drove past the van close enough to spit on it.

"He's coming by again, real slow. Stand by." Travis turned the radio volume off. O'Neal drove past and Travis re-adjusted the radio. "He's by. Take him away."

Jake cursed softly. Another player entering the deal posed significant problems. He wished there were two additional cars on the team, but with no other agents available he had been forced to settle for four vehicles. Four might've been enough, but the van was burned and couldn't be seen by O'Neal again. Scratch one vehicle. And the drug dealer may have noticed Lisa's car when he drove by, so she would have to keep her distance. Scratch another. That left two cars to do the work. Two didn't cut it. They ran a solid risk of burning the entire surveillance, or worse, losing O'Neal (and the drugs) in traffic.

Jake knew if O'Neal took the package into an apartment or office building, the narcs couldn't keep tabs on the evidence and it would be lost. He grabbed the radio. "If he goes to an apartment building, stop him and take the dope. If he goes to a house, we'll set up on it. We won't worry about Lurtz right now."

Sal and the Postal Inspector were a block and a half behind O'Neal. They were in luck. It was a short surveillance. Minutes later Sal reported, "His right turn signal's on." Then, "He pulled into a driveway in the three thousand block. We're driving by the house now. He's out of his car, taking the package inside. We're by. The guy looks paranoid. Gave us a hard stare." Sal then called out the house number for the other agents.

Jake turned to Travis. "We lucked out on this one." Then he got back on the air. "Ken, park on the street and take the eye. I'll call Kiel and give him the new address for the warrant."

Ken found a spot, and the agents waited for Kiel to arrive.

Inside the house, O'Neal peered out the windows with a pair of binoculars. A black man sat in a car a block down. Not doing anything, just sitting there. O'Neal studied the car and its driver, wondering what the hell. No black families resided in that area. Was the guy studying the street? What was he looking at? Why was he there?

It struck him like a blast of windblown sewage. The narcs were onto him! Approaching its saturation point, his typical state of general paranoia expanded rapidly. They must have set up that delivery, and now they knew he had it. Probably getting ready to hit his door. Swearing violently he kicked a chair, sending it flying across the room. Where was his gun? The nine millimeter would play hell with anyone who tried to bust in. He found it on a lamp table, grabbed it and worked the action. A round jumped out of the chamber, onto the floor. He retrieved it. Yeah, the gun was loaded and ready.

He peered out the window at the car once more, then dwelled on his predicament. If narcs hit his place, it wouldn't be just a couple of 'em. It'd be a swarm of 'em, and they'd all have guns. *Pop a cap at them and I'll be decorating a slab at the morgue before the evening news.*

O'Neal forced himself to regroup. Think this over. *What would it feel like, lead tearing through my guts? Dying by the hands of those fucking narcs*

And then the ultimate insult popped into his head: His blood soaked body sliced and diced by some coroner. O'Neal suddenly had a lot of second thoughts. *No. There has to be another way.*

He fought to keep his fiery temper in check. To think rationally. *Can I get that coke out of here so the narcs will see it leave?*

If he could swing that, they wouldn't have any reason to come into his place. O'Neal had other dope, worth a lot of money, in the house. If the coke was lost . . . okay. The price of doing business. It hadn't been paid for, and now it never would be. But if narcs raided his house and ransacked the place, it would be one hell of an expensive set back.

An idea came to him. Cramming the pistol underneath the couch, he picked up the phone.

Fifteen minutes later Ken got on the radio. "Hey, I've got a Brooklyn Center police car pulling into the driveway. One uniform in the car. He's out and going up to the house."

Jake looked at Travis. "What the fuck." To Ken. "Okay, keep calling it."

The police officer left twenty minutes later, with the package. Ken could see the package had been opened. Some of the brown paper dangled loosely as the officer carried it to his car. Ken called him away.

Jake got on the radio. "Everybody stay put. I'm going to talk with that cop."

He flagged the officer down a half mile from the house. The officer stopped and looked at Jake curiously.

The two agents got out of the van and held their badges out for the officer. He closely examined their credentials.

Jake started the conversation. "Look, we're doing a surveillance on the house you just left. That package was delivered under our direction. It's evidence. Could you tell us what happened in there?"

Officer Morgan looked amused as well as puzzled. "Yeah. I got a call from our dispatcher that this guy, David O'Neal, called and requested a police officer come to his house to check out a suspicious package someone gave him. Said the package had been mailed from Colombia, and he surmised someone wants to set him up. I went there and we opened the package together. It's a book with a lot of coke concealed in the covers. Anyways, I guess it's probably cocaine."

Morgan looked at his notes. "The package was addressed to Angela Lurtz on Earl Brown Drive, not too far from here. O'Neal said she called him and told him she got the book in the mail from a friend of hers. Said her friend wrote her earlier and told her he was mailing her something from Colombia that would make a good souvenir. She doesn't read much, and didn't have any use for souvenirs from Colombia, but she thought O'Neal might want to look at it. He's an avid reader, or so he says. He told me when he got back to his house he started thinking this whole thing smells like a set up. Says anything from Colombia is suspicious to him. So he called us. Seemed real happy about my taking it off his hands. I was going to turn it over to one of our detectives. I guess you can have it. All I need is a signed receipt."

"What a crock," Jake said angrily. "We've got a search warrant on the way for that guy's house. As soon as it gets here we're going to kick his door. I'd appreciate it if you'd come along and assist."

Morgan said he would, and notified his dispatcher. As the officer was talking, Kiel drove up with the search warrant. Jake got on the air and had everybody meet several blocks away from O'Neal's house. When the team joined up, Jake brought them up to speed.

O'Neal continued to watch out the window, hoping he had solved his problem. His heart sunk when he saw the agents' cars, followed by the marked police car, coming down his street. That half pound of heroin stashed in his house would be damn expensive to flush. Son of a bitch, he thought. Got no choice.

He ran into the kitchen and retrieved a pail full of dirty rags from under the sink. The heroin, contained in a plastic bag, was concealed beneath the rags. He had just gotten into the bathroom when the agents came screaming through his front door.

"Federal Agents! Search warrant!"

It all happened within the space of a few seconds. While opening the bag of junk, O'Neal kicked the bathroom door shut with his foot. Kiel entered the house first and heard the door slam. He ran straight to the door, heard the flushing noise of a toilet, and kicked in the door. O'Neal, about five inches taller and thirty pounds heavier than Kiel, watched the baggie with its contents circling around the toilet bowl as the agent came through the door. Hoping to buy just a few more seconds, O'Neal lunged at Kiel, grabbing his gun hand. Kiel tried to pull his arm free while fiercely hanging on to his pistol. O'Neal slammed the agent's hand onto the porcelain sink, knocking the gun loose from Kiel's grip. *Clunk!* The pistol clattered down to the bottom of the sink. They wrestled and punched until O'Neal slammed Kiel's head into the edge of the sink. A stream of blood spurted from Kiel's forehead.

Jake rushed into the bathroom to see O'Neal reaching for Kiel's loose pistol. Without slowing down, Jake wrapped his arm around O'Neal's neck, and his momentum carried him and O'Neal backwards into the bathtub, with Jake on the bottom, and O'Neal lying on top. Jake banged his head on the chrome fixtures as he fell, and blood gushed out of the side of his head, spewing all over. He hung on to O'Neal's neck, nearly strangling him. The drug dealer fought desperately, kicking wildly and elbowing Jake in the ribs. Badly dazed by the blow to his head, Kiel latched on to the sink, trying to recover his bearings and unable to help.

Travis reached the door just as Jake fell into the tub. He holstered his pistol, and stormed in.

As O'Neal floundered and struggled in the bathtub he looked up at Kiel, whom he apparently blamed for his sorry predicament. "I'm going to get you, you fucking bastard," he yelled just before Travis got to him.

Kneeling down next to the tub, Travis delivered two solid blows to O'Neal's stomach. Then, locking his hands together, he delivered a devastating punch to the man's balls.

The drug dealer groaned loudly and his face turned white. Travis pulled him out of the tub, grabbed his ponytail, and dragged him from the bathroom. In the living room, Travis executed a perfect hip toss. O'Neal did a complete somersault and landed heavily on his back. Travis rolled him over onto his stomach and slapped on the cuff. Then he put his boot onto the back of the man's head, pressing his face hard into the floor, and yelled, "Hey, Fungus Lips! You through yet?" He was pumped.

Gasping for air, O'Neal couldn't talk. He managed a slight nod, and Travis removed his foot.

Lisa helped Jake out of the bathtub, then ran to her car for a first aid kit. Ken, Sal, Mattson and Morgan began searching the house. Kiel and Jake sat on a couch and tried to get their heads straight.

The search of the small house didn't take long. Except for the pistol underneath the couch, they found nothing of significance. And the pistol wasn't illegal. Not in this state.

When they finished, Jake said, "Lisa, I want you and Sal to take O'Neal in and have him charged for assaulting federal agents. We didn't get any dope, but at least we've got that."

Lisa, Sal and Mattson took O'Neal back to the office and placed him in a detention cell. Then they met with the prosecutor. Morgan took Jake and Kiel to the ER at North Hospital. After they were patched up, he took them back to their van.

Jake and Kiel arrived back at the office at five, exhausted, sporting bad headaches and wearing thick gauze and white tape on their heads. And they were hungry. Lisa greeted them with a glum look.

"So what happened?" Jake asked grouchily. He didn't like her expression.

"The prosecutor declined to charge O'Neal for assault. Said he thinks O'Neal will claim he was using the bathroom, didn't hear us identify ourselves as we came through the door, and had to defend himself from armed intruders. Everything else was the result of fear, adrenaline, and the heat of the moment."

"I don't believe this crap," Jake moaned. "Where is that sack of maggot shit?"

"We kicked him loose about a half hour ago," Lisa answered reluctantly.

She could see Jake becoming surly. "Sorry guys. By the way Jake, you got a message on your desk."

Walking over to his desk, Jake massaged a large lump on the back of his head. The message had the word *URGENT* at the top, underlined several times. It was from someone named Debby Hornacek. Lisa took the message shortly before Jake and Kiel returned. Jake turned to Lisa and asked, "Who the hell is she?"

Lisa regretted not waiting until the next morning to give Jake the message. He needed some time to regroup. "She seems to know something about Frenchy Deveroux. Wants to talk to the agent investigating the triple homicide. Said it had to be right away. That's all she would say."

Jake returned her phone call, and a short time later he and Kiel dragged their sorry butts back onto the street. Hornacek wanted to talk. She might change her mind if they waited until tomorrow.

It was ten thirty by the time Jake finally pulled into his driveway. He'd had about one hour of sleep in the past thirty six, and was double marathon tired. His eye lids were heavy. Legs, rubbery. Head, sore. And his stomach growled from being ignored.

Melissa opened the door for him. "My God, what happened to your head?"

"I'll tell you about it later."

Just then their oldest daughter came into the kitchen and had the same question. "Daddy, what happened to your head?"

"It's a long story, Melanie," he said.

She knew that meant he wouldn't be telling her any more, and eagerly changed the subject. "Hey Daddy, can you come down stairs? I have to show you something." She snickered as she said it.

Although he would never admit it, Melanie, now looking forward to her sophomore year in high school, was his favorite. He had two other daughters; nine year old Suzanne, and twelve year old Kimberly; and two sons, Jake Junior at thirteen, and four year old Jeffrey. Jake frequently felt troubled by a gnawing sensation in his gut that the rich rewards of fatherhood were passing him by. A perplexing problem, it plagued him more and more as the kids grew older. They were exploring life with all its problems and successes, and his participation could contribute a great deal. But with the demands of his job, it seemed the weeks just didn't have enough hours for his family to get their fair share.

Melanie knew the way to his soul. She looked into his tired eyes, waiting for his response.

He fought back his exhaustion and even surprised himself with a fresh smile.

"Sure thing Hon. I'm right behind you."

His daughter led him down the stairs to the nicely finished basement, where the boys had their bedrooms. As he walked past his older son's bedroom, Jake saw his son toiling with his homework. "Hi, Junior."

Jake Junior immediately noticed the wrappings on his dad's head, and came rushing to the door. Jake gave the boy a reassuring pat on the back and said it was no big deal. His son gave him a hug and returned to his studies.

Melanie led her father into little Jeffrey's room, where Jake saw Jeffrey, sound asleep. He had both his arms wrapped around 'Mutt,' a stuffed toy puppy. Mutt's nose snuggled against Jeffrey's face. Every time Jeffrey exhaled, his breath had a windmill effect on the whiskers of the dog, causing them to flutter up and down in tune with his breathing.

"Mutt and Jeff," Melanie said, giggling.

Jake remembered watching Melissa sew the toy for Jeffrey's second birthday. Jeffrey and Mutt had since become inseparable. Seeing the stuffed toy cradled in his son's arms made him forget his aches and even drew a laugh out of him. The laugh made him feel better, and watching his innocent four year old gave Jake a much needed shot in the arm. Sometimes he needed that to get him through the day as he fought in the trenches of a drug plagued world.

Jake went back up to the kitchen and raided the refrigerator. When did he last eat? Couldn't remember. He grabbed a jar of mayo and a squeezie of mustard, then found the summer sausage. After cutting off a half dozen thick slices of meat, he spread some of the mayo and mustard onto two slices of wheat bread and carefully placed the slices of meat so they covered all the bread. He returned to the fridge and found a cold bottle of beer. Then he joined Melissa at the table where she watched his every move.

"You're going to eat all that, then hop into bed?" she asked, snickering.

Jake nodded. "It can't do too much damage to my arteries. I haven't put anything else into them all day."

"How the hell do you guys stay healthy with your screwed up hours?"

He took a huge bite out of his sandwich, chewed it for a while then reached for his beer. "I'm sure I'll pay for it later in life."

Melissa frowned. "What's with all that gauze on your head? What's going on? I haven't talked to you for a couple days?"

He relived the fight in the bathtub, then the ass chewing he'd undergone earlier in the week.

"Things don't look too good for our side right now, Mel. I don't know what Alan's problem is, but I know he's got it in for me. I wouldn't be surprised if I got orders out of here within a few months. If assholism were a competitive event, Ravich would be an Olympic contender."

Melissa didn't want to hear that. "My God, Jake, is he that bad? Isn't there something you can do to smooth things over?"

"Probably not. I'm sure as hell not going to kiss his ass, and that's about the only thing he respects."

Melissa frowned. "I don't want to think about a transfer. I love this place. When we came here, you said we'd probably stay in Minnesota until you retired. If we moved, we'd have to pull the kids out of school, and they're all doing so good now. They give you orders, why don't you just quit? Find something else to keep you busy."

Jake took another chunk out of his sandwich and studied her while his teeth worked it over. He loved Melissa. She was a great companion and a super mother. At thirty-six plus, they were close to the same age. Orphaned at eighteen when her parents were killed in a boating accident near her home town of San Diego, she inherited the estate, close to half a million dollars, which she placed in a variety of successful mutual funds. Money was not a serious concern.

He washed his last bite down with a couple chugs of beer. "Don't ask me to do that, Mel. I've put sixteen years of my life into this career. I can't just walk away because I've got a lousy boss. He's not the first, and probably won't be the last. But this job has too many good things to offer."

She shook her head. "Yeah, like the freedom to work twenty-three hours a day and free treatment in the emergency room. You must be crazy, Jake. Come on, let's go to bed. I'll give you a chance to work off some of that cholesterol."

Don Nelson

CHAPTER 12

Jake stumbled into the office shortly after ten thirty the next morning. He had just poured his first cup of coffee when Harold Sampress beckoned him.

Harold looked at Jake's patched head and greeted him with a sympathetic smile. "Lisa told me about the O'Neal raid. How's your head?"

"The Doc says I'll live. You know, controlled deliveries aren't very controllable. They're more like a controlled Chinese fire drill."

"Sometimes we eat the goose, sometimes we get goosed. I hear you had another late one last night. What happened on your meet with Debby Hornacek? The message sounded like she had a hot lead on the Frenchy Deveroux angle."

Jake began briefing his supervisor on the two hour meeting he and Kiel had with Hornacek. "I don't know how hot it is, but it's something. She's a lesbian. Had a long term relationship with Nikki, the one that was gunned down in Deveroux's basement. Debby said she never went to Frenchy's house, and he didn't know her. But Frenchy left town quite often on business, and then Debby and Nikki got together. Nikki liked to talk, made a habit of telling her what was going on in Deveroux's house. Said Frenchy was really big time. It kind of scared her living with a major heroin dealer, but he worshipped her. Always treated her nice, bought her fine things, expensive meals, all that crap. Debby said Nikki had it made. She loved coke, but when he left he always locked it up. She knew about the floor safe, but didn't want to risk Frenchy's wrath. Enter Debby. She had a source she copped from every week. Turns out he was Desmond Reinhart, one of the guys involved in the murders."

Harold nodded as he soaked it all in. "Desmond found out about Frenchy from Hornacek?"

"Yeah. Six weeks ago, while testing some of Desmond's blow, she accidentally let it out she knew of a high level heroin dealer. After hearing that, he kept quizzing her every time they met. Says she didn't realize she told him as much as she did. He's smart and maybe she's not in his league. So the other day she reads about the case in the papers. Sees Desmond's mug, and puts it all together. Blames herself for the murders. Says she'll testify, the whole nine yards. That's one bitter broad."

"What's she know about Frenchy's operation?"

"Just what Nikki told her. Frenchy got his heroin in shipments of two to three kilos from a pair named Eddie and Dominique. Occasionally they'd come to Frenchy's place, Eddie more often than Dominique. They'd either come together, or Eddie by himself. Says Eddie drives a red sports car. Doesn't know what kind. Nikki lived with Frenchy for the past two years, and Frenchy dealt with Eddie and Dominique that whole time. Six months ago Frenchy got real excited because they started getting their junk from a new source, and the shit was a lot better. He made a big deal of it. Nikki told Debby that Frenchy had at least two guys selling his junk, but she never met them and doesn't know anything about them."

Harold nodded. "Some of that squares with what Black Jack Mike's wife told us. Didn't she say Roosevelt's man changed his source about six months ago?"

"Sure did."

"Eddie huh? Think you can do anything with that red sports car lead?"

"Don't know, but at least it's another piece to the puzzle. Maybe it'll develop into something."

Harold mulled it over for a few seconds, then said, "I'll talk to Alan. Tell him how impressed I am with the job you're doing." He didn't like Alan Ravich any more than the others did, but tried his best to conceal his attitude, acting as a buffer between the boss and the workers.

Jake figured Harold was simply trying to smooth things over following the ass reaming by Alan after the Black Jack Mike raid. He simply nodded and gave his boss a 'thank you' smile.

When Ravich came to the office, Jake had serious reservations. Like the others, he found the new boss's work habits disappointing. Alan generally came in late, often hung over, and then left early. For a staff that normally put in twelve hour days, it was unsettling to see the boss walk out after five hours or less behind his desk. What was the man's agenda? Jake had a talent for reading people, and Alan Ravich read like bad news. If Harold wanted to tell Ravich that Jake was doing a fine job, so be it. And if Harold didn't say a word . . . no problem. Normally it would be desirable for the boss to hear good things. But Jake's gut told him with Ravich it didn't matter. He didn't know about Alan's other world, but in this office the man's people skills tank ran on fumes. And the fumes had a bad odor.

Harold changed the subject. "You liked working with Kiel, huh?"

"Yeah, we've got good chemistry."

"I hear you, but we've got other considerations. Travis could benefit from working alongside some experience. Would he cramp your style?"

"Not at all."

"Good. I'm pairing you two up. He's your partner now. Take him under your wing on this heroin case."

"Okay, boss."

As Jake turned to leave, Harold said, almost as an afterthought, "Say, Jake, you've uncovered some pretty good leads in this case. You got your eyes on any more rocks we can dig under?"

Although Jake didn't know it at the time, the next big lead was in the works in the Fargo-Moorhead area, an agricultural region a few hours driving distance northwest of Minneapolis.

Charles and Elizabeth Abercrombie had a sugar beet farm in Clay County, just outside of Moorhead. Although not especially large, it provided a decent living for their family. They were very content, growing sugar beets and raising two children. Then, during the month of May, the bottom fell out of their lives, first when their three year old was killed in an accident, and second when they came home to a trashed house following the funeral.

The Sheriff's office sent two deputies to investigate. They walked through the house while the Abercrombie couple tried their best to describe the missing items. Then, as they sat down and began discussing the burglary, Elizabeth broke down, sobbing hysterically. Charles fought hard to control himself.

"You going to get the bastards?" he asked. His words dripped with venom.

"We're certainly going to try," one of the deputies answered, "but I have to be frank with you. Burglars are pretty hard to catch, and our detective bureau is short-handed. We've seen a ton of burglaries lately, and many of them occurred while the family attended a funeral."

The two deputies finished and headed back to their office.

Meanwhile, Lonnie and Donnie Dissel, twenty-one year old identical twins, walked out of a small building on Fargo's west side after fencing the goods stolen from the Abercrombie's home. Their habits for the next week had been bankrolled. The two paid a heavy price for those habits. They looked unhealthy and shared skeletal like features, neither having much excess flesh. Eating just enough to survive, a big chunk of their money went into their veins.

Tanya's place in north Fargo was their next stop. They got into their rusted van and drove her way. Donnie exercised caution as he drove, making extra turns, circling blocks and constantly checking his mirrors. If he brought heat to her house, he and his brother were literally dead meat. The bitch would see to that. Finally satisfied, he turned north onto a quiet street. Approaching the two story house, they saw two other junkies walking out the door. No doubt the two just scored some smack. It was the only reason to go to there. The twins occasionally saw other junkies leaving. Fargo wasn't a large city, and most of them knew one another.

Parking in front, they walked up the rickety wooden porch and Donnie knocked on the door. Tanya let them in, they went to the kitchen and sat down at the table.

The house, an old turn-of-the-century model, had hardwood floors needing work, walls in need of paint, and high ceilings stained by a leaking roof. Two men sat at a warped, gray card table in a spacious living room adjacent to the kitchen. One wore his long, light brown hair in a pony-tail. The other had coal black, greasy looking hair dangling straight down, brushing his shoulders. They appeared to be in their twenties, and watched Lonnie and Donnie indifferently, through lifeless eyes that could've been transplanted from a couple of apathetic fish. Although the twins saw the two every week for three years, they never exchanged words. Donnie, the cautious one, always felt apprehensive when coming here. These were scary people.

Tanya seemed preoccupied, even less talkative than usual. Placing two small baggies on the table, she said, "Each bag has a quarter ounce. Weighed them myself. Price hasn't changed."

Lonnie and Donnie each produced fourteen hundred dollars.

Tanya carefully counted it and smiled. "Have a good time. See you next week."

"Yeah, later," Donnie said, now anxious to get the hell out of there.

The twins headed towards the door. As they walked out, Lonnie gave the two men a long look. The curious one, he wondered just how bad they really were.

They returned to the rat hole they called home in south Fargo. Their small, bug infested apartment reeked from odors of garbage, uneaten food, dirty clothes, and bodies that hadn't bathed in weeks. A dead mouse, lying in a corner next to the refrigerator, contributed to the stench. The twins sat at the table and quickly dipped into their bags. Lonnie measured a hit of heroin into a crusty, blackened tablespoon. Its bent handle formed a loop so it could sit on its own without spilling its contents. He added some water and held a cigarette lighter under the spoon. As the mixture heated, the heroin dissolved, and he set the spoon down. Lonnie drew the solution into a syringe so he could shoot it up. Wrapping a belt around his upper left arm, he tightened the tourniquet until his veins swelled. The syringe found a good spot and the heroin mix went slowly into his arm. Releasing the belt, he sat back with a sigh. Feeling the effects of the drug, a mellow smile wrapped his face as he watched Donnie begin the same procedure.

"You know Bro, I wonder if there's something we could do," Lonnie said.

"What are you talking about?"

"Tanya and her friends."

"What about 'em?" Filling his syringe, Donnie's eyes narrowed as he looked over at his brother.

Lonnie stared vacantly across the room, his contented look a barometer of the high he felt. Finally he said, "You know, that's a hell of a lot of money she's making. You can bet your ass Tanya and her goons don't really live in that house. They live someplace else. Where that is, there's gotta be a pile of dough, and a big motherfucking stash of dope."

Donnie thought about what his brother said and set the syringe down. "I don't like where you're headed. Sounds like smack talking."

"Think about it," Lonnie persisted. "All we got to do is set up on that house, follow them to where they live, and case the place just like we always do. If it looked right, we could hit it and they wouldn't have no reason to think it was us. Fuck!! We'd probably have enough junk to last us a year."

"Are you fucking nuts? There is no motherfucking way I'm going to screw with them. Let me remind you of the first time we met up with her. Tanya held that big-ass fucking knife to my crotch and said if we ever tried to mess with 'em she'd cut off my nuts and stuff 'em down your throat. The bitch wasn't joking."

"You're not believing that crap, are you?"

"Hey, you don't think she's treacherous? And what about those two goons?"

"Yeah? Well they'd have to get past this first," Lonnie said, picking up his Beretta. He waved the pistol, pointing it at imaginary targets and barking, "Pow! Pow! Pow!" The gun barrel moved about the room until it was aimed at Donnie's face. Lonnie mimicked another gunshot.

Donnie saw red. "Put that fucking thing down, asshole!!" he yelled.

Lonnie set the pistol down.

"You know, you're fucking crazy," Donnie growled, scowling viciously. "If you ever, I mean *ever*, do that again you'll be eating those bullets."

Lonnie stared at his brother. "Hey Pal, you ain't gonna do shit and we both know it. So just forget about it."

"Look, we're not gonna fuck with them. Your idea sucks. I like my dick where it is." Donnie grabbed his syringe.

Later that afternoon, Donnie looked at a batch of newspapers sitting on the table and said, "Let's check the obits. Maybe we got some easy pickings."

The two browsed through some of the local newspapers covering eastern North Dakota and western Minnesota.

Finding a prospect almost immediately, Lonnie snorted, "Hey bro, check this out. Anderson family outside Valley City. Son got killed in a tractor accident. Says here the funeral is going to be in West Fargo. Why would a family living in Valley City go all the way to West Fargo for a funeral? Sixty miles away. Might make it easy for us. We'd have the whole morning to go through the place."

After Lonnie and Donnie left, Tanya and her two pals, Frankie and Charlie, hung out at the house for a couple hours. Relaxing as they sucked on bottles of Bud, Tanya and Frankie were lying on a thick shaggy rug that once was white, but now bordered a dingy brown-gray thanks to years of ground in dirt.

A few feet away, Charlie stretched out on an old, unsightly, blood red recliner. He broke the silence. "Tanya, you really trust those guys?"

Tanya raised onto her elbows and looked over at him. "It's funny you should ask that now. We been dealing with those junkies for years."

"I know. But it's been growing on me for a couple months. I never did like their vibes, and they were stronger than usual today."

When something rubbed her wrong, Tanya's large, brown eyes instantly flashed rage. Now Charlie was doing the rubbing. Had they been at the farm, she would have deferred to Big Al. He was the boss. But this was her turf. He never came to this house.

"Hey asshole," she said fiercely. "Big Al and me decide what we do and who we do it with. You do as you're told."

"Hey, I'm telling you I trust my instincts. If I don't like somebody's looks, bells ring inside my head. And when those guys come around, the alarm blares. How did you meet them anyways?"

Tanya stood and approached Charlie from the rear. Once behind his chair, she snatched an empty beer bottle, smashing it hard against a table. Hearing the noise, Charlie tried to scramble. Too slow. Grabbing his pony tail, Tanya pulled him back and stuck the jagged bottle up against his throat.

"You fucking dog turd," she said, staring into his startled eyes. "You question me and it's going to be your turn in the cage. You got that?"

Charlie turned ghostly white. Trying to brace himself, his fingers dug like leeches into the chair's arm rests. He felt strongly about his hunch, but he liked his neck more so he backed off just enough. "Hey, okay. You got it. But if we don't watch what we're doing, we're all fucked. And that includes you. I'm not trying to cause any shit. I'm just telling you. We all got a lot to lose."

Mesmerized, Frankie took a huge swallow from his bottle and watched his two companions. That woman was totally unpredictable, and he wasn't about to open his trap. He had seen Tanya in action, had been at her side as she slashed a man's throat with a razor sharp knife. A broken beer bottle added a new twist to her style, but someone at the wrong end would be just as dead. He knew his place in the pecking order. Charlie should've known too. Had to be crazy to blow off like that.

Smirking, Tanya threw the bottle onto the floor and stepped in front of Charlie. She had made her point. Time to smooth things over.

"Yeah, I'm hearing what you're saying Charlie. It's well taken. But I think they know what would happen if they fucked with us."

"Yeah, you're right." Charlie exhaled in relief.

"Okay, so do you trust us or don't you?"

"You know I trust you."

"Okay then. Follow me."

Tanya grabbed Charlie's hands, pulled him off his chair and led him upstairs to one of the bedrooms. When they came down forty-five minutes later, Charlie was sweating heavily.

"Come on you two. Time to get back to the farm," Tanya ordered.

They got into the van. At the farm they would give Big Al all the drug money they had taken in. Then they would go south and search for another lamb.

Stephanie, a fifteen year old run away, wanted to hitchhike to the lake region of Minnesota. Her last ride, an over the road trucker, dropped her off at 2:00 AM at a rest area off the freeway. He would continue east on I-90. Stephanie planned to go north to Fargo, 200 miles away, and then east from there. All alone in the rest area, she slipped on her jacket to ward off the frigid night's chill. Standing outside the building in the middle of nowhere, the frightened young girl became overcome with depressing thoughts. Tears flowed down her cheeks as the loneliness brought back ugly visions of the home she had so eagerly left.

Shaking it off, Stephanie contemplated what to do next. The freeway held light traffic at this hour. Would somebody actually stop to pick up a hitchhiker in the dark? Would they even see her? Would it be wise to hop into a vehicle at night when she couldn't see who, or what was inside? No! She went inside the building and sat down on a bench. It would be a good place to wait out the night and consider her predicament.

An hour later she saw two vans enter the rest area from the north. A couple got out of one van and came into the building, both giving her a good once-over as they walked to the rest rooms. The woman came out and approached Stephanie.

"Hi," the woman said. "Are you okay?"

"Yeah. I'm headed to the lake country, and my last ride dropped me off here.

"What's your name?"

"Stephanie."

"I'm Tanya. If you're hitching, we'd be glad to help you. We got turned around. We're heading north, to Fargo. You want to ride with us?"

"I'd really appreciate it."

The afternoon following Stephanie's abduction, Big Al sat at his desk contemplating the full moon and sharpening his sacrificial knife. His pager buzzed. He took his feet off the desk and read the phone number on the little screen. It was the number of an answering machine in one of his houses in Fargo. He dialed the number, uttered a verbal code into the phone, and waited for the messages. Only one message sounded. Al recognized the voice. Eddie Pellegrino.

The message was short. "Big Al. Call me five at five."

He was to call Eddie at pay phone number five at five o'clock. The Grandfather clock on the opposite side of the room read two forty-five. Al turned to his credenza and punched a few keys on his computer. The screen revealed the phone number for pay phone number five, which was in the Minneapolis area. He scribbled the number down on a scrap of paper. If he left in one hour, he'd get to a pay phone in Fargo with time to spare.

The West Acres shopping mall on Fargo's west side held numerous pay phones. He would go there, call Eddie, and then have a good meal before returning

Al stuffed the scrap of paper into a pocket, and then someone knocked on his door. "Come in," he responded. He had a raspy, baritone voice; his speech, slow and deliberate.

Tanya walked in brazenly and closed the door. Al gestured for her to take a seat across from his desk while he studied her body language. She's really feeling the need, he thought. Well, he would soon take care of that.

"You came back in the early hours. I did not expect you so soon. You accomplished your mission?"

Tanya gazed expressionless across the desk at the man twenty years her senior. "Everything is all set on my end," she said, her voice cold and concise. "Our little lamb is secure. Mac, Fernando, and Juleen are back from Detroit Lakes, and they'll be going out tomorrow to find the heifer. They've got money for you."

"Tell them I'm waiting. I'll meet you at the barn in forty-five minutes. By the way, did everything go well?" Al asked.

"Everything was simple and easy with the lamb. Her name is Stephanie. She'll be a fine one for El Diablo."

"Give her some water with the usual amount of valium. No food. She'd barf it up anyways. It will be a couple days before we get to her. Anything else?"

"Yeah, there's something you should know," Tanya answered stiffly.

"Go on."

"Charlie and me had a tiff yesterday at the house. He questioned our judgment with Lonnie and Donnie. Says he doesn't trust them."

"And why's that?"

"Says alarms ring when he sees them. He can't point to any specific reason. Just plain paranoia I think."

"I see. What else?"

"I don't like Charlie doubting our decisions. Lonnie and Donnie are our call, not his. Maybe his mind's not right and you should look into it. I got him under control, but you never know."

Turning his chair around, Al faced the window, looking towards the river. With his eyes focused on the compelling scenery, his mind contemplated the clan, Charlie, and all the dirty secrets concealed on the farm. Anyone taking exception to one of Big Al's laws might soon become one of the dirty secrets. Here, Manfred Alphonse Culpepper was the Sheriff, Congress, and Supreme Court all wrapped up into one tidy bundle.

He reached his decision slowly, then faced Tanya. Sternly, he responded, "You will stay on the farm with Charlie and Frankie for the next two days. Charlie will not leave the grounds. I will deal with this at the full moon."

At the mention of the full moon, as if on cue, Tanya got up from her chair and walked around the desk to Al. Suddenly a meek, vulnerable young woman, the transformation could not have been more striking. Getting down on her knees, she placed both of her hands on his legs and pleaded, "Big Al, please be my daddy."

Al played to her needs. "Tiggy, I am your daddy. I have been your daddy for years. Your other daddy hated you. He was cruel to you. He got what he deserved. Lucifer's domain is now his home, along with your mother. I have some very important business to take care of this afternoon. This evening I will take care of your needs."

Tanya got up off her knees and stepped back. The transformation ended, with Tanya again all business. "I'll be at the barn," she said brusquely.

"Good."

Tanya walked out of the office, closing the door behind her.

Big Al picked up the knife and tested its edge with his thumb. Not quite satisfied, he grabbed the honing stone and began massaging the blade of the knife against the stone as he had done earlier, first one side then the other with a squelchy, *Errrrrip, Errrrrip, Errrrrip.*

Several minutes later another knock sounded on his door.

"Come in."

Mac entered the office carrying two battered briefcases. A wiry young man, he had bushy, sandy colored hair, a pre-maturely hardened face and a thin, scraggly beard that tried, unsuccessfully, to conceal the rough, patchy scar of a burn inflicted on him during his childhood. He placed the briefcases on the desk. Al gestured for him to sit down.

"Were there any problems?" Al eyed him closely.

"Everything went well."

"Tell me about it."

"We sold a pound to our man in Detroit Lakes. He paid on delivery, and the deal went down real smooth. On to Brainerd. Unloaded a kilo there. Everything was cool. Grand Rapids next. Rick introduced us to someone new. Guy named Gregory. Rick said he's known him for years. I believe him. Didn't sell to the guy, but we talked business." Mac noticed Al was about to speak, so he abruptly stopped.

After a few seconds of silence, Al looked directly at the man and said with more than a hint of admonishment, "You know meeting somebody new is one of the most dangerous things we do."

It wasn't a question.

Al went on, "New customers are essential for our business. But this is also the time to exercise extreme caution. Always remember, when you meet someone new you must consider he might be an undercover agent, a snitch, or a rip-off. You cannot be too careful. Does Gregory use dope?"

The question was of fundamental importance. An undercover narc wouldn't use hard drugs such as heroin. If Gregory used heroin, it wasn't an absolute green light. Someone using junk could still be a rip-off or a snitch, but Mac could eliminate at least one of the threats.

"Yeah, he's a junkie. We sold a quarter pound to Rick and he gave the guy a hit. Gregory shot it up in front of us. I gave him the standard greeting. He took it straight, and I'm sure he got the message. He'll be okay. It'll be good to have another customer in Grand Rapids. Told him we'd have an Oh Zee for him when we came back, and gave him the routine we expect. Next time we're there we'll take an extra day to make sure he's straight. There shouldn't be any problems."

"Be careful. If he's a junkie, that's good. But junkies can be extremely treacherous. Their only loyalty is to their monkey." Al let this sink in for a few moments, then slightly tilted his head. "Continue."

"We sold a pound to our other people in town. Went smooth. They said they could handle more the next time around. Grand Rapids is a hot spot right now. Unloaded a half pound in Hibbing and then a kilo in Duluth. If we had it, we could have sold more in Duluth. Market's wide open up there." Mac opened up the briefcases. They were filled with bundles of cash, predominantly hundreds, totaling nearly a half million dollars.

Putting down his knife, Al pulled the briefcases across the desk and briefly examined their contents. Resting snugly inside with the bills all arranged face up, the neat stacks of currency conveyed a message of the efficiency demanded by the clan's leader.

"Good," he uttered, as he contemplated putting the currency through the money counter. "Anything else?"

Mac thought for a few seconds. "Can we get bigger quantities?"

"I'll see what I can do. Take care of the heifer for us. The lamb is waiting. The full moon approaches."

To Mac, the words "full moon" from Al's lips carried the kinetic energy of a falling piano. When they struck, Mac's eyes opened wide, his nerves shimmied, and his speech turned hollow and monotone, mirroring Tanya's earlier stance. "Yes. We'll be ready."

Al looked steadily at Mac for ten seconds, then said indifferently, "I have other business now."

"Okay, Big Al." With the grip now released, Mac became Mac. He left the office.

Looking again at the money Al's eyes glowed, like a little boy watching a speeding fire truck. He returned the knife and honing stone to the drawer. That job could wait. Al had other things in need of attention.

After securing the briefcases in his vault, he walked out to the barn and rejoined Tanya. It was a barn befitting a once successful dairy operation. In the interior all of the cattle stalls, holding pens, and utility rooms had been removed, leaving one huge room. A discerning nose could still detect a faint, but not unpleasant scent of cow manure. The area outside the barn, once fenced, now comprised a large manicured yard. Between the barn and the river sat the two double-wide trailers, installed by Big Al after he moved onto the farm.

With a grim smile, Al said, "Let's have a look at her."

They entered the barn and walked over to the trap door leading to the cellar. The floor of the barn, built with heavy landscaping timbers, made a solid ceiling for the room below. The two walked down the stairs, opened the large door and entered the cellar where they saw Stephanie, sitting in the same cage Roxanne had occupied a month earlier. The captive's eyes had a drugged appearance as she stared through the steel bars at the two people entering the stench filled room. But the valium in her blood wasn't sufficient to mask her fear. Like those before her, Stephanie was no longer a pretty picture. She immediately recognized Tanya as the one who had betrayed her at the rest area. She hadn't before seen Big Al's face; one she'd rather not remember.

With Tanya watching in eager anticipation, Big Al fixed his predatory eyes on their lamb. Then, giving Tanya a look of deep reflection, he said, "You know Tiggy, I can see a strong resemblance between her and your mother when she was a girl."

Tanya recoiled as she heard these words, her eyes flashing rage. She angrily looked at Stephanie and hissed, "You fucking bitch."

The astonished fifteen year old stared at Tanya. "You don't know me," she whispered.

CHAPTER 13

Ignoring Stephanie, Al turned to Tanya. "Let's go. I've got an appointment."

Both retreated up the stairwell and out of the barn. Tanya disappeared into the house. Al went to the garage, started his black Mercedes and drove to Fargo.

Finding an unoccupied pay phone proved easy. As usual, he and Eddie would keep their conversation short. No longer than a minute. The organization had a number of hard and fast rules from which they never deviated.

At five o'clock he dialed the number for pay phone five. Eddie Pellegrino answered on the first ring.

"Yeah," Eddie said gruffly.

"It's me," Al said. "What is it?"

"We need to meet. I'd like to come to the farm."

"You want to come here? Is something wrong?"

"Not from where you're standing."

"Okay. Tomorrow at noon?"

"Noon it is."

They hung up.

After the phone call, Al went to the Golden Gate Restaurant, a five fork establishment located on the outskirts of Fargo, where he relaxed over a steak dinner. Later, when he returned to the farm, he found Tanya waiting in the living room.

Al approached her and said flatly, "Are you ready for me, Tiggy?"

"Yes, Daddy." Tanya keyed on the name her father called her when she was young.

"Upstairs to my bedroom," he said sternly.

When Al moved to the farm he had the large house remodeled, converting four second floor bedrooms into two, with his bedroom taking up three of the previous rooms. Tanya occupied the other room.

He walked up the stairs with her following submissively. Entering his bedroom, Al turned around and slapped Tanya's face with his open hand, leaving a red mark on her left cheek. She recoiled from the blow but rebounded.

"Why did you do that, Daddy?" she asked haughtily.

"Because you've been a very bad girl. You've been a whore. You must be punished. Strip off your clothes."

Tanya quickly undressed.

He looked at her sleek naked body. One side of this woman, a highly efficient, calculating machine, devoid of fear, eagerly did his bidding. A different woman embraced the other ego, a woman overwhelmed with needs that had to be regularly stoked, needs that only he could fulfill. And when satisfied, they were the fuel that fed the machine.

Yeah, the machine is hungry. Time to feed it. "Go to the punishing pole," he said abruptly.

The punishing pole, a round wooden pillar, extended from floor to ceiling. Tanya meekly went to the pole and reached for a leather loop, fastened on the pillar two feet above her head. The loop was slightly larger than one of her hands, but she could squeeze both of her hands in one at a time. With the leather loop now tight on her wrists, she waited.

Stripped naked, Al took out a long leather strap from a closet. Using the strap, he struck her several times on the buttocks, leaving red welts. He then yelled, "So, you've been fucking those guys your mother has been sending to your room. Haven't I told you I'm the only man you're going to fuck?"

"Yes, Daddy," she whimpered.

He struck her twice on her bare back. More angry red welts instantly appeared.

"You've disobeyed me. Your mother is a pimp. Why do you obey her and not me?"

Tanya wailed, "I had to, Daddy. She made me do it. She was mean to me. She doesn't love me."

The whipping stopped.

As if transfixed, Al reached over to the loop, releasing her hands. He picked her up and carried her to his king-sized bed, gently placing her head on a pillow. "Tiggy, I forgive you," he said softly. "And you know I love you."

She melted. Big Al knew how to push her buttons. Her real father had never said things like that. The closest might have been, "You got nice tits," as he forced her legs apart, never offering the slightest hint of affection. He would screw her, slap her around and then leave, making her feel cheap and worthless. This continued until her teen years when an agency removed the girl from her parents' custody. She bounced around from one foster care home to another, but none of those folks had a clue how to handle her. By the time she turned seventeen, the police in the Twin Cities knew her well. Around that time, Big Al entered her life.

Al and Tiggy made love, then cuddled on the bed. She loved lying next to him.

Big Al is my real Daddy. I'd die for you, Big Al.

Al looked at her and could sense her thoughts. Propping himself up on an elbow, he said consolingly, "Your mother will be punished for what she did, Tiggy."

"Yes, I know."

"And who is going to punish her?" he asked in a quiet voice.

"You will," she answered meekly.

"That's right. I will take care of your needs, Tiggy."

Smiling inwardly, Big Al knew he owned her. She was his slave; both her egos. What a remarkable find. He recognized her potential from day one, and his talents were up to the challenge. She was the best. But the others were also good. He molded them, surrounding himself with people who would do anything for him. They lived for him and would die for him. Yeah, he was truly a genius.

Big Al considered it a tragedy nobody else knew this. He had wealth, but no recognition. Genius un-shared meant genius un-recognized. His anonymity, essential for his operation's success, deprived him of another important prize. What was the proper balance? He would mull over that later, not now.

The tone of his voice changed. "Tanya, make sure Charlie doesn't leave us before his time. We'll get dressed now."

Tiggy responded to the change and reverted back to her alter-ego. "Yes Big Al." She dressed and left the bedroom, not looking back.

At high noon, Eddie Pellegrino arrived in a burgundy Corvette convertible. Al went outside to greet him. They shook hands, then embraced.

"Man, you're looking good Al," Eddie said, smiling broadly. He took a deep breath of the fresh country air. "You know, I should get up here more often. Getting out into the country is invigorating."

"Eddie, you are always welcome. Just make sure you call me first. One of these times we should try fishing the river."

"Yeah. Fishing is good for your soul."

"Soul is what this place is all about. Come in. We'll talk."

Entering the house, Al led Eddie to his office and motioned him to sit on a plush, upholstered chair. He then walked over to the bar where he poured Scotch on the rocks for them both. "So, what is this visit about? I sense urgency."

"Several things you should know. Our operation is affected, but you might benefit for a few months."

Al handed Eddie a drink and sat down on the couch.

Eddie savored his drink for a moment and then continued. "First the bad news. The DEA hit Black Jack Mike's place. Gunned him down. I guess he put up a fight. His old lady and one of his people, a guy named Jeremy, were also in the house. Jeremy is still in the slam, the old lady bonded out. Neither of 'em knows exactly who I am, and if Mike played it right they've never heard of you. There shouldn't have been anything in the house pointing to us, but I'm watching real close. If there's any heat I'll let you know."

Big Al stirred in his chair but didn't interrupt.

"Losing Black Jack Mike hurt, but a week later Frenchy Deveroux got himself killed too. That leaves me in a hell of a spot until I find people to take over their action. As you know, good help is hard to find. In the meantime, I gotta find some way to pick up the slack. Do you think you can handle six more keys a month?"

All this was a big load for Big Al to absorb at one time. "How'd Frenchy get it? DEA onto him too?"

Eddie shook his head. "No. It was some rip-offs. Killed him in his house along with a couple broads. The DEA is looking into that too, but there shouldn't have been anything in his place that would lead to us. Like I said, if I feel any heat you'll be the first to know."

Big Al swore under his breath. "Six more keys a month with no advance notice is gonna be tough. I'm not set up for it."

Eddie nodded sympathetically. "Al, I hear ya. But I'm worried if I cut down the size of my shipments the people down south will be asking why. I can't tell 'em the DEA is breathing down my neck. They hear that they'll cut me off. I got to carry on with business as usual. Right now, you're my only outlet."

Al looked out the window, not saying a word. Finally the silence became louder than Eddie could stand.

"Okay, look. I'll give you the extra keys at a twenty-five percent break. How the hell can you turn that down?"

Al faced Eddie, deep in thought. "Twenty-five percent, huh? Okay, I'll do it. But if you get the slightest hint of any heat, I need to know fast."

"I got you covered, Al. Remember, I'm at risk too. No way do I want to go to that damn joint again. I've been rehabilitated."

"You may be forgetting. I was there too."

The atmosphere in the room suddenly changed as the two shifted away from business and back to old times.

"I see you haven't lost those big prison biceps," Eddie said, looking at Al's muscular arms. "Still working out, huh?"

"They convey a message. I've installed a gym in the basement. Physical conditioning keeps me mentally sharp."

"You always were the mental type," Eddie said respectfully. "I guess that's what intrigued me when you got to the joint. There were a few guys in there with college degrees. But you were the only one I knew with a Masters in psych. I always wondered why you didn't go on. Maybe get a PhD. Be legit."

The compliment left Al elated, but he maintained a deadpan look. The day before saw him regretting that nobody fully appreciated his genius. Eddie's visit gave him a chance to crow. He wouldn't tell Eddie everything, but to a man hungry for recognition this was like a hot Thanksgiving meal to a homeless person.

"That's a very interesting subject," he began, as he prepared to talk about himself. "I took psych because I wanted to know what made people tick. But I never would have made a good doctor. They care about people. I don't. As far as I'm concerned, if somebody gets sick that's tough shit. Selling dope is as close to being a doctor as I want to get. The money is much better, and with my people the work is definitely easier. They are very good."

"So your college background put things in motion?"

Al could see fascination in Eddie's eyes. The man had struggled to get a GED in prison, and Al provided him considerable coaching. And now Al was helping him get rich. He smiled inwardly. Without Big Al, Eddie was nothing.

Al nodded at Eddie's last question and then poured it on. He recalled the Come Together group home, where he managed to get a job as a counselor after his release from prison. "The degree got me the job. I took over from there."

Eddie took a swig of whiskey. It was twelve year old, top shelf Scotch, and he enjoyed its mellow warmth as it traveled down his gullet. He held the tumbler on his knee and resumed his conversation. "And that's where you found your people?"

"Yes," Al said. He talked about his clan, their non-functional homes and screwed-up parents who abused, and even tortured them, as punishment for having been born.

Al paused as he took a long swallow of his drink. "So you can see where I'm coming from. The system took them from their homes or wherever and tried to make things right. But the kids saw incompetence, agencies that always seemed to do the wrong things for the right reasons. At Come Together, things got smoother after I arrived. The staff needed my abilities. They loved me and forgave me immediately for the indiscretions that landed me in the joint. What a bunch of bleeding hearts! They especially liked me because I could handle the incorrigibles. The kids related to me because I had been in the joint. Didn't consider me part of that system. When I got ready to make my move, I selected the ones I wanted and brought 'em here. Now they're all super-charged, and I know how to channel their energies."

"How'd you get a handle on all this?"

"Suffice it to say I know what I'm doing. I've found the key."

Eddie politely nodded, but his curiosity ballooned as a silent alarm stirred deep within his memory banks. "This farm is the key?"

"You might say that. I provide them with a secure setting; a roof, clothing, food. All the basics. And I give them a sense of discipline, and direction. I run a tight ship. They fear me and love me at the same time. Teaching them the drug business is part of it. We've been highly successful. So far not a single one has gone down. And if one were caught, I know the cops wouldn't get anything on me."

Al continued talking, looking out the bay window as he rambled on about the training of his followers, his continued drilling on the necessary precautions, techniques, all the do's and don'ts they had to remember while selling his dope. Yeah, he had done one hell of a great job.

As Al spoke, a gut-wrenching flashback struck Eddie hard, dousing him with anxiety. His frame stiffened. Cold sweat gushed out of his pores. An old memory, it hadn't visited him for many years, and caused him to reflect. What the hell was going on here? Was this farm the base for a cult? No way could he be a part of that. His guts trembled as he fought to maintain a stoic face. But he had to know more.

Eddie blinked and reasserted himself, dumbfounded that he had lost it for a few moments. Had Big Al noticed? Thankfully, no. All caught up in himself and his brilliance, the man had been looking away as he spoke. Grabbing a handkerchief from his pocket, Eddie wiped his eyes and face, trying to regain his composure.

Big Al turned around just as Eddie put away his handkerchief. It was a break for Eddie. Al would have interpreted Eddie's temporary transfixion as a sign of weakness, something to be exploited. In this world, the players and their roles were always subject to change.

Al stopped talking and looked at Eddie, obviously expecting a response.

Eddie cleared his throat. "I'd guess a lot of this was made possible by my attorney. I'm glad I put you two together."

Al stared into his whiskey, feeling some satisfaction while at the same time chagrined that Eddie tried to take any credit. Reluctantly, he let it pass. "Vondermolte did use his connections to get me in the door at Come Together. As I think about it, Vondermolte has helped me in a number of ways. He must owe you a lot. Whatever I want, I get."

"Yeah, he owes me big time," Eddie said. "I kept him out of prison. He knows he'd be doing ten to twenty if I would've cooperated with the feds. The man is plenty grateful. He's the one who hooked me up with Dominique after I got out. Dominique had the connection and I had the outlets. Marriage made in heaven. I told Vondermolte to help you out."

Big Al smiled. "And that he did. His law firm is the legal, registered owner of this spread. Everything is in the name of the firm . . . taxes, phones, vehicles. Everything. Set it up that way for the benefit of nosy cops. In this world I don't even exist. If the cops come to him for information, he'll tell them to get fucked, or whatever attorneys say to cops."

Eddie grinned. Then he thought of Tanya. He met with her briefly once a month in Minneapolis when they exchanged money and drugs. He considered her generally bizarre. This meet cleared away some of the fuzz. If she was a cult member, she was probably psychotic. Eddie decided to probe in that direction.

"So how's Tanya doing? My old lady saw her once. She was intrigued by Tanya's black lip stick . . . that whole gothic thing."

"Tanya is my greatest success. She lives in the house with me. The rest stay in the trailers."

Eddie didn't push it, again changing the subject. "Who does your handy work?"

Fast Freddie was Big Al's handyman. Eddie knew the man from prison, and Big Al realized Eddie hadn't put it together. Best to keep it that way. Freddie was some kind of a handyman genius. When Big Al bought the farm, Fast Freddie set it up the way Al wanted. It wasn't cheap. Al paid him twice the going rate for all the work. Now the man enjoyed a constant retainer. No need to go into that, no reason for Eddie to know about the tunnels and the other rooms.

Big Al liked Eddie asking questions. It gave him the opportunity to brag. On the other hand, too many questions violated the sacred creed of drug dealers. He considered his answer.

"There's always people looking for a buck or two."

Eddie seemed satisfied. "So how did you happen to pick Kindred, North Dakota? You're out in the middle of nowhere."

"That's what's good about it. They don't have much of a crime problem in these parts. It's not heavily populated. Real simple equation. No crime problem equals not many cops. And I really like the plains. Sitting in that cramped prison cell I could only see four walls. I like going out into my yard and enjoying a fine view with open spaces. Plus, I've got privacy. You probably noticed, trees hide my place from three directions. The closest neighbor is a mile west, and he can't see us. The road you came in on is a quarter mile away. The driveway circles through the trees. Somebody driving past doesn't see anything. And the river is to the south. More trees. Had to pay a hell of a price for the place, but it was worth it."

"So, how about showing me around?"

"Be glad to."

Al gave Eddie a guided tour, but left out the important areas. They were none of his business. After the tour, Eddie left the farm and returned to Minneapolis.

CHAPTER 14

The evening was perfect for the ceremony. The sky was clear. Nothing would interfere with the strange, mystical powers of the full moon. By eleven o'clock, the bright moon rising in the heavens tempered the darkness of the night. The clan members felt giddy with excitement.

Al beckoned Tanya to his office.

As usual, her eyes were keenly focused. She carried a black, hooded robe. "Is it time, Daddy?" she asked.

"Yes, Tiggy. It's time to punish your young mother."

"Everybody's ready."

"How about Charlie?"

"He doesn't have a clue."

"Good." Al stepped to the refrigerator, took out the zip lock baggies, and handed Tanya the usual ration of psilocybin mushrooms and sinsemilla marijuana.

"Begin the ceremony. I'll see you in the barn."

Tanya left, joined the other clan members and handed out the drugs. After they finished with the joints, the ceremony commenced.

"Light the torches," Tanya commanded.

As before, Frankie struck his lighter and seconds later the ghoulish shadows danced across the grounds. The clan followed Tanya with their loud, haunting chant.

"Lucifer. Satan. Beelzebub. We've sharpened the knife. It's in your honor we'll snuff out a life.

"Lucifer. Satan. El Diablo. We ain't gonna fail. Come pay us a visit. There'll be blood in your pail."

Twenty minutes later the group again stood in a half circle before the alter, all of them stoned except Tanya. All of them eager to see blood spilled.

They stood in silence, waiting. Shortly, they heard the chains clatter up the stairs beneath the trap door. The trap door slowly opened and their chant resumed, its volume reflecting their state of frenzy. Then, seeing El Diablo rise out of the floor with their lamb securely in his arms, they added the third verse:

"El Diablo, El Diablo! Bring on the knife. This is your night. Come take a life."

Al placed Stephanie on the alter, then held up his hands to silence the group. With every eye riveted on him, Big Al addressed the clan, giving them his usual spiel. He then turned his attention to their lamb. A short time later she was gone.

He looked over the group. Charlie stood at the far end of the line. Al picked up the pail with the mixture of blood, along with the cow's tail, and walked to the end opposite from Charlie. As always, he stopped in front of each clan member, painting their faces. They moaned and bellowed as they licked the blood.

At that point, the routine changed.

Al stopped in front of Charlie, who looked at him unsuspectingly. "Satan has given me a warning. There is one of you who is no longer worthy to be among us. One of you doubts me. Satan's wrath has been called."

Following Tanya's lead, the group returned to their chant.

" . . . . Come take a life."

Charlie, as stoned as the others, didn't suspect he was the one. He continued the chant along with the rest.

Al set the pail down and punched Charlie in the chest. He doubled over in pain as air exploded from his lungs. With one quick movement, Al slashed Charlie's neck. Charlie collapsed to his knees, futilely trying to catch his blood with his hands, wishing he could jam it back into his veins, unable to comprehend why Big Al would do this.

The others filed over to Charlie, putting their hands into his blood, then to their faces, mouths, and the others' faces. Yelling, "Traitor," they took turns kicking him as he lay bleeding to death on the floor.

Al's face beamed. Time to go back and savor the moment with a bottle of Scotch in the peace and tranquility of his bedroom. He returned to the tunnel. The clan would stay up all night, working off the effects of the hallucinogens, while Tanya closely watched over them.

At first light the clan members would bury the two bodies in the woods near the river. After three years of ceremonies the area was littered with shallow graves.

Two weeks after Memorial Day, Tanya returned from the Twin Cities with another load of dope. She brought it directly to Big Al's office.

"Any problems?" Al asked.

"Everything's cool."

"How's Eddie doing? Did he mention anything about heat?"

"He hasn't felt any."

Al nodded but said nothing.

Tanya looked perplexed. "I hope we can get rid of all this shit." She placed ten kilos of heroin, six more than usual, on Al's desk.

Thoughtfully, Al studied the dope. After they cut it, they would have twenty kilos to dump. The normal load, after being cut and packaged, was eight. The product was great, but hell, there had to be a market. Al knew he had a problem. He would have to put pressure on the clan members to sell more, find new customers. Maybe the schools were the solution. A few high schoolers used his dope. But a few wasn't enough.

Shifting his gaze back to Tanya, he said, "We'll cut the product this afternoon. Mac, Fernando, and Juleen are leaving tomorrow. They will take four additional kilos with them. Mac found a new buyer in Grand Rapids. That's good news. And he tells me the market in Duluth is expanding. He should be able to unload even more there. But we're going to have to modify our strategy a little. We got this junk at a discount, so we have some wiggle room. I want all of you to have your distributors focus on the school kids. Tell them to find out where the kids party, go where they hang out and give 'em free samples for a couple weeks. Get 'em hooked. Teens should be an easy market. If it's done right, twice the money will come in."

"We'll do our best."

"I know, Tanya. You are the best. I will always take good care of you."

The following day Mac and his crew drove to their assigned territory. Mac and Juleen drove together in the van. Fernando followed, alone in a new Dodge. Big Al always felt it a good idea to have two cars available for additional security on these trips.

"We got our work cut out for us," Juleen said to Mac. "Never handled so much before. You think it'll go okay?"

"Yeah," Mac answered confidently. "It went smooth as silk last time, and I got no reason to think it'll be different today. Gregory, that new guy, was in Rick's house and he had his money waiting. Gregory said he could handle more this time if we could come up with it. He might open up some new avenues. Push it, and I think they'll lighten our load. Then, when we're all happy, we'll talk to them about expanding their market like Big Al said."

Juleen knew all this. She accompanied Mac and Fernando on all the runs. But she listened intently, wanting to make sure she hadn't forgotten something important. "Everything's looking good. We already got one new buyer, there's more product to sell, and it shouldn't take too long for the free samples to do the trick with the school kids. I think we're gonna make Big Al real happy." she said with satisfaction. A contented Big Al made life sweet for all of them.

They made their usual stops in Detroit Lakes and Brainerd. After spending the night in a motel, they hustled on to Grand Rapids. Coming to the city limits, they stopped at a gas station.

"You gotta make a pit stop before we go to Rick's place," Mac asked Fernando.

"Nah," Fernando said. "Let's just go do it and get out of here."

"You got it," Mac said eagerly. "I'll go in and meet with Rick and Gregory. I'm bringing a kilo into the house. This is the biggest load we've ever sold there, so stay on your toes."

"Yeah," Fernando said. "I know the routine."

Rick's house was located in a sparsely populated, low income area outside the city limits. Mac stopped in front and got out of the van. Juleen took the wheel and parked a distance down the road. Fernando sat in his car directly in front, as Mac quick-stepped to the side door of the small house and knocked lightly.

Rick answered the door. "Hey Mac, we've been expecting you. Come on in."

"How you doing," Mac said. "Gregory here too?"

"Yeah, he's ready to do business. Is that the shit?" Rick pointed at the paper sack Mac held in his hands.

"Yeah. I brought a kilo this time. Gregory said he could handle more. When this deal's down, I got some other things to talk to you about." Mac said, placing the bag on a table.

At that time Gregory walked in from another room, accompanied by a man Mac didn't know. Both held pistols.

Mac knew immediately it was a rip, and his mind scrambled. He wasn't about to tell Big Al a kilo of heroin had been lost without a fight. He'd rather take a bullet than follow Charlie's fate. Hoping for a lucky break, he quickly grabbed for his pistol. Not a chance! Gregory and his partner were each on a hair trigger. Seeing Mac attempting a quick draw, they began shooting. Bullets riddled Mac's chest and stomach before he could level his gun. He dropped dead on the spot.

"Let's get the guy in that Dodge. He's probably got more dope," Gregory said quickly. Then he pointed his pistol at Rick's head and said, "Don't you fucking touch this," as he gestured towards the bag of dope.

Rick's entire body quivered. Beads of cold sweat appeared on his forehead. Dark stains had already formed around his armpits. "You guys didn't tell me you were going to do this," he stammered.

Gregory's partner hammered his fist into Rick's face and yelled, "Just do what you're told!"

Rick staggered backwards and put his hand on his throbbing cheek where the guy punched him.

Fernando heard the shots and knew they had big trouble in the house. He grabbed his pistol while frantically waving to Juleen so she'd be ready for whatever. Then Gregory darted out the door. Fernando knew that meant bad news for Mac. Seeing a gun in Gregory's hand, Fernando slammed his car in gear, fired a couple shots towards the house, and burned rubber as his car screamed down the street. Gregory ducked as two bullets struck the front of Rick's house.

Trying to keep up with Fernando, Juleen jammed her foot down on the gas. The van's tires screeched and smoked as the vehicle lurched forward. Seeing Gregory crouched down, Juleen also fired a couple rounds in his direction as she roared by. As long as he was in that position he wouldn't be shooting back. By the time he stood up, both vehicles were well down the street.

Gregory watched them disappear and growled to his partner who stood just inside the door, "There were at least two people out there. Maybe we were lucky."

He darted back into the house, peered into the paper sack, and his disposition quickly changed. "Yeah, he did us right," Gregory gloated. Then he looked at Rick, totally ignoring what they had just done to him, and said, "We'll give you an ounce of this shit. Won't cost you a thing. But you take care of the body. Don't fuck this up. We don't want nobody connecting this to us, you got that?"

Rick knew he had no choice. Lots of lakes and rivers around here, he thought. *Throw him into the drink, maybe the fish will eat him. If not, I'll be long gone before anybody finds him. I'm getting the hell out of Dodge.*

Fernando and Juleen sped out of town, taking a direct route back to North Dakota. They stopped at a rest area a few miles out of Grand Rapids, where Fernando filled Juleen in on what he saw and heard. For sure Mac had been on the receiving end of those gunshots.

"There's nothing we can do about it except tell Big Al," Fernando said bitterly.

"Yeah, we'll tell him and he'll decide what to do," Juleen said. Nothing like this had ever happened. It scared her. Like Fernando, she dreaded seeing Big Al angry. Hopefully, he wouldn't take his anger out on them.

They drove straight to the farm and dutifully made their report.

As expected, Al became livid. But gratefully, he didn't condemn them. "Go get Tanya," he said to Juleen.

Within minutes, Tanya walked into the office and Fernando told her the news. She looked at Al with revenge in her eyes, awaiting his orders.

"Tanya, take Fernando, Juleen, and Frankie back to Grand Rapids. Take any firepower and whatever else you need. Find Rick and make him tell you about the rip-off. Then take care of it. Try to get our dope back. But send a message to Grand Rapids. This won't happen again."

They immediately loaded a van with weapons and accessories and left for Grand Rapids, arriving at Rick's house at two the next morning. The house was dark and desolate, with no cars around.

"Looks like Rick's not home," Tanya said. "Let's go inside. If nobody's there, we'll wait. Juleen, take the van and park it down the street. I don't want them seeing it. Then join back up with us." She turned to Frankie and Fernando. "You guys stick with me."

Tanya picked the lock on the back door and they entered. Within minutes, Juleen returned on foot. When she walked in she saw them standing over a large, dried dark stain on the kitchen floor.

Pointing to the floor, Tanya said, "This is where Mac got it. Nobody's here. We'll sit tight and see what happens. Maybe we'll get lucky."

Shortly after sunrise a car pulled into the driveway.

"This has to be him," Tanya said eagerly. "Take your positions."

Rick entered the house. Halfway into the kitchen he paused and looked down at the floor. "What a fucking mess."

Tanya came around the corner and pointed her nine millimeter in Rick's face. The rest of the group followed, guns ready.

Startled, Rick threw his arms up over his head and said, "Okay, okay. I can explain everything." He had a large, dark bruise on one cheek.

Fernando walked past Tanya towards Rick. "That's right, motherfucker. You're going to explain everything." He smashed his fist into the other side of Rick's bruised face.

Rick hit the floor hard, landing on his back. Expecting another blow, he rolled over onto his side and covered his face with his hands. Tanya walked over and landed a solid kick to his balls.

He moaned in pain, then blubbered, begging for mercy. "I told you I would explain everything!

Tanya pulled him onto his feet. "Who pulled the rip, and where are they?"

Rick told them everything he knew about Gregory, then pleaded, "But I don't know anything about the other guy. All I know is he's a junkie."

His answer didn't satisfy Tanya. Taking a small pair of pruning shears out of a knapsack, she said to Fernando, "We'll see how truthful he is."

Rick saw the shears and wailed, "That's all I know, honest! That's the truth!"

Fernando punched Rick hard in the stomach, causing him to double over, fighting for breath. Then Tanya kneed him in his ribs and he fell to the floor. Forcing one of Rick's arms out on the floor, Fernando knelt on it and stared into Rick's bulging eyes.

"This is the most effective lie detector I've ever seen. Let's see if you agree."

With Rick unable to move, Fernando cut off one of Rick's fingers, then a second. Rick's eyes opened as big as golf balls. He screeched in agony and begged them to believe him.

"Okay, I believe you," Tanya said calmly. She looked over at Frankie. "Put some gauze over the stumps so he don't bleed in the van. Then tape his mouth." She shifted towards Juleen. "Go get the van."

Frankie reached into his knapsack and pulled out a pack of thick gauze padding and some duct tape.

Five minutes later they drove to Gregory's house. Handcuffed, Rick lay in a fetal position on the floor. Fernando sat on the bench seat. One of his size fourteens rested heavily on Rick's head.

Gregory lived in an old rental house on the north side of town. The group arrived there at nine thirty. An old Ford occupied the rear of the driveway.

Fernando pulled Rick up to the window and hollered, "Is that Gregory's car?"

Rick nodded and slumped back on the floor.

"Let's do it," Tanya said.

Juleen parked in the driveway behind Gregory's car. Leaving Rick in the van, the four went to the back door. Fernando kicked the door in and they stormed into the house. It was a small one story with two dingy bedrooms. Armed with the information Rick gave them, Frankie and Juleen checked out the second bedroom, while Tanya and Fernando quickly went to Gregory's bedroom. They found him asleep under a dirty blanket littered with cigarette burn holes and food stains. Tanya grabbed his blanket and pulled it off. Gregory awoke with a start. His eyes flared when he saw the gun barrel pointed at his head.

Tanya yanked him out of bed by his hair. "You've got our heroin, motherfucker! We want it back!"

Gregory tried to remain calm, knowing he had a powerful card to play. If only he could get to it. "Okay, don't shoot me. You can have it back. No problem. I'll get it for you."

"Yeah, I'll bet, shithead," Tanya said. "Take us to it."

As he came within arm's reach of the dresser, Gregory lunged for the top drawer. Fernando saw it coming. He drove his fist into Gregory's face, sending him straight to the floor. Tanya pulled the drawer open and saw what Gregory wanted: A nine millimeter pistol. Grabbing the pistol, she discovered a bag filled with heroin lying beneath it. It appeared to be half of what Mac lost.

Frankie and Juleen ran into the bedroom, joining them. "The other room's empty," Frankie said.

"Where's the rest of the shit!" Tanya screamed.

Gregory, sprawled on the floor, realized his ace in the hole had just gone down the toilet.

"Pete's got it. We split it fifty-fifty. He went to peddle his share."

"How long before he's back?" Tanya demanded.

"Got no idea. Sometimes not for days. Depends on how high he gets, where he goes," Gregory said.

"Where's your money," Fernando asked roughly.

"Drawer. Next to the junk," Gregory answered, sobbing.

Juleen looked in the drawer and found a wad of cash inside a dirty sock. She counted it. "Eight hundred dollars," she said. "I'll give it to Big Al."

Tanya glared into Gregory's eyes and said, "Okay, shithead. Since you've been so cooperative, we'll give you the choice where you die. Your call."

Gregory blubbered louder, "Jesus Christ! Shit, no! I'm sorry. We didn't mean to kill him. It was an accident. When Pete gets back, I'll get your dope. I promise."

"Yeah, you're sorry all right," Tanya said contemptuously. "Since you can't make up your mind, we'll do it here." She glanced at Fernando. "Pick him up."

Fernando grabbed him by his armpits, stood him up and handcuffed him. Gregory stood there with every muscle in his body quivering violently. Scowling, Fernando punched him in the stomach. "That's for Mac."

Gregory doubled over and fell to the floor, gasping for breath.

Tanya pulled a knife from her sheath and danced the blade back and forth in front of his nose. As his eyes exploded in fright, she slashed a deep gash in his throat from ear to ear.

"Get Rick," Tanya told Frankie.

Shaking badly and with duct tape over his mouth, Rick stumbled into the bedroom. Seeing Gregory's body flopping in a pool of blood, Rick began heaving with fright.

Tanya held the bloody knife in front of Rick's eyes. "We told you, don't ever fuck with us. This is why."

Her blade sliced through Rick's throat like butter. He collapsed, his blood pooling with Gregory's. Tanya and her crew returned to their van.

"We're not done yet," Tanya said. "We know nothing about Pete, and we probably never will, but he's not going to get away clean. We got to leave him something to think about. Frankie, you and Fernando get the assault rifles. As soon as I back out onto the street, I want you to empty a couple magazines into the house."

At ten o'clock that morning, Paula Johnson pushed her

three year old daughter on a makeshift swing hanging from a thick tree branch in their back yard.

Little Megan laughed with delight, yelling, "Faster Mommy, faster."

"Okay, how's that, Honey?" Paula pushed the swing faster and higher. Then she heard a stream of what sounded like loud firecrackers coming from the direction of the troublesome rental house bordering her backyard. Instinctively, she looked in that direction before her mind processed the situation. *Oh my God! That's gunfire, not firecrackers. We're in danger.*

Instantly she grabbed for Megan, wanting to run like hell. Too late. Megan's lifeless body had dropped to the ground. Blood poured onto the dirt.

"Megan! No, no! Megan! AAAARGH!"

CHAPTER 15

Alan Ravich folded the newspaper, rolled it up, and twisted it in his sweaty palms. Disgusted, he walked around his desk, and in a fit of temper slammed the newspaper at the desk top.

Earlier in the week, two reporters came to his office to interview him. At the time of the meeting he was nursing a hangover. Wasn't in a mood to talk. After he gave 'em the bum's rush, they decided to shove their story up his ass. And they had a great deal to shove. Their report filled two pages in the newspaper, harshly criticizing the drug enforcement efforts in the state, and illustrating in gut wrenching detail the problems and heartbreak brought on by the drug epidemic.

"Those bastards can't do this to me." He paced, ranted and raved. "Fucking press. They're nothing but slime. What the hell do they know about drug investigations. Come in here, pumping me for information, then turn on me like vipers. If they would've told me what they had in mind, I would've played their game. Maybe could've helped 'em out. Dung heaps, that's what they are. The fucking dung heap duo." Alan's yelling to no one carried on, his epithets louder and louder, echoing throughout his office.

His secretary, wincing on the other side of the closed door, whispered to the typist at a nearby desk, "Get ready to duck. That fan might be blowing our way!"

The reporters' articles were vivid. After rehashing the Black Jack Mike debacle and the Frenchy Deveroux tragedy, they zeroed in on the Abercrombie burglary. The reporters liked that story, thinking it would tear at the readers' guts.

"Farm Home Ravaged by Junkie Burglars While Parents Attend Funeral of Young Daughter."

The headline bellowed right above Natasha's photograph. The little Abercrombie girl could have been a model for a "Precious Moments" image, and the couple's state of depression was so severe it had apparently brought the mother to the brink of suicide.

Quoting the Sheriff, the article said, "The burglary devastated that poor family. Everything indicates it was drug addicts again. I promise you, we'll get 'em. But it seems for every one we put in jail, five more pop up to take his place."

The next article detailed a burglary in Valley City, North Dakota. Close enough to Minnesota to be considered next door. The story's bold headline glared:

"Farm Burglarized, Hired Hand Murdered While Family Attends Funeral of Breadwinner."

The article recounted how the oldest Anderson boy, in his early twenties, had died in a tractor accident. The kicker was he had been heading up the farming operation because his dad died just a year earlier. The article quoted the young man's mother, who told the reporter, "I don't know what I'm to do now. I'm a housewife. I've been busy raising five children. I don't know how to farm. I can't even drive a tractor. And that poor hired hand. Our neighbor loaned him to us just to help out. He never hurt nobody."

Next was a story about Megan, a toddler in Grand Rapids. Another gruesome headline wrenched at the readers' innards.

"Young Girl Gunned Down While on Backyard Swing."

The mother was currently under medical treatment for shock and extreme emotional distress. The city's populace, outraged. The police, exasperated. A detective disclosed when they investigated the shooting of Megan, they discovered two more bodies, both junkies. "It was a grisly scene inside that house," he said. "And two days later another body, riddled with bullet holes, bobbed to the surface in Big Hand Lake. It looks like a drug war is going on."

Turning the page, the stories continued. The next, describing an ugly murder at a shopping mall in Duluth, carried another bewildering headline.

"Woman at Mall Watches in Horror as Fiancée Clubbed to Death."

The police chief said, "We're certain the two perpetrators are junkies. They bludgeoned the young man with a tire iron, stole his wallet and then cut off the woman's finger to get her diamond ring. She ran for help after they took her new car. We found the vehicle near Lake Superior, littered with used syringes."

Similar accounts followed. The reporters placed the blame for the entire mess on the shoulders of Mr. Alan Ravich, the head of the DEA in Minneapolis. *"Why Doesn't the DEA Do Something?"* the headline screamed. And immediately below: "Why won't Mr. Ravich meet the press? What is he hiding?" Then they tossed some ideas into the stew, hoping to further pique the readers' attention. Mr. Ravich had been in Minnesota for six months. Couldn't the DEA find someone more effective? Is the DEA's fine reputation just a lot of hype? Maybe Minnesota had been short changed. Shouldn't the readers write their congressman?

Alan glared at the mangled newspaper. Headquarters would cut his balls. Fuck his ideas of a big promotion. The chances of landing a posh assignment now were about as good as that woman sprouting a new finger. Hell, the brass reads this and he could be *demoted.* Ravich thought about it for a moment. Demoted and transferred to some shit hole office, working as a grunt. The idea made him shudder. "Damn it," he growled. "Heads will roll before that happens."

A cold, calculating smile formed on his face. Someone would pay, if not those fucking reporters, then somebody else. His agents would have to get their collective asses rolling in high gear if they wanted to escape his wrath. He was the boss, and the buck bounced here.

He pushed a button on the intercom.

"Yes, Mr. Ravich," the secretary answered unsteadily.

"I want every agent inside the war room in one hour."

"Yes sir."

Exactly one hour later, Harold Sampress sat glumly at his boss's side while Alan evil-eyed the agents. After giving them a quick rundown on the newspaper articles, he zeroed in on the first head he would see roll.

"Jake, who was Black Jack Mike's source?"

"It looks like it was a guy named 'Eddie,' boss."

"But, you don't know. Black Jack Mike is dead. Right?"

Jake braced himself. Ravich was headed down the same path as before when he had Jake standing tall.

"What about this Frenchy Deveroux. Where was he getting his junk?"

"Same guy."

"Okay, I'll give you that. So tell me, who the fuck is Eddie?"

"Boss, I don't know."

Ravich took a deep breath and exhaled slow. "Damn it. You're the heroin man, right? This is your case. For the past two months you've done nothing right. You're clueless. I need answers, and you don't know shit."

"Alan, I don't think that's a fair assessment."

Ravich huffed and puffed and drew in his breath, inflating his chest to match the girth of his paunch. Raising his voice, he said, "I'm the boss here. I'll decide what's fair. We're paying you to investigate. What do I get? Dead bodies! The press can do that. They're doing a better job than you. Now those bastards are on my ass, blaming me and the DEA for your screw-ups. I'm tired of watching you piss into the wind. I want progress! I want fucking results! I want the press off my ass! Start kicking butt. Your clock is running."

Looking around the table, Jake saw the same dismay on the faces of all of the other agents except Scott, who was grinning. Jake looked at Alan, thinking, *What's with this guy anyways? He comes to this office six months ago with timber log chips on his shoulders, and tries to turn a harmonious, hard working office into a discordant hell hole.*

Jake had reservations about the man from the start. Now he knew why. Ravich's ideas on motivation were skewed. Working for him was like having a jagged thorn poking through one of your Nikes. Far from making you run faster, you had to make a supreme effort to keep from slowing down.

Ravich, like a cat ready to pounce, turned on Lisa. An equal opportunity despot, he spread the heat around. Holding little respect for women in general, he felt especially contemptuous of female DEA agents.

"Lisa, what about your undercover deals? You find out anything about this asshole called Big Al? He's supposedly controlling the junk market in the northern half of the state. Go make some buys off him."

She shifted in her chair. "I'd love to boss. I don't know who he is. Might make some headway tomorrow. Got a buy set up with Fergie the Slob."

"Who the hell is Fergie the Slob?"

Lisa's next thought was *Who the hell are you?* But she held her emotions in check, wishing there were some way to lighten the atmosphere. "A heroin dealer in Eagan. The guy has never seen soap. His house is a dump. Don't think he's a big dealer, but he's probably well connected. Our strategy is to make a solid case and then get him to flip." She managed a smile. "I'm thinking Eddie might be perched at the top of Fergie's ladder."

"Eddie, huh? Do you have anything concrete that makes you believe that?"

"No, just a feeling. All I know is Fergie sells heroin, and he stinks. If you follow a rat, sooner or later it'll lead you to garbage. I'll keep Eddie in mind as we move along with the case."

"It sounds like you don't know shit either, but I'm going to hold you to that. Your clock is ticking too."

Ravich slid his chair far enough away from the table so his gut didn't brush it when he stood. He slowly shifted his menacing glare from one agent to the next. "The name of this game is 'Powder on the table.' I want to see it. I don't want fucking excuses, people. I want powder on the table! You don't produce, I'll get people who can." He stormed out of the room.

With the meeting done, the agents staggered out in a state of disbelief. Returning to their office, Travis edged over to his new partner's desk where Jake tried to make sense of Ravich's tirade.

"You know, I see hate in that guy," Travis said in a low, confidential voice.

Jake struggled to control his disgust. "I hear you. It's times like these I don't know who the enemy is."

Lisa Sanchez had been a senior high school teacher in Orlando for two years, when she decided the life of a PhyEd instructor and girls' basketball coach was too slow. A high spirited thoroughbred, she needed a faster pace. So she joined the DEA, and undercover work became her panache. But it came with a price. One of her undercover assignments in Orlando left her with haunting visions. She requested a transfer and soon arrived in Minneapolis, where she battled her ghosts along with the bad guys.

The day after the staff meeting, Lisa and Kiel headed to Eagan, a southern suburb of Minneapolis, to make the buy from Fergie. Lisa had been at Fergie's one time, and didn't relish returning. A few minutes in the same room with him had given her a solid understanding why they called this a dirty job. She believed two more heroin buys from the anti-hygiene activist would tighten the legal noose around his grubby neck.

The informant who introduced Lisa to Fergie was a hooker known on the street as "Ginger." A street-wise junkie, she had connections throughout the Twin Cities. Fergie was one of 18 junk dealers Ginger had introduced to Lisa. They all sold dope to the agent thinking she was cool. Lisa didn't know how much longer this could continue, but wanted to drag as many dealers as possible into the trap. Ginger accompanied Lisa the first time they went to Fergie's. After doing the deal, Fergie said, "You're cool Lisa. Come back for more when you need it."

She obtained the preliminary results of the lab analysis of the dope she got from Fergie on the buy and she was elated. It was real kick ass shit, much better quality than the junk she had been buying. Its purity indicated a dynamite connection. "The better the dope the closer you are to the source," was a rule of thumb with DEA agents. Lisa called the slob and set up another deal.

Her plan was for Kiel to provide close cover outside in his car while she went in to make the buy. Fergie, like the others, felt comfortable with Lisa but didn't like the idea of her bringing a man into the dope deal. Other backup agents would set up in the area to help if she got into a jam, but they had to keep their distance. Strangers hanging around a dealer's place of business spelled trouble with a capital T.

The two agents left the office, and with Lisa riding shotgun, Kiel turned onto Highway 77 and headed south. "You know we're partners, but you still haven't told me about Orlando. Maybe it's something I should know," he said.

Lisa shuddered. "Yeah, well I don't like talking about it. Orlando bothered me more than you can imagine."

"I'm listening," he persisted.

Lisa reluctantly began telling her story. "I had an undercover deal targeting two Cubans. I made a purchase from them a week earlier for ten grand. It all went down smooth. Looked like they were big time players. But for some reason I had a bad feeling." She grimaced, slightly shook her head, and paused for a minute. Finally she continued. "Nothing I could put my finger on, just that something seemed wrong. My boss said to raise the ante, so I started talking larger quantities. We settled on three keys for fifty grand. Arranged to do the deal at a truck stop south of Orlando. I met with them and they wanted to see the money before they showed me the dope. I had the buy money in the trunk of my car. Typical deal, you know how it goes," she said, thinking back.

"I raised the trunk lid, opened the duffel bag holding the money, and then heard one of the Cubans behind me say to his partner, 'Ahora.' That's Spanish for 'Now.' I knew by the tone of his voice it was a rip. I turned around, grabbed for my .38 inside my waist band, under my sweatshirt."

"You ever been in a gunfight?" she asked, thinking about her actions.

"No," Kiel answered simply.

"Well in a situation like that, your focus is incredible. Everything slows down."

"Yeah, I've heard that."

"It's amazing," Lisa said, staring out the window. "By the time I had my hand on my pistol, the Cuban had his nine millimeter pointed at my chest. He saw my piece and dropped the hammer on me. All my senses were moving at the speed of light. I see his finger squeeze the trigger and in the space of an instant a hundred things flash through my mind; all the while I'm still bringing my gun up. I hear the hammer of his pistol hit. My brain is racing. I think, 'He's got me.' But then that's all I hear. Just a 'click' and nothing else. It was so loud it echoed in my head. His gun misfired. We figured he had bad ammo. I can still see the look on his face when he knew he was screwed. I pointed my revolver at his chest and shot a couple rounds through his heart.

"Then I see his partner reaching for his gun. He must have thought the other guy had me, 'cause his gun was still in his belt. Lucky break for me. He pulled out his gun and . . . you know, I shot them each twice, all within the space of a second. They fell, blood spurting and splashing, and I stood there, a smoking gun in my hand, and watched them wriggle and flop. I'm thinking, 'My God, I've just killed two people.' But then I think, 'Hell, they almost killed me.' So then I'm in kind of a daze. Like the whole thing didn't really happen, it must be a dream. But it was more like a nightmare.

"For months the sight of those two guys collapsing on the pavement, their faces staring at me, kept creeping back into my mind. Just couldn't get them out of my head. Every place I went, there they were. And then I started doubting. Could this have been avoided? Never came up with an answer, other than not doing my job. Other thoughts haunted me. Maybe I'm not cut out for this stuff. But I love this job. Why should a couple dirt bags force me out?"

She shook her head, staring out the window into the distance for a few moments, then continued. "I needed out of Florida, so I asked for a transfer. Here I am. Talk about a change. And you know what? That experience in Florida seems to have fine-tuned my intuition."

Creases formed on her brow and she took a deep breath, exhaled, and looked over at her partner, wondering how he would deal with her story.

"You got it out of your system? I mean, you've been here for a year." Kiel's voice was steeped with concern.

She nodded her head. "For the most part. I'm dealing with it. If a similar situation came up again . . . yeah, I'd shoot the bastards."

Kiel drove across the bridge over the Minnesota River to Eagan. Finding the exit to Rahn road, he drove past Fergie's dilapidated rat trap to see if he had company.

Everything looked good. He backtracked and parked. Lisa casually walked up to the house like she was visiting a friend, and knocked on the door.

"Lisa, come on in," Fergie said. As he smiled, his fat face grew.

In his twenties, he was big. Big fat, not big muscle. His tattered jeans, and dirty T-shirt with yellow sweat stains under his arm pits, were tell-tale evidence why people called him Fergie the Slob. His pungent body odor slapped at her as soon as he opened the door.

She stepped into a small, dingy living room, with the kitchen in the rear and two bedrooms off to the right. The blinds were shut, and in the poor light she could hardly see him until her eyes adjusted. Light from a cheap portable TV caught her eye. It sat on a metal folding chair in the corner. Jammed into the top of the television was a twisted coat hanger serving as its antenna. The only other pieces of furniture in the room were a ratty looking sofa sitting against a wall, with a small coffee table that overflowed with trash and fast food wrappers.

Lisa surveyed the room. *What a pit.* She gave him an engaging smile and said, "How's it going, Fergie?"

She wouldn't be too inquisitive during this meet, but intended to get as close to the line as possible without stepping out of bounds. When making a buy, undercover agents always tried to leave with something besides the dope. Even if only a clue. Get enough tidbits and you might have a solid lead to the next rung on the ladder.

"Hey, everything's cool here," Fergie answered. "You said you wanted an ounce?"

"Yeah, a full Oh Zee," Lisa said. "My customers really liked the last shit I got from you. Is this the same stuff?"

A fair question. Lisa had a legitimate right to know about the junk he would sell her. She wanted Fergie to say more than he should.

Fergie studied her closely. Lisa expected it. No doubt he would size her up, searching for a sign, deception in her face, an overly inquisitive nature, anything that might indicate a threat. She impassively accepted his stare like it was a whole lot of nothing. Her training and experience called for attitude and ice cubes, without being overbearing. Lisa wasn't an actress. Never wanted to be. But in Hollywood, her undercover performances would have been Oscar material.

"Yeah, same stuff," Fergie finally said, evidently now at ease. "My source is steady, always has it when I need it, and his junk is righteous. You got the bread?"

"Yeah, right here." Lisa pulled a roll of hundreds out of a pocket, showed it to him, then put it back.

After seeing the wad, Fergie said, "Okay. Come into the back room and I'll show you what I got."

Lisa cautiously followed him into one of the bedrooms. The small room stunk even worse than the living room. The dingy hardwood floor and dresser were cluttered with garbage, moldy food, and piles of smelly clothes. She thought she might vomit.

Fergie turned around and faced her. "You know, I always sold the shit to Ginger at a discount. Did she tell you why?"

Lisa suddenly became uneasy. "Uh, no. She never mentioned anything about a discount."

"Well, I sold it to her at a discount because I always got some pussy from her. And I want the same from you." Saying that, Fergie reached with both hands and grabbed her breasts, giving each a rough pinch.

Fergie, three or four inches taller than Lisa, weighed a hundred pounds more than she. But she had speed and considerable athletic ability. Her ice cube demeanor melted, immediately replaced by steam.

"Get your slimy hands off me, you motherfucking slob," she said, slapping both his arms down.

Fergie saw red. She wanted rough, *he* could play that game. He threw a vicious punch towards her face. Lisa was ready. Blocking his swing with her left arm, she drove her knee straight into his balls. The blow was solid. A loud moan spilled from his mouth as he staggered backwards, and doubled over. Moving quickly, she grabbed his hair and slammed her knee hard into his face.

Crunch!

Lisa knew she broke his nose. *Good!* Then she saw his blood gush onto the faded pants legs of her brand new levis. *Not good.* Now she was even more pissed off. He'd pay for that too, damn it.

Fergie straightened up.

He was a mess. He was livid. He was getting his ass kicked by some bitch half his size.

Bright red fluid flowed from his nose, down his shirt and onto the floor. This really sucked. Time to turn things around.

Not if Lisa could help it. She whacked his left shoulder with her right hand. The blow shoved him off balance as his weight shifted onto his right leg. Driving her foot to the inside of his right knee, Lisa stepped back and watched as Fergie's leg crumpled and he crashed to the floor in a heap.

She saw more of his blood had now splattered onto her gray sweatshirt. Her adrenaline flowed. Eyes flared. Nostrils twitched. She struggled to contain herself. The slob had violated her. Pinched her nipples. He tried to rape her. She felt contaminated, not only from being groped, but also by his blood. Fergie, a junkie, lived by the needle. Who knew what festered inside his veins?

"Don't make me kill you, you stinking sack of pus!"

Their eyes met for an instant, hers as wild as his. In his she saw dismay and fear. In hers he saw frenzy and determination.

Fergie lay on the floor and continued to moan, not knowing what hurt the most. He had wanted to fuck this good-looking bitch. Not anymore.

She decided he no longer posed a threat. Peering around the room, she spotted a small box sitting on the cluttered chest of drawers. Inside the box she discovered two zip-lock baggies, each containing brown powder, alongside a thick stack of hundred dollar bills. She briefly examined the money, maybe around twenty grand she thought. She took the box and its contents. It would leave with her. Fuck him.

Lisa walked over to Fergie. "Listen pusface, you put your hands on me and that's going to cost you, big time. Nobody puts their hands on me if I don't let them. You cause any problems over this and you'll be seeing me again. This is nothing compared to what I'll do to you next time."

Fergie looked up at Lisa as she latched onto the box containing his money and junk. Although in serious pain, he still held some fight. The fucking cunt was bent on ripping him off. He had to do something. If he could get her down on the floor, he'd have her. The bitch would die right here.

He reached for a leg. Lisa jumped back and he missed. She stomped on his damaged knee. His face turned white. Howls of agony pierced the air. Pulling her pistol out, she shoved it in front of his face and pulled back the hammer.

"You just don't fuckin' learn do ya, you fat ass piece of shit," she yelled. "How would you like some of this?"

Fergie looked up at the gun barrel and surrendered. "Just go," he whined. "Get the fuck out of here!"

In the worst way, she wanted to drop the hammer. Send the pecker head straight to hell where he could swap stories with those two dopers from Florida. For a moment she feared she just might. She held the pistol in his face for a very long five seconds, then decocked the weapon and walked out.

Kiel saw her scramble out, and checked his watch. He needed the time for his report. Then he noticed the blood on her clothes. Something wasn't right. He instinctively felt for the piece in his shoulder holster, not knowing who else might come through that door. When Lisa approached the car, Kiel could see she was as mad as an evicted swarm of hornets.

"Damn, what the hell happened?"

"Just take me to the surveillance van. Fuck this guy," she said tersely.

"You got it."

He drove a couple blocks away to the van. Lisa got out of the car.

"Come with me," she said.

Jake opened the van's sliding door, a curious look on his face. Lisa promptly handed him her pistol, the box full of dope and money, and the buy money out of her pocket. Then she stripped off her bloody clothes, tossed them onto the street, and jumped into the van wearing nothing but a bra and panties. With an embarrassed expression, Kiel followed her shapely bottom through the van's door.

"Look," Lisa said in an angry, staccato voice. "The filthy motherfucker tried to rape me. I beat the shit out of him, but the jerk bled all over my clothes. He paid the price for grabbing me. Probably won't ever walk right again. Looks like a couple ounces of heroin in that box with the stash of money. Might be twenty grand in there. You can see I'm not carrying anymore." She thought for a moment then said, "I gotta have some clean clothes. There's a mall a couple miles down the highway. Let's go there and one of you can buy me some."

The agents all looked at Lisa as she sat nearly naked on the bench seat, and tried to absorb what she had just told them. She caught Travis ogling her and their eyes met. It wasn't hard for her to read his thoughts. He wanted to maintain his professionalism, knowing this was a very difficult moment for her, but at the same time he undoubtedly found it highly intriguing that beneath her baggy sweatshirt and washed out blue jeans she wore sexy, Victoria's Secret lingerie.

Jake quickly took charge. Taking off his shirt, he told Kiel to do likewise. Handing them to Lisa, he said, "Here put one of these on and the other over your lap."

She slipped on his shirt. It was a pull-over short sleeve that ended just below her crotch. Grabbing Kiel's shirt, she placed it over her legs. She now felt at least a little more at ease.

Jake noticed Travis scoping out Lisa's tender skin, and didn't bother to hide his irritation. "Travis, get to that mall. You can go in and buy what she needs." As an afterthought he added, "And keep your eyes on the road." Then he told Kiel, "Follow us. As soon as Lisa gets dressed, you can have your shirt back."

"Okay," Kiel answered. He opened the van's side door, then closed it behind him. Getting back into his own car he examined the passenger seat, wanting to reassure himself that none of Fergie's blood lurked inside his car. He couldn't see any, but when he got back to the office he'd spray it with disinfectant. Just in case.

Travis put the van in gear and headed to the store while Lisa called out her sizes.

As Jake repeated the sizes to make sure Travis had them right, Lisa took a deep breath, closed her eyes, and wished for the day to be over. The thought of Fergie touching her made her shudder. But there was more. Something else figured into her serious stress. Thankfully, nobody else would know how close she came to dropping the hammer on that guy. The two Florida ghosts still made an occasional appearance, and she sensed their presence now. She sure as hell didn't need a third. Another thought struck her. To kill someone in self-defense was defensible. To shoot somebody while in a fit of rage? Probably not. Blowing him away while he laid on the floor moaning would amount to murder, no doubt about that. Talk about a sick twist of fate. Fergie's ghost sending *her* to prison.

Jake noticed Lisa closing her eyes as she sat on the bench seat in the rear of the van. Real damned uptight, he thought. But then, who wouldn't be? He had to admire her. Practically nude as she stepped into the van with three men, she did a good job of keeping her composure. Many women would have been humiliated or felt dirty. Lisa simply accepted it as part of the job. No signs of embarrassment. Her clash with the dope dealer made it quite obvious: Lisa could take care of herself. Jake agreed with her decision to shed those bloody clothes. Who would sit on a seat stained with Fergie's fluids?

And he wouldn't summarily fault her judgment about who may or may not occupy the rungs on Fergie's ladder. Lisa felt Eddie had some involvement in this drug ring. If true, the agents were close to making real progress. In previous cases she had demonstrated what Jake dubbed 'intuitive conjecture,' that was simply uncanny. While outraged at what had happened, he had to consider its ramifications on the case and what they should do. So what now? Go arrest the bastard? Not yet. If they did, both Lisa and Ginger would be burned. It would be the end of her undercover heroin operation, and the other dealers in the net would have to be taken down immediately or the agents would play hell finding all of them. On the plus side, Lisa did make one buy off the slob, and then confiscated another two ounces. That made for a pretty solid case, with Fergie now staring at some heavy time. Might be enough to scare him into doing the right thing.

After weighing the options, Jake decided to simply get Lisa some new clothes and head back to the office. Nothing more to be gained out here today.

Lisa opened her eyes. "Jake, you know when we arrest him he'll claim I stole his money."

Jake knew that. Drug dealers constantly made allegations against the agents who busted them. Sometimes it was their only defense. "You've got no problems. It was dope money, we've got custody, and Fergie has no rights to it."

She nodded and stared out the window, trying to contain her anger.

CHAPTER 16

Back in the office, Lisa locked up the evidence and the confiscated money. Then she briefly met with Harold and described, in graphic detail, her UC encounter with Fergie. Her edgy state made Harold feel uncomfortable too. Like Jake, he felt sympathetic towards her and infuriated with Fergie. But he refused to allow emotions to dictate the direction of the investigation.

"I know the afternoon is still young," Harold told her. "But I want you to call it a day. Go home. Get cleaned up. Unwind. In the morning we'll all think this over with fresh minds."

Lisa didn't have to be told twice. Harold always seemed to make sense, and she liked what he said. The day had dumped a load of shit on her. Time to unwind and work it out of her system. She knew the best way to start. In less than an hour she walked through her front door.

Feeling a sense of urgency, she hustled to her bedroom, put on her running clothes and went outside. Her spacious house, located south of the cities a few miles outside of Burnsville, brushed up against a little used country road. Lisa loved running along the scenic hilly countryside, an area in which she saw only an occasional car or truck. Quite often on these runs she would spot a deer or two, maybe even some rabbits and wild turkeys. The fresh air and peaceful solitude always gave her soul a boost. She needed it now. After stretching she began her run starting with a moderate pace, then faster, harder, and finally sprinting as she relived those moments, trying to purge them from her brain. Her heart churned, her breathing became loud and forceful. She kept the pace for several minutes, then slowed to her normal jogging speed. Her stride was long. Fluid. Graceful. It felt good. But her thoughts were heavy.

Fergie had stolen an intimate feel of her body. His

greasy hands actually came in contact with her breasts, and they were sore. It was only for a second, but the assault shook her right down to the marrow in her bones, and the degradation shattered her sense of wellbeing. In return, she almost splattered his brains. Lisa felt grateful for the thick sweatshirt she had worn during the deal. It provided her with some insulation when the slob pinched her. The speed with which he had grabbed her breasts amazed her. His hands were quick. Lightening quick. He must've been rehearsing that move since he first met her. Maybe that's why he so eagerly cut the informant out of future deals.

Her mind moved forward. Although she had nothing concrete to go on, the generalities of the investigation, along with the high purity of the junk she purchased, made her suspect Eddie had his hooks planted somewhere along Fergie's chain. But throwing Eddie's name into the mix wasn't much more than a premonition, with one part wishful thinking and one part gut feeling. When she confided in Jake, he didn't challenge her. She knew that he had come to respect her intuition.

Even so, she never should've brought it up during that office meeting. She wished she could buy those words back. Stuff 'em into a sock and eat 'em. If only she had kept her big mouth shut. Ravich didn't have to hear her premonition about Eddie and Fergie. But he sure picked up on it, and would no doubt use it, when the time was right, as leverage to undermine her position as an agent. Now the cards were stacked against her. If it turned out she was wrong, Ravich would jump on her case royally, and her evaluations would really suffer. *"Jumps the gun,"* he would say. *"Exercises poor judgement."* And if she was right, Ravich would hammer on her because the undercover meet didn't work. She could imagine what *that* evaluation would state. *"Lacks the requisite skills for this job."*

Lisa knew what spurred her to bring up Eddie's name. The atmosphere in the war room had been suck-city. She had hoped to inject an optimistic note into the negative tone. Just get the guy to ease off. Obviously her judgment fell short in *that* respect. Where was her ESP when she needed it?

She now sat on the hot seat alongside Jake, and it looked like the two of them might slide down a banister littered with slivers. If things didn't work out and Ravich had his way, her future in Minneapolis, and possibly the DEA, looked as murky as the waters of the Mississippi. The boss clearly didn't like women agents.

Travis called him the "Hate Man." Lisa wasn't sure if it was because Ravich seemed to hate everybody, or if everybody hated him. Well, not everybody. His mother might love him. But in the office, except for Scott, there was nothing but animosity towards Ravich.

The only bright spot would be if Fergie cooperated, they made their case on Eddie's organization, and the entire investigation ended as an overwhelming success.

Yeah, right! And all the agents in the office lived happily ever after!

A few yards ahead, a rabbit appeared along the side of the road. Lisa saw its nose twitching. The rabbit saw her coming and scampered down the ditch, disappearing into the tall grass. Lisa smiled. "Hey, Bugs," she called out, running past the spot. "How's your day been? Better than mine, I hope."

Her thoughts returned to the investigation. A major problem with Fergie's attack and her reaction to it dealt with the central case. What happened in Fergie's house could fuck up everything. So, what next? The best case scenario would have been to keep the buys going. Lisa knew she had a genuine knack for wheedling information out of people. A few morsels elicited from Fergie, combined with more buys and solid surveillances, might've led them to Eddie. But there wouldn't be any more undercover meets with Fergie.

She thought it possible Jake might flip the guy and convert eau de skunk into a fine French perfume. Jake had that ability. But *she* wouldn't be a part of any deals with that jerk. After what happened she wanted nothing but distance, and a prison wall, between her and him.

Lisa continued running, her mind spinning. She arrived at her halfway point, a farm's driveway exactly 3.1 miles from her starting point. A frequent runner in 10-K events, Lisa checked her watch. At this pace she'd finish the course in less than thirty-eight minutes. She smiled, pivoted and headed home. She hit the finish line, marked by a towering oak tree, did her usual cool down and entered her house.

After locking the door the agent headed straight to the bathroom. A warm, lingering soak in the tub would feel great. She pushed down the drain stopper, poured a scented bubble bath into the tub and opened the faucets. As the tub filled she walked over to the refrigerator, reached in and retrieved a bottle of wine: Colombia Valley Reisling. She looked at the label and smiled. Lisa preferred white wine, and she had grabbed her favorite.

Opening the bottle, she selected a wine goblet, slipped a James Taylor CD into her stereo, and headed back to the bathroom where the tub was now full and topped off by bubbles. Perfect. She poured her first glass of wine, set it on a ledge and stepped into the tub, sliding comfortably beneath the foam and using a thick towel to cushion her head.

The bath water felt sudsy. Slippery. Soothing.

Lifting the goblet to her lips, she began nursing the wine as her mind returned to the events of the day.

She remembered the shirts Jake and Kiel handed her in the van. A thoughtful thing for them to do, and not surprising that they did it. Either would readily give the shirt off his back to any agent in need. She had a lot of respect for Kiel. A sensitive, loyal, hard-working guy, he probably felt deeply embarrassed following her into the van. Lisa's thong panties and low slung bra left very little for the imagination. Occasionally he'd go off the handle. Maybe lose it for a minute or so. Hell, join the club! Lisa was certainly no stranger to that department. Like in Fergie's house. Sometimes, going ballistic was the appropriate thing to do.

She felt the same sense of respect for Jake. He held a lot to like. With the job, a professional, no bullshit kind of guy. With his family, a different person. His devotion to his wife and kids was painted all over him. While pulling long surveillances together, Lisa and Jake had shared more than a few laughs as she listened to him talk about his kids' antics, or something his wife had said that struck him as particularly funny. She envied his having a warm family to go home to after work, while she went home to an empty house.

Reaching for the bottle, she refilled her glass. "Damn, you're gonna get drunk if you don't watch it, Lisa." She thought about it a moment. "What the hell." Taking another sip, she focused her thoughts on Travis.

At least her nights weren't spent in a van. What an enigma, that guy! She had worked next to him for a year, but still didn't have a real feel for him. He could be irritating, irreverent, and yet likable all at the same time. After a couple of their verbal duels, she knew she had met her equal. When Travis saw her step into the van, he probably had a hard-on as stiff as the gear shift lever. Lisa figured he could be quite the stud, but he never pranced like God's great gift to women. Thankfully, he wasn't a self-centered loud mouth like a couple of guys she had dated in the past.

Lisa had become exceedingly particular about her male company. She hadn't had a real relationship since she came to Minneapolis, and had dated only three men during the past year. All of 'em disappointing fizzles. The FBI agent seemed to have only two loves in this world: himself and his badge. She only dated him once, and couldn't wait for the evening to end. Then came the Minneapolis cop who seemed to think playing the macho role would pave the way into her pants. What a total bore! Another one-time date, and for a while she thought she might have to kick his ass before the night ended. The last one? Lisa recalled the computer guy she met in church. She actually dated him twice, thinking he must have a personality hiding in there somewhere. But on the second go around she verified she was wrong. He was just vacant, and didn't have much to say about anything.

Her thoughts returned to Travis. She knew he had a thing for her. And she had to admit she liked what she saw. But she knew about his women, and just couldn't lose the suspicion that a relationship with him would be rocky and painful. She didn't need that. Over the past two years her life had seen enough pain. Still . . .

Lisa emptied her goblet and reached for the bottle.

Several days later Ginger called the DEA office. Lisa took the call.

"Hi, Lisa. This is Ginger. I got a phone call from Fergie. He told me not to bring you around anymore."

"Well, no shit," Lisa said, amazed at Fergie's apparent stupidity.

"Yeah, I don't think he likes you. What the hell happened, anyways?"

Lisa glared into the phone. "There's no need to get into it. Just stay away from him, okay?"

"Yeah, sure. I never did like the creep. But I got another one for you. Her name's Leslie. I haven't dealt with her for a while. I forgot all about her until today when I went through my black book and saw her name. Gave her a call. She's still dealing junk and said to stop by. Told her I'd bring a friend and she's got no problem with that. You want to do it?"

All the dealers Lisa and Ginger had sucked into their trap flashed through Lisa's mind. She now added 'Leslie' to her mental list as a smile crept onto her face. "How much can she do?"

"We could start with a half Oh Zee," Ginger answered eagerly.

"Okay, tell me what you know about her."

Ginger told Lisa everything she could remember, and they made arrangements to buy a half-ounce the following day.

The next morning Lisa, Kiel and Ginger, tailed by several surveillance agents, drove to Robbinsdale, a northern suburb of Minneapolis, to meet with Leslie. Kiel drove to her house on France Avenue as Ginger gave directions. They made the usual pass, then parked in the driveway.

"This shouldn't take too long," Ginger said. "Leslie's waiting and she's got everything set to go."

"Be careful," Kiel said, as the two women got out of the car.

Lisa and Ginger were in the house only ten minutes when another car drove up and parked directly in front of Leslie's house. Kiel watched as a man got out of the car and walked towards the house. He immediately recognized him. Kiel's hand instinctively reached to his head, remembering the hurt when his head got slammed into a bathroom sink by this man.

It's that fucking David O'Neal, Kiel thought. Without a doubt O'Neal remembered Lisa and Kiel. If he got inside the house, who knew what would happen. This maggot was violent. Something had to be done. Now!

Kiel stepped out of his car just as O'Neal walked past. "I've been waiting for you, O'Neal. Let's see what's in your pockets."

Recognizing Kiel, O'Neal saw red. A malignant smile surfaced as he looked around and saw the narc, all by his lonesome.

The drug dealer rushed Kiel. "Let's see how tough you are when you're by yourself, fuckface!"

O'Neal threw a punch, which Kiel blocked with his left arm. They punched, kicked and scrapped for all they were worth, until O'Neal, bigger and a little stronger, gained the advantage and managed to slam Kiel onto the ground with a loud thump.

He had his undercover weapon today, a revolver concealed beneath his belt, in the event Leslie would agree to meet both him and Lisa. The pistol flew across the grass.

O'Neal lunged towards the gun. Kiel lashed out with both legs. O'Neal tripped, falling on his face. His outstretched arms reached for the pistol, two feet away. Kiel scrambled, wrapping him up as they rolled over and over.

Inside the house, something drew Lisa to a window. Looking out she saw the scuffle and recognized O'Neal as he threw a punch. She quickly forgot about the dope deal and darted out the door. She saw the pistol on the ground, a few feet away from the men. The drug dealer looked up and saw Lisa. If he could get his grips on that pistol, he'd punch her number too.

Lisa raced towards the two men. The drug dealer scored one more blow and was up on one knee when Lisa arrived. She smashed her foot into his chest, broke a few ribs and sent him sprawling. Glancing at Kiel, she saw blood pouring from his nose.

"You piece of shit," she screamed, and raced towards O'Neal, now on his hands and knees, trying to stand up. Lisa danced up to him and landed another solid kick into his stomach, sending him hard onto the ground once more. Moaning in pain, he looked up at her with a feeling of déjà vu.

While Lisa was breaking O'Neal's ribs, Ken Washington, maintaining a roving surveillance, drove past. Seeing the fight, he grabbed his radio mike and came to a screeching stop. "One UC is down. They need help," he yelled.

Ken grabbed his gun, bolted out of the car and rushed to Kiel, who was shaken and struggling to get up. Jake and Travis arrived moments later. Ginger, in a state of shock, stood in front of the house with her hand over her mouth. Leslie had just stepped out of the house and watched the spectacle, wondering what was happening.

Jake quickly surveyed the scene, and recognizing O'Neal, surmised the damage done to this investigation and possibly to many others. They all involved Ginger. This could burn her. If it did, the dealers would know they had been sucked into a trap and sold dope to the Man. The Man, in this case, being a woman.

Jake's eyes met Ken's. "Take Kiel and O'Neal to the hospital to get treatment. Stay with O'Neal. I want him in jail for assaulting a federal agent. Tell Kiel to call me as soon as he's patched up, then I'll talk to the prosecutor."

Being careful not to let O'Neal hear, Jake turned to Travis. "Take Ginger to the office. Stay with her 'til we get on top of this. Next, Jake motioned to Lisa to follow him. It was time for damage control. They approached Leslie, hoping to salvage the undercover operation.

"Leslie," Jake said in a low voice, "We're DEA agents. Let's talk."

Leslie turned pale and started shaking. Inside, they sat down in the living room.

Jake began. "Leslie, here is the deal. You just sold heroin to an agent and now you're fucked. Federal judges hammer heroin dealers. You're staring at fifteen years. I'm sure you don't want to do a hard fifteen. You don't want to go to the slam at all. You need someone on your side. If you work with us, we can help you. Play ball and we'll go to bat for you with the prosecutor and the judge. Maybe little or no jail time. But I gotta know now. Otherwise you take your chances."

Fighting off tears, Leslie peered at Jake and then Lisa. She sat in silence for several minutes, her brain numbed by Jake's devastating words. Her worst nightmare had just come true.

"Okay," she finally whimpered. "I can't go to jail. What do you want?"

Jake's words softened. "To begin, tell us everything you know about the heroin dealers in this area. Then we'll figure out if you can help us nail some of them. The more you give, the more we'll be able to help you. Your attitude is very important. Be straight with us, we'll be straight with you. If you lie to us, you're in serious trouble. You'll only get one chance. Make the most of it."

"Okay," Leslie began. "O'Neal used to be my connection. When you guys hit his house a couple months ago you really fucked him over. He flushed a bag of junk down the toilet when you busted in, and lost that key of snow you took from him. Angela Lurtz is on his case to pay her for taking that coke through the mail. And the shit he flushed was given to him on a front. Owes a big chunk for it and can't pay because he's got no dope to sell. His connection won't deal with him because of the heat. I think they're really careful. David's really pissed. Used to sell me dope, now he's trying to score from me. He was coming over to pick up a couple grams to get back on his feet. Can't even pay for a couple g's. How bad is that?"

"What do you know about his people?" Jake studied her closely.

"Well, before you guys raided his place his connection was getting his junk from Frenchy Deveroux, that guy in Elk River. I don't know much about the connection, but one time David was bragging. Said he was into this huge heroin organization. He told me the people supplying Deveroux had a lock on the smack market in Minnesota. The big man is a guy named Eddie. He never told me Eddie's last name, but said he lived in the Twin Cities. I think Eddie's bringing the junk up from South America. After Deveroux got killed, David's connection got elevated. He's in tight with Eddie. If things go good, he'll be operating at Deveroux's level real soon. David was set to follow his man onto the fast track when you guys struck."

Jake's ears tweaked. Eddie, he thought. That son of a bitch's name pops up like weeds in Grandpa's garden. But Jake didn't have the impression he was closing in.

"So who is your source now," Lisa asked quietly.

"Got no regular source since David got cut off. Know a lot of people around the cities. When I'm dry I just make the rounds 'til I find someone who's holding. Got an ounce a couple days ago from a guy down by the West Bank, near the University. Sold some of it yesterday, then the half I sold you. Just had two grams left. David was going to get those."

"You have two more grams?" Lisa asked, raising her eyebrows.

Leslie frowned. "Yeah. In that cabinet."

"You'd better give it to us."

Leslie reluctantly went to the cabinet and handed Lisa the dope.

Lisa said, "So, what you're saying is your main connection is out of the picture, and there's nobody else you could turn us on to?"

"Yeah, that's the way it is. You still gonna help me out?"

"We'll help you out," Jake said. "But only if you work with us. You can't tell anybody about Lisa or Ginger. Is that a deal?"

"You got my word. No way am I going to talk about this to nobody," Leslie said earnestly.

"Okay," Jake said. "That's a start. Can you tell us if O'Neal knows anything about Ginger?"

"As far as I know, no. I haven't seen her myself for six months or so. I was surprised to hear from her."

"Leslie, we won't take you downtown if you agree to stay in contact with us, and out of touch with everyone else. O'Neal will confront you about Lisa. Play dumb. Tell him you met Lisa, but didn't sell to her because something didn't seem right. And you're out of the dope business. You won't be selling anymore to O'Neal or anybody else. You got that?" Jake's voice reflected his deadly serious attitude.

Jake and Lisa headed back to the office. Lisa was too hyped to concentrate on traffic, so Jake drove. As he turned onto the freeway, she looked at him with wide eyes and said, "My God, can you believe I had to beat the crap out of two guys within a week. I'm probably seeing more hand-to-hand action than the average Marine."

Jake and Lisa arrived at the office just as Kiel called from the hospital. Jake talked to Kiel about the brawl outside of Leslie's house, and after he had a firm understanding of the situation he asked Kiel about O'Neal.

"He's still in ER. One of the doctors said he's got broken ribs. That dirtbag is hurting," Kiel said with a laugh.

"Okay," Jake said. "I'll talk to somebody in the US Attorney's office about charging him with assault. You and Ken stay put until I get back with you. Don't let O'Neal out of your sight."

Jake conferred with the prosecutor and then called Kiel. "They won't charge O'Neal. Said this appears to be a feud between the two of you. The prosecutor warned us not to bother O'Neal again unless we have something significant. I think we've just been slapped in the face. But it's not like O'Neal got off easy. Talking to Leslie, he's as broke as his ribs. My guess is he'll resurface. We're not through with David O'Neal."

CHAPTER 17

Jake sat at his desk, dictating, when a secretary transferred a call to his phone.

"Hi Jake. This is Terry Monnisett. I'm the Sheriff of Becker County in Detroit Lakes. How's everything going in the Twin Cities?"

"Oh, we've got plenty to keep us busy, Terry. More than enough bad guys around. How are you doing up there in the lake country? Are the fish biting?"

"Not yet. But two weeks ago we caught a couple burglars ripping off lake homes. We had to coax one of them out of the lake. He tried to rabbit on us, and actually ran out into the water. Not long ago that lake was under two inches of ice. What a moron. Almost died of hypothermia. They're sitting in my jail. Both of 'em are junkies, and until I got a hold of 'em they had sizable habits. They finally got their systems cleaned out, and this morning they decided to cooperate. It looks like they got information that might interest you. I'm wondering if you could make your way up here and talk to them. It's about heroin, and lately we seem to have one hell of a problem with that shit."

It was another possible lead into the heroin plague, this time involving the northern part of the state. Jake welcomed the opportunity. His leads were fizzling like the Vikings in post season.

"Terry, I'll be there noon tomorrow."

"Look forward to meetin' you Jake. Whatever I can do to help, let me know."

Hanging up the phone, Jake back-pedaled his chair over to Travis' desk and told him the news. Detroit Lakes was a four hour drive northwest of the cities. A heavy foot could knock a chunk off that. They were debating what time to leave when Jake's phone rang a second time. He returned to his desk and took the call. It was his wife, and she was hysterical.

Two minutes later, Jake hung up the phone and returned to Travis' desk. Travis looked up and saw a different person. Jake's face had turned ghost white.

"That was Melissa. There's been a bad accident. It's my daughter, Melanie. An ambulance just rushed her to Metro Memorial. I've got to go there."

Travis' voice turned heavy with concern. "What happened?"

"A horse threw her. She's unconscious. Look, go to Detroit Lakes. Interview those two meatheads and find out what they've got. I'm really interested to see if Eddie's name comes up, or if they've got anything that leads to the Cities. When you get back, meet with me and we'll decide where to take it. I'll probably be at the hospital. And tell Harold for me, will you?"

"Yeah. Go take care of your family, Jake."

Jake hustled out of the office and sped to the hospital. He found his wife in the waiting room near the surgery suite. Melissa's eyes were red, her face drawn and heavy.

They hugged for several minutes and then Jake asked, "So what happened? How did Melanie get thrown by a horse? She's an experienced rider."

"I know," Melissa sobbed. "She went to the stables to ride her usual horse, but the horse had something wrong with its leg or hoof or something, so they gave her a different one. She was riding with two friends. They weren't far from the stables when her horse got skittish. Melanie couldn't control it. The horse started bucking. She went flying. Her head hit a rock. One of her friends rode back to the stable to get help. She's been unconscious since she fell. The doctors are doing surgery to relieve the pressure on her brain."

An hour later the surgeon came into the waiting area and met with them. The doctor explained Melanie's problems. He had inserted a shunt to relieve the pressure in her skull caused by excess fluid buildup.

Melanie was comatose, but stable, and was now in recovery. They could see her in a few minutes, the doctor said. Her prognosis is uncertain. She's on life support.

The words jolted Jake and Melissa like an earthquake.

Prognosis uncertain.

They hugged and broke into tears. After regaining their composure they went to Melanie's bedside. The nurses had just wheeled her into an intensive care room. Tubes led to her nose, more tubes led from her arm to an IV solution hanging on a rack, and wires connected her to a monitor and other devices. Her face had no color, and bandages covered much of her head. And she was asleep.

Looking at her, Jake and Melissa broke down again. Their daughter, who appeared to be at peace, was in big trouble.

That damn horse, Jake thought. Why the hell did the stable give her a skittish horse? They know their horses. That's their job. Just a couple of months ago she had asked for her own horse. Why didn't we do it? This wouldn't have happened. Jake now realized he hadn't even discussed it with her, and thought he might never forgive himself.

Melissa reached down and gently picked up Melanie's hand. It was limp. She bent over and kissed Melanie on the cheek.

Jake saw a tear drop fall onto Melanie's face and handed Melissa his handkerchief. He looked down at his daughter. His mind seeped with guilt.

I should have asked her about the horses in the stable. Maybe she would have told me they weren't steady. What an investigator! I should've looked into it, made sure that place had their act together. I didn't take the time to talk when she needed me. I let her down.

Melissa returned his handkerchief.

Jake choked up, tears welled in his eyes.

I was hung up at the office. Lost sight of my home. What are my priorities? The job competes with the time I have with my family. They depend on me, but I can't just chuck my career. The work is too damn important and the job is a huge part of my life. But Christ, this is my family.

Clearing his throat, he asked, "Where are the kids?"

"They're at home. The neighbors said they would step over and make sure they're doing okay. The kids will have supper with them."

The rest of the day and much of the night dragged on as they sat by their daughter's bed side. When Melissa went home to tend to the others, Jake stayed with Melanie, watching her closely and praying for an encouraging sign. The next day Melissa rejoined him early in the morning and they spent the entire day watching Melanie sleep. Nothing changed.

That evening Travis walked slowly into the room. He gave them a warm hug. Looking down at Melanie, he asked, "How's she doing?"

Melissa just shrugged as tears formed in her eyes.

Jake's face, covered with two days growth, looked drawn. "We don't know yet. The Doc says her prognosis is uncertain. Let's go down to the cafeteria. We can talk there." He kissed Melanie and told Melissa they'd be gone for an hour or so. "If anything changes, page me right away," he added as they walked away.

"Okay, Hon. Bye Travis. Thanks for stopping by."

The two agents walked to the cafeteria. It wasn't crowded, with only a couple tables occupied by stragglers eating snack foods. Jake found a large coffee urn and poured two cups of steaming coffee. He paid the cashier and they found a table in a secluded corner, away from the other folks.

Jake tested his coffee. It nearly burned his lips and he set the mug down. "You do any good in Detroit Lakes?"

Travis furrowed his brow. "Hard to say. The mopes I talked to are a few gallons short of a full tank. They're burglars, specialize in lake cabins. Sheriff's deputies caught 'em in the act. They've both been down before, so they're looking at some hard time. I could tell their hearts weren't into cooperating, but they told me a little. They share an apartment in Perham, a small town about a half hour or so from Detroit Lakes.

"Mope Number One did most of the talking. He told me he and his partner are both junkies with big habits. About a year ago at some party they met a guy named Mitch. They were in a hurt, and couldn't get a hold of their man. Mitch offered to sell them some junk and they've been buying off him since."

Jake nodded. "Mitch got a last name?"

"That's one thing that's causing me a problem. They said they don't know his last name, where he lives. Really don't know anything about him. I figure after a year they'd know something. They're probably blowing smoke up my ass as far as Mitch goes. Trying to protect their source so they've got someone to take care of 'em when they get out."

"Okay. I guess that's nothing new."

Travis nodded. "Yeah, probably not. So this Mitch guy would stop by their place every few days and they'd each buy a quarter ounce. They said after doing business for a few months, Mitch started bragging about how much he could handle. Said he got the shit in pound quantities. They agreed it was the best stuff around."

"So if Mitch has the best stuff in town, but they don't know anything about him, how does that help us?"

"Good question. That's what I asked. I was starting to get pissed, thinking I drove that distance just to listen to a lot of bullshit. So then Number One tells me, 'Look, I can't do anything about Mitch, but I think I can help you with his source.'

"So now I'm listening. He tells me a few months ago Mitch stopped by their place, stoned on his own shit, bragging again about the quantities he could handle. So the mopes ask him how much he's got available and he says he's out, but he could have a pound in a couple days. They give him a "Yeah, right" look, and so he asks them to let him use their phone, like he wants to prove his point. Mitch dials a number and they figured by the way he talked he was hooked up to an answering machine. All he said was, 'This is Mitch. I need another pound. Call me six at seven.' The mopes figured it had to be some kind of code. That made 'em curious, so when he left they wrote the time down, thinking they'd check the phone number when they got the bill. A week later the bill arrives and they figured out where he called. It's a Detroit Lakes phone, Jake. They were surprised. Both of 'em thought he got his stuff from Fargo. So Number One tells me, 'If you want Mr. Big, he lives in Detroit Lakes. And if you want to know where, check out the phone records, because Perham to Detroit Lakes is a long distance call."

Jake shook his head, skeptically. "What'd the Sheriff say?"

"Says he never heard of a junk dealer named Mitch. And he doesn't think the market around Detroit Lakes is big enough to support a wholesale dealer who sells in pound quantities. If there *were* someone, and he sold pounds to Mitch, he'd have other customers in that area. That would be a number of people buying pound lots for resale. Detroit Lakes has a population of about ten thousand, and it's the largest town in the county. Sheriff says they've got a heroin problem, but not that big."

Jake nodded, picked up his coffee cup and tested it again. It was cooler, and he took a careful swallow. "You know what, Travis? You may have wasted your time. Look, let's track down that call. Get a subpoena and go after those phone records. If we can show they're lying, we'll know not to waste more time on it."

"You got it. So, how's your daughter doing? What's this prognosis uncertain all about?"

"Melanie's really hurting. The doctor did surgery, put a shunt in, and now she's in a coma. You know, we have so much. But a person tends to lose sight of what he has until it looks like he might lose it. A person shouldn't take anything for granted. With this job, you and I know our number could come up any time; but we don't really think the same thing applies to our family. There's no guarantees for any of us. I didn't even see my daughter yesterday morning. Actually, I didn't see any of my kids, just my wife. They were all asleep. Now, Melanie is on life support. What if I never get the chance to talk to her again? It's really tearing at me. A lot of things are ripping at my stomach. I should have investigated the stables better. Maybe I could've prevented this. Now my family's in a crisis. And if that's not enough, I got Ravich on my ass. The way he's acting, I might be staring at transfer orders real soon. My family sure as hell doesn't need that."

Travis thought for a moment, then said, "You're a family man, Jake. I never was. Tried a couple of times, but could never make the commitment. When an agent is a family man, he's got to keep his two worlds separate. When an agent is alone, like me, he doesn't have to deal with any separation. Maybe that's why I'm alone. Didn't want to be shackled with that responsibility. Do I regret it? Sometimes. It would be nice to come home to a wife and loving kids. But for some reason the slow track was never for me. The price for my lifestyle is high. My life's a mess and the future doesn't look any brighter. Look at me. I'm living out of a van for Christ's sake. The office is my home."

He picked up his mug and tasted his coffee. It was okay, and he drank some.

Jake nodded, saying nothing, and waited for Travis to continue.

"I envy you, Jake. You have somebody to come home to. How about taking some advice? You can't blame yourself or the job for Melanie's accident. If you need a place to lay blame, put it on the horse. And don't let the job get you down. Your family depends on you. I wouldn't waste one second of my time frettin' about the Hate Man. What makes Ravich tick is a mystery, but it's obvious he's a miserable person. Don't keep him company."

"Yeah, you're right. So many things going on and now this happens."

"I'll deal with getting those phone records. You take some time off and deal with your daughter's health. Don't worry about this Detroit Lakes thing."

CHAPTER 18

A few days after the scrap with O'Neal, the swelling around Kiel's eye dissipated, but he boasted a visible shiner. But his black and blue face wasn't a big concern. His wife, Lucie, and their marriage weighed heavily on his mind. He had been stewing over their relationship ever since his conversation with Jake during the Black Jack Mike deal. Lucie was never happy.

"You take your damn job too seriously," she had told him on numerous occasions. "Your priorities are all screwed up. I don't know where I fit in your life any more. And what about your daughter? Lucinda hardly knows you."

Her attitude disappointed him. What he wanted was her support. Kiel entered the DEA shortly after they were married, and she started complaining about his hours and their life together a few months after he graduated from the academy. The demands of the job and his time away from home were something she just didn't want to accept. This surprised him. She had a degree, had been a teacher when they got married, and he had assumed she was tuned into the work ethic expected in his profession. Any challenging career demanded a sense of dedication and personal commitment. The DEA certainly fell into that mix. Kiel truly believed once he established himself there would be more time for his family. Until then, the sacrifices he made weren't just for him and the job. He wanted to secure their future. And damn it, didn't she realize they had bills to pay?

Lucie continued to sulk around the house, acting miserable whenever she had an audience. Then, a couple months ago she stopped complaining about his job and began grousing about their car. He welcomed the change. Admittedly, the car seemed to be in the shop every other week.

Sitting at his desk, Kiel came to a decision. He could deal with the car issue. *I'll surprise her with new wheels. Maybe that will make her life a bit more pleasant.*

He walked over to Lisa's desk. "How about a favor?"

"Sure, Kiel. What do you need?"

"I'm going to take the rest of the day off. Could you give me a ride to Bloomington and drop me off at a car dealership. We need a new car. I'm going to pick one out this afternoon and surprise my wife."

Lisa looked at Kiel's bruised face, and remembered how he got it. She certainly owed him one. "I'll put my stuff away and we're out of here," she said.

Minutes later they were heading south towards Bloomington. "So how is Leslie's attitude holding up?" Kiel asked. "She going to stay true to her word, or is she going to fuck us over?"

"So far she's holding steady," Lisa answered. "I'm just hoping she'll keep cool, at least for a couple weeks until after the roundup. Can you imagine the mess we'd be in if she started running off her mouth?"

"Yeah. Leslie doesn't know the trouble she could cause."

Lisa thought about it, then said, "O'Neal showing up was bad timing at its worst. But Jake handled it and Leslie got the message. She's looking after her own interests, and fortunately they fall in line with ours. Her priority is to stay out of prison, not fuck us over."

"So what's your feel on the defendants? You've probably got a handle on every one of 'em. After the bust goes down, how many will do the right thing?"

"You never know who's going to turn." Lisa mulled it over for a bit, then bit her lip. She really hated to say her next words. The memories of her encounter with Fergie still burned her guts. But DEA agents, as a matter of necessity, would work with practically anybody if that person could get them what they wanted. Although she would never personally work with him, Lisa was willing to do her bit and surrender some hard earned feelings for the good of a greater cause.

"I figure the Slob is our best bet. He could do some good things for us." Lisa pictured Fergie for a second and frowned. "I bet his knee will be fucked up for life. Serves him right. What an asshole." Her frown changed to a smile.

Arriving in Bloomington, Lisa dropped Kiel off at a car dealership. He went inside, browsed for a while, and selected a Bonneville sedan that was ready to go. An hour later he drove home in his new car.

Kiel had a newer house on a quiet street in Bloomington. As he approached his driveway, he saw Lucie tossing suitcases and other belongings into their car. *Now what the hell is this about?*

He parked behind her and stepped out of the car. Lucie barely looked at him, appearing surprised but not stopping. Anger adorned her face.

"Lucie, where are you going?"

"What the hell do you care?"

"Whoa! Are we having some kind of problem?" Kiel asked.

"Some kind of problem! Some kind of problem," she repeated. "Have you heard anything I've been saying for the past six years? Have I been talking to a brick? Of course we're having a problem. You're never home. You're always working. And when you're working, you don't call. I never know when to expect you, or if I should expect you at all. Lucinda knows the neighbors better than she knows you. When you do come home, you're so fucking exhausted you just sleep. And recently you've been coming home wrapped in bandages. What's wrong with you? Are you nuts or something? What kind of a life is this Kiel? Maybe you like this bullshit, but I don't. I'm fed up. I've had it! I want out!"

"You mean you're leaving, just like that? You weren't even going to talk to me about it?"

"You haven't been listening. I left you a note on the kitchen table. Read it, then help me finish packing the car."

Lucie was in her late twenties, and slim like her husband. She stood a couple inches taller than him, and he looked up as he listened to her. Lucinda, their blonde four-year-old, stood in the doorway, watching. She knew her parents were fighting, but didn't know why.

Stunned, Kiel looked at the house and seeing Lucinda said, "You're taking Lucinda with you?"

"Well, no shit! I suppose you thought I'd leave her here so she could feed herself and get off to pre-school by herself. Maybe go out and do the shopping for you. What the hell do you expect? You're never here."

Kiel took it hard. The words hurt a hell of a lot worse than O'Neal's best punch. He slowly walked into the house, picked up Lucinda and went over to the kitchen table to find the note.

Reading it added to the seriousness, the finality, of the moment. As the full meaning seeped in, Kiel felt his world caving in.

He had always taken Lucie, and their life together, for granted. Had assumed she would always be at home for him. Putting Lucinda down, Kiel stared into space, now experiencing the dismal emotions of defeat. He loved his job and put everything he had into it. He considered the work he did essential to the community and the country. It wasn't a mediocre career. Nor was it a career for the mediocre. It demanded a person's dedication and focus, time, energy and resolve. They both knew that. It should've been a family commitment. Lucie should've accepted the challenges. But she didn't. She was leaving. His wife was a quitter.

He stormed back to Lucie, who was struggling to put a heavy suitcase into the back seat, and yelled, "Okay, quitter! Leave! Just walk out on our lives! But I never let you down. You're the one who failed this marriage, not me. You should be supporting me. You never did. All you've done is gripe."

Lucie looked up at him and said simply, "Whatever." She put Lucinda into the car and strapped her seat belt. "I want a divorce Kiel," she said evenly. "I'll be getting an attorney. He'll be in touch with you. We'll be living with my mother until this all gets ironed out. Good-by." She looked over at the shiny new Bonneville parked behind her. "And move that car. It's in my way."

Kiel opened the door and kissed Lucinda goodbye. Muttering, he walked back to his car. He then noticed several of his neighbors had suddenly found they had urgent yard work in the front of their homes. Kiel flashed them the bird as he got into the Bonneville.

About a five hour drive from Bloomington and a few miles northwest of Fargo, North Dakota, another conflict had been brewing. For years Jim Olson's neighbors called him a cantankerous old coot. After his wife passed away, Jim became a loner. He retired from farming at sixty-two and rented out his acreage rather than selling it off piecemeal, while continuing to live in his childhood farm house.

Retirement didn't suit Jim. He developed an unfriendly, even hostile, attitude. Most of his neighbors ignored him. But ignoring him was tough for the neighbor living only three quarters of a mile due west. In this heavily Scandinavian area, the name 'Olson' was quite common. That neighbor had the same name.

Neighbors and other farmers in the area distinguished the two by referring to them as Hermit Jim and Farmer Jim. With six mouths to feed, Farmer Jim could only dream of retiring some day. It really irritated him that every week he experienced a mix up with his mail. Managing a farm required considerable focus, and Farmer Jim didn't like time consuming distractions. Talking with the mail carrier didn't help.

"Maybe you should change your name," the carrier suggested.

Hermit Jim contributed to the problem. Whenever he received Farmer Jim's mail, he simply threw it in the trash. Farmer Jim suspected such, and several times confronted the crusty old hermit. But with no proof the confrontations were fruitless. If anything, Hermit Jim became more hostile.

The mail delivery gaffe hit once again after one of Farmer Jim's children died of pneumonia. Reading of the death, Lonnie and Donnie immediately started on their homework. The groundwork included locating the farm. Looking at the plat maps, they discovered two Jim Olsons on the same road. They decided to target the family that received the sympathy cards.

The twins were parked in their van, a mile east of Hermit Jim's farm, when the rural mail carrier drove past. Donnie watched the mail carrier through binoculars. The carrier delivered Hermit Jim's mail and moved on. Quickly, Lonnie and Donnie went to the box. Donnie pulled up close, and Lonnie reached in and grabbed a handful of envelopes. Then they drove off to examine the evidence.

Lonnie could feel his adrenaline surge when he ripped open an envelope that appeared to contain a card. "Yeah, this is it," he said eagerly. "It says, 'With deepest sympathy for your loss.' We'll hit it in the morning."

The funeral would begin at ten o'clock in Fargo. Shortly before ten, the twins entered Jim Olson's yard. Hermit Jim had just dragged his bony frame out of bed when they drove up. Looking out his upstairs bedroom window, he spotted the van. *Now, who the hell is this? Hmm. A couple trashy-looking punks. What the hell kind a business they got with me?*

Hermit Jim kept a twelve gauge shotgun handy, and he hustled to the closet to grab it. He found some shotgun shells on a shelf and began loading the gun.

While the old man fumbled with the shotgun shells, the twins knocked on his front door. The hermit ignored the knocks. Just as Jim had shoved in the last shotgun shell, his front door came crashing down.

The spry old man moved quickly out of the bedroom to where he could see the front door. He saw the twins just as they saw him, and they all reacted simultaneously. The hermit had just raised his shotgun when Lonnie fired two quick rounds. Hermit Jim ducked around a corner, shooting as he moved.

Lonnie fired two more rounds towards the old man, and then said to Donnie, "Let's get the fuck out of here. This can't be the right place."

Hermit Jim took a quick peek and fired again, hitting nothing but wall.

Lonnie returned three more shots, and as the old man ducked back around the corner, Lonnie and his brother bolted out the door and into their van.

Hermit Jim ran back into his bedroom and watched the two punks scramble. "Son of a bitch," he muttered, and dropped the shotgun. "Them bastards ain't going to get off that easy."

He reached for his Winchester 30-06 deer rifle. In his younger days he had been a pretty good shot. He moved to a different bedroom window and saw the van leaving via the long driveway. Jim tried to open the window but it wouldn't budge.

"Son of a bitch," he said again. With the van rapidly approaching the county road, Jim knew he had to act fast. He smashed the window glass with the rifle butt, raised the rifle to his shoulder, put the crosshairs on the back of the van and fired. The van had just reached the road as the shot exploded. "Dirty bastards," he spat. "Maybe I can make out the license plate."

Hermit Jim centered the crosshairs of the telescope on the tag as the vehicle began turning east, towards Fargo. His vision wasn't sharp, but the scope helped. He repeated the license number several times while searching his room for pencil and paper. Then he called 911.

When the dispatcher answered the call, Jim gave her a description of Lonnie, Donnie, their van, and its license number.

"They was headed east, towards Fargo, and driving fast," he said frantically. "I got a bunch of bullet holes in my house, and they got a bullet hole in their van. You tell your deputies to hurry up. They'd better be careful."

The Cass County Sheriff's office received the information from the 911 dispatcher and quickly ran down the license plate. The information went to the deputies on road patrol, and the Fargo Police Department. Within minutes the van was the subject of a hot alert.

Donnie drove. They pulled onto the county road when the high caliber bullet struck. *Crack!* Obviously the old man was still shooting. Turning, Donnie saw his brother slump forward against his seat belt, a bleeding mess. He jammed his foot on the gas and pushed 90 miles an hour.

"Lonnie, you okay? Lonnie, where you hit?"

No answer.

Donnie managed a quick glance at his brother as he tried to maintain control. Blood spilled out of his brother's mouth, onto his shirt and pants, and splattered the dashboard. A gaping bullet hole told the story. Donnie's heart pounded. His twin brother, his only friend on earth, had just taken one hell of a hit. Donnie was frantic.

"Don't die on me, Lonnie! Please don't die! You're going to be okay, I promise. I'll get you some help right away. Just don't die on me! You hear me?"

Two Fargo uniforms had just delivered a pregnant young woman to the ER of St. John's Medical Center in Fargo. Walking out to their squad car, their faces beamed. Then they saw the speeding van pull up.

Donnie saw the two officers standing right where he had to go, but didn't care. His brother needed immediate medical attention. The hell with the police.

Coming to a screeching halt in front of the officers, he scrambled out of the van and ran to his brother's door. The two officers noted the van's license plate and knew these turkeys were the subjects of the alert that just went out.

After spending all night and most of the morning in the hospital with Melanie, Jake returned home to freshen up, spend some time with the rest of his family, and meet with Harold and Travis. Looking out the window, he saw them pull into his driveway. He went out to greet them.

"Hi, Jake," Harold said as he extended his hand.

Jake shook Harold's hand and returned the greeting. Then he turned to Travis. "How you doing, Bud?"

Travis looked at Jake with a genial smile. "I'm okay, but how are you all doing? That's the question."

Jake shrugged. "Come on in."

They went into the kitchen, sat down, and Jake poured coffee.

Harold started the conversation. "I dropped by to visit Robert yesterday. Doctor says he's healing fast and should be ready to go back to work in a month. He's hobbling around in a walking cast, but his arm's pretty much healed. His grandmother says the kid's starting to get ornery just sitting around all day like a pent up tiger. Robert says he's raring to go."

"That's good to hear," Jake said.

Harold nodded, then asked, "How's Melanie?"

"Still the same. No better, no worse. Melissa and I are going to the hospital in an hour to spend the afternoon with her."

"Okay." Harold nodded compassionately. "Look, you do whatever you think you have to do. I'm with you all the way. There have been some developments in your heroin case that need immediate attention. Travis is doing a good job, but I'm sure you're aware Alan Ravich may be a problem. With you gone, he's been talking about turning the case over to Scott. I've been holding him off. We went around on it again this morning. I wish it were up to me. I don't want Scott working this case. It's way over his head, and besides, it's your investigation. If you think you'll be back in the next day or so, I'm pretty sure I can hold Alan at bay. I hate putting pressure on you like this Jake, but I have to know soon."

Jake frowned. "What's going on with the case?"

Travis answered. "I got the information from the phone company on that number in Detroit Lakes. It's in an apartment complex. The Sheriff looked into it and said the entire complex has a bad reputation. The police are constantly called over there. The landlord is shady. Sheriff said the man can't be trusted, so we're not going to talk to him.

"I dialed the number and got an answering machine. Had a real short message. Just said, 'Leave your message.' Kind of a strange sounding ring to it too. I got the telephone toll records from the phone company. Strangest thing. The exact minute I called the number, that phone placed a call to a number in Fargo. So I talked to the phone people. Turns out the telephone is set up for call forwarding to the Fargo number. I want to go to Fargo and talk to our guys there. We should look at that number, see what's cooking. It looks like we're dealing with a fairly sophisticated operation. The phone company says the phone in Detroit Lakes is a non-pub, billed to Vondermolte and Marney. That's a law firm in Fargo. We'll have to look at them too. We should probably get on it."

Jake felt a tremendous tug inside himself as two loyalties went to war. Melanie hadn't recovered from her comatose state. What if she regained consciousness and he wasn't available? What if her condition worsened and he was up North? How could he expect Melissa to shoulder this entire burden?

But then, this heroin investigation demanded his full attention. People were dying all over the state. He had accepted the assignment, with all its responsibilities, and people were counting on him. Scott couldn't investigate the contents of a cereal box. If the investigation went to hell, it would be tough living with that.

Priorities. Sometimes life was really a bitch.

"Okay, Harold," Jake said finally. "I know you understand my crisis. And I understand the stuff going on in the office. Let me talk to my wife, and I'll get back to you in the morning."

"Sure, just give me a call."

Travis put his cup down and looked across the kitchen table. "Oh, by the way, Kiel's wife left him. Said she was getting tired of his long hours. Told Kiel she wants a divorce, and her attorney will be in touch. Kiel asked me if I wanted to move in with him while he still has a house. I told him maybe he should wait for a while. Lucie might come over to talk and they could have a chance to turn things around . . . you know, like a kiss and make up session. If I was there it would complicate things. He's pretty upset. Says she caught him completely off guard."

"Yeah, he called me and told me all about it. This is a real blow," Jake said. "Kiel's dedicated to the job. I guess Lucie had different ideas."

Harold and Travis both shrugged, said goodbye and left.

As Jake watched them drive away, Melissa walked up behind him. "So, tell me about it," she said, stroking his shoulders.

With a grim look, Jake turned around. "What the hell am I supposed to do? Melanie is in the hospital. Who knows what's going to happen. Then I've got you and the rest of the kids to think about. We can't neglect them, and I can't neglect you. Things are starting to break open on this heroin investigation. Harold just told me he needs an answer in the next couple days about how long I'm going to be off. There's big pressure on him."

Melissa looked up at her husband, tears forming in her eyes. The past week had been hell. Her first born lay in a state of perpetual sleep. Maybe Melanie would live, but maybe God had other plans. These were very trying times. Jake's strength had helped see her through it. She didn't know how she could manage all this by herself. And she had other children who needed attention. They were traumatized by their sister's accident.

But Melissa knew her husband's office needed him. His co-workers depended on him. It was a crucial time. After a long pause, she said, "Jake, I can't handle a narcotics investigation, but I can handle things at home. I understand your need to be at the hospital if something develops, but Melanie isn't the only one counting on you. If there's something that needs to be done, I'll be there. And don't forget, Sally and Steve are coming over every day to help. They're the best neighbors anyone could have. If you're gone and I'm at the hospital, they'll be around to keep tabs on the kids."

She paused for a moment. Jake reached over and held her hand. It felt cold. He looked into her eyes. They were moist. He let her talk.

"I know the importance of this case," she continued. "You can't let your office down. Come with me to the hospital this afternoon. Then tomorrow it's time to get back to work. Trust me to handle this. There's nothing you can do, really, as far as making Melanie better. But you *can* deal with the heroin problem. If that's where you can make a difference, you should be there. We'll just let things follow their course."

Jake looked into his wife's moist eyes and found it difficult to control his emotions. He took a deep breath. "No wonder I love you so much."

CHAPTER 19

The DEA office in Fargo didn't compare in size to the one in Minneapolis. Aris Kosteckle, the Resident Agent-in-Charge, held the same rank as Harold Sampress, but as the head of a small office he had numerous tasks that would never touch Sampress' desk. The call from Jake Shaunessey made for a welcome respite to business as usual. Their paths had crossed on several occasions and Aris liked working with Jake. During the call Jake briefed Aris on the heroin investigation, telling him the ring appeared to have strong links to Fargo.

"Travis Shepherd is my partner," Jake added. "We're coming to Fargo tomorrow to follow up on some leads. You be around?"

"I'll have some coffee ready when you get here."

The following day, after drinking coffee and exchanging small talk with Aris, Jake briefed the man on the investigation, providing him with all the details. Aris listened intently.

"We've definitely got an epidemic on our hands," Jake told him. "If someone in Fargo is supplying pounds of heroin to Detroit Lakes, there's no reason to believe it stops there."

The three agents discussed the Vondermolte and Marney Law Firm, and the telephone number called from the Detroit Lakes apartment. Aris said he would put his resources to work, and the Fargo office joined in the investigation.

Lisa Sanchez hadn't yet left the office when Jake and Travis returned from Fargo. After checking his messages, Jake bee-lined it home. Seeing Lisa at her desk, Travis decided to stick around.

He plopped down on a chair next to her and said, "It's been a long day. How about a couple drinks and something to eat."

Lisa looked at him coyly. "Does this mean you're buying me dinner?"

He tried to conceal a disappointed expression on his face and said, "Uh, well, that would be a problem."

"Travis, you ask me out for dinner and then tell me you're broke? You know, you're a real piece of work!" Lisa sat back, a devilish grin on her face, and said, "Okay. I'll take pity on you. Let's go eat."

Travis leaned back in the chair. She had a knack of pissing him off, but at the same time he had to admire her. Still, he couldn't let her get in the last word. "Lisa, why do you always have to try and act so fucking macho? Did your dad always tell you he wanted a boy?"

She scowled. "So, who the hell do you think you are? The office shrink? You know, this will be the first time I've gone out with a homeless person." After pausing a few seconds for effect, she asked, "Where do you want to go? Sergeant Joe Friday's?"

Travis gave her a dry look. "No. I'm not in the mood for one of the office watering holes. How about a place where we won't know anyone? I don't want someone from the office listening to us argue about who's the better man."

"Oh, fuck you Travis!"

He smiled sweetly.

They stared, neither blinking, and then burst out laughing.

"Okay, where we going?" Lisa said when she regained her breath.

"I know a great place in St. Louis Park," he said.

A half hour later they were ordering their drinks and starting to relax.

Travis sat back savoring the moment. He hadn't had a date since his last girlfriend gave him the boot. Their waitress arrived with their drinks and prepared to take their orders. Travis scanned the food menu. A steak looked good, and what the hell. Lisa was paying. He ordered the steak.

Lisa laughed inwardly. Admittedly, she had agreed to foot the bill. Nothing to be gained by counting the pennies. Wanting to keep things on a positive note, she ordered the same, while telling herself this wasn't exactly a date but it sure felt good.

The waitress left and the two agents spontaneously lifted their glasses in a toast to whatever.

"So how do you like your house?" Travis asked.

Lisa's large brick house had once been part of a farm. When she first moved in it needed a lot of work. Over the past year she had made many improvements. The place took a big bite out of her paycheck, but she considered it as much an investment as a home.

"I like it. But it sure takes up most of my personal time."

"I should be so lucky."

Lisa took a sip from her martini and scrutinized the restaurant, a routine practice for cops.

Looking over the bar towards the booths on the opposite side of the room, Lisa spotted Kiel's wife. "Hey, look over there. Isn't that Lucie?"

Travis looked across the room and recognized Lucie sitting in a booth with someone. "Yeah, but I can't see who she's with."

Lisa shifted, straining to see. "It's a guy. Whoever it is, he's got slicked back red hair. Oh shit, you don't suppose?"

Travis jumped to the same conclusion. *Scott*!! He turned rigid. "I'll go see."

Travis walked the long way around to the men's room. Lucie looked up and recognized him. She became acutely embarrassed when their eyes met and quickly looked down, not wanting to enter into a conversation. Travis stopped at the booth and eyed her companion. Scott Hookman!

Travis glared at the agent, but said nothing and didn't acknowledge his presence. Then he looked at Lucie and said scornfully, "Hello Lucie. Who's taking care of your daughter tonight?"

Lucie didn't even look up. Travis then continued to the men's room. Scott quickly joined him.

"Look, I can explain."Scott said.

Travis walked up to Scott, placed his hands on Scott's chest, and shoved him hard against the wall. "You're a fucking slime ball. I've always thought that. Now you've proven it. Get the hell out of my way."

Scott regained his balance and started to approach Travis. Travis' eyes narrowed as he pointed a finger at the other agent. Not wanting to be carried out on a stretcher, Scott stopped in his tracks. Travis walked out seething. He told Lisa and they sat in their booth, depressed, staring into their drinks.

"Well, we're going to have to do something about it," Lisa said, exasperated. "Kiel hears about this, there might be bloodshed. We can't have that."

Travis took a long pull from his drink. "I know. I'll take care of it tomorrow."

They canceled their food order and asked for the bill. The evening had been ruined.

The following morning Travis went into work early and joined Harold for a closed door meeting. Harold then met with Alan Ravich. By the time Scott got into the office his fate had been sealed. Harold came out of Alan's office and approached Kiel's desk.

"What's up Boss?" Kiel said, looking up at Harold.

Harold placed a piece of paper on Kiel's desk. "I got a tip last night that someone driving a red Cadillac is supposed to show up at this address before one o'clock today. The driver is to pick up five keys of coke. The caller was specific about the car and the physical description of its driver. I want you to go there. Spend a few hours and see what develops. If the car shows up, contact me and I'll send help. This could lead to a nice seizure."

Kiel examined the paper Harold gave him. He pulled these surveillances quite often. Occasionally they worked out, but generally not. This tip had evidently been obtained from someone on the inside. Harold hadn't said anything about the reliability, or the identity of the tipster, which probably meant the person was unknown. An anonymous tip held the least potential for success. It might have been generated out of revenge. Or, maybe someone wanted to eliminate his competition. But right now, the informer's motive didn't really matter. Harold wanted a surveillance, and that's what he would get. Kiel hoped for luck.

"I'll get right on it Harold," Kiel said eagerly. He cleared off his desk and hit the street.

Harold called Scott into his office.

"Close the door," Harold said brusquely.

Scott sat across from Harold.

Harold ignored Scott for five full minutes, doing routine paper work. Let the son of a bitch squirm, he thought.

Finally he looked up at Scott, who had actually begun to sweat. With a piercing look he said, "Scott, tell me there is nothing going on between you and Kiel's wife."

Scott looked at Harold, but said nothing.

"Okay," Harold said tersely. "Your personal affairs are of no concern to me unless they have an adverse effect on the operations of this office. When that happens, they become my concern. Your fucking around with the wife of another agent is my concern, and I'm going to take immediate action. I just cleared it with Alan. I don't want you around here anymore. What you've been doing, in addition to your other screw ups, is just plain stupid. You could get yourself killed."

Harold watched Scott grimace, then went on. "The best place for you is anywhere but here. We're always getting calls from Miami requesting agents to assist in their operations. You're gone! Officially this is just a temporary assignment, but that will change as soon as we get through the paper work. You won't be coming back. I want you out of this office within a half hour. Report to the Miami office tomorrow morning."

Scott walked out of Harold's office without saying a word.

Several minutes later Alan Ravich walked into the agents' work area. He glared at Travis, then looked toward Lisa and the others. "I want to see powder on the table," he bellowed. "Powder on the fucking table!" He gave his words a minute to soak in, then stalked out the door. While still early in the day, he needed a drink.

Aris Kosteckle jumped headlong into the investigation after receiving a call from a prisoner in the county jail. Donnie Dissel had decided to spill his guts.

When Aris went to the jail, he first spoke with the chief jailer. Aris told the jailer Dissel had contacted the DEA, and the deputy eagerly ventured his opinion. "Well, I know you guys in the DEA got a tough job to do. But trust me, this guy is really a piece of shit." The deputy then told Aris about an earlier altercation with Dissel in the jail.

The Clerk of Court had presented the jailer with papers signed by Cass County Circuit Court Judge G. A. Hammer, ordering the Sheriff to release Dissel. The deputy read the release order and then read it again. He found it baffling that Dissel could have raised fifty thousand dollars for his bond.

Dissel was lying on his narrow cot when the deputy unlocked the heavy cell door. He looked up impassively as the jailer entered the cell, but said nothing.

"Okay, dirt bag," the deputy said. "Your attorney posted your bond this morning, and His Honor, Judge G. A. Hammer, has ordered us to release you. Get up! You're outa here!"

This came as a complete surprise to Dissel. During meetings with his attorney, a public defender, the subject of posting bond had never even come up. "What the hell are you talking about? My attorney never mentioned anything about posting bond."

The deputy took a deep breath. He held up the release order, naming the law firm of Vondermolte and Marney. "I don't really give a fuck. His Honor wants you out of here, and I'm going to give the judge what he wants. Now get your ass up and follow me!"

Dissel slowly stood up. As much as he wanted out of this shit hole, something didn't add up. Why would some attorneys he'd never heard of post fifty grand to get him out of jail? Why would *anybody* pay fifty grand to get his ass out of this joint? Who did he know that even had that kind of money?

Then it struck him. The only people he knew with that kind of cash were Tanya's organization. Yeah, they'd have it. And Tanya and her tough guy buddies had never been particularly friendly to him or his brother. If they wanted him out of jail that badly, it wasn't in the spirit of good will. He knew who their customers were, and other information about their organization. Nearly every time he and his brother went to their house they learned something. Put enough minor details together and a person could tell quite a story. That was it. They wanted to shut him up! His brother was dead. If Donnie left this jail, he'd be paying Lonnie a visit. Dissel tried to think. What the hell should he do? It didn't take but a flash for him to figure it out.

He stood by his bed and said, "I'm not leaving. I want to stay right here."

"Hey, dirt bag," the deputy replied condescendingly. "In case you haven't figured it out, you're not in charge. Nobody really gives a flying fuck what you want or don't want. The judge says you're leaving, so you're gone."

As the deputy approached the prisoner, Dissel took two steps towards the deputy and struck him in the stomach as hard as he could. But the junkie had a powder puff punch. The deputy took the punch and came back like a human sledge hammer, pounding his fist into Donnie's face. Dissel hit the floor, blood spewing from his mouth.

The jailer looked down at him. He didn't understand Dissel's reaction, but he knew the scumbag wouldn't be leaving today. Not after this.

"Okay, asshole, have it your way. You'll be looking at additional charges. How does felonious assault sound?"

Dissel spit a glob of blood into the small sink along with a tooth. What next? he wondered.

A short time later he had a long talk with Aris.

At 4:30 AM the following day the roundup began. The DEA office in Minneapolis buzzed with law enforcement personnel. Every state and local narcotics agency in the seven county metro area was represented, along with all of the DEA agents and a few US marshals. A number of plain-clothes detectives and uniformed officers also made their presence known.

An assortment of donuts and rolls sat next to a tall coffee urn on the table in the war room. All of the agents, detectives, and uniforms helped themselves as they tried to sharpen their early morning focus on the day's event.

Harold ran the show, dubbing the roundup "Operation Screwdriver," because the DEA was putting the screws to twenty heroin dealers Lisa had bagged. The group had been divided into arrest teams, with each team assigned a team leader. Twenty arrest packets were distributed amongst the teams, each containing pertinent information and court documents regarding one of the defendants.

When everyone had their coffee and rolls, Harold gave the group some general information. "Okay everyone, listen up please. Many of these people have violent histories. Most are addicts, and they're all dangerous. Timing is crucial. We crash their doors at six. If there are any questions, I'm here to help you. Good luck and please be careful."

Jake and Travis were assigned to Fergie. They were joined by two Eagan police detectives and two uniforms. They huddled together in a corner and Jake gave the team some final information.

"Lisa believes Fergie's the most significant dealer of the lot, and if he's handled properly he might flip. We'll meet a couple blocks north of Fergie's house, and go through his front door at six o'clock. Travis will handle the sledge hammer, then I'll lead the way." Speaking to one of the detectives, Jake said, "Can you have one of your uniforms cover the rear in case Fergie tries to escape out the back door?"

"Got it covered."

The detectives studied their package, and then the team headed to Eagan.

Harold coordinated the action. At five-fifty he conducted a roll call over the secure radio system. All the team leaders were in place and ready.

At six o'clock Jake's team rolled up to Fergie's house and scrambled out of their cars. Jake pounded on the door yelling, "Police," and quickly moved out of the way. Travis sent the door crashing in with one blow from his hammer, and the crew stormed into the house.

Jake and Travis went directly to Fergie's bedroom. As they entered the room, they heard Fergie snoring like an elephant. The odor in the bedroom might have been elephant dung. Travis turned on the lights and Fergie woke up staring at the muzzle of Jake's gun. Wanting to ensure the man wasn't sleeping with a gun, Travis yanked Fergie's filthy blanket off the bed. Fergie wore a pair of badly stained boxer shorts, a dirty T-shirt, and a steel leg brace, but had no gun. Travis stood him up and handcuffed him while Jake read the man his Miranda rights.

While Jake watched over Fergie, Travis checked the room. Crutches leaned against the wall, next to the bed. On top of the dresser sat a small box, about the size of a shoe box, filled with money. Next to the box were a drug scale and two baggies containing brown powder.

"Check this out, Jake," Travis said tauntingly, as he lifted up the two baggies of heroin. "Our timing was right on this one. Fergie, I got to tell you. You're fucked!"

"Son of a bitch!" Fergie blared.

"Looks like you owe us about twenty years or so," Jake said matter of factly. "You're going downtown."

Jake sensed that Fergie, who looked downright depressed, was ready to fold. He poured on the pressure. "It's like this, Pal. One of our undercovers, Lisa, got a couple ounces of junk from you after you tried to rape her. The assault charge hasn't even been considered yet by the grand jury. They just indicted you on the junk."

Fergie's mouth opened wide. "Lisa," he said. "She's DEA?"

Jake looked at him sternly. "You got it. And you pissed her off."

Gathering his thoughts, Fergie said, "Okay. Look, can't we make some kind of a deal?"

"We're listening," Jake answered flatly.

"What's in it for me if I cooperate?"

Jake looked at him intently. "We could help you. But you have to make it worth our while."

"How about some specifics," Fergie said.

"I'll spell it out. You could buy back a portion of your life. Or you'll be spending a big chunk of time looking at prison walls. It's up to you."

It didn't take long before Fergie began to sing. "There's this guy named Elwood Royal. We all call him ER 'cause he's kinda like the medicine man, you know. He's my man. Deals some real kick ass shit. Stuff comes straight from South America. You know that guy who got killed out in Elk River? Dealer named Frenchy Deveroux? Well, Elwood got his stuff from Deveroux. Those rip offs closed Deveroux's book, and ER moved up a notch. These people have a huge operation. I never met any of them, but I can give you ER. You get him and you're knocking on their front door. How's that?"

"You help us get inside this organization . . . yeah, that would buy you something," Jake said. "Could you take me to ER?"

"Yeah. ER really trusts me. But if he finds out I've been busted he'll shut me out. This guy's really careful. And dangerous. I think he's killed people, but I don't know who. Just word on the street, you know?"

"Sounds like he's the paranoid type."

Fergie nodded. "I'll tell you how ER thinks. Sometimes he hangs with this guy named Dave. He's a real bad ass too. Can't remember his last name, but you guys know him. A couple months ago you took his coke, and the story is he flushed some junk before you could get into his house. Well, Dave got his shit from ER. Then this thing went down with you guys. ER got real paranoid after that. Said it sounded like bullshit; like maybe what really happened was you guys got the dope, arrested Dave, and now he's snitching. ER still hangs with him, but he won't sell to him, and he won't let the guy into his place. Says he has to be a hundred percent on Dave before he'll go back to business as usual. He's just watching him real careful, you know."

Jake looked over at Travis. "Stay with Fergie. I'll call Harold."

Shortly after ten thirty, Jake and his team returned to the office without Fergie. He had been given an official reprieve.

CHAPTER 20

Driving back to the office, Jake rehashed the latest developments. "So now we know about ER, and we know that Eddie's dope funneled down to Fergie. I go undercover and maybe we'll get Eddie. Lisa's hunch was right on the money. When she retires she oughta become a psychic."

Travis nodded. "How the hell does she do it?"

Jake shrugged. "Good question. She must have some extra neurons jumping around inside her brain."

A day later, Fergie met ER in a Bloomington bar and arranged to introduce Jake. They sat in a booth and talked business over a couple cold beers.

ER had a rough, gangly appearance with long, stringy blonde hair, a pale, cadaverous face, and dark eyes that were later described in a DEA report as 'rodent-like.' As he talked he squinted, and his eyes constantly flitted around the room like a wary mouse trying to locate the cat. His arms were littered with poor quality tattoos: A spider web covering a large area around one elbow, a woman's head above two large breasts, an eagle flying above the words, "Free and Clear." On the four fingers of his left hand were the letters "F" "U" "C" "K." The fingers of his right hand said, "Y" "O" "U."

Staring at Fergie's leg jutting out from the booth, ER asked, "How's the leg?"

Fergie frowned. "Hard to say while it's in this damn brace, but the doc says it's healing," Fergie answered glumly.

"I never thought a person could fuck up his knee just falling down some stairs. Looks like your nose got it too. Better be careful with those steps after this, huh?"

"For sure."

"Have you read the papers?" ER asked curiously.

"You mean the big bust?"

"Yeah. Nineteen people got popped. I never dealt with any of 'em direct, but about half of 'em were dealing our shit. This is going to play hell with distribution."

"You think it'll set you back?"

ER toyed with his beer glass, then looked back at Fergie. "Yeah."

Fergie considered his words carefully. "Maybe we better lay low for a while."

ER shook his head. "Can't. The shit's coming in every month and we gotta unload it."

Fergie nodded thoughtfully. "Then I might have a solution. I've got a guy I've been selling to for almost a year. He wants to move up."

They talked about it, then Elwood left, agreeing to meet Jake at two o'clock the following afternoon in the cocktail lounge of a bowling alley in Bloomington.

Fergie drove to the other side of Bloomington and met with Jake and Travis.

"I set it up the way you wanted," Fergie told them. "If the deal goes down and the two of you agree to do your own thing, I'll get five grand for the interduct."

Prior to the deal the next day, Jake held a meeting with the surveillance team. Jake had invited the Bloomington police to send one of their narcs to help out. Bloomington gave the assignment to Stuart

Klamm. A police officer for eight years, he had recently been assigned to the narcotics unit but hadn't worked with the DEA.

At the meeting, Stuart introduced himself to the other agents, and then Jake made the assignments. "Kiel, you'll be inside the lounge, covering the meet. Stuart, you assist the agents conducting the moving surveillance of ER."

Stuart nodded.

"Travis, Lisa, Ken, Sal and Jerry are the surveillance team, along with Stuart. Six cars are plenty. I'll meet ER and show him the money. Hopefully, he'll leave the bar and go to his stash, then bring me an ounce of junk. Surveillance will follow him and try to get a fix on his stash."

Jake turned to Stuart. "I know you've never been involved with us on a moving surveillance, so we'll give you one of our portable radios. Here's how we do things. Everybody on the team will be changing their positions so ER doesn't see the same vehicle too often. We try to blend in with the rest of the traffic on the street. Use other cars for cover. If one of us has the eye and thinks ER's seen him too much, he calls it out and somebody will replace him. The one who has the eye calls out every move so the others know what's going on. What are you driving?"

"A red Ford Mustang. "

"Okay. Glad you're here. It'll be a pleasure working with you."

Before Jake arrived at the undercover site, the surveillance agents positioned themselves around the bowling alley so they could watch ER's arrival and departure. When ER left to get the dope they'd be on him like feathers on a duck, hoping he didn't lead them on a wild goose chase.

At 1:30 PM Kiel arrived at the cocktail lounge ahead of Jake. He wanted to see who was there, and avoid giving the impression he and Jake were together. The lounge wasn't crowded. A couple sat at the bar, and Kiel found a seat several stools down from them. Looking around, he saw two small groups, bowlers left over from the morning league, seated at one end of the lounge. They were loud; making it obvious they had been drinking for some time. Kiel sensed ER didn't have anybody inside.

Jake arrived fifteen minutes late, typical of dope dealers. He saw Kiel sitting at the bar, and took a seat in a booth.

A washed out looking waitress with a deep dimple in her chin came over to Jake's booth. He ordered a beer. ER and Fergie arrived at the same time as the beer. Both sat down opposite Jake, with Fergie on the outside to accommodate his cast.

Fergie made the introduction. "Jake, this is ER. He's my man."

Jake and ER grunted and cautiously shook hands. Before saying anything, ER lit up a Marlboro and studied Jake, who looked quite relaxed.

Fergie decided to firm up the introduction a bit. "Jake is cool."

A records check Jake conducted the day before revealed ER had done time for selling heroin. His tattoos and quirks confirmed it.

"Fergie tells me you're from the cities," ER said.

"Yeah," Jake answered succinctly. Then he tried to take over the direction of the dialogue. "Seems you got some of the best shit around."

ER ignored Jake's effort. "So, if you've been dealing smack in the cities for over a year, how come I never heard of you?"

"I'm a cautious man. Never been busted. Those tattoos. Looks like you done some time."

"That doesn't concern you. Who are some of your customers?"

"That's not your business. Like I said, I'm careful."

"Okay," ER answered uneasily. "Fergie says you're cool, then you're cool. You're right about my dope. Comes straight from South America. You can hit it twice and your customers will still love it. What kind of quantities you talking?"

"An ounce to start," Jake whispered. "If I like it and the price is right, I'm good for half pounds."

"You use?"

Jake shook his head. "No, I don't do the shit. When you start dipping into your bag, your motherfucking business goes to hell."

"How do you test your shit?"

"I got a couple whores. They know their shit."

ER nodded. "Okay. My price to start is six grand an ounce. You got the bread?"

Discreetly, Jake reached into his pants pocket and pulled out a wad of hundreds. ER reached for it but Jake pulled back, then fanned the wad of bills for ER's benefit.

ER's eyes lit up. Grinning, he said, "I'll be back with the shit. Fergie will stay here. When I return, I'll come in and get you and we'll go someplace and do it."

ER left the lounge and got into a black Porsche. In a corner of the lot, Travis, who had the eye, crouched down in his car trying to be inconspicuous. "Subject is out of the building," he said evenly. "He's getting in his car. The car's moving and he's north onto Lyndale Avenue. Northbound on Lyndale," Travis repeated. "You got him, Ken?"

Ken Washington proceeded north a couple cars behind the quarry. "I got him." He continued calling out ER's location as he moved north. The remaining surveillance vehicles fell in behind Ken, mixing with the traffic. Ken maintained a distance behind ER, but didn't let him out of sight.

"He's approaching 494. Now he's entering the freeway," Ken announced. He followed the Porsche around the cloverleaf. "Westbound on 494. He's kicking it. We're going to have to punch it to keep him in sight."

With the traffic not too heavy on the beltway, ER stomped on the gas. His Porsche answered, screaming down the freeway. Quickly doing seventy-five, well above the limit, he weaved in and out of the lanes. The agents struggled to keep pace.

A drunk, driving a white Chrysler, entered the freeway, cutting across two lanes. It struck the right side of a Lincoln. The Lincoln skid into the path of Ken Washington. Ken tried to avoid the car and hit the median barrier. He bounced back into the left lane. The two cars collided. Ken smashed into the median again. He spun around and faced the opposite direction. His car stopped. It now occupied both the shoulder and the left lane. The Lincoln swerved into the path of Lisa and Sal. Lisa crashed into the Lincoln. Sal crashed into Lisa. Two other cars directly behind Sal managed to stop. Several cars behind them couldn't. A chain reaction pileup blocked all of the lanes.

Only three surveillance vehicles remained. Stuart drove his red Mustang onto the right shoulder and around the accident, with the other agents following close behind. Travis viewed the chaos as he approached and saw Lisa waving them on.

ER generally watched the traffic behind him, and when he saw the cars crashing into one another he nudged on his brakes. He enjoyed a little mayhem whenever he had the chance.

It surprised him to see a red Mustang emerge from the pileup and continue on. At first ER thought it strange the driver didn't stop to help. But then he saw two more vehicles dodging the clutter. Warning signals sounded in his brain. The three cars were the only ones behind him.

Stuart noticed ER's Porsche slowing dramatically, so he also slowed down, not wanting ER to get a good look at the Mustang. "I'm on him," Stuart said gravely. "I'll take the eye."

ER accelerated and continued west with the Mustang matching his pace. He exited the freeway to see if it stayed with him.

Seeing ER pull off the freeway, Stuart slowed down. He would take the same exit but didn't want to be on the ramp right behind ER. Stuart got to the exit just as ER approached the end of the ramp. "He's turning right, going north."

Travis, the last in the short line of cars said, "Okay, Stu. I'll go with ER on the turn. You and Jerry take a left, then double back and follow me. I've got the eye."

After hanging a right, Travis called it out. "He's going slow, a couple blocks up." About a half mile north he saw the Porsche turn. "Now he's making a right." Travis approached the street where ER had turned and did likewise. "I've still got him. Now he's turning left. I'll let you know the street when I get there." Stuart and Jerry picked up speed. Not wanting to follow the Porsche through two turns, Travis called it, then went straight. "The street is Gleason. I'm going by. Jerry, you take him."

Jerry turned on Gleason. He couldn't see the Porsche because the road curved a short distance ahead, so he picked up his speed. Rounding the curve, Jerry was confronted by the Porsche, parked at the curb with ER staring into the side-view mirror. The agent continued past

ER, warning the others. "He's parked at the curb looking in his mirror. Don't come down this street."

Too late. Stuart had already rounded the curve as Jerry spoke. ER watched the red Mustang drive past. Now he knew. Son of a bitch. Narcs were all over his ass! He calmly thought things through. What brought this on?

The answer was obvious. A major DEA drug bust had gone down, then Fergie brought in somebody new. Some guy with big money. Fergie had to be a damn snitch. Jake was probably DEA. ER had just negotiated a dope deal with an agent. Still on parole, negotiating with a federal narc would send him back to the joint. Now what the hell?

ER slowly digested the causes of his problem. Eddie continued to bring in a huge supply of heroin, but his dealers were falling like bowling pins. ER felt pressure to develop more outlets, and he got careless. Now he needed a strategy. He put his Porsche into gear and thought as he drove back towards the freeway. He remembered Dave O'Neal's situation. Dave had contacted the cops and used them to take off some of the heat when the narcs were breathing down his neck. ER had an idea. While his circumstances differed from Dave's, maybe a similar approach would work.

Stuart got on the air as soon as he reached the next intersection. "I just went past him. Couldn't avoid it. He stared at me. We're burned."

Travis swore under his breath. "Okay, let's drop the surveillance. Maybe Jake's undercover thing will still go if ER doesn't see us again."

ER drove back to the freeway, then east into Bloomington. Pulling into a gas station parking lot, he wheeled up to a pay phone and called the Bloomington Police department. A desk sergeant answered the phone.

Several minutes later, Lieutenant Moffett, the chief of the detective bureau, called the DEA office and spoke with Harold Sampress. Harold hung up and beeped Kiel, who continued to watch over Jake and Fergie. Kiel called the office, then slid alongside Jake in the booth, opposite from Fergie.

Kiel joining them could only mean bad news. "What's going on?" Jake asked.

Frowning, Kiel told Jake about the pileup on the freeway and the shattered surveillance. The news got continually worse. "A guy called the Bloomington PD. Had to be ER. Said he was an ex-con who got sucked into a drug conversation that he wanted no part of. Played along so he could get a good description. Told the desk sergeant if the police came to this bowling alley they'd find a heavy weight with a pocket full of drug money. He gave them your description. It's over, Jake."

After making the call to the Bloomington cops, ER tackled the rest of the problem. Fergie was a snitch. No doubt about that. But ER didn't know about Dave O'Neal. Maybe he was, maybe he wasn't. Now ER could find out, and possibly kill two birds with one bullet. He'd contact Dave, then go to Las Vegas for a few days while Dave took care of things. If Dave did good, ER would know the score.

CHAPTER 21

For once in his life, Eddie Pellegrino felt genuinely ecstatic. Dominique brought him (finally) to Colombia to meet the heavies on their ranch two hundred kilometers from Bogotá. Eddie expected to see wealth, but this surpassed his imagination. The secluded compound rested on three thousand acres of heavily wooded rolling hills, lush, dark green meadows, and pastures for a stable of thoroughbred horses. A nearby waterfall cascading down into a rushing stream provided a spectacular view. The hacienda, as the Colombians referred to it, consisted of several tan stucco buildings which formed a giant horse shoe shape, nearly surrounding the main house.

Dominique and Eddie sat at a table overlooking a large swimming pool, enjoying the deep blue sky, the great view, and each other's company. Eddie took a sip of his Scotch and set the glass down. "I hate to go back. The past few days have been great. You going back with me?"

Dominique grinned. Eddie would have to fly to Minneapolis on a commercial jet, not the Lear. Might as well break it to him now. "No. When I leave I'll be going to Berlin to meet a group of Russians. Minnesota won't be seeing my face for six weeks. I'm sure you'll continue to do your excellent job while I'm away."

Eddie concealed his disappointment. He had been counting on a return flight in Dominique's private jet. "Of course. Sandra's about due with the next load. In three months I'm hoping to up the shipments by several kilos. I promised her more money for each key when we make the jump. She's a good mule."

"I like your style," Dominique said with his easy smile.

Sunrise wouldn't arrive for another hour and a half. The Twin Cities were still shrouded in darkness. But to David O'Neal, everything looked bright and cheery. He felt exuberant as he thought about how this day would change his life.

ER met with Dave three days earlier and offered him the chance to prove himself. They hooked up in a parking ramp at the Mall of America. Before talking, ER frisked him for bugs. Then, before getting down to business, he first insisted on moving to another level in the huge garage. Finally, they talked.

"Fergie is a DEA snitch," ER said bitterly. "He knows a lot about both of us. Introduced me to an undercover narc. I'm going to Las Vegas. I need a vacation. I hope while I'm gone you can fix the problem. If you do, you'll be rock solid again."

O'Neal knew what ER expected, and welcomed the words. Not only could he gain some revenge on the DEA, he would be back in the money. Life would be good again. Add to all that, this job would be enjoyable. He never liked Fergie. The slob always smelled bad, looked dirty, and acted weird. It came as no big surprise to O'Neal the guy was a snitch. O'Neal hated snitches.

He parked in the driveway at the rear of Fergie's house. Before getting out of his car he put on a pair of latex gloves and tucked a thirty-eight revolver into his belt. Then he put a set of brass knuckles into the pocket of his windbreaker. Testing the back door, he found it locked but not real sturdy. Putting his shoulder against the door, he gave it a hard shove and it opened. He thumbed the switch on his penlight, then stopped to listen for signs of life. He heard Fergie making like a freight train. Obviously sleeping. Good. This would be a piece of cake. Making his way to the bedroom, he grimaced at the noxious odor. Ignoring the stench, he pulled out his thirty-eight and located the light switch. There lay Fergie, spread out under a ratty looking blanket. Stepping to the side of the bed, O'Neal held his pistol inches away from Fergie's head and sat down, shaking the bed.

Fergie's eyes opened, looking into the business end of the revolver. He tried to sit up but O'Neal pushed him back. "I'll tell you when you can get up, you motherfucking snitch."

Fergie's eyes flared with fear. "Dave. What's this about?"

Moving his revolver to his left hand, Dave slipped the brass knuckles onto his right. "You want to snitch to the DEA? Well try snitching your way out of this."

Dave slammed the brass knuckles into Fergie's mouth. Four teeth shattered. Fergie's jaw broke. He grabbed Fergie's hair and pulled the man's head up. Fergie slobbered blood and teeth onto his blanket. Dave stood up and pulled the blanket off the bed, then smashed his brass knuckles into Fergie's ribs. He heard them crunch as they shattered. Fergie moaned and gasped for air.

"Take your shorts off."

The excruciating pain nearly paralyzed him, making every movement difficult. But a thought flashed through his mind: As long as he was alive he still had hope. He slowly, painfully reached down and pulled his shorts off.

Looking at the disgusting underwear, Dave felt thankful for the rubber gloves. Crumpling the dirty shorts into a wad, Dave jammed them into Fergie's mouth. Fergie choked and gagged.

Time to do it, Dave thought. He rammed the revolver's barrel into the kneecap of Fergie's bad leg. Fergie flinched. Dave pulled the trigger. Fergie's entire body convulsed with pain. Fergie automatically brought his hands down to his ravaged knee. O'Neal slammed his brass knuckles into Fergie's left arm. Fergie's eyes were psycho-wild. Reality had set in. With one last effort, he brought his arms up to cover his face.

Dave knocked Fergie's arms away and looked straight into his eyes. "That's right you fucking piece of shit."

He screwed the gun's barrel tight against Fergie's temple and blasted his brains across the side of the room.

Several days after the disastrous surveillance of Elwood Royal, the agents involved in the car crash were still battered and bruised, but none sustained serious injuries. With three cars in the fleet totaled, Harold worked overtime getting them replaced. He was putting the finishing touches on some of the paperwork when his secretary transferred a call to his desk. Several minutes later he called Jake and Travis into his office. He didn't like telling them the bad news.

"I just got a call from the Eagan Police Department. They received an anonymous tip earlier this morning telling them to check out a house on Rahn Road. Fergie's address. The PD sent a couple guys out there. They went inside and found Fergie murdered. Whoever did it beat the hell out of him, then shot him in the knee and head. The detectives are there now, going over the scene. They figure the killing's related to our investigation. I agree. My guess is it's ER. Probably had someone do the hit for him. It's interesting about the phone call. They figure Fergie had been dead only a couple hours, so whoever did it wanted him found quickly. The informer also called the Tribune, and the press got there in a flash. TV crews too, and it'll be on the news this evening."

Jake and Travis looked at each other. Their wide open mouths revealed the devastating effect of Harold's words. Harold paused for a moment, then continued.

"I told Eagan we'll assist them in every way. They'll want to look over your reports, Jake. Give 'em everything they want. If we can't get ER on a heroin charge, maybe we can get him on a murder rap."

While Jake and Travis spoke with Harold, Kiel took a call from his wife.

"Kiel, this is Lucie," she said in a cold, all-business tone. "I have to discuss something with you."

Kiel's heart started pumping, but he wasn't sure if it was excitement at the possibility of resolving this mess with his wife, or anger pushing up his blood pressure. "Sure, Lucie. Should we meet for lunch?"

"Not hardly," Lucie replied. "I'm in Miami."

Blood pounded in Kiel's head. "Miami. What the hell are you doing there?"

"Lucinda and I have moved here. I'm living with Scott Hookman. We plan to get married."

Kiel slammed the phone down, swore violently and pounded his desk with his fist. Then he kicked his office chair, sending it hard into another desk.

During this tirade, Jake and Travis were walking out of Harold's office. They stared at Kiel then moved in, prepared to restrain him. Now realizing what he had just done, Kiel calmly walked over to his chair, picked it up and returned it to the desk. Then he sat down.

"I'm sorry guys," he said. "I just got off the phone with Lucie. She's run off with Scott. Can you believe it? What a miserable slime."

Jake and Travis weren't sure which slime Kiel was referring to, Scott or Lucie.

Travis shook his head. "Let's go get a drink. Jake's buying."

The week Fergie died it was hot in San Diego. Approaching the US Customs station at the port of entry, Jose Garcia de Lopez pulled behind a long line of trucks awaiting inspection. Short and thin with fine features, Jose had oiled down black hair, and aging brown eyes. Sitting in his rig, just breathing seemed like a struggle to the drug smuggler as he tried to deal with both the tension and the acrid air. The atmosphere felt almost soupy as the heat combined harshly with the exhaust hanging over the causeway and the Mexican smog. Jose watched the heat rise in hazy waves off the concrete, and wondered if everyone else trapped on the causeway felt as miserable. Occasionally he slipped the truck's transmission into gear, crept a few feet forward, and then sat back and tried to settle his nerves. After a seemingly endless wait, Jose, growing increasingly more fidgety, finally reached the customs station booth.

Two Customs Inspectors approached his rig, one of them handling a sniffer dog named Ranger. Seeing the dog sent heavy throbs of fear ripping through his chest, down to his bowels. His boss had told him they packaged the heroin so water couldn't damage it. But he warned Jose it could be detected by a Customs sniffer dog. Jose's tense hands gripped the steering wheel as though doused with crazy glue.

Ranger, a large, black and tan, badge carrying German Shepherd, had a nose for trouble, and his handler took great pride in the dog's demonstrated skills. Ranger eagerly sniffed the front of Jose's truck, while his handler held onto his thick leash.

Slowly approaching Jose, the second Customs Inspector's eyes zoomed in on him and held an icy gaze for what felt like an eternity. Attempting to appear as calm as possible, Jose managed a weak smile. Visions of confinement scared him, making his attempt at indifference difficult. Fifteen years if he got caught with this stuff. An eternity of gray walls, steel bars, endless boredom, fear and loneliness.

The inspector walked directly to Jose's door. "Get out and open the rear doors."

Jose did as instructed, while watching the dog handler help Ranger climb onto the driver's seat. Opening the rear doors, Jose moved to the side, trying to watch the dog's progress. Ranger quickly finished with the cab and jumped down to start his search under the trailer bed. Shortly, he started whining.

The dog handler yelled, "Hey Howard, grab him. We've got something!"

Howard hadn't yet climbed into the rear of the truck, so he simply reached over and latched onto Jose's arm, escorting him to the front of the rig.

The dog handler gave Ranger a command and the shepherd sat down, staring threateningly at Jose, who was now visibly trembling and fighting to keep from wetting his pants. Howard walked into the customs building, returning with a set of tools. Minutes later he removed six kilos of heroin from the hidden compartment.

"You're coming with us." Howard slapped the cuffs on Jose's wrists.

The inspectors suspected the six bundles, each wrapped with white paper tape, contained heroin. But it might be cocaine. "Only one way to find out," the dog handler said, placing the parcels on a desk in the back room of the office.

Howard locked Jose in a cell and joined his partner. Using a knife, the dog handler sliced through the tape on one of the packages. He discovered a large zip lock bag containing a light beige powder.

"Heroin," he said, grinning.

But they had to check it further. Howard retrieved a small packet, made of thick transparent plastic, from a desk drawer. It contained a narcotics field test kit consisting of three small, delicate glass vials. Each held a chemical that responded differently in the presence of opiates. He placed a small amount of the powder into the packet, closed the top, and separately broke each vial. As each one shattered, the chemical released and mixed with the powder. The presence of heroin would cause the mixture to change to a different specific color with each broken vial. The field test proved positive.

"Heroin," he repeated.

An hour later two DEA agents arrived at the customs building. After talking to the inspectors they interrogated Jose, giving him the usual pitch. "We caught you with a load of dope. Judges hate heroin smugglers. You can count on spending a big chunk of your life in a federal prison. There's only one way out. Cooperate."

Eager to give them what they wanted, Jose spilled his guts. The agents quickly realized they would have to hustle. Mark Teneras, the senior agent, called his office and requested several agents to assist. "We're interested in Sandra Walton. She's somewhere in the area waiting for this load. If we don't move quickly she'll spook. We want to catch her holding," he told his boss.

Mark, a twelve year veteran, was responsible for showing his rookie partner the ropes. With less than five months on the job, this would be Charlie's first controlled delivery. Charlie listened attentively as Mark spoke to Jose in fluent Spanish. Mark explained exactly what the agents needed. If Jose followed the instructions to the letter, Sandra would soon be listening to her Miranda rights, and Jose could breathe a hell of a lot easier when he stood before the judge. After the agent finished his initial interview with Jose, the shaken smuggler returned to the detention cell. Mark and Charlie then went to the back office and waited for the other agents.

"Here's what we're going to do," Mark told Charlie. "We'll hit Sandra's pager, and Jose will meet with her. When she leaves with the dope, we'll take her down."

"So, we catch her with the dope in her car and we've got our case?"

"That'd be a good case, but we're gonna try to make it better. We want Jose to coax her into a conversation. If she says one of the magic words, like heroin, junk, or kilos, it'll be the same as a confession."

"How we going to do that?"

"Piss her off."

Charlie chuckled. Damn, he loved this job.

The agents brought Jose back into the office and hid a transmitter under his clothes. About that time the additional agents arrived.

Looking at Jose, Mark said, "Okay. Let's do it."

Jose dialed Sandra's pager, then punched 12121.

The smuggler drove his truck to the warehouse in Chula Vista, followed by several DEA vehicles. Jose parked out of sight of the building. The agents established a discreet surveillance, with Mark taking the eye. Jose got out of his truck and sat back against one of the truck's wheels.

Sandra arrived and pulled her car close to the truck. As she got out, Jose stood up and approached her.

"You're late, Jose. Is everything okay?"

Jose pointed at a front tire of the tractor and replied, "Flat. Sorry."

"Okay," Sandra said irritably. "But now I'm late too. Let's see it."

With a couple tools in hand, Jose crawled under the bed of the trailer. A few minutes later he handed Sandra the duffel bag she wanted.

Sandra looked inside. "You're short. Where's the rest of the junk?"

Jose suddenly became ignorant of the English language. "Que?"

"The sixth kilo," she said. "Where's the rest of the fucking heroin?"

"I don't know. This all they give me."

Bewildered, Sandra stared at Jose, then at the contents of the bag. If they were only going to send five kilos, they would have told her. It had always been six. Why were there only five? Her mind began to short circuit. Was Jose fucking them over? She would get a thousand dollars less for making this trip. What would Eddie say? Would he blame her? Realizing she was on the verge of losing control, Sandra slowed down and regrouped. Obviously this damn wetback wouldn't tell her anything. She would have to make the trip with a short load. If Jose had cheated them, Eddie would deal with it. Without saying another word, Sandra closed the duffel bag, placed it in her trunk and headed to the usual dumpster.

Mark and Charlie watched the exchange and listened to the conversation, while keeping the others informed. All were smiling as they followed her away.

Sandra stopped and the agents watched her take something out of the trunk.

Mark keyed his radio. "Take her down!"

While moving the kilos from the duffel bag to a suitcase, Sandra heard the screeching of tires. Looking up, she knew what had happened to the sixth kilo.

CHAPTER 22

Jake arrived at the office, poured a cup of fresh coffee and sat down at his desk to ponder his strategy for the day. His phone rang.

"Jake, Mark Teneras. How the hell are you? It's been a long time."

"Hey, Mark. You still in San Diego?"

"Yeah. You still freezing your ass off up there in the forbidden wilderness?"

"Hey, Minnesota is one of our country's best kept secrets."

"I'm glad *somebody* likes it there. Maybe they'll let me stay *here*."

Jake and Mark had worked together years earlier in San Diego. Before getting down to business, they caught up on each other's lives.

Finally Jake asked, "So what's up?"

"I've got something for you that looks good," Mark said with relish. He told Jake about the Sandra Walton bust. "At first she wouldn't give us the time of day. We laid down some heavy talk, put her in jail, and the court appointed a lawyer. I spent yesterday afternoon with Sandra and her attorney. Our case against this girl is solid. The attorney could see that. He worked on her for a while . . . finally got her to come over to our side. You ever heard of a guy named Eddie Pellegrino?"

Jake's eyes lit up. After a long pause he answered slowly, "We've been working a major heroin investigation for a while. It seems the big man is a guy named Eddie, but we haven't identified him. The 'Eddie' we're looking for is hooked up with a guy named Dominique."

"Walton mentioned Dominique along with Eddie. I bet these are your targets," Mark said exuberantly. "Sandra brings the dope to Minneapolis on a bus. From there she takes a cab to the Medallion Suites hotel in Bloomington. Does that sound right?"

"There's a hotel in Bloomington by that name," Jake told him.

"Okay. So far it looks like she's being straight," Mark continued. He told Jake about Sandra's routine. "She really likes this Eddie. Didn't want to do him."

Jake digested this for a moment and then said, "Where can we take this, Mark?"

"That's why I'm calling you so early in the day. The time element is critical. I've made arrangements to bring Walton to Minneapolis with the heroin, assuming you want to run with it. If you do, all we have to do is get there in time.

"Normally, she would arrive at the hotel this afternoon. If Sandra doesn't show up on schedule, Eddie will know something's wrong. We can be there this afternoon, then it's your baby. Set things up at the hotel, and when Pellegrino comes to her room to pick up the load you can take him down. It should work."

"This might be the break we need. Let's do it."

"See you in a few hours, Jake."

Jake sat for a few minutes, letting his mind process the information and toy with the possibilities. Then he walked over to Travis' desk.

"What's going on, partner?" Travis asked. Jake filled him in. Travis liked it.

The next step was lining up additional help. Jake called the Bloomington PD and spoke with Lieutenant Moffett. They discussed the plan and arranged to meet later at the Medallion Suites.

Eddie Pellegrino wasn't in a good frame of mind when his flight finally touched down in the Twin Cities. He had been guilty of poor judgment. After Dominique informed him he would be returning to Minneapolis alone, Eddie delayed making flight reservations. That cost him a full day because when he finally called the airlines, the flights were full. Sandra would arrive in Minneapolis that afternoon, and Eddie should already have been in place. With caution his top priority, Eddie always allowed enough time to make sure of everything. He had lost that edge.

He walked quickly to the crowded baggage claim area and waited impatiently for his luggage. Once his suitcases appeared, he hustled over to the parking ramp and located his Corvette. Taking his cell phone off its cradle, he dialed ER's pager.

ER immediately called back. "Eddie?"

"Yeah."

"ER. Where you at?"

"I'm at the airport. Got held up. Things under control?"

"Yeah. Her room is waiting. I took care of our room too. I'm here right now. I got all the stuff we need. She beeped you yet?" ER asked.

"No. It's late so I'm not going to stop by my place. I'll come straight over and wait for her page. What room we got?"

"Four eleven."

"See you in twenty minutes."

"Okay."

Their hotel was a mile down the strip from the Medallion Suites. When the shipment arrived, Eddie always brought the heroin there. Eddie and ER would cut it once, turning the six kilos of pure heroin into twelve. Its value was roughly two and a half million dollars. A portion of that would find its way back to South America. The profit margin for smugglers was several times that of the distributors, because the risks associated with getting the dope out of one country and into another were much higher. Eddie and Dominique split the profits fifty-fifty. ER's payment had been a half pound, which he would cut a couple times and sell for about a hundred grand. This time around, due to the deaths of

Black Jack Mike and Frenchy Deveroux, ER would get an additional pound to unload. He would pay for that as soon as he got the money.

ER could scarcely contain his elation over Frenchy Deveroux's death. It meant more money for him. "As soon as you develop the customers to handle the load, you'll be working at the same level as Frenchy," Eddie had told him. Yeah, Fergie turning snitch presented problems, but they had been resolved, Dave O'Neal had proven himself, and Eddie had been kept in the dark. ER's confidence in his organization was firm once again. He also felt confident in what his future had in store.

Eddie felt much the same. After they weighed and packaged the heroin, Eddie would page Big Al, who would send Tanya to the cities to get his share. Eddie and ER wouldn't leave the hotel until the heroin had been distributed. Then, Eddie would just sit back and count the money. He liked the way his life was laid out.

For Sandra Walton, the decision to ruin Eddie's life had not come easily. Her attorney had been the deciding factor. Like the agents, the attorney could be very persuasive. But in contrast to the narcs, the attorney's concern dealt with Sandra's welfare, not putting dopers in jail. Sandra told the attorney she loved Eddie. Her attorney had a different view.

"Sandra, you don't owe this guy anything," the attorney told her. "He placed you into harm's way. You mean nothing to him, other than a way to get his dope from here to there. And you can bet your ass if Eddie were faced with the same choices, he would turn on you in a cyber-second. This is a major heroin trafficking ring, and the Feds are going to attack it aggressively. They're offering you a chance to start your life over. You had better take them up on their offer. Otherwise, my guess is you'll be spending the next ten to fifteen years in prison. Do you know how many minutes there are in fifteen years? That's how many times you'll be kicking yourself in the ass if you don't take my advice."

The following morning she boarded the plane with the two agents. Jake and Travis were in Minneapolis waiting for them. Travis studied Sandra as they greeted the trio. With her straight hair, God awful glasses and baggy clothes, she was as plain as unbuttered toast. Mark had earlier told Jake whenever Sandra and Eddie met at the hotel, sex always came before drugs. Travis' curiosity grew. This woman had the sex appeal of a soggy muffin. Eddie, undoubtedly a multi-millionaire, should have no problem finding a gorgeous sex pot. So why her? This little puzzle was just one of the countless nuances that made the job so interesting for Travis. Certain he would figure it out at some point, he tucked the thought away for another time.

After making introductions they drove to the Hotel, talking strategy. Sandra was squeezed between Mark and his partner in the back seat. Jake occasionally glanced at Sandra in the rear view mirror as he spoke.

"Sandra, you'll stay in your room at all times. We'll bring you your meals. Don't ever forget you're in custody. The fact you're in a hotel room instead of a jail cell doesn't change that. You're on the third floor, so don't think about jumping. And if Eddie calls and you get a sudden change of heart, you better think it over. Warn him and it'll mean one more charge against you."

Sandra nodded. "Don't worry. We got an agreement. I ain't gonna fuck myself like that."

Jake checked her out in the mirror again. Her face looked pretty somber. He was confident he had gotten through. "Good. Your room will be bugged, so when Eddie meets with you we'll be listening and recording every sound."

Sandra's lips spread apart, exposing a pearly set of teeth. "You guys'll have an interesting time. You know the first thing Eddie wants when he gets to the room is a good fuck. All you're going to hear for the first hour is fuckin' an' suckin'." She laughed while the agents tried to stifle their chuckles.

Travis turned around for a quick glimpse of Sandra's face. *Maybe she does tantalizing things with her lips.* Fighting the urge to take yet another look at her mouth, he faced forward and fixed his eyes on the freeway.

"Okay, I hear ya," Jake said. He paused for a few seconds, then said, "Look, none of us gives a rat's ass about your sex life." *Except for Travis*, he guessed. "But when Eddie looks at the product we want to hear some conversation. That should be easy because you'll only have five kilos and Eddie is expecting six. Put all the heat on Jose. Tell Eddie how pissed off you were. Try to get him to talk about what he intends to do about it." Jake let that soak in, then moved on. "You think Eddie will open the other five packages and inspect the junk when he finds out he's been shorted?"

"He never has in the past. You can tell right away if the packages have been fucked with. But I don't know for sure. I mean, this has never happened before."

Jake nodded. "Okay, here's the game plan. If Eddie doesn't open the packages but just takes them and walks, we'll take him down in the hallway. If he starts opening them to inspect the junk, we're going to come through the door. I don't want him panicking and throwing powder all over the room. If we come in, it's going to be fast and loud so be prepared and stay out of our way."

Creases formed on Sandra's brow, her face totally serious. "I understand. Listen, if you want this to look realistic, I've got to clean up and change into something else when I get to my room. Eddie's expecting to see me looking sexy, not like this. You guys are gonna be seeing tits."

Jake stole a quick glance towards Travis, who was grinning, then said, "Whatever you gotta do, Sandra."

They arrived at the hotel and Sandra checked in. They got on the elevator and went to her floor. Sandra had her room to herself for a while so she could clean up. Mark Teneras and his partner took over the adjoining room, with the common door wide open, while Jake and Travis went to the room directly across the hall and met with the other agents and the detectives from Bloomington.

Jake briefed everybody on the plan and passed out photographs of Eddie Pellegrino. One was a mug shot, the other his driver's license photo. "Kiel, Ken and Lisa will be in the parking lot with an eye out for Eddie. Motor Vehicles tells us he drives a red Corvette. Should be easy to spot." Jake looked over at Lieutenant Moffett. "I'd like one of your people to be in the lobby at all times. If Eddie comes into the hotel with a few extra guns, we'll need a heads up. I'll be in the adjoining room with Travis. Mark and Charlie will keep a close eye on Sandra and the dope because they've got official custody. The rest of you will be here."

Moffett assigned two of his detectives to cover the hotel lobby. They'd stay there two hours on, two off. Anybody going up to a room had to pass through the lobby. The couch at one end of the expansive lobby made a good surveillance site.

Occasionally, everybody has a bad day. Shannon Kubicek was having a bad month. Six months earlier she became engaged to a stockbroker with a promising future. Shortly after their engagement they rented a large, stately house overlooking Lake Harriet in south Minneapolis.

But one evening her fiancée, busy entertaining a client, had a few too many drinks. On his drive home he ran a stop sign. The truck that killed him had the right of way. At that point Shannon's life started to unravel.

For days after the funeral Shannon couldn't sleep. One night she gave up trying and decided to go for a stroll around the lake. It would give her a chance to collect her thoughts, and maybe help her snap out of this damned funk. The bright moon, nearly full, reflected off the water which doubled its illumination. It gave Shannon sufficient light to find her way. Arriving at the paved walkway she began her hike. With heavy thoughts and slumped shoulders, she looked down at her feet. Her depression seemed irrepressible as she walked down the path.

At times, the walkway paralleled the road encircling the lake. Engrossed with her pain, Shannon paid little attention to the two vans slowly driving past. But a few minutes later, when a van drove by from the opposite direction, it caught her eye. She thought it strange seeing vehicles at this hour. Hearing two car doors close, she became uneasy. The noise came from the direction of the last van.

Tanya, Frankie, and Fernando rode in two separate vans cruising around Lake Harriet. The radiance of the moon lent a sense of urgency to their mission. Normally, by this time in the lunar cycle their lamb would be safely tucked away in a steel cage, awaiting her fate.

The moon's brightness plus a park light allowed the predators to spot their prize: A woman all alone. Tanya and Frankie drove down the road, with Fernando following, in the same direction Shannon walked. When they were a safe distance ahead, Tanya stopped the van and Fernando pulled alongside to hear her plan.

"Me and Frankie will double back," Tanya said almost in a whisper. "We'll get out on foot. You wait for her here. If she gets away from us, you take her. Make sure she doesn't scream."

"She won't do no screaming."

Tanya and Frankie turned around and drove to the last place they saw Shannon. Fernando watched them drive off, wondering where to position himself.

A couple hundred yards down the street Tanya and Frankie spotted their lamb still walking along the pathway. Tanya's body quivered with excitement. She considered the thrill of the hunt as electrifying as the full moon ceremonies. They drove another hundred yards, then parked and quietly ambled towards their prey.

By now Shannon had picked up her pace.

After a couple minutes, Tanya and Frankie still couldn't see her.

"Let's hustle," Tanya whispered. "She's up there somewhere."

Their heavy steps clashed against the stillness of the night.

Thud . . . thud . . . thud . . . thud

Shortly, they spotted Shannon's silhouette in the moonlight.

Shannon heard footsteps and turned around. To her horror, she saw two people closing in, about twenty yards back. She sped away like a spooked rabbit.

Tanya also felt alarmed. Their prey might escape. Seeing the woman bolt, they broke into a dead run with Tanya out front.

Frankie felt no enthusiasm for this venture. He had developed serious misgivings about the ritual they went through nearly every month. He remembered his buddy, Charlie, lying on the floor of the barn bleeding to death during the last ritual. All the clan members kicked him, adding to the condemned man's misery. Charlie had been their friend, but Big Al had ordered it done and it was so. That incident placed a tremendous weight on Frankie's conscience. Caught up in the moment, under the controlling effects of the drugs, he had kicked his dying friend just as the others did, while denouncing him as a traitor. Why? The question obsessed him. Since Charlie's death, Frankie knew if Big Al wanted it to happen, the same fate could await any of them. Big Al was an evil person.

And ditto with Tanya. You never knew what to expect from that psycho. At times she might be strung tighter than a hangman's noose, or as frenzied as a phone booth full of cats and dogs. A short time later she might be as tempered as someone's pet rock. Like at the house in Fargo. There she was, within a hair of using a broken beer bottle to convert Charlie's throat into a mess of mottled hamburger. Then a couple minutes later she became Miss Congeniality, taking him upstairs and fucking his eyeballs out.

Frankie had to admit he was in awe of the woman. She could move as quickly as a rattlesnake, and her strength probably equaled that of a Rottweiler. And man, could she handle a blade! In a nutshell, as wacko as she was, she was damn efficient. The mystery he couldn't sort out was Tanya's relationship with Big Al. She was his puppet. Why did Tanya allow herself to be so dominated?

Big Al and Tanya were a fearsome combination. Frankie figured he was little more than a prisoner, not much different from those people in the cellar of death. He wanted out, but how? Until he came up with an idea, he had to survive by doing as he was told. Right now that meant helping Tanya chase down another victim. Frankie hoped the woman would disappear into the darkness.

Shannon pulled further and further away. Tanya and Frankie were running out of steam.

"We'll stay on her," Tanya said. "She'll run right into Fernando."

Fernando, a dark tan Hispanic, had a tall, stocky frame with broad shoulders, made to order to support his role as an enforcer. Anybody seeing him would never forget his pock-marked face with its cold black eyes and coal black hair. Tanya didn't like him, but always made him her first choice for a tough assignment. Unlike the others, he didn't fear Tanya. He feared Big Al.

He left his van and walked to the paved trail, selecting a thick tree near the path. As good a place as any, he'd hide behind the tree and wait. Minutes later, hearing heavy footsteps and forced breathing, Fernando grinned savagely, exposing a mouthful of very bad teeth.

Scanning the path, he saw a silhouette approaching at a dead run. Timing it perfectly, Fernando sprang out just as Shannon arrived. She didn't have time to swerve. Fernando's fist struck her squarely in the face and she dropped like a brick.

Tanya and Frankie arrived twenty seconds later.

"You didn't kill her did you?"

Fernando detected a threat in Tanya's voice but it didn't rattle him. "Nah."

Kneeling down, Tanya leaned close to the girl's mouth. She heard a moan.

"Yeah, she's okay. Good job."

They placed Shannon on the van's bench seat.

"To the farm," Tanya ordered.

CHAPTER 23

Eddie joined ER and they waited. About three hours later Eddie's pager vibrated. He checked the number. 30303. Sandra had arrived.

He looked at ER and smiled. "It's her. Everything's cool. Time to go to work."

Picking up the phone Eddie dialed one of the cleaning maids, his primary contact in the Hotel. Beaumont Lenihan seemed sharp enough, but Eddie felt the fewer people he called the better. So he had Shirley contact Beaumont.

Fifteen minutes later she returned Eddie's call. "This is Shirley," she said curtly. "Something's wrong here. Your girl is in the room, but we got instructions from the manager not to disturb two other rooms on the same floor. One of the rooms is next to hers, and the other is directly across the hall. I called your man downstairs. He told me he saw some lieutenant with the Bloomington police come in earlier with a few other guys. They met with the manager. He knows the Lieutenant. Comes to the hotel occasionally on police business. They left one guy sitting in the lobby reading a newspaper, and the rest of the group went upstairs. Your man thinks they're all cops. This whole thing stinks."

Eddie turned white and hung up the phone. He looked at ER, who was sitting on the bed watching the tube, and said, "I think we're fucked. Sandra is in her room, but the hotel is crawling with cops. They got rooms on the same floor."

"Damn. For real?"

"Yeah. I got two people in the hotel, and both got strong indications."

Eddie rubbed his eyes. "My first guess: they took Sandra down and she turned. Now they're waiting for me to pick up the dope. Another possibility: they haven't arrested her, but somehow got onto her and are watching her real close. I have to think about this. Until I sort it out, I'm not taking any chances. I want you to gather up this stuff. Get the hell out of here and wait for my call. I'll get you on your pager."

For Jake and his team the wait began when Sandra walked into the adjoining room looking like a lingerie ad. The thick glasses were gone, her glistening hair looked healthy and full, and (Sandra had been truthful) her full breasts with their wide nipples were quite visible through a sheer night gown that ended well above her knees. Travis looked her over and couldn't disguise his astonishment. Eddie's questionable taste in women had been vindicated. He forced his eyes away and looked toward Jake.

Jake caught himself staring. "Okay. Hit his pager, Sandra."

She beeped Eddie and they waited. Mark and his partner stayed with Sandra, while Jake and Travis remained next door. Eddie often didn't arrive until the latter part of the following day, but they couldn't count on that. He might come knocking within minutes and they had to be ready.

With all the tech equipment in place, and the suitcase full of heroin under Mark's watchful eye, Jake sat back on the bed, resting against the headboard. Travis parked himself on a nearby chair.

"Mark had to jump through a bunch of hoops to take Sandra and the dope into another jurisdiction," Jake said quietly. "He and I go way back, so he was willing to stick his neck out for me. What we're doing is out of the norm."

Travis nodded. "You used to work with him in San Diego?"

"Yeah. I was his senior partner. I broke him in."

"Think it'll work?"

"You never know. It seems like the odds have been stacked against us every turn. Sooner or later things have got to shift in our favor."

Travis nodded. "You know, this thing could go down any number of ways. Eddie might change his MO for some reason and show up with a crowd. Or he might smell a rat when he meets Sandra, and blow her away."

Jake shrugged. "I suppose. Or maybe rip-offs get wind there's six kilos of junk sitting in that room and hit the place ready to rock and roll. We can't discount anything Bud, but I'll tell you what. Eddie shows up here, he's either going to jail or the morgue. And if anybody other than us walks out of here with that dope, it'll be over my dead body."

Travis glanced towards the open common door, hoping that Sandra couldn't hear them. "You ever shoot anybody?"

"No, and I hope I never have to. But if it comes to that, I'm ready."

Saying that, Jake adjusted his shoulder holster so it wouldn't dig into his ribs. The damn thing always worked itself into an uncomfortable position whenever he sat down for any length of time. He needed a different rig.

Something else dug at him: Melanie. Nothing had changed, still unconscious, still plugged into life support. He shuddered and fought back the thought that he shouldn't be here. He should be at the hospital, manning the vigil. He felt his eyes mist, and struggled to push that part of his life back into its corner. This surveillance demanded he remain focused and alert. Hard to do for an extended period of time, but he knew they wouldn't be holed up in this room for more than a couple days.

Eddie studied his watch and fretted over his situation. Many hours had passed since his pager sounded. By now he should have picked up the packages and Sandra should be back in California. He contacted Shirley several times during the day. Things looked bad. Beaumont told Shirley people were occupying that couch in shifts. He had quizzed the manager, who told him to ignore it.

By late evening of the second day Sandra's nerves started to unravel. Eddie should have been there. Mark asked Jake to join them. Sandra needed to talk.

In a troubled voice, she said, "He still hasn't come. What should I do?"

"What would you normally do under these circumstances," Jake asked earnestly.

"Well, I guess if this was a regular trip and he hadn't shown up yet, I'd hit him on his pager again."

Jake looked at his watch. It was eleven o'clock. "Okay. Go ahead and page him. If he calls you, or if he shows up and asks why you called him twice, you can just tell him the obvious. You weren't sure if he got your first page."

Sandra called Eddie's pager again, leaving the same coded message of 30303.

At eleven o'clock Eddie saw Sandra's coded message light up his pager a second time. 30303. That meant, "Everything's okay. Let's do it." Sandra had never paged twice. Damn! Two and a half million riding on this. With so much at stake, he couldn't afford to draw the wrong conclusion and forfeit all that dope. The Colombian had held up his end. He would expect payment regardless.

But the latest information from Beaumont seemed damn conclusive. Undoubtedly, cops were in that hotel. It had to be his mule. The more he thought about it, the more convinced he became. Sandra flipped, and the narcs were onto him. Probably knew his name, where he lived. That he had done time. Maybe they had his mug shot floating around in the hotel. But they didn't have him! Even if they had the dope, and Sandra's mouth had been running like a finely tuned Swiss watch, he should still be okay as long as they didn't catch him in this trap.

At three in the morning he made his decision. Abandon Sandra and the heroin. One hell of a setback, but he'd make up the money. When the heat died down, he and Dominique would pick up the pieces. But where could he go now? He had to get away from this claustrophobic room and find a place to calm down and think.

Eddie pulled out his wallet and counted the bills. Just under a thousand bucks. He couldn't live on that very long, yet he didn't dare go home. For sure they had his house under surveillance. And he didn't dare call his old lady. The Feds undoubtedly had a tap on his phone. No any contact with the home front would be fatal. With Sandra and the dope in town, that might be all the Feds needed to raid his place.

Wouldn't they love to get their paws on his mountain of money! Use a credit card? Nope. Too easily traced.

It slowly dawned on him he had only one place to go. The farm. Al would be pissed off, but damn it this was an emergency. Eddie recalled when they first started doing business. He and Dominique ranked above Al in the pecking order. They were his source of supply and held the key to his business. Al respected that, but at the same time he made it clear his business was his domain. The man had an iron clad personality and wouldn't tolerate anybody who tried to meddle. For sure, if he went to Al's place unannounced it would have to be with hat in hand. But if Al slammed the door in Eddie's face, the man would have to find another source. When Dominique returned, they could find other outlets.

By midnight Eddie still hadn't responded. Jake instructed Sandra to get some sleep. Leaving the common door open, the agents went into the adjoining room.

By now the narcs were starting to feel the sharp jabs of frustration that always accompany deals gone awry. Eddie was a no show. They did have six kilos of heroin taken off the street. But considering the prize that slipped away, they didn't feel much comfort there.

With a voice filled with disappointment, Mark said, "I'm calling the airlines. If Eddie shows up we'll just miss the flight." After completing his call he said to Jake, "Our flight leaves at eight-thirty. If this thing doesn't go, I'd be anxious to learn what went wrong. I've got to know how to deal with Sandra. It's possible she withheld information. If she sabotaged our plan, she's fucked."

The next morning they were confronted by the obvious. The deal was dead. Jake and Travis took Mark, his partner, and Sandra to the airport for their flight back to the coast.

Checking out of the hotel, Eddie drove four hours north to Fargo. He got off the freeway and headed through the city to a truck stop. He ate a big breakfast, unsuccessfully tried to read a newspaper, then went to the farm, arriving at ten o'clock. Parking in front of the house, he knocked on the door.

The sight of Eddie at the door brought Big Al a load of instant heartburn. Eddie most certainly should have hit Al's pager, not show up at his door. An unannounced visit could only mean bad news. Al gave Eddie a hard stare.

"What's this about, Eddie? Why would you come here without calling first?"

They went to Al's office. Al sat down at his desk and motioned for Eddie to take a seat. He didn't offer Eddie a drink.

Eddie gathered his composure. "Al, we've got problems. It appears the DEA is onto our main mule. She's sitting on six kilos of junk in a hotel room, and narcs are all over the place waiting for me to show up. I can't go home. All my money's stashed and I can't get to it. I need a place to stay for a couple weeks 'til everything cools down. I couldn't think of any other place."

Al's anger surged. Eddie should have been smarter. Okay, so the narcs were on to him. That happens to nearly everyone in the drug business at one time or another. Occasionally a person gets caught. Selling dope is a gamble.

But if Eddie felt major heat, why the hell did he come to the farm? This farm was Al's sanctuary. Now he had heat. Al sat in his chair, speechless, wondering how to handle this calamity. Finally he looked closely into Eddie's eyes. "So, how do you know you weren't followed?"

"Look Al, I've been down in South America for the past couple weeks with Dominique. We flew down there in his Lear. My car's been at the airport all that time. As soon as I got back, I drove directly to a hotel. Didn't go home. When I left the hotel, I came straight here. They had no way of finding me. They couldn't follow me if they didn't know where I was. I checked my mirror all the way up here. Nothing. I'm telling you, I didn't bring no heat."

Al's lower lip quivered as he made every effort to contain himself. "Do you think it's a safe assumption the cops know what you're driving?"

"Who the fuck knows?"

Al made his decisions and smiled for the first time since Eddie arrived. Number one, Eddie would die. Number two, the money had to be moved. And number three, Al would temporarily shut down his operation. He needed to know if they were watching him. And when he resumed, he'd find another source. But that might not be too difficult. In a few months he would meet with Dominique and explain everything. Dominique, an astute businessman, would be appalled at Eddie's indiscretion and sympathetic to Al's decision. Friendship had nothing to do with it. This was business.

"Okay," he finally said. "I'm not happy you came here with the DEA on your ass, but we've known each other for a long time. That's good for something."

Eddie felt a surge of relief. "It sure is."

"You can stay here for as long as you think necessary. Two weeks, three weeks, whatever. But under one condition: You have to stay in the house. You can't go out for any reason. I don't want you seen. Do you agree to that?"

Eddie nodded. "That's fine with me, Al. Whatever you say. In the future, if there's ever anything I can do for you, just ask. I've got some powerful contacts."

"I'll keep that in mind, Eddie. I'm going to get one of my people to help you get comfortable. He'll bring a spare bed and furniture from one of the trailers, and you can set up housekeeping in my basement. There's a bathroom and a shower down there. I'll try to make you as comfortable as I can."

Al picked up his phone and dialed Fernando's pager. At the beep he punched his special code of 00001. Come immediately.

Five minutes later Fernando walked in, the picture of humility. "You called for me, Big Al?"

"Yes. This is Mister Eddie Pellegrino. He is going to be staying with us for a while. Take him to the basement and help him get comfortable. Later this afternoon bring in some of our spare bedroom furniture. Stay with him and get him whatever he needs."

"Yes sir," Fernando replied.

Fernando motioned for Eddie to follow him, and they walked down to the basement. As soon as they left, Al dialed Tanya's pager.

CHAPTER 24

It was 9:30 AM when Jake and Travis arrived at the office. They met with Harold to brief him on the fizzled deal. When they finished, Harold looked concerned.

"You guys look awful. Go home and sleep. We'll go over this whole thing again tomorrow. I'd say Pellegrino's security did us in. He's not going to abandon six kilos of pure heroin without knowing it's really lost. We'll talk about it after you guys get some rest."

Exhausted, Jake and Travis did a quick exit and headed for home. For Travis, home was now Kiel's house. Shortly after Kiel's wife and daughter moved to Florida with Scott, Travis gratefully accepted Kiel's invitation.

Jake got home at eleven. Melissa was preparing to go to the hospital. Jake held her briefly before collapsing into bed. At four o'clock the phone rang.

"Um, yeah," Jake muttered.

"Jake, this is Harold. Are you awake?"

"Uh, I don't know. Who is this?"

"Jake, wake up. This is Harold."

"Harold? Sorry. I was sleeping really hard. What's up?"

"Jake, I just got a call from Aris Kosteckle in Fargo. He needs to talk to you. ASAP. It sounds like this might involve Eddie Pellegrino. Have a cup of coffee, then call Aris at his office. He's waiting. Have you got that, Jake?"

Harold's words jolted Jake out of his semi-slumber. *Eddie! What the hell is he up to?* "Yeah, Harold. I'll call him right now."

A minute later Aris and Jake were on the line.

"Jake, I just talked to Harold. We might be onto something pretty interesting."

"I'm listening."

"Okay. Here's the background. There was this burglary duo operating up here. Donnie and Lonnie Dissel. Identical twins. Both junkies. Recently they got in over their heads during a burglary, and Lonnie got shot by a farmer. He went to the morgue and Donnie went to jail. A short time later an attorney, S. Lee Vondermolte, tried to post Donnie's bond. Vondermolte is not Donnie's attorney. Do you remember S. Lee Vondermolte?"

"Yeah, sure," Jake answered. "He's the attorney renting that apartment in Detroit Lakes. The tracer we did on the incoming calls for that apartment linked it to a house in Fargo, and it turned out Vondermolte owns that place too."

"Exactly. Now, I'll take you a step further. I got the telephone tolls for the house in Fargo and did a tracer on its incoming calls. I connected the house with a farm outside of Kindred. Turns out Vondermolte also owns the farm."

"This is getting real interesting, Aris. What's the connection between Donnie Dissel and Vondermolte?"

"Yesterday I had a long talk with Donnie at the jail. The Dissel twins got their junk from a hard core bitch named Tanya. Whenever they scored from her, it was out of that house in Fargo. That's where Tanya and her thugs hang out. He believes Vondermolte is a crooked attorney hooked in with Tanya's organization. The court had set Donnie's bond at fifty grand. No way does he have that kind of money. The only people he knows who do are Tanya and her bunch. Donnie spooked when the jailer tried to release him. He's certain they're trying to get him out of jail so they can kill him before he talks. Donnie told me Tanya and her crowd are big time. He's real scared of her. Said she's a psycho."

"Did Eddie's name come up?"

"Not from Donnie. But it looks like he may have just entered the mix. After I talked to Dissel I decided to look at the farm. Drove past it and couldn't see a damn thing. There's a thick grove of trees between the buildings and the road. One of the Fargo narcs is a pilot, and I asked him to fly me over the place. We went up early this afternoon. Saw a nice looking house, a big barn, and two double wide trailers. I counted eleven vehicles parked in the yard. And get this. There was a burgundy Corvette sitting next to the house! When I told Harold, he almost choked. Said you'd just tried to set up a heroin dealer who drives a red 'Vette, but the guy's in the wind. This has got to be Eddie, Jake. He's at this farm right now."

There was a long pause while Jake wondered if he was still asleep and just dreaming. "My God, Aris . . . a burgundy 'Vette. It can't be a coincidence."

"Yeah, that's what I thought. I want to go up again tomorrow to take a good look at it. Can you meet me here in the morning?" Aris asked.

"Sure. Travis and I'll be there first thing. I'll bring our digital recorder. Maybe we'll be able to focus in on the license plate of the 'Vette."

"See you in the morning. Now go back to sleep."

Big Al and Tanya had discussed the same series of events.

"We've got problems, Tanya," he told her. He then brought her up to date on Eddie's situation. But he had some good news. "Starting now, I'm making you my partner. Don't let me down. You're going to learn all my secrets. I've got a safe house in Fargo you don't know about. After we get Eddie caged, you and I will go there. I've decided to hide the money in that house, but we have to do some remodeling. You feel like doing some carpentry work?"

Al's words nearly brought Tanya to a state of orgasm. He would make her his partner! He trusted her! She concealed her glee. "I'm ready for anything."

"Go to the cellar and get the collar. We'll take care of Pellegrino."

Tanya returned shortly, and they went to the basement. Eddie sat on a couch. Fernando, loitering near the small gym, looked up as Tanya and Al came into the room. Seeing the collar, with its long attached chains, he knew Al's intentions. He crossed the room and joined them.

Eddie looked surprised. "What's going on, Al?"

"Eddie, you said if there was anything you could do for me, just ask."

Eddie looked at Al intently. "That's right, Al. Whatever you need."

"Good. I want you to put this collar around your neck."

Eddie edged towards the stairway. "What's this about?"

Fernando and Tanya moved in to block his escape. Eddie rushed directly at Fernando, hitting him squarely. The impact knocked Fernando down, but also slowed Eddie's momentum. He started to run again but Tanya tossed the chains at his legs. Eddie tripped and fell hard to the floor. Al and Fernando held him as Tanya latched the collar on his neck. She grabbed one of the chains, Al snatched the other.

Eddie got up slowly. "Okay, Al. Just what do you want?"

Al gave him a cold look. "I've decided to move you to different accommodations. Please follow me."

"Do I have a fucking choice?"

"No."

They pulled him to the barn and down the steps below the trap door. In the cellar Eddie saw two cages in the middle of a dirt floor. Shannon sat, shivering, in one of them. Eddie shuddered and broke out into a cold sweat.

"Al, you fucking piece of snake shit, nobody fucks with me like this. Get me the fuck out of here or you'll pay big time. That's a promise."

Ignoring Eddie's plea, Al opened the door of the vacant cage and motioned him inside. Eddie didn't move. Tanya kicked him hard, shoved him into the cage and latched the door.

Al said, "Eddie, you did the unforgivable. You jeopardized my entire operation. I will not tolerate this stupidity. Sleep well tonight. It will be your last."

Numb, Eddie watched the three leave. Now he and this young woman in the other cage were alone. Ignoring her, he began swearing violently and talking aloud to himself. "I wish the DEA *had* caught me. If I was in jail I'd have a chance. With a team of smart lawyers I could have beat it. Al's right. I *was* stupid."

Shannon listened. "Just who are you and what the hell is going on here?"

Eddie narrowed his eyes in her direction, his contempt all encompassing. "So what did you do to these people?" he asked. "Rip them off? Narc on them?"

Shannon became indignant. "You're a drug dealer, aren't you? You screwed up and so they're going to kill you. Well, I'm not some low-life. I didn't do anything wrong. I shouldn't be here."

"So why are you here? Who the hell are you?"

"I'm Shannon. I was walking in the park last night and these monsters kidnapped me. That guy, Al, told Tanya I look like her mother when she was young. Tanya went bonkers. She's crazy. She told me they're Satan worshippers, and every month at the full moon they sacrifice a human. Said Satan himself does it. I'm the next guest of honor. You're tied in with these animals?"

Shannon had pushed the right button. Her words tore through Eddie's guts as he realized his suspicions were on the mark. A cult *was* at work here, doing all the wicked, nightmarish absurdities that cults do. And Al called the shots. Even worse, Eddie was a part of it. Not directly maybe, but a knot on the same rope. Eddie's mind churned and his stomach heaved. He grabbed the bucket. The stench got to Shannon. She covered her nose. Embarrassed, Eddie watched her as he wiped the sweat off his forehead, trying to regain his composure.

Ignoring the dark bruise under her eye, he felt captivated by his cellar-mate's face, which had the smooth appearance of a twenty year old. With her long dark hair, she reminded him of his sister who had died a grisly death while he watched. He hadn't been able to save her, but if he could save Shannon then maybe part of that debt would be paid. And maybe he could save himself in the process. The big question: How? There had to be a way.

Driving his Mercedes, Al and Tanya went through Kindred on their way to Fargo. Al surveyed the town. "Such a small town. If these people only knew how much money would be going down their street tomorrow. Knowledge is a powerful thing. With it, a person can do anything."

Tanya felt very uncomfortable. "Do you think the DEA's coming after Eddie?"

Al shrugged. "Well, they didn't catch him with any dope. If they want Eddie, they're going to have to do a lot more than just catch his mule."

His ambiguous reply confused her. "How long before we know?"

He shrugged again. "It's a guessing game, Tanya. They're making a run at him, so we've got to be careful. I'm going to shut down and wait. After a few months, if it's cool, we're back. My problem is not knowing. I can't take any chances."

In the city, they drove to a well-kept, one story house on a large corner lot. He pulled the Mercedes into the driveway and stopped. A tall wooden privacy fence enclosed the large back yard. A steel gate, secured by a padlock, blocked the driveway. He pointed at the padlock and handed Tanya a key. She opened the gate, and closed it after he pulled in. He led her inside the house. In the basement, Al measured a wall. Then he made a phone call.

Eddie's mind worked overtime. He wished he had recognized Al as the psycho he was. As a child, Eddie had been victimized by a cult. Thinking about it, he now saw similarities between Al and the leader of the cult that cremated his sister.

Looking at Shannon's battered face, empathy and guilt immersed him. "Shannon, I'm not innocent. Al is a heroin dealer and I supplied him. Now he's got it in for me. They want to kill both of us, but for different reasons. It's this cult thing that concerns you. I've got some experience with cults."

"I don't understand. You mean you used to be a cult member here?"

"No. Back when I was eleven years old I had an older sister. She was a runaway. Neither of us was happy at home, and she came back for me about a year after she split. It turns out she had joined a satanic cult in North Carolina. The leader of that cult sent her for me. My sister didn't know his intentions. She brought me there, thinking I would become another member.

"They lived somewhere out in the boonies. When I got there they took me in for a couple weeks. Made me feel at home. Then one day they grabbed me and tethered me to a stake. They burned their victims at that stake. I was next. It was mid-afternoon, and the ritual was to take place at midnight.

"My sister was able to free me. 'Eddie,' she said. 'Run and don't look back.' I ran like hell. The cult members saw me and chased me into the woods. I found a hollow log and crawled inside. At one point they were just a few feet away, and I heard them talking about me and my sister. They said if they couldn't find me, they were going to burn her in my place. They searched for me until dark, then gave up. I tried to go back for her, but it was too late. They had her tied up to the stake and the ritual had begun. I watched from the edge of the woods. They piled wood under her feet and burned her alive. After that, I had nightmares for years."

Shannon turned white. "That's terrible."

"Yeah. I wandered through the woods for a couple days, miserable as hell. Then I stumbled upon a road. Some people drove by, picked me up and took me to their place. Turns out they were heroin dealers. I stayed with 'em, and they taught me the business. Started out by making deliveries. Years later the Feds caught up with me and I went to prison. That's where I met Al."

"Is he crazy?"

"He's a man with no conscience."

Shannon nodded. "Do we have any chance at all?"

Eddie shrugged. It sure as hell didn't look good.

Late that evening, Big Al and Tanya returned to the farm. Parking in the garage, a smug smile formed on Al's lips. "We're halfway there, Tanya. In a couple days this place will be clean. The Feds won't find shit."

Early the following morning Aris sat at his desk, mentally chewing his notes, when Jake and Travis arrived. They grabbed some coffee and sat down across from Aris' desk.

"Welcome back to Fargo. How was the drive?"

"Kind of long," Jake answered. "Neither of us got enough sleep to undo the damage of the last couple days. But we're here, raring to go."

"Good. While you're having your coffee we can go over my interview of Donnie Dissel. Sergeant Bauer will meet us at Hector airport in two hours. He'll take us on an airborne tour of the farm. Had one hell of a storm rip through here last night, knocking trees down, raising hell. I wasn't sure we'd be able to go today. It's still a little windy, but Bauer is a great pilot. We won't have any problems. You bring your digital recorder?"

"Yeah."

"Great. When we get back, we'll plug it into our computer. If the Corvette's still there, we might be able to make out its tag. Maybe we'll get lucky and capture some of the farm's residents on video."

Travis swallowed some coffee. "I've got good vibes on this one."

Jake looked at Travis and grinned. "Good. Maybe they'll slant things our way. If it is Eddie Pellegrino at that farm, I'd say there's a good chance that's where we'll find Big Al, whoever that is."

Aris nodded. "Yeah, Big Al is the missing link in all this. We might be closing in on the monster's head."

Jake and Travis started reading the interview notes. Flipping to the third page, Jake stopped and looked up. "Says here every time the twins went to that house to score dope, Tanya was there with these same two guys. Then, a couple months ago, one of the guys was replaced by an Hispanic. Any idea what happened?"

"Nope," Aris answered flatly. "All he knows is the guy dropped out of sight. Said the Hispanic is even scarier than the guy he replaced. Has crazy eyes."

An hour and a half later the three agents drove to the airport where Sergeant Bauer was doing a pre-flight check. He flew a Cessna four-seater with an ivory colored fuselage and bright red wing tips. Aris made the introductions and they climbed in. Aris sat in the co-pilot's seat, with Jake behind Bauer. Soon they were airborne, heading southwest. A moderate wind with frequent strong gusts made for a choppy flight. But the sky shone a magnificent blue, with unlimited visibility.

Within a short time, Sergeant Bauer announced the approaching farm.

Aris pointed to ten o'clock. "That's it. Behind it is the Sheyenne River."

They were a half mile away when a brown van pulled out of the farm's long winding driveway. It turned onto the county road and went east. Everyone saw it.

On a strong hunch, Jake changed the game plan. "Hold on. I'd like to follow that van. Might be an opportunity. The farm will still be here when we come back."

The sergeant maneuvered his craft high behind the van, reducing the plane's speed and keeping to the rear of the vehicle where they probably wouldn't be seen. Twenty minutes later the van entered Fargo's city limits. The agents watched it drive through the city. A few minutes later the van pulled into a driveway.

Aris grinned. "This might get interesting. Here is a house we don't know about. Can you get a fix with your GPS?"

The sergeant punched some buttons on the plane's GPS system. "Got it."

At two thousand feet he began flying in a wide circular pattern as they watched. The plane flew counter clockwise so Jake and his digital recorder had a constant view of the property. Travis leaned over Jake's shoulder, looking out the same window through a pair of binoculars.

Everybody saw a person get out of the van and open a gate. The van drove in. The plane bobbed and weaved through the strong air currents, while its occupants studied the ground.

CHAPTER 25

"Let's get to work," Al said.

He and Tanya got out of the van and began toting cardboard boxes, covered with newspapers, into the house.

"I've counted twelve trips into the house. That's twenty-four boxes so far," Travis said curiously. "And I bet they're not finished."

"What's our altitude," Jake asked.

"We're at two thousand," the sergeant answered.

"I'd like to get a picture of their faces. Can you take it down to a thousand feet and do a single pass? Then we'll head back to the farm."

"Going down," the pilot said.

"Almost through," Al said. He heard the drone of an aircraft flying directly overhead, and looked up at the sky.

Tanya, lifting a heavy box out of the van, ignored the plane. Al grabbed the last of the boxes and they walked towards the back door. Midway, a strong gust of wind blew the newspapers off the boxes, exposing the bundles of money.

"Fuck!" Al exclaimed. "Come on, let's get these inside!"

They carried the boxes down to the basement and stacked them alongside the others against a wall. On one side of the basement a false wall had been nearly completed, with an open space on one end. A section of drywall, cut to fit that spot, stood in the corner next to tools and nails. They stashed the boxes into the gap and nailed down the final piece of dry wall.

The surveillance plane turned on a south-westerly course as the agents resumed their original plans. Minutes later Sergeant Bauer said, "We've got the farm coming up. I'll do a fly by."

Flying over the farm at two thousand feet, Jake recorded everything.

Peering over Jake's shoulder, Travis was elated at what he saw. "There's a dark red Corvette down there, next to the house."

"I think we're up a little too high to get that tag," Jake said. "How about taking another pass at one thousand feet."

The pilot circled and came through again, while Jake focused the recorder.

When they completed their pass Jake set the camera down. "Okay, I got it. Let's head back to the office."

Travis leaned back in his seat. "I saw two people standing next to the barn. I wonder how paranoid they are."

They returned to Hector Airport and twenty minutes later the agents walked into Aris' office. Sergeant Bauer went to locate the house in Fargo and get its address, then rejoined the agents.

Aris interfaced the digital recorder with the computer. The picture, excellent in quality, provided the agents with a classic bird's eye view of the house and yard. They watched intently as the two people in the video carried boxes into the house. Then they saw something they hadn't seen from the plane. Paper had been blown off the boxes by the wind, exposing the contents.

Aris' eyes lit up like campfires in the night. "Hey, this might be good. Maybe we can see what they've got."

Jake enhanced the picture, and the computer screen displayed the contents.

"Damn," Jake said, astonished.

"It's money," Aris said excitedly. "Boxes and boxes of money."

Jake stared into the screen. "We hit a home run."

"They made thirteen trips before we left," Travis told them. "That's at least twenty-six boxes. We're looking at Fargo's version of Fort Knox."

Jake looked up, his eyes scanning the others in the room. "We're going to take action on this. We need to guard that house just in case someone's coming to move the money. The place might be a temporary holding site."

Aris nodded. "I can put two of my guys out there." Then to Sergeant Bauer. "Can we get some help from your department?"

"You bet. I take it you're planning on a search warrant."

"You got it," Jake said crisply. "And I'm hoping to get one for the farm too. If that's Pellegrino's car, getting a warrant shouldn't be a problem. As soon as we analyze these images, we'll know."

Aris manned the computer. "Here's the farm coming into view."

Details on the grounds became clearer as the plane drew closer.

"Okay, you can now see the car."

In a few seconds the image of the sports car took over the screen. Aris directed the computer to focus on its license plate. The computer did its magic, and they had what they wanted. "It's got the right plate. That's Pellegrino's car."

Their jubilation could have been heard well down the hallway of the building, where people might have thought the folks in the DEA office were watching a major sporting event on television. Aris stood up and everybody in the room gave each other high five's as they shouted, "Yesss!!! and Alright!!"

Jake turned to Sergeant Bauer. "I'll get started on the affidavit for the house."

Bauer nodded. "I'll get my people out there."

When Al and Tanya returned to the farm, Fernando and Frankie rushed over to the van. Al noticed their concern. "Is everything okay?"

They shook their heads. "We're not sure," Fernando said. "When you left earlier, a small plane came from the north. It was white with red wing tips. When you turned onto the road, the plane followed you. An hour and a half later the plane returned and flew over the farm. Then it circled around and flew by again, only a lot lower. I think it was cops."

Al pulled Tanya aside, out of hearing range of the others. "That fucking Eddie," he exclaimed. "The plane flying over us in Fargo was white with red wing tips." His face turned pale. "Leave me alone for a while." He stormed into the house.

Going directly to his office, he plopped down in his high backed chair and looked out the window, studying the wooded terrain near the river. He couldn't let himself panic. *Maybe it was just coincidence. Planes were always flying around. Who knew what they were about? Besides, what could someone see from that distance? So they saw us in the back yard of the house. What would that give them?*

He swiveled around and faced his desk, wringing his fingers and cracking his knuckles . . . anything to relieve the stress. *But what if they followed Pellegrino here? They know he drives a Corvette, and they see it here? What would that mean? If they had an arrest warrant for him, they'd be here by now. If they didn't, then they're not going to come here. They've got nothing on me. They don't even know I'm alive. But still, it was the same damn plane flying over the farm and the house. Something is going on. Could they see what we were doing? Is my money safe?*

Al needed answers. Decisions had to be made. But how could he make the right decisions if he couldn't see the whole picture? He didn't dare jump to conclusions based on assumptions.

He decided to go back to the house. If the police were there, he was screwed. If everything was quiet, maybe the cops didn't have jack.

He turned around, again looking out the window. He would have to hustle before it got dark. The moon was full, and they had to deal with the two captives, one way or another. Walking out of the house he saw

Tanya, sitting with Frankie on the grass beneath a thick oak tree. "Keep a close eye," he said tersely. "I'm going back to Fargo."

Al went into the garage, slipped a helmet on and started his motorcycle. Twenty minutes later he turned onto his street in Fargo. His worst nightmare stared him in the face. "Cops! Son of a bitch! They're all over the place."

He rode his bike slowly past the house and studied the scene. Five marked police cars on the street, and two unmarked cars in the driveway. The gate stood open, with a van in the back yard. Several men, wearing black jackets with large, white letters across their back identifying them as DEA, loading boxes into the van. A group of uniformed policemen, carrying shotguns, milling around in front. Al's questions were answered.

His priorities immediately changed. With all his savings now gone, he had to concentrate on saving his skin. That meant taking care of the lamb, Eddie, and the witnesses. The entire clan had to go, with one exception. Tanya. He still needed her. He had to clean up the house so the Feds couldn't pin anything on him. He wondered how he could possibly get all that done in one night.

Al's muscles quivered. His mind raced. He sped back to the farm.

Riding the motorcycle west on I-94, Al formed his plan. Maybe not an ideal plan, but the situation compelled him to improvise on very short notice. To his knowledge, the Feds knew nothing about him. It must stay that way.

Tanya and the clan members were near the trailers when they saw Big Al return. Tanya left the group to meet him. "Are we in trouble?"

He removed his helmet, grim-faced. "Yeah, big time. The DEA took our money. But don't let on. I think we can save ourselves. I have a plan. Let's meet with the others. It'll be dark soon and we have much to do."

Al approached the other clan members. They appeared anxious, and Al surmised each hoped to hear they had nothing to worry about.

"I just returned from Fargo, where I checked with my sources," Al stated in his commanding baritone. "The plane you saw was just some people doing an agricultural survey. Nothing to worry about. But I did learn something that concerns us: Eddie Pellegrino. He is a traitor. He came to betray us."

This brought murmurs of anger and disgust. Tanya remained stone faced.

Al held up his hands. "Furthermore, I just learned Pellegrino had made arrangements to meet and collaborate with someone here. One of you is an informer. As yet I don't know who, but we'll soon find out. The informer must die tonight, along with Pellegrino. The lamb will have to wait until we deal with them."

Fernando looked around. Juleen stood just a few feet away, and he gave her a menacing look. Juleen sat at the top of his list. She always liked Charlie. That rotten traitor got what he deserved, but maybe Juleen wanted some payback. Fernando had tried many times to get close to her. But the bitch always resisted his moves. Very suspicious!

Juleen felt his stare and glared back at him. Has to be Fernando, she thought. He always has that psycho look. Yeah, he'd betray us. I'll watch him real close.

Seeing Juleen staring at him, Fernando began looking over the others. His eyes rested on Frankie. Could be him. Fernando never liked Frankie either. Always had the feeling the little dog turd didn't fit in with the family. Him and Charlie were real tight. Maybe the two of them were plotting before Charlie died. For sure it was either Frankie or Juleen.

Frankie had different thoughts. When referring to Pellegrino as a traitor, Big Al caught Frankie's full attention. Those words were reminiscent of Al's treatment of Charlie, who certainly wasn't a traitor. If Big Al wanted the clan to believe Pellegrino wore the same label, the man had another agenda. Something didn't square. All of a sudden an informer lurked in their midst? Along with a traitor? What the hell is the difference? And that poor girl in the cellar. Big Al intended to kill her too. What a psycho!

Fernando stepped forward.

"Yes, Fernando. What is it," Al asked indifferently.

"Big Al, how can we deal with the informer if we don't know who it is?"

With utmost seriousness, Al looked over his clan. "None of *us* knows. But I assure all of you, *Lucifer* knows. Tanya and I are going into the house to communicate with him. Remain here until Tanya returns. At that time she will show you the path to revenge and justice. The moon will reach its peak of enlightenment at midnight. Its power will illuminate your senses. Then we'll take action."

Al and Tanya went directly to his office. With a grave face and a somber voice, he told her what he saw in Fargo. His story horrified her.

"You and I are going to leave here unscathed," Al said. "But we have to take care of the loose ends. The house is full of records. Everything must be destroyed. This whole thing has to stop here. End of story!"

Tanya studied him. She had never seen him look so worried. "How are we going to do that, Big Al?"

He poured himself a tall tumbler of Scotch. His hand shook as he lifted the glass. He took a huge swallow. Then another. "I'll move our van so it's close to the front door. After midnight we'll move our records and essentials into the van. Then we'll torch the place. I've got ten gallons of gas in the garage. We can't let the Feds find anything to identify us. When we leave here, we'll go to Fargo. You drive the van. I'll drive the Mercedes. We've got to hit Vondermolte. He knows too much, and if the Feds put the squeeze on him he'll spill his guts. We'll dump his body in the Red River. In a couple days he'll be feeding the fish up in Canada."

Tanya glared at the floor. Eddie had ruined everything. She looked up at Al. "How much time you suppose we got?"

"If worse comes to worse and the heat storms in here tonight, you and I can still escape. We'll motor down the tunnel to the woods on my trail bike. Then we're history. We'd be miles away before they started searching by the river. However, that is one contingency plan I don't think we'll have to use. Sure, they got our money. I don't know how they found out about it. Probably just dumb luck. But what else do they have? Even if they somehow identified Pellegrino's car outside, that wouldn't be enough. The Feds need more. But at some point I'm sure they'll hit our farm. We can't be here when it happens."

He took another chug from his drink and refilled the glass. "At eleven-thirty I want you to go out and meet with the clan. This is what you tell them." Al gave her specific instructions on what to say.

He picked up his glass, drained it, then rose from his chair. "Go get your fake ID's. We'll put them in the secret room."

Tanya left and returned a couple minutes later.

"Okay, let's go," Al said.

They crawled into the secret room. He quickly unlocked the door to the tunnel leading towards the river.

"We'll leave everything open in case we have to get out of here fast."

He flipped on a light switch, illuminating a corridor made of concrete blocks. Although its entire length was lit up, Tanya could not see the other end. Parked next to the door was a Honda motorcycle. Two helmets sat on the bike.

Al gestured towards the tunnel. "It comes out about twenty yards from the river. The end is concealed by a fake tree stump, made of fiberglass and plastic but very realistic. Two latches hold it in place. We just release the latches and push it up. Then we follow the river east for a mile, until it comes to a small road where we can ride either north or south, depending on the heat."

They walked over to the gun rack. A knapsack dangled from a hook near the rack. "The emergency money's in there. Put all your identification inside. Mine's already there. We don't want to look for that stuff if we're scrambling."

He pointed to the weapons. "Everybody gets a nine millimeter, some ammo, and a flashlight."

He grabbed two more knapsacks and filled them with hardware. Then he checked his watch. Eleven-fifteen. "Let's get this upstairs. It's almost time."

They carried the knapsacks to his office. Al opened the refrigerator door and retrieved two large zip-lock bags. He counted out a number of joints and mushrooms, put them into a small paper bag and gave them to Tanya.

"Give them the hardware first. Then, each gets one of the joints and two mushrooms, double the usual. Once they've finished the mushrooms, tell them what must be done. Then return here. They'll be psycho after fifteen minutes, and the rest should take care of itself. We'll go out later to check and take care of any survivors. My money says Fernando will be the only one. It'll look like the clan began feuding and shooting each other, with the lone survivor killing Eddie and the lamb, and then dying of his own wounds. The autopsies will reveal they were stoned. You and I will be long gone."

CHAPTER 26

Tanya went outside and joined the clan. The full moon shone brightly, the sky brilliant with the twinkling of countless stars. Juleen held a flashlight while Tanya distributed the dope. Everyone lit up.

The double dose of mushrooms put Frankie on guard. His mounting suspicions caused him to refrain from using the dope. Not this time. Following the example of a prominent politician, he puffed, but didn't inhale.

When they finished with the joints, Tanya directed the group to eat the mushrooms. Frankie palmed his and faked it.

After waiting for the drugs to take effect, she addressed the group.

"Big Al and me have communicated with Satan. Lucifer knows the informer, but he left it up to you to figure it out. He's testing us. You've been watching each other, looking for signs of betrayal. Trust your instincts. In a few minutes it will be midnight, and your trial will begin. The power of the full moon will help you make the right decisions. The informer must be discovered. The informer must die.

"One hour after the informer is killed, Lucifer will rise up from the depths. When he appears, we will know we have rid our clan of the infidel."

Tanya returned to the house.

Frankie watched Tanya walk away, dumbfounded at what she just said. He thought it through. She wants the clan members to kill each other. If they follow her instructions, there'll be mass murder committed here. And with everybody stoned, they can't see through it.

The shooting will begin any minute, and then its everyone for himself. Totally incredible! Frankie quickly devised his own plan.

While the other clan-members warily shined their flashlights on each other, Frankie edged away from the group, towards the barn. Just as he reached the barn door, the first shots rang out.

Al and Tanya heard the shots. Tanya found the cautious smile now on her lover's face to be quite comforting.

"Every gunshot puts us closer to safety," he said. "Let's get to work."

He tucked his Beretta into his belt and they began gathering all the important papers. It was a time consuming task, occasionally punctuated by the sound of gunshots. At every report, they looked at each other with increased satisfaction.

Several hours earlier, Shannon and Eddie had reached the point of despair. Both lay on the floor of their cages and hoped it would soon be over. Neither had been given food since they were locked up, only water, and they suspected the water had been drugged so they drank sparingly. Then they heard the gunfire.

"Gunshots," Eddie said.

"Something is happening out there. I wonder if it means our time is up," Shannon replied slowly. "How do you think they're going to do it. Shoot us, or cut us up?"

"I don't think I want to get into it. We'll find out soon enough."

Then they heard the door. "Someone's coming," Eddie whispered.

The door opened slowly, its rusty hinges an instant giveaway.

Creeeeeek.

Shannon and Eddie watched the door, wide eyed, as a pistol crept into view, then two arms, and finally a man. Shannon recognized him immediately. Frankie, one of the rotten bastards that kidnapped her. He had come for them.

Frankie edged through the door and, looking around, saw he was alone with the two captives. He put his pistol into his belt.

"Let us go, murderer," Shannon yelled.

Her attitude caught him off guard, and Frankie flinched. Obviously they hadn't been drinking their water. "Shut up," he said. "I don't want anybody to hear. I'm not going to hurt you. I'm gonna save you."

Eddie didn't trust him. "Yeah, right! If you want to save us, give us those keys and let us out of here. We'll save ourselves, you miserable two-bit punk!"

Frankie held up a hand, motioning him to quiet down. "Look, you have to believe me. But I can't let you out of these cages. Not yet. It's very dangerous out there. You're a lot safer in those cages."

The two prisoners were both incredulous. Eddie's voice rose. "You're nuts! How can you possibly say we're safe sitting here in these cages. Just unlock the damn doors and get the hell out of the way!"

Frankie gave him a determined look. "No, you'll both get shot. As long as I'm alive I can protect you. The two of you will have to go along with that. But I'll tell you what I will do."

He walked over to the wall and grabbed two keys. "Here's the keys to those collars. Take off the chains. When it's time to leave, you'll have to run for it."

They went to work on their collars. Moments later, they sighed with relief.

"Well, it's a start," Eddie said. "Now what?"

"Now we wait. If someone comes in the door, I'll blow him away."

Eddie shook his head. "That's your plan? Someone comes in the door, you blow him away? I think you don't get it. There's a bunch of psycho nuts on this farm besides you, and they plan on murdering us. And your plan is just to sit here and wait?" He stopped talking for a moment, appalled at the absurdity of it all. Then he looked gravely at Frankie. "Look, this is way over your head. Just open these cage doors and let me handle it."

"No! You don't know what's going on. We'll do this my way."

Frankie sat where he could watch both doors. One led to a tunnel, presumably leading to Big Al's house. The other door, where he had entered, led up to the barn. He had to be ready for anything.

They waited for hours. Shannon didn't say a word, reluctantly going along with Frankie's instructions. Eddie wasn't so easy, but every time he started to talk Frankie put his finger to his lips. Eddie finally gave up, lay down on the cage floor, and watched the door to the barn.

The telltale sound caught their attention when the door leading up to the barn slowly opened, its hinges again creaking like soprano bullfrogs. Frankie aimed his pistol at the door. Shannon and Eddie watched a scene unfold like a replay of earlier. A pistol slowly appeared, then someone's arm. Then a man's torso.

Fernando!

Frankie already had the man squarely in his sights when Fernando saw him sitting on the floor. The first bullet caught Fernando squarely in the chest, then another directly above the first. A third bullet struck him in the middle of his forehead. It was a classic triple tap, fired in less than two seconds.

Shannon and Eddie watched as the bullets struck, the blood splattered, and Fernando's body hit the floor. Shannon screamed, from both relief and shock. Eddie remained silent, curious about what was next.

Frankie dragged Fernando's lifeless body into the room so he could close the door. He looked at his watch. Five-thirty. Light enough outside to see. If something more was going to happen, it would be soon. Fernando was undoubtedly the lone survivor of the melee. Thankfully, Fernando posed no threat. That made things easier. But two bigger threats remained. Unlike Fernando, Big Al and Tanya wouldn't be stoned. Frankie made a decision.

"I'll open your cage doors," he said grimly. "The others are probably dead. But I expect more trouble. I'm certain Big Al and Tanya will be coming down. Stay in the cellar. If you go outside, they'll gun you down. In here, we might have a chance."

Their cages open, Shannon and Eddie felt stunned with this surprising opportunity at freedom. Shannon tried to gather her wits, while Eddie snatched Fernando's pistol. Two guns improved their odds.

Al and Tanya looked out the window. In the distance they could see the results of the sporadic gunfire they heard during the night. One body lay close to where Tanya had left the group, another slumped against a trailer, and several others lay motionless on the grassy yard.

Al went to his office and returned with two more weapons; one a MAC-10 machine pistol, the other, a nine-millimeter Beretta like the one under his belt. He handed the Beretta to Tanya. "You got your knife?"

"Of course," Tanya said patting her ankle.

"Okay. Let's go"

After seizing the money, the agents returned to Aris' office. The clock chimed midnight when they walked inside. Jake called Harold Sampress, asked him to send some more manpower to Fargo, and then settled in at the computer to work on the second search warrant.

An affidavit for a search warrant often has to withstand the close scrutiny of a bevy of attorneys and judges, weeks or months after the door is kicked in. At that time the defendants' attorneys have the luxury of second guessing the adequacy of the document, as they argue to another judge that the first judge sat in error when he approved the search. And if they were trying to raid a house belonging to an attorney, the standards would be unofficially raised. All the t's would have to be expertly crossed, the i's dotted to perfection. In court, an affidavit has to stand on its own. It's either sufficient or it's not, and at that point it's too late for the agent to plug in additional facts. While Jake felt a sense of urgency, not knowing how much longer Pellegrino would remain at the farm, he also knew this constituted a onetime shot. To pass muster, Jake's affidavit had to include many details of the investigation beginning at its inception. As he began a brief narrative of what he learned from the Black Jack Mike raid, Jake mentally prepared himself to spend most of the night staring at the computer.

The distance from the house to the barn was the length of a football field. Al and Tanya were mid-way when they heard the vehicles.

"What the hell," Al said. His eyes and ears studied the long driveway.

Then he saw the first of a string of cars pull through the thick grove of trees. Its telling red light flashed.

Struggling to fight off panic, Big Al's mind began spinning. The Feds knew. They were coming for him. He had to act fast if he wanted to snatch escape out of the jaws of prison. Or worse. A tiny bit of relief crept into one corner of his mind. He had prepared for the unexpected. But he had to rely on Tanya to help him pull it off. He knew he couldn't make it to the house before the cars got to him. At his age, speed had long ago deserted him. But Tanya was young, her legs quick. She'd make it. "Get to the house. Torch the van and the house, then take the bike and meet me at the end of the tunnel in the woods."

Tanya nodded and sprinted to the house. Just before entering and catching her breath, she turned around and looked at the police cars. Had to be a dozen of 'em. And some cops were already out of their cars, running towards her. "Shit . . . this is gonna be close," she said to nobody.

She and Big Al had poured gasoline into coffee cans scattered throughout the house. It was ready. But not the van. She'd grab a can of gas and toss it into the vehicle along with a quick match. Then torch the house and disappear through the tunnel. She darted inside.

Big Al scrambled past the barn, his mind racing again.

He had to get to the grove of trees...

He had to get to that fake tree stump...

He had to run like hell.

A couple steps short of the tree line, he looked over his shoulder. Three agents were closing in fast. He turned and fired. His MAC-10 spit a stream of bullets towards them. One went down. *Good! Two to go.* He faded into the trees. As he disappeared, bullets shredded the bushes and branches around him.

When the shooting began, Frankie, Eddie, and Shannon were waiting for Al and Tanya to come through the cellar door. Frankie was familiar with gun sounds. Machine guns, shotguns, pistols; all had their own peculiar resonance, their own characteristics.

"That's not the clan shooting at each other. That's a fucking police raid. I'm going up," Frankie said. He rushed to the door.

Shannon followed close behind him. If the police were there, she'd be saved. She wasn't going to wait for them to find her. With Eddie in the rear, they ran up the stairs into the barn, and then toward the large door facing the house. The trio found themselves confronted by Aris Kosteckle, two Fargo police officers and a deputy sheriff.

Frankie and Eddie immediately threw their pistols down and raised their arms. "Don't shoot. We surrender," Frankie yelled.

Shannon didn't consider herself one of them, and ran across the barn floor towards Aris, yelling, "Help, please save me."

He trained his pistol on her, saying, "Stop where you are and put your hands over your head."

Seeing the gun pointed at her, Shannon fainted and crumpled to the floor.

Kiel, Ken, and five uniformed officers ran to the house. They saw someone sprinting in that direction as they drove up. Nearing the structure, they slowed down. Caution was the key at this point.

Kiel prepared to enter the open doorway when he paused and said, "I smell gas." As the words left his mouth, a coffee can struck him in the chest and drenched him. "Gas," he yelled, diving away from the door.

Seconds later the interior of the house exploded as the gas ignited. They scrambled out of harm's way.

"My leg. I'm hit," Lisa said. Her left leg crumpled beneath her. She fell to the ground. Blood poured from a vicious wound.

Jake and Travis saw the man disappearing into the woods. They emptied their magazines, firing rapidly in the direction of his fleeting shadow.

"Take care of Lisa," Jake said crisply. "This guy's mine."

Travis knelt down to help Lisa, and Jake ran to the trees.

Jake reached the tree line. He heard Big Al stumbling through the woods. The sound headed south. Jake followed the noise. He ran in a half-jog. Dodged branches. Stepped over tree roots. Every few yards he paused. He listened. He let his mind work. While the man ran there could be no ambush. The sounds read like a story-book map.

He was getting closer.

Big Al ran. Only one cop chasing him. *No sweat. Look for a place to ambush the guy, riddle him with lead, then meet Tanya.* He stopped to catch his breath. It came loud and heavy. Although muscular, he had little stamina. He heard his pursuer hot on his trail, but couldn't see him. He continued running, while looking for a good spot to set up an ambush.

Jake paused. He tried to get a fix on the man. The woods had suddenly gone quiet. Jake couldn't ignore the warning. He carefully scanned the area. The noisy chatter of a squirrel broke the silence. Jake instinctively looked in that direction. A sparkle of light reflected off an object near a pile of dead brush about thirty yards ahead. It lasted only a split second, but that was enough. Jake crouched behind a thick tree stump just as a barrage of gunfire let loose. Bullets sprayed the trees and brush near him. The gunfire stopped briefly then resumed, now much slower. It sounded like a different weapon. *His machine gun must be empty.*

He peered around the tree stump. Nothing. He fired several rounds with his Sig-Sauer into the brush pile. Still nothing. Then Big Al jumped up from behind the trees, fired more rounds in Jake's direction, and bolted. Jake sprang to his feet, quick-stepping towards Big Al, firing on the run. One bullet struck home. Big Al yelped in pain and swore, but didn't slow down.

Jake ran faster. He spotted his foe in the distance. Saw the man's left arm dangling. Saw the man stop again. Jake stopped. He fired several rounds in Big Al's direction. Big Al fired a volley at the agent. Jake ducked behind a tree. Bullets whined as they zipped by his face. One round ricocheted off the tree trunk just over his head. He shot back, through the brush and tree branches, until his pistol was empty. He changed magazines and watched Big Al race away.

Charging after him, Jake's foot caught an exposed tree root. He crashed to the ground. His head banged against a tree trunk. Dazed, he crawled to his feet and felt his head. Blood gushed from the wound, pouring onto his hand and the ground. Ignoring it, he tried to run. Sharp pain shot through his foot. He realized he twisted or sprained his ankle. Sucking it up he moved on, limping.

Big Al came up to the river and ran east. He'd soon see the fake tree stump. *About 200 yards to go.* But he had to do something about that damned cop before joining Tanya. *Time to make a stand.* He spotted a thick tree near the river bank. Its trunk would give him adequate cover. He might get a clean shot. *Gotta get behind that tree.*

After dousing Kiel with gasoline, Tanya dashed back into the house, kicking over a couple gas cans as she darted to the basement stairwell. She fumed that she didn't have a chance to torch the van. But Big Al would understand. At the stairs, she lit a cigarette lighter and tossed it onto a puddle. Cans exploded. Inside, a raging inferno. Searing flames licked the walls and ceiling. Smoke billowed and filled the room, quickly spreading throughout the house. She raced down the stairs. A minute later the Honda screamed through the tunnel.

Arriving at the other end, Tanya heard bullets flying. With them came questions. How many cops were on Big Al? Would he reach the tree stump? How long would it take? She grabbed her Beretta, worked the latches and pushed the stump open. Another volley of shots. Her muscles tensed.

Jake could see the river now, but Big Al was gone. Jake last saw him running towards a tall oak tree. *That's probably where he is.* He looked around for cover. Spied a part of Big Al's head and shoulder along side of the tree. Spotted Big Al's pistol aimed towards him, ready to fire. The agent dove to the ground. A barrage of bullets blasted the dirt to his left. He rolled right. More bullets tore up the dirt, following his roll. The last one struck inches from Jake's bleeding head. Then they stopped. Jake saw Big Al running. Lying on the ground, he emptied his magazine. Big Al lurched, and staggered toward the river. Jake slammed his last magazine into his pistol. Only fourteen rounds left.

A bullet tore through Big Al's left leg. With his left arm shattered, now he had a gaping hole in his thigh. Both wounds bled heavily. He could no longer walk. His pistol out of ammo, Big Al watched Jake closing in. He looked at the river. Debris, tree branches and leaves, the result of the storm, charged past in swift water. Twenty feet off shore he spotted a fallen jack pine tree. Branches and spikes jutted out at various angles. It was his only chance. Big Al tossed his gun onto the ground and jumped backwards into the water, hoping somehow he could make it to the tree before it drifted past.

Half floating, half swimming, Big Al struggled valiantly to reach the floating tree. The current caught him and kept him even with its branches. He had trouble keeping his head above the surface. He floundered. Swallowed water. Choked. Retched. Spit. Finally, he grabbed a tree branch and pulled himself to the tree's trunk as he coughed up water and gasped for air. He wrapped his good arm and leg around the trunk, tangling them in some branches.

Where the fuck are you, Tanya? Get your ass over here! Take out that fuckin' cop! Get me the hell out of this! Help me, God damn it!

His weight caused the tree trunk to roll. His body slipped beneath the surface. Spikes tore through his clothes.

He struggled. He became entangled. He held his breath.

Desperately, he tried to free himself from the tangled mess. But two bullets had ripped through his muscle tissue. An arm and leg were useless. He lost considerable blood. He could no longer move.

Jake watched Big Al throw his gun down and flop into the river. By the time Jake reached the river bank, the man had traveled twenty yards downstream to a floating branch. He saw the man desperately pull himself onto the floating tree. A puddle of blood covered the ground where Big Al last stood. A cloud of red followed him in the current. Limping along the shoreline, Jake followed Big Al downstream. He watched the log roll over and pull the man under water. Jake stayed even with the floating debris, watching the man's arm jutting grotesquely out of the water for a hundred yards.

Big Al was dead.

Jake stood on the riverbank, catching his breath, fighting the pain and wondering if the man floating down the river was Big Al. Then he heard Travis yelling.

"Jake, you okay?"

Jake looked up and saw Travis and Aris running towards him.

"Not really. But I'm doing a lot better than the other guy. I shot him and he's tangled up in a tree, floating down the river. He's dead. I'm thinking its Big Al. How's Lisa?"

"She took a round in the leg. An ambulance is on the way."

Jake nodded grimly, pressing a handkerchief onto his head wound. "Let's get back to the farm. I'm not jumping into that river."

Tanya could hear their loud conversation through the stillness of the woods. She fought to contain her shock. Her world had collapsed before her eyes. Looking at the river she saw the tree and Big Al's arm protruding from the water. Yeah, he was dead all right. Time to take care of herself.

With Jake's limp getting progressively worse, the slow trek back was accompanied by a whole lot of hurt. When they reached the farmyard, Jake saw what Tanya had left in her wake. Orange flames mingled with a mountain of black smoke that obliterated the sky above what remained of the house. The first of many fire trucks had arrived. Sirens pierced the early morning air. Jake also saw a Fargo police officer on his knees, tending to Lisa's wound.

Lisa looked up at Jake's bloodied face. "My God, look at your head! Did you get him?"

Jake nodded, temporarily forgetting the pain. "He's floating down the river. We'll have to get a crew from the Sheriff's office to retrieve his body." He looked around at the corpses littering the farm yard. "What the hell is the story here?"

"We've got two prisoners in the barn," Aris told him. "We might learn something from them."

Jake's foot needed a rest, and the gash above his forehead required medical help, so he remained with Lisa and the police officer. Travis and Aris returned to the barn. Shannon had regained consciousness and sat on the floor, sobbing. Eddie and Frankie, handcuffed and guarded by two Fargo cops, also sat on the floor some distance from Shannon. Aris walked over to the two prisoners, while Travis approached Shannon.

"Is it over?" Shannon asked.

Travis looked at her curiously. "Who are you?"

"Shannon Kubicek. These animals kidnapped me. They're a bunch of drug dealing devil worshippers. Is it over?"

"Yes, it's over Shannon."

Then Shannon told Travis about the cages in the cellar. Travis frowned. Maybe it wasn't over. He quickly caught Aris' attention. "There's a cellar below us. We have to check it out."

Travis and one of the deputies drew their pistols and inched their way down into the cellar. Opening the door, the stench collided with their nostrils. They spied the chains. The cages. The pail, its surface blackened and crusty with rancid, dried blood. And Fernando's body.

Travis shook his head in horror. "What the hell was going on here?"

The deputy was equally shocked. "Holy shit! This has been going on under our noses. What kind of animals are these guys?" he asked.

Travis shrugged. "That gal upstairs says it's a cult." He pointed at the steel door on the other side of the room. "I wonder where that leads to." He tried the door. It was solidly secured. "Let's go see what they want to do."

They returned to the barn and rejoined the others. Travis told them about the cellar.

Aris grimaced and pointed to the two prisoners, as though they were trophies of a big game hunt. "Yeah, that fits with what these two told me. They know all about this place." He motioned his hand towards Eddie. "This is Eddie Pellegrino. He was in one of those cages, preparing to meet his maker. The other one is Frankie Cello. Cello wants to make music, and Eddie wants to make it a duet."

Watching Jake limp into the barn, Aris shifted his thoughts. "Jake, you were right. Big Al was here. His full name is Manfred

Alphonse Culpepper, and I gotta believe he's the one you chased through the woods. It seems we missed a lot of action last night. A regular civil war. We've got bodies all over. Frankie says there's a grave yard in the woods next to the river. Figures there's close to thirty victims buried there, most of 'em young girls. These psychos have been killing people for three years." He pointed towards Shannon, now sitting on the dirt floor a few yards away, talking to a Fargo cop. "She was to be their next victim, but Big Al spooked when Pellegrino showed up. And there's someone we haven't found yet. Big Al's partner, Tanya."

Kiel chimed in and told them about the woman who had doused him with gasoline then ran into the house, setting it in flames. "One of the firemen hosed me down. I'm glad I had a change of clothes in my car. It had to be Tanya. She's probably a crispy critter now. We'll have to sift through the ashes to find her."

Putting the fake tree stump back in its place, Tanya gave a parting glance to her surroundings. Through the thick vegetation she could barely see the barn and trailers. Looking past the barn, the violent orange flames and the black smoke held her gaze. She smelled the smoke, her nose confirming what her eyes could see. Sirens continued to wail, some nearby, some in the distance. Goosebumps raised on her arms as she thought about all the havoc she had caused, all the attention she and Big Al were getting. She started her Honda, rode slowly and quietly through the woods, reaching the county road ten minutes later. The road went north-south. Hearing sirens to the north, she would have to take an indirect route to Fargo. She headed south.

An east-west county road was two miles away. Tanya reached the road within minutes, turned east and cranked up her speed to sixty. As she rode, Big Al's image haunted her. A DEA agent had gunned down the only man she'd ever loved. She heard his partners call him 'Jake.' Heard Jake say he had hurt his ankle bad. And it sounded like Big Al shot one of the agents in the leg. A woman they called 'Lisa.' Good! Big Al had gotten in his licks.

Tanya would remember them.

CHAPTER 27

Tanya's first priority upon entering Fargo? A different set of wheels. Her destination? Minneapolis. A city she knew. The lamb might still be alive, and could give the police a very good description of her. She would forget about Vondermolte. He had never met her and wasn't worth the risk.

She wondered if anyone besides her survived, if anybody remained to talk about her. Big Al figured there would be one, most likely Fernando, but Tanya didn't believe he would be captured. He would have gone down shooting, and was dead. She didn't think Frankie would have made it. Too damn weak. What about Juleen? She was tough, and hated Fernando. Juleen and Fernando probably squared off right away.

And then she thought about Eddie, the person responsible for all this.

Could Eddie still be alive? Probably not, but if he survived he'd be eager to spill his guts. He knew a lot about her. Initially, they'd assume she'd been killed in the fire. But when they discovered the tunnel, they'd know. Then the search would be on. She'd have to change her appearance.

She made her way to a motel near I-29. It boasted a cocktail lounge, a popular nightspot for the younger crowd. An ideal place to get rid of the bike. Tanya parked and looked around. Through the glass windows she saw a man in the process of checking out. Taking off her helmet, she began tinkering with the motorcycle's engine. Minutes later the man walked past. He seemed the unassuming type. Easy prey. She watched him stroll across the lot.

He went to a gray mini-van. Under Tanya's watchful gaze, he put his suitcase into the rear of the van then walked to the driver's side. She approached him.

"Excuse me, sir. I'm having problems with my bike. You wouldn't have a screwdriver I could use, would you?"

The man displayed a friendly smile. "Yeah, I have a tool box here someplace. Let me see if I can find it. Your motorcycle won't start?"

"No. It's temperamental. I know what's wrong. I need a screwdriver to make an adjustment. Just take a minute."

The man opened up the sliding door and located his tool box. While he was occupied, Tanya scanned the parking lot. Satisfied they were the only ones in the lot, she reached down to her ankle.

"Okay, here it is. I guess if your bike is so temperamental maybe you should have one of these," the man advised, turning around to hand her the screwdriver.

"You're right. The only thing I carry is this," Tanya said, shoving her blade deep into his heart.

He didn't bleed much as he fell into the interior of the van. She returned to the bike and removed its license plate, leaving the keys in the ignition. Some jerk walking past won't be able to resist stealing it, she thought. By the time the police find it, if they ever do, they'll never link it to this motel.

Tanya got behind the wheel of the van and slowly drove away, returning to the freeway. Her next destination was a county road on the northern fringes of the city. From there she drove east several miles to the Red River. Arriving at a bridge, she stopped and stripped the man of all his identification. Then she studied the road. No cars in sight. Things were going her way. Looking down at the river, she saw the water churning. The northward current ran strong. With any luck, his body would be crossing into Canada by the next morning.

She draped the body over the railing of the bridge and gave it a hefty shove. The sound of the splash brought a satisfied smile to her face. She continued east, through Moorhead, and found her way to I-94 and Minneapolis.

A feverish scene consumed the farm. As the firefighters sprayed water onto the burning house, Ken and two Fargo officers removed the boxes from the van, and other officers examined the various crime scenes surrounding the corpses scattered around the farm yard.

Frankie and Eddie were separated and questioned by Jake, Travis, Kiel and Aris. After the fire was extinguished and the smoke cleared, the four agents put their heads together.

"I'd say it's gonna take us a few days, maybe a week to search this place," Aris said. He decided to begin their search by investigating the door in the cellar.

Travis retrieved a sledge hammer from his car and they returned to the stench of the dingy room below the barn. With the others looking over his shoulder, he smashed the door down with the hammer.

"Hey, it's a tunnel," Travis said, unnecessarily.

They could smell the remnants of smoke, but the tunnel was clear. Turning on their flashlights, the agents followed the tunnel to the secret room in the basement. There they found the second tunnel. Tanya had left the door wide open in her hasty escape. Following this tunnel, the agents made their way towards the river where they discovered the fake tree stump.

Spotting fresh tire tracks, Jake said, "I don't think we're going to find that woman's bones in the house."

Aris took charge. "I'll talk to the sheriff. All these homicides are his jurisdiction. My guess is he'll need a lot of help from the state. They'll be working here 24 hours a day until they finish. We'll help out where we can. Jake, you should go to the ER in Fargo and get yourself patched up. Come on back when you can. We're gonna be here a while. Travis, call that motel in town and reserve a few rooms for us so we got a place to rest when we get the chance."

Five days later the search of the farm and the woods by the river was completed.

"Twenty-seven bodies," Jake commented to Aris as they walked out of the woods for the final time. "What a nightmare for those people."

Aris nodded. "Makes you sick, doesn't it? Come on, let's go meet the press."

The raid received extensive coverage in the media, locally and nationally. Once the investigators finished their work, they allowed the media onto the farm to televise and photograph the scene. All the officials were quizzed extensively.

Finished with the interviews, Jake, Aris, and the others huddled together before leaving.

"Some of those reporters were spooked and some of 'em loved it," Jake commented to Aris.

"I noticed," Aris replied. "That's the most gruesome press conference I've ever been involved in. A satanic cult, kidnappings, sacrificial murders, a grave yard stuffed with bodies, cardboard boxes stuffed with millions of dollars. And all of it tied to heroin. That's gonna give the media something to chew on."

Jake grimaced. "Let's go see how Lisa's doing."

They went together to the hospital to visit her and tell her what they found.

"Thank God we arrived when we did." Lisa managed a smile.

"Yeah," Jake agreed. "And that's not all. Eddie tells us he's got millions stashed in safe deposit boxes throughout the Twin Cities. He's scrambling hard to avoid being charged as an accessory to what went down at the farm. He's got information on Dominique LaForte, the Colombian cartel, and other members of the organization in the Minneapolis area. He mentioned ER's name, but nothing about the hit on Fergie. And then there's Frankie. That guy knows he's fucked, so he just wants to get it all off his chest. Can't wait to tell us about Al's heroin customers around Minnesota and North Dakota. We found a lot of records in the van. They will probably support what he says. This is going to keep us busy for a year."

Lisa chuckled quietly to herself as a thought she had entertained earlier in the year revisited her:

Yeah, right. And all the agents in the office lived happily ever after!

Then: *Huh! Who woulda thunk? I guess it's appropriate they're telling me this story while I'm in bed.*

Travis stood at the head of Lisa's bed and gently put his hand on her shoulder. "How are you doing Lisa? What about your leg?"

"The bullet broke a bone. They did surgery. They say I'll probably want cosmetic surgery later. My leg's going to be weak, and I'll have to do some rehab to re-build the damaged muscles."

Travis frowned. "At least you're still with us. I guess you were lucky."

Lisa looked at Travis and then at Jake and the others. "Get a load of this guy. I'm lying here on a hospital bed with a bullet hole in me while he came through without a scratch, and he says I'm the lucky one. Huh!"

Travis shook his head in wonder. "She gets cut down by a machine gun and she's just as sassy as ever." He looked at Lisa. "What's it take to slow you down?"

"I'm not ready to slow down," Lisa said. "When that happens I'll look for another line of work."

The exhausted group finished their visit and left the hospital. "A motel bed is going to feel great," Kiel said. "When was the last time any of us slept for longer than a couple hours?"

"You know, I can't even remember," Aris answered. "I could probably sleep straight through the next twenty-four."

Jake stifled a yawn. "Yeah, I hear that."

"Say, how are Melissa and Melanie doing," Ken asked.

"The same. Melanie's still in a coma. Melissa is getting pretty worn down, going back and forth to the hospital plus taking care of the other kids." Jake saw a very tired look in Ken's eyes, but it seemed to be more than just a lack of sleep. He had again been touched by death.

"How about you, Ken? How are you doing?" Jake asked, concerned.

"I'm not sure. I'm going to think about it for a few days. Then I'll let you know. How are all your wounds?"

"My foot will mend. My head got scraped but it's okay."

Ken looked at Jake's heavily wrapped foot and nodded, saying nothing.

They approached their cars and stopped. "Let's meet at Aris' office at noon tomorrow," Jake said.

Tanya had also kept busy during the past five days. She first stopped at the Mall of America in Bloomington. In the Mall she purchased cosmetics, a razor, and scissors at Macy's, then went to a shop called The Wig-Wam where she purchased a red hair piece. She checked into a motel under a phony name and shaved her head.

Next, she had to find a place to live. For no reason in particular, Tanya decided to look for a home north of the cities. She wanted a place in the country, away from curious eyes. Her search ended two days later when she pursued an ad in a local paper which led to a house in the country outside of Forest Lake. After renting the house, Tanya went to several banks in the area and opened checking accounts. She made cash deposits of slightly less than ten thousand dollars in each account.

This accomplished, Tanya drove to St. Paul where she abandoned the stolen van in a high crime area near the capitol. She left the keys in the ignition and the doors unlocked. A ten-minute walk brought her to a bus stop on University Avenue.

A bus dropped her off near a car dealership two miles away. She walked into the used car lot and began browsing. Tanya liked the business man's van; small and maneuverable. She decided to get another. The dealership had one in good condition, and an hour and a half later she drove it back to Forest Lake. Then the jitters started. She felt the need.

It was an overwhelming compulsion, with two separate forces attacking her senses. One involved the usual: a need to exorcize her demons. In that regard, Al had been her savior. He always knew what had to be done. Early in their relationship, Al found her demons could be tamed by human blood. The second force demanded revenge. And it held a powerful thirst for information. She continually surfed the tube for news.

Initially, the raid received thorough coverage, but never enough to satisfy her. After several days she became greatly irritated. Nothing more about the farm. Frustrated with the lack of information she threw half a pizza across the room, where it splattered against the wall and dropped onto the floor in a messy glob. Then she unloaded her hostilities at the news anchor on television. "Big Al told me knowledge is power. Why don't you assholes do your job?"

She paced the carpet, violently swearing at the DEA, Jake, Lisa, and the others whom she didn't know. Finally, she forced herself to calm down and focused on what to do next. If she wanted revenge, she would first have to learn more about those agents. She knew two names. That bitch, Lisa, had been shot in the leg and probably used crutches now. Should be easy to get a make on her. A smile replaced Tanya's angry scowl. She knew what she had to do. Find Lisa and she'd find Jake.

With the initial interviews of Frankie and Eddie completed, Jake and Travis drove back to Minneapolis.

"What are you planning when we get back," Travis asked.

"Spend some time with my wife and family."

"Good. They need you. Melanie needs you."

"Yeah. If I only knew what was going on in her head. I got a theory. I'm thinking if she were given the proper stimulation she'd snap out of it. Maybe there's a key to open her door. I talked to the docs. They said they weren't sure, but if it makes me feel better, what's to lose? The rest of the kids are beginning to feel neglected. I'm going to have to work something out with Harold."

Travis nodded. "Yeah. You know, I'm worried about Ken."

Jake agreed. "He seemed depressed. I think he's got problems."

Glancing over at Jake, Travis took his eyes off the road for a second. "I hear ya. All that death. He wasn't ready for it. How about you, Jake? Now you've killed somebody. How you doing?"

Jake thought about it for a few seconds. "As I watched him drown, the adrenaline was pumping so hard I never gave it a thought. Then later, after I had time to think it over, shooting that piece of slime didn't bother me at all. I wish we would've got Tanya. That's my regret."

Early that afternoon they met with Harold in his office. He couldn't contain his enthusiasm. "Welcome back. Park your butts. You all did one hell of a good job on this case and I'm proud of you. Hell, the entire state of Minnesota should be proud."

They spent the next hour filling Harold in on the details of the raid.

Finished with the update, Harold asked, "How's that ankle doing?"

Jake shrugged. "It's a bad sprain. The doc said no permanent damage."

"Glad to hear that."

"Harold, I need to work shorter days for a while. How about taking me off the overtime schedule. I need time with my family."

"No problem. You can cut out of here every day at five if that's what you need. If it's pressing, you can leave earlier.

"By the way, there've been some developments. First, Ken asked for a leave of absence. I'm not sure when he'll be back, if at all. Next, Robert Little's doctor cleared him to return to duty. He'll be coming into the office tomorrow. I spoke to him on the phone this afternoon. He's elated."

Jake smiled. "That's great. With Scott Hookman gone and Ken Washington on a leave of absence, Robert can help fill the void. Anything else?"

"Well, you just sort of mentioned it. I don't know exactly what the hell is going on, but the boss sent a wire to Florida bringing Scott back here for a few days. Supposedly it's for consultation on a marijuana case. I looked the file over and Scott's involvement was practically non-existent."

Harold looked straight at Travis. "After you told me about Scott and Kiel's wife, I went into Alan's office and we had some strong words. I told him Scott had to go immediately. He wasn't hearing it at first, but I got his attention. Maybe a bad career move, but it worked. He told me to do what I had to do, but now he pulls this little maneuver. Consultations! What a load of bull shit!"

Just a notch away from losing it, Harold's voice began to thunder against the walls of his small office. He caught himself, stopped, and took in a deep breath. After a long pause he said, "It's like this. Alan doesn't like either of you. And after this thing with Scott, he's got a major league hard-on for me. If there's any way he can shove it up my ass, he will. I won't accept a transfer. If I have to leave here under a cloud, I might as well pull the pin. The brass don't like supervisors who aren't company men, and that's how Alan would portray me. But don't count me out. I've got some things going. If it works out we'll be okay. In the mean-time, I have to keep Kiel away from the office for a few days. I don't want him to know Scott's in town. But I'm not sure how I'm going to do it."

Jake frowned, slightly shaking his head. "That'll be a tough secret to keep."

Harold's eyes became dead serious. "We've got no choice. Kiel sees Scott hanging around here, he's likely to draw his nine-iron and ventilate the guy's head. I'll figure out something, but I don't want any whispering going on out there. Take care of it, Jake."

"I'll see to it, Harold."

"Close the door behind you."

Jake sat down at his desk and tried to digest everything his boss had said. Harold also saw the hand writing on the wall. The three of them might soon be packing their bags. What a crazy world! He shook his head in amazement. Then his phone rang. It was Sudden Sam O'Grady. Jake smiled. He liked that guy.

"Yeah, Sam. It's been a while. How's everything?"

"Great. And it sounds like good things have been happening with you too. You guys have been monopolizing the news. Hell of a job! It's my impression this heroin ring you busted is the same bunch Frenchy Deveroux was involved with."

"That's right, and you were a big help Sam. We really appreciate what you did. They won't be bringing any more heroin into this state."

"Well, the city hasn't shut down my club and I'd like to thank you for that."

Jake smiled. "In all honesty, I didn't ask the PD to leave you alone. But when we gave them five hundred thousand of the money we seized from Black Jack Mike, I mentioned you were working closely with us."

"Ah! Well, I did you guys a favor, you returned the favor, and I guess that's the grease that oils the wheels. I'm calling you again to help keep the wheels churning. Drug dealers still come into my club. I know a lot of 'em. Most are small timers, but once in a while I see someone you might want to look at. I think I can help."

"What do you have in mind?"

"If you could send an agent to the club during the evenings, I'd set it up so he could watch the patrons. Whenever I spotted a significant dealer, I'd tip the agent. Then he could do his thing. I'm not an investigator, but I got to think the more you guys know, the better off you are. Something might come of it."

Jake thought for a few moments and a bright smile took over his face. This was perfect. "Okay, Sam. I'll talk this over with my boss. Thanks for the call."

"Bye, Jake."

Jake walked over and knocked on Harold's closed door. Through the window he could see Harold hanging up his phone. Harold looked up and motioned Jake in.

Sitting down on the chair he had just vacated, Jake told Harold about the conversation with Sudden Sam. Harold liked it.

"I'll give the assignment to Kiel. The surveillance will be his full time responsibility for the next week, and until he's through with it he doesn't have to come to the office. I'll let him think I'm giving him a break. Robert's itching to get back onto the street. I'll pair 'em up."

Harold looked at Jake suspiciously. "You know Jake, a good agent makes his own luck. But you did this in a matter of minutes. How'd you do it? You got some kind of magic powder you sprinkle on your phone or something? Things aren't supposed to be this easy."

CHAPTER 28

Kiel and Robert drove together to the Saddle Club. Kiel's watch said six-thirty. The club would start to buzz in about a half hour. After three nights on this assignment, they were beginning to get their system down pat, although with mixed results. So far they didn't have anything noteworthy. On the plus side, they had been spending long evenings on this surveillance, and Robert felt like an agent again.

Kiel had a portable radio concealed under his light weight jacket. When Sudden Sam recognized a drug dealer in the club, he would walk over to Kiel's table and give him a sign. Kiel would watch the individual, and when the person left the club Kiel would key the mike on his radio as the doper walked out. Robert watched the exit. When he heard the mike click, he would match Kiel's signal with a body. He had to identify the person's car and record the plate number. Later, he and Kiel would compare notes and times.

It didn't always work. Sometimes the subject came with someone else, and they rode in that person's car. Other times the individual drove another person's ride, leaving the agents with nothing but a big question mark. But they gave it their best shot. When finally finished, they'd put it all down on paper and let the boss decide what to do with it.

Kiel eased out of the car, closed the door and then ducked his head back through the open window. "Okay, Robert. Good luck out here."

"You too, Kiel. Watch yourself."

Kiel nodded, walked into the club and took his usual table. Sam brought him a glass of coke and joined him for a few minutes.

"How's it going, Kiel?"

"About the same, Sam. Going to be crowded in here tonight?"

"I hope so. I'll be helping my bartender for a while. One of my regulars called in. He's got car problems and he'll be late."

"Okay. You know where to find me," Kiel said. Nursing his coke, he sat back and waited for the show to start.

A few hours later Kiel's jaw dropped when he saw Scott Hookman walk in. Not seeing Kiel, Scott took a seat at the opposite end of the room. Kiel's nerves began bouncing as he fought to maintain his cool. *What the hell is that bastard doing here? He's supposed to be in Florida. He'll be sorry he came back.*

Scott ordered a drink while Kiel fumed. Then one of the strippers, a stacked beauty who seemed to know Scott well, came over to his table and sat down. Kiel watched as she slid her chair close to Scott's and began running her hand up his leg.

Kiel's blood rushed to his face. *That miserable motherfucker. He runs off with my wife, and then when he comes back here he's screwing whores. What a piece of shit. And my daughter's got to live in the same house with him.*

The agent's animosity swelled as he watched Scott and the hooker groping each other. On the verge of storming over to Scott's table, he stopped short when he saw two other people he knew arrive. One was ER, whom Kiel recognized from the bowling alley surveillance. ER had no way of knowing him. But the other guy knew Kiel quite well. Seeing him, Kiel's eyes swamped with hostility.

David O'Neal!

Kiel's rancor instantly focused in a different direction; towards the two new players. He watched closely as the drug dealers took seats at a table near the stage on the opposite side of the room from Scott. The three tables occupied by the agents and drug dealers formed a triangle. Like Scott, O'Neal had not seen Kiel.

Assholes, Kiel thought. ER had Fergie murdered. You can take that to the bank. And there he is with O'Neal. I'm betting O'Neal pulled the trigger. This club is full of slime tonight.

Instinctively, Kiel brought his hand up to the side of his chest to check on his pistol, while he mulled over this new development. As much as he hated ER for having Fergie murdered, his grudge against O'Neal stacked much higher. *I hope I'm the one who arrests O'Neal. I still haven't had a decent chance to kick his ass. I wonder if they're packing heat.*

Sam saw Kiel looking intently at the two people who had just entered. Sam had seen both of them individually, but never together. He knew nothing about them except they were occasional patrons, but the way Kiel had focused in on them was revealing. They had to be drug dealers, possibly already under investigation. He had planned to walk over to Kiel's table, but quickly dismissed the idea. No sense drawing attention to Kiel. Sam had also seen Scott Hookman come into the club. No surprise, as Scott had contacted Sam earlier and made arrangements to be with one of the girls that evening. Sam knew Scott well, although he hadn't seen him for a while and knew nothing about Scott's transfer.

Sam sensed the atmosphere thicken inside the club. He recognized a real life drama unfolding before his eyes, but he couldn't get a grip on the plot. He wondered if Kiel and Scott were working together, but for some reason hadn't told him. Didn't seem likely. They hadn't even acknowledged each other's presence. But then, if they were on a surveillance they probably wouldn't. Maybe they were working on two separate cases. Nah. If that were true, Scott wouldn't have set it up with one of the girls. No way would Scott be using one of Sam's girls for cover. Sam decided Scott had come to the club to enjoy himself and knock off a piece. Pure and simple. Kiel's presence in the club at the same time? Coincidence. Sam decided to stay in the background.

O'Neal and ER huddled at their table, talking animatedly. Their waitress delivered their whiskeys, and they started working on their drinks. Then O'Neal noticed Kiel sitting alone at a table. They caught each others' eyes.

O'Neal nudged ER. "That's one of those fucking DEA agents," O'Neal said, his voice dripping with animosity. "His name is Kiel. Two times I was kicking the motherfucker's ass, but he always gets rescued by his buddies. He's one of the bastards who put the screws to us. Fucking sawed off midget. And now he's here, watching us. I've had enough of his shit."

They downed their whiskeys, flagged down the waitress and ordered two more.

ER didn't know Kiel from someone just off the bus. But he knew he'd been royally fucked, and it felt good to put a face on one of the nameless bastards who'd been doing it. He took a hard chug from his fresh drink. He liked the feeling the booze gave him. His emotions became stronger, his thoughts more vivid. He felt fully in control. Whatever he wanted was his.

Right now he wanted payback.

He leaned towards O'Neal. "They fucked over our entire organization. I can't even take a crap anymore without wondering if they're in the shitter looking up at me."

They glared at Kiel. The waitress came by and they ordered a third round. She returned shortly.

ER took a sip from his fresh drink. "Rotten motherfuckers!"

O'Neal took a sip. "Fucking narc piece-of-shit!"

Kiel watched them closely. Seeing the hatred in their eyes, he matched it with his own. He reached under his jacket and stroked his Beretta, now half wishing they'd start something. He'd finish it fast enough.

O'Neal noticed Kiel's movement, and the whiskey started talking. "The bastard's taunting us. I suppose he thinks we don't have guns. I'll show the son of a bitch." He reached under his jacket to pat his piece.

ER nodded approvingly. "Yeah, he ain't the only guy in here that's got a gun." He reached under his jacket and glared at Kiel.

Kiel was taking his hand away from his piece, when he saw ER and O'Neal reaching under their jackets. Yeah, they *were* starting something. They were going to take him out. Already on red alert, no way would he let them shoot first.

Kiel pulled out his gun. ER and O'Neal both had their hands on their guns when they saw Kiel draw his.

"Take him," ER growled.

ER and O'Neal pulled their pistols, pushed back their chairs and stood up. Kiel brought his Beretta up as ER and O'Neal leveled their guns on him. Kiel shot first, striking O'Neal squarely in the heart. The drug dealer dropped backwards onto his chair, his gun hit the floor with a heavy clunk.

ER would have been a wiser choice for Kiel's first bullet. He was handy with a gun. As Kiel's shot rang out, ER fired twice. One of the bullets struck Kiel in the chest. He slumped to the floor.

The club instantly transformed into a state of bedlam. The waitresses shrieked and hit the floor. The stripper on stage dropped down and scurried on hands and knees to safety. Chairs flew as the patrons dove under their tables.

Scott had been totally involved with the hooker when Kiel stood up. He hadn't noticed Kiel, and was amazed, not only that Kiel was there, but that he had his pistol out. He saw two other men aiming their guns at Kiel. Then the bullets started flying and Scott saw one of the men go down. He looked towards Kiel and watched him drop. Scott grabbed his gun.

The hooker seated with Scott saw him reach for his gun, and panicked. "Scott, no!" She dove to the floor.

ER heard the woman yell. He turned her way, saw someone else with a pistol. He whipped his gun in Scott's direction and fired. The bullet tore through Scott's chest. The agent went down.

As he stood behind the bar, pouring drinks, Sam watched. When he saw ER and O'Neal had both drawn guns, he darted towards the other end of the bar. Just as Scott fell, Sam grabbed his revolver from under the cash register.

ER saw the movement. He leveled his nine millimeter at Sam's head. He pulled the trigger.

Nothing! Jammed!

He tried to clear the pistol's action. Too late.

Sam's .357 magnum thundered. Once . . . twice . . . three times. Two of Sam's bullets struck home. The first hit ER's arm and his pistol clattered to the floor. The second went through one of ER's eyes and out the back of his head, which exploded in a torrent of blood and brains.

Sam didn't waste time. Keeping the revolver in his hand, he yelled over to the bartender. "Call 911!! Get an ambulance! Officers shot!"

He ran to Kiel. Badly wounded, the agent lay in a red pool, blood pouring from his nose and mouth. Sam knelt down, feeling helpless. He cradled one of his large hands under the agent's head.

"Take it easy. You're going to be okay," Sam lied.

Kiel knew better. He looked up at Sam, wanted to talk, but coughed up a mouthful of blood. He tried again. It took all the strength he had. "Sam . . . tell my daughter . . . I love her."

"I will, I will."

"And tell my wife . . . she made a big mistake. Scott is a loser."

Sam was puzzled. What did Kiel's wife have to do with Scott? He looked helplessly at his friend as Kiel wheezed and groaned in pain. "I don't understand," Sam said desperately. "Your wife? Scott?"

Kiel clutched Sam's shirt. "Just tell her! Tell her!"

"I'll tell her, Kiel. I promise. I'll tell her."

Two days after the shoot out, Jake and Melissa were in Melanie's hospital room.

"When is Kiel's funeral," Melissa asked.

"In two days. Harold called Lucie, Kiel's wife. She's flying in tonight. I suppose she'll be spending most of tomorrow in the hospital visiting Scott. I don't think she had much feeling left for Kiel. What a rotten relationship they must have had."

"What about Sudden Sam? His club got all shot up. What's he going to do?"

Jake shrugged. "Harold talked to him after the shooting. Sam's taking it hard. I think he feels snake bit. Earlier in the year one of his girls was murdered. Now this. Both incidents were tied into our heroin investigation. Sam hates drugs, but he's got no problems with hookers. Unfortunately, the drug dealers like to frequent his place. How does he keep one, and eliminate the other? I guess that's one of the reasons he was so eager to work with us. But things don't always turn out the way they should, do they?"

"No, they sure don't," Melissa said sadly. "Is his place closed?"

"Yeah. He's got workers cleaning. Sam told Harold he would probably keep it closed for six weeks, until the publicity fades. Then he'll see about opening again.

"Sam is a different kind of guy. He's involved in some things that are illegal, but I don't picture him as a crook. The man just has his own set of values. He's going to the funeral, by the way. Said he had a message to give to Kiel's wife and daughter. Wouldn't tell Harold what the message was. Said it was personal."

Melissa's eyes opened wide. "A personal message for Lucie?"

"Yeah, I guess. Kiel and Sam had been close the past days. Sam is the loyal type. Maybe they talked about her while Kiel was there."

Melissa looked down at Melanie and began squeezing Jake's hand.

Instinctively, Jake looked over at his wife and saw that her face was turning white. "Mel, what is it?"

"Melanie," Melissa whispered.

Jake looked down. Melanie's eyes were open and moving around. She was conscious.

The church was packed. Every DEA agent from Minnesota and the four surrounding states attended the funeral, along with 31 agents from Chicago. Add to that all of the state, city, and county narcs, along with several from the neighboring states. Forty-six uniformed officers also dotted the assemblage. Scott Hookman didn't attend. He remained in the hospital, recovering from his wound. ER's bullet had nicked his lung.

Kiel's minister gave a compelling eulogy praising Kiel as an individual, and condemning the scourge of drugs that caused his death. Harold, Jake, Ken, Travis and Lisa sat in the front of the church, next to the brass from headquarters.

Except for Harold, all of the Minneapolis agents mulled over the same question: "Where the hell is Alan Ravich?" They hadn't seen him all day.

After the burial, people drifted away. Travis and Lisa spotted Lucie standing apart from the crowd with her daughter and Sudden Sam. The club owner was kneeling in front of Lucinda, talking to her. Then he stood up and briefly talked to Lucie, who didn't appear to be grieving. To the contrary, she looked angry. They watched Sam walk away from her, a confused look on his face.

"We should at least go talk to her," Lisa said to Travis.

"Okay."

Travis and Lisa approached her as she tried to comfort her daughter.

"Lucie, I'm very sorry," Travis said softly. "Kiel was a close friend of mine. We're all going to miss him a lot."

Lucie looked up and snapped, "Travis, I want you the fuck out of my house."

Travis looked down at Lucinda, who was in tears, then back at Lucie. His eyes narrowed. "Lucie, how about you and I having a little talk away from your daughter," he said tersely. "Lisa," he said, "Can you watch Lucinda?"

"Of course," Lisa answered as she took Lucinda's hand.

Lucie started to object, but changed her mind. "It's okay, Lucinda. I'll just be right over there. You stay with this lady, will you?"

Lucinda nodded tearfully, and Lucie and Travis walked over to a nearby tree.

"I don't think Lucinda should be subjected to that kind of language," Travis said. "And how about you showing some respect for the moment."

"Mind your own fucking business. I want you out of my house. Kiel doesn't live there anymore. And make it by six o'clock this evening."

"You know what, Lucie? I'm really sorry I ever met you. You're a disgrace to Kiel's name."

Lucie slapped Travis' face.

He ignored it. "When Kiel was killed, Scott was in the club getting it on with a hooker. Scott's a loser, Lucie. You fucked up, big time."

Lucie tried to slap him again, but he caught her wrist and gave it a pronounced twist. She winced and drew a sharp breath.

Travis looked into her eyes, his words harsh and angry. But still cognizant of Lucinda, he held his voice down. "You only get one freebie with me, Bitch. I feel sorry for Kiel's daughter, but you and Scott deserve each other."

He left Lucie and rejoined Lisa. They walked over to where Ken Washington was talking with Jake.

"So, you're going to turn in your badge?" Jake asked Ken.

"Yeah, it's what I have to do, Jake. I've been thinking about this whole ordeal ever since I got back from Fargo. The farm was unreal. So much death. It tore me up. I've been going through all the same flashbacks I dealt with after the Black Jack Mike thing. It's just not worth it to me and my family."

"I understand."

"You know, I'm a very religious man. I believe in the Bible, and the Ten Commandments. 'Thou shalt not kill.' Had I arrived at the door to that house a couple seconds sooner, I would've shot Tanya. I want to take myself away from those situations. Most people believe that devil-worshipping thing was all just a lot of hocus-pocus. I don't. Satan possessed that farm. He had control. Big Al Culpepper worked as his flunky. I'm not going to give up the fight. I'm just going to attack it in a different way."

"What are you going to do?" Jake asked.

Ken smiled. "Join the ministry. I believe the solution is spiritual. That's where the fight really is."

Jake held out his hand to Ken. With a melancholy smile, Jake said, "The war on drugs has to be fought on many fronts. The best of luck to you."

"Thanks, Jake. Say, how is Melanie doing now?"

"She came out of her coma two days ago. The doctors are very optimistic. She can't talk yet, but she's alert and responsive."

"That's wonderful. I've been praying for her all along. Give her my love."

Travis and Lisa stood nearby. Ken's plan of joining the ministry was news.

Ken looked their way. "How about you guys?"

Lisa smiled. "If you're looking for my blessing, you've got it."

Travis added, "Promise to stay in touch, okay?"

"Sure," Ken said with a crackling voice.

Harold walked over and pulled Jake and Travis aside. "I've got some news for you two. I'll tell the office tomorrow, so keep this to yourselves until then."

The two agents looked at Harold intently. "Okay Harold," Jake said.

"Alan is gone for good. He sent in his retirement paperwork yesterday."

Jake nodded approvingly. "This have something to do with your plan?"

"Yeah. Alan's relationship with Scott really disturbed me. Just couldn't figure it out, but I knew it wasn't right. Scott couldn't find his ass with his right hand, but Alan always ran interference for him. Wouldn't let me do my job. When I learned for a fact that Scott and Kiel's wife were getting it on, I wasn't satisfied with simply sending him to another office, even after Alan relented and gave me his approval. I called OPR and talked to them. They conducted a pretty thorough internal investigation, and then confronted Alan. He copped out, told them everything. Scott is Alan's son. Scott's mother is Alan's cousin. After Scott was born, Alan married another woman. She got pregnant too, but Alan beat her up one night, threw her down some stairs, and she had a miscarriage. She divorced his ass, but didn't press charges. Alan never remarried, and he developed a close relationship with Scott. He's Alan's only child. That little snot is all that Alan has in this world."

Jake and Travis looked at each other. Amazement visited their faces.

Harold paused for a moment, then continued. "Scott never should have been allowed to come to this office with Alan in charge. It's a total violation of DEA's nepotism policy. To make things worse, Alan wasn't shy about favoritism. It made my stomach turn when I saw some of the things Alan did. Scott's on the way out too. As soon as he's back on his feet, I'll give him the word. You guys won't have to pack your bags after all."

Harold walked away, grinning at their dumbstruck looks.

Shaking his head, Travis said to Jake in a conspiratorial tone, "I bet the Hate Man hated that."

"Yeah. See you tomorrow," Jake said, walking away.

Lisa and Travis headed for Travis' van.

"Care to go with me to Kiel's house?" Travis asked, as he fastened his seat belt. Then he told Lisa about his short conversation with Lucie.

"That slut," Lisa said.

Travis nodded. "And now I'm homeless again." He turned out of the cemetery and merged into traffic.

"Well, there is another option. I've been giving it some thought. Why don't you move in with me?"

Travis tried to conceal his smile, without much success. Lisa saw his grin and smiled herself. "How about it?" She didn't have to ask again.

"I can't think of anything I'd rather do. If you're sure."

"I guess now is the time, huh?"

"You've got a roommate!"

Lisa giggled. "By the way. I like to do my housework in the nude."

"Well, I guess that's something I'll just have to get used to."

CHAPTER 29

Jake hadn't had time to reinvigorate himself, and the funeral drained what little energy he had left. He had taken care of Kiel's final arrangements, and when not busy with that he stood vigil in the hospital. The next morning, looking over the back log of work in his in-box, he felt overwhelmed. He wanted to ignore it, go home and just kick back for a few days.

The day consisted of filing reports and other paper work. It made for a long eight hours. Everyone felt grateful when the clock on the wall finally made it to five o'clock. Jake, Travis and Lisa walked out together. Jake's limp was still obvious, and Lisa used crutches to take the strain off her injured leg. Their cars were parked in a lot across the street. Stopping at Jake's car, they talked about the week's events for a couple minutes. Then it was time to go. Rush hour had begun.

As Lisa and Travis walked away, Jake called out, "Go easy on that leg, Lisa."

"I will Jake," Lisa said. "I guess we're the walking wounded. You go easy on your foot."

They didn't see the woman watching from inside the parked mini-van. Spotting a woman hobbling on crutches, Tanya keyed on the three agents. She heard them speaking loudly, and smiled in grim satisfaction. Two of the three were limping. Big Al had left them something to remember him by. She zeroed in on Jake. *You wanted to follow me and Big Al around, huh? Okay. Show me where you live, motherfucker.*

Jake's concentration level had plummeted. Just making the routine drive home was a challenge. Merging onto I-94 near the domed stadium he realized he couldn't even remember driving the past half mile.

At the same time adrenaline drenched Tanya, her energy level exploding off the charts. The hyper woman could barely keep from bouncing in her seat while gripping the steering wheel. She eagerly followed Jake down the busy street. He was three cars ahead. A sign indicated the on-ramp would put them on the east-bound freeway.

Jake proceeded east on I-94, driving over the Mississippi River and past the University of Minnesota campus into Saint Paul. The heavy traffic worked in Tanya's favor, but possibly more to her advantage was Jake. In his exhausted state he didn't check his rear-view mirror.

A half hour after merging onto I-94, Jake arrived at the 694-494 clover-leaf. Tanya watched in eager anticipation as her target moved over into the right lane.

Jake merged onto the clover leaf and then went north, with Tanya's van not far behind. A short time later, she saw Jake turning onto highway 36, heading east.

Within a few minutes Tanya passed a sign announcing the city limits of Stillwater. She continued into the downtown area. The traffic remained heavy until Jake turned. Then he was all alone on a quiet residential street.

The surveillance now became tricky for Tanya. She had to keep tabs on his car without him noticing her. Her van slowed to a crawl. Irritated drivers, forced to stop behind her, pounded on their horns. Ignoring them she slowly crept into the intersection where Jake had just turned. From a distance she watched him proceed up a hill, over the crest and out of sight. Making her move, she turned rapidly and quickly drove to the top of the hill where she spotted his car turning onto another street. Her pulse quickened.

She sped up just short of the intersection, then slowed down dramatically. Slinking into the intersection, she looked off to her left and saw Jake's car turning into a driveway. Noting the name of the street, Tanya continued straight, driving around the neighborhood for several minutes, giving Jake time to go inside. Then she returned and drove past the house, making the assumption he lived there.

Dominating the end of the street, a mansionesque house built in the 20's stood as a sturdy reminder of the town's historical heritage. Converted into a Bed and Breakfast, according to the sign posted in the front yard, it was one of several in Stillwater. Curious, Tanya pulled into the driveway and checked it out. A three story affair, it had several windows facing Jake's street. Excellent! Tanya's brain clicked into high gear as she drove home. The following day she returned and rented a room with the view she needed.

Tanya spent much of the next two days in her room, watching the street and taking notes. Then she reviewed what she had learned.

The man had a wife and four kids. His wife left every morning at about ten-thirty, and returned home around two. Tanya wondered what Jake's wife did every morning. Jake arrived home around six, then he and his wife left at six-thirty. The neighbors never came around, but once in a while the neighbors' kids came over. Jake's kids played in the front yard with the neighbors, and occasionally they went across the street to another house. Jake's two boys liked to play Frisbee with the neighbor's dog. Tanya felt thankful Jake's family didn't own a dog.

She also gave some thought to her victims. One of the boys looked like a teenager, the other quite a bit younger. The two girls were just what she needed. They appeared to be middle-school age, and wouldn't give her much trouble. It seemed everybody was home when Jake and his wife left in the evening. But it concerned her that she didn't have a feel for how long they were gone. One night they were away for an hour and a half. The next night it was three hours. Tanya figured the best time to go in was shortly after they left.

Her plan wasn't complicated. She would knock on the door, and one of the kids would open it. Once inside, she'd kill the boys and tie up the girls. The garage would have an empty space, and she would move her van inside. Then, simply throw the girls into the van and split. Tanya figured it would all take about ten minutes.

For a few minutes she indulged herself, considering the rewards.

The girls and me have a date with destiny. They look like good lambs for my personal ritual. If I do it right, El Diablo will rise up and join us. He'll be pleased, and the demons will disappear. Big Al will be avenged. I'll do it tomorrow evening. It's not a full moon, but my need is too strong to wait.

The following day, Jake arrived home shortly after six o'clock, still tired and somewhat grouchy. The evening meal was prepared, with Suzanne and Kim seated at the table. The boys had been at the Kowalski's, their backyard neighbors, all day. Steve Kowalski, trying to give Jake and Melissa a helping hand, would take the boys to a ball game that evening. They wouldn't be home until dark.

Putting the meal on, Melissa said, "Little Jeffrey asked us to take Mutt to Melanie. Thinks she might need some company other than us."

"She's got a half-dozen stuffed animals with her now."

Melissa eyed her husband. He was on the surly side. A couple weeks of R&R would sure do him good. "I know, but it's important to him, Jake. The little guy really misses his biggest sister. He wants to do something for her."

"No problem."

Forty-five minutes later Jake and Melissa said good-bye to the girls and left.

"Right on schedule," Tanya verified with a sinister smile. She put on her knife sheath. She wore it on a belt, concealed under a sweatshirt.

After leaving the office that evening, Travis and Lisa decided to have dinner in one of the downtown restaurants just two doors down. They walked, with Lisa hobbling and Travis keeping a slow pace at her side. The restaurant specialized in chicken lunches. Due to its fast service and good food, the establishment did a thriving business with the lunch hour crowd, but wasn't very busy in the evenings. Within a few minutes, they were sharing a half chicken.

"Do you mind if I take the leg?" Lisa asked.

"That's fine with me," Travis replied, dipping his fork into a mound of potato salad. "I've always been a breast man." His eyes soaked in her boobs.

The look, maybe a bit too obvious for Lisa, mildly irritated her. "Jesus, Travis. Don't you ever get your fill?"

"My appetite for objects of beauty is unlimited."

"Are you saying you view me as a sex object?"

"That's a loaded question. You're a whole lot more than sexy."

She tried to hold back a smile. "You are soooo fulla shit. You'll probably be a hell of good narc once you get your cherry popped."

"What do you mean by that?"

"You'll know when it happens." Lisa decided to change the subject. "It seems like months ago since we spotted Scott with Lucie. I'm thinking Kiel never returned to a warm home after work, just a cold shoulder. And this nightmare Jake and his family are going through has really been bothering me. I bet there's not much warmth in his house either. He and Melissa have been going through hell this summer. I wish there were something I could do to help them."

"Yeah," Travis answered sympathetically. "Jake is a strong person, but there are limits to what a person can take."

Engrossed in thought, Lisa abruptly tossed her chicken bone onto the table. "Travis, I want to go visit them. I think they need some company. Let's go."

Her impulsive decision caught Travis off guard, but he had no objections. "Uh, yeah, if you like. Why not? They're probably at the hospital, but we could entertain their kids 'til they got back."

Five minutes later they were driving to Stillwater.

"You ever been to Jake's home," Travis asked.

"No."

"Ever been to Stillwater?"

"Nope."

"It's a quaint town."

Suzanne was upstairs in her room when the doorbell rang. Kim answered the door. "Yes."

Her system flooded with adrenaline, hatred, and the overwhelming need for revenge, Tanya wasted no time with words. She grabbed Kim by the neck, shoving her backward and pushing her into the house. Kim started to shriek, but Tanya quickly put her knife to the girl's throat.

"Not a sound, you understand?" Tanya said quietly.

Kim nodded, and Tanya hastily put a strip of duct tape over her mouth. Looking around, she saw no one else in the room. She tied Kim's hands and feet, then went upstairs to find the others.

The second floor had three bedrooms. The first one Tanya came to was obviously the master bedroom. She glanced inside, then continued down the hallway. The second room was also empty. Tanya heard a girl humming softly in the third bedroom.

She entered the room and spotted Suzanne seated at her dresser, brushing her hair. Seeing Tanya in the mirror, the young girl screamed but had no other defense. Shortly, Suzanne lay next to her sister. Tanya hustled down to search the basement.

Jake and Melissa were just a few minutes away when Melissa realized they hadn't brought little Jeffrey's stuffed toy. "Jake, we forgot Mutt."

He looked over at his wife with a trace of impatience in his eyes. "Can't we bring him tomorrow?"

"Honey, I promised. Please go back."

"Yeah, I guess you're right." He turned the car around. Arriving back at the house he told Melissa, "I'll get it. Just be a second." He limped into the house.

Opening the front door, fear drenched him when he saw Kim lying on the floor, bound and gagged. He reached for his pistol, but it wasn't there. Jake didn't like carrying a piece in the hospital while visiting Melanie, so he had left it in their bedroom. He quickly scanned the room. Seeing no one else, he reached down to pick up his daughter, wanting to whisk her out of the house. As he picked her up, Tanya came into the house from the garage where she had just stashed Suzanne.

"You!" She screamed. Tanya pulled out her knife and charged.Jake had to set Kim back down without dropping her on her head. It placed him at an enormous disadvantage. Tanya charged him like a mad rhino.

Her motions were fluid and quick as she lunged at Jake with a razor sharp knife. Still lowering his daughter to the floor with his left arm, he raised his right arm in defense of the blade. The knife caught him in the forearm. Pain seared through his body. Tanya's momentum pushed him back several feet. She stayed in close, pulling the knife out of his arm, wanting to cut him again. Blood spurted all over. Onto their hands, faces, clothes, and the floor.

Jake regained his balance, shoved her away, then kicked her in the gut with his right foot. But with his weight on his bad ankle, he couldn't put much force into the blow. Still, it knocked her back against the wall. Ignoring his wound, he quickly glanced around for a weapon. With his left hand, he grabbed the only thing within reach: an eighteen inch ceramic vase.

She lunged at him again. This time Jake parried with the vase, slamming it hard against the woman's knife hand. The knife flew onto the floor. Hissing like a wild cat, Tanya glared at him with wide, psycho eyes. She moved to recover the knife. Jake anticipated her movement and swung at her head with the vase. But she dove to the floor and the vase slipped out of Jake's bloody hand, whizzing past her and shattering harmlessly. She reached the knife and Jake dove on top of her, locking onto her wrist, wanting to control the weapon. They rolled on the hardwood floor, both becoming bloodier as they grappled with one-another.

Tanya chomped down hard on his left arm, then grabbed a wad of his hair and pulled it out, ripping a chunk of his scalp with it.

Fighting for his daughters' lives as well as his own, Jake's adrenaline masked the pain. But he knew he was losing ground. Tanya's knife had made his right arm useless, one of his ankles was so bad it couldn't support his weight, and he was losing blood. He felt himself weakening.

Travis and Lisa pulled into the driveway behind Jake's car. Seeing Melissa inside the vehicle, they were happy they got there before Jake and his wife had gone for the evening. They walked up to her window.

"Hi, Melissa," Travis said. "We stopped by to see if there was anything we could do for you guys."

"Oh, hi Travis. Hi, Lisa. We were on the way to the hospital but we forgot something. Jake went inside to get it. I don't know what's taking so long."

"Mind if I go inside and help him look? He was kind of groggy today. Maybe he needs another set of eyes."

"Go right ahead. I'll stay here and talk to Lisa."

When Travis entered the house he first saw Jake's daughter on the floor, next to a bright red hair piece. On the other side of the room he saw his partner on the floor, desperately struggling with a bald headed woman. Travis knew it could only be Tanya. He raised his pistol hoping for a clean shot, but none was possible. Jake and the woman were rolling back and forth, locked close together as they struggled for control of a knife. Travis closed in, waiting for his chance.

Then Tanya managed to get up on one knee and wrenched the knife away from Jake's weakened grip. Anger distorted her face. Tight, twisted lips testified to her fierce determination, and frenzied eyes mirrored her hatred as they locked onto Jake's pupils. She raised her knife, preparing to plunge it into Jake's neck.

Travis launched himself, feet first, straight into her head and torso, ripping her away from Jake. She tumbled across the floor, landing on her back but still clutching the knife in a death grip. Travis landed on his side in a slippery, crimson puddle, and slid into the wall, his pistol lock tightly in his hand.

Tanya, still full of fight, struggled to her knees, trying to regain her balance so she could spring on him before could use his weapon.

Travis was equally furious.

Although in an awkward position, he leveled his nine millimeter at her head and squeezed the trigger. Balanced on all fours, Tanya faced him like a mad dog ready to pounce. His bullet caught her between the eyes.

EPILOGUE

Stepping out of his car, Jake limped across the cemetery lawn, obviously favoring his left leg. Bags hung below his bloodshot eyes, his ankle throbbed, and his right arm was in a sling. Still, he could finally wear both shoes. With that thought, Jake looked down at his feet. The caretakers had mowed the lawn recently and his Nike's, saturated by the early morning dew, were cluttered with clumps of freshly cut grass.

Approaching the newly placed tombstone, Jake grumbled, "Should've worn my older pair," thinking they'd already been through hell and it wouldn't make any difference if they got trashed.

His attention turned to the gray stone. Running his hand along the top of the stone, he slid his fingers over the rough edges while his eyes traced the letters sliced out of marble.

The stone was thick. Solid. Cold.

A thick lump settled in his throat as he mouthed the words on the tombstone. Without success he tried to swallow. "I never had a chance to say 'good-bye,' he whispered. "So I guess this will have to do."

He looked down at the freshly planted grass. "I know you'd be happy to hear this. We've identified people all over the state who were involved in this heroin ring, and we're going to kick some ass. I'd say Minnesota will be a much safer place. And Eddie Pellegrino turned over a huge pile of money. He won't need it where he's going. Was it worth it? I'm not the one to answer that. Not as I look down at your grave. But I will say we saved a lot of lives. I wish yours could have been one of them. Damn it Kiel, I really miss you. Rest easy, Bud. You'll be in our hearts forever."

Jake limped back to his car where Melissa waited.

Made in the USA
Monee, IL
13 November 2020